THE FLYLEAF KILLER

THE FLYLEAF KILLER

William A. Prater

Book Guild Publishing
Sussex, England

First published in Great Britain in 2007 by
The Book Guild Ltd
Pavilion View
19 New Road
Brighton
BN1 1UF

Copyright © William A. Prater 2007

The right of William A. Prater to be identified as the author of this work has been asserted by him in accordance with the Copyright, Designs and Patents Act 1988.

All rights reserved. No part of this publication may be reproduced, transmitted, or stored in a retrieval system, in any form, or by any means, without permission in writing from the publishers, nor be otherwise circulated in any form of binding or cover other than that in which it is published and without a similar condition being imposed on the subsequent purchaser.

All characters in this publication are fictitious and any resemblance to real people, alive or dead, is purely coincidental.

Typesetting in Baskerville by
SetSystems Ltd, Saffron Walden, Essex

Printed in Great Britain by
Antony Rowe Ltd, Chippenham, Wiltshire

A catalogue record for this book is
available from the British Library

ISBN 978 1 84624 123 9

CONTENTS

Chapter 1	The Book	1
Chapter 2	A Taste of Revenge	20
Chapter 3	Teenagers	33
Chapter 4	Noises	46
Chapter 5	The Body in the Garden	55
Chapter 6	Beast	77
Chapter 7	Investigation	95
Chapter 8	Preparation	123
Chapter 9	Assassin	133
Chapter 10	The Old Church	142
Chapter 11	Francis, R.I.P.	161
Chapter 12	Abducted	192
Chapter 13	Missing Persons	207
Chapter 14	Fugitive	230
Chapter 15	A Promise Made . . .	251
Chapter 16	Come into my Parlour . . .	259

Chapter One

The Book

The boy was a little below average height, but sturdily built, fit and muscular. Heavily bespectacled, sallow and prone to spots, with straw-coloured, slicked-back hair—greasy from too much gel—his unpopularity had little to do with his appearance, even if it had once been a contributing factor. Sullen, bookish and introvert, frequently shunned by his schoolfellows, or else taunted and teased unmercifully, he avoided the playground as much as possible.

It wasn't as if he sought to be disliked. On the contrary, in earlier years he had striven desperately for the approval of his classmates, even resorting to bribery. But apart from the few who probably felt sorry for the unhappy boy, most treated him and his advances with contempt—and rarely missed an opportunity to let him know it. None of the teachers liked him, despite his scholastic ability, and he was regularly singled out to be the butt of their sarcasm.

He suffered particularly at the hands of the school bully and his henchmen, who delighted in making his life a misery. There was little he could do: they were all older and stronger than he. But he was intelligent, quick to learn and possessed an extraordinarily retentive memory. He loved reading and excelled in most subjects but, paradoxically, hated the school, its system, and everybody connected with it.

Things were better at home, though not especially so. He had given up trying to please his mother as far back as he could remember. Nothing he did seemed to satisfy her no matter how hard he tried. There was little comfort from his father—habitually indifferent to his son's well-being, he was authoritative and equally hard to please. It was better to keep out of his way.

The unpopular, miserable little boy had grown into a teenager

1

with a burgeoning personality complex. At thirteen, Robert seemed destined to enter adulthood an embittered loner.

One afternoon in September 1998, another of those depressing days when little went right, Robert came out of school just before 3.30, earlier than the rest of the class as a reward for better than average marks for an essay—not that he was particularly bothered. Disconsolate and moody, he automatically began to head for home—his mother always nagged him not to loiter. Then, for some inexplicable reason, almost of their own volition, his feet overruled all other considerations and turned instead in the direction of town. Ignoring twinges of conscience he strolled on, unresisting. And as he walked he deliberated: What punishment might he expect for such 'downright disobedience'—besides nagging, that is? Grounding? Guaranteed. No tea, bed by 7.30 and no supper? More than likely. Oh well . . . He ambled on resignedly, but then brightened. The library was close to the town centre and, no matter what, the detour was at least an opportunity to pick up a couple of new books. His reading tastes were wide-ranging: science fiction, Westerns, adventure, thrillers, educational material, even the classics. Dickens' *David Copperfield* was a special favourite. An avid reader from an early age, Robert was always on the lookout for new subjects and authors.

He walked past a succession of high-street stores, idly kicking a pebble and pausing should something in a window catch his eye. Reaching Woolworths on the main parade he stopped. Should he retrace his steps and go home? There was time yet to escape his mother's wrath, and he could visit the library whenever he wished—subject to permission in advance. But the compulsion that had brought him thus far was not to be denied. He shrugged, blew a raspberry at his reflection in the window, then found himself going in the direction of the library at a considerably faster rate.

He came to and passed the model shop without a sideways glance, despite the array of planes, helicopters, trains and ships that he would normally have found irresistible. His pace quickened, accelerated by the same inner urge he had yet to recognise. Crossing the service road, he arrived at the last block of five shops: newsagents, ladies' hairdresser, ironmonger, a boarded-up space owned by the post office which had been relocated after a fire in 1996 and, finally, a dingy carpet warehouse.

Beyond lay the imposing town hall and council offices complex whose extensive grounds contained Robert's favourite destination, the public library. At least that was the way things had been the last time he had changed some books, about two weeks ago.

Remembering that the library closed at 4.00 and no further visitors were allowed in after 3.50, he checked the time by the town hall clock. It was 3.42. Abandoning the pebble, he broke into a trot but on reaching the former post office site he stopped dead in his tracks, stunned, amazed and massively intrigued. The hoarding was gone and the space had been transformed into a brand new shop—and what a shop! To a lonely boy whose only real pleasure stemmed from reading, this was no ordinary shop:

'HENRY PLOWRITE – BOOKSELLER'

the sign above the door announced and lettered across the window in bold, red capitals were the words:

WE HAVE THE BOOK *YOU* REQUIRE

In Robert's eyes, the attraction was nothing short of magnetic. Behind the glass lay a window display engineered to grab a booklover's attention and hold it. Nose to glass, Robert scanned rows of volumes avidly; they were artistically arranged on glass shelves extending the width of the window and a comprehensive selection of publicity leaflets was pinned across the window-back, each promoting merits of a newly-published title. Magic!

Absorbed in window-shopping, he forgot about the time. Eventually, dragging himself back to reality, he told himself firmly: Better get to the library, Robert my boy, or there'll be no new books for you today.

He stepped back a couple of paces to bring the town hall clock into view—3.48pm. Too late! Even if he ran at top speed, the library doors would be locked before he got there.

'Bother, what a twit!' he exclaimed, gaining a puzzled look from an elderly passer-by.

Disappointed, annoyed with himself for having dallied, Robert returned to the window where his eye was drawn to the central display and a book he hadn't previously noticed. Wow! A gold blocked, leather-bound copy of *Oliver Twist*, one of Dickens' most famous novels. Robert stared, hungrily. 'How the heck did I miss seeing that?' he wondered aloud.

As with most people, addressing oneself in times of doubt is far from uncommon, but Robert wasn't 'most people' and today, as on other recent occasions, he was privileged to receive an answer. *No point in wishing*, an inner voice observed, and went further—much further: *A magnificent book. A fantastic book—and it could be yours, Robert Strudwick—today! Oliver Twist. A wonderful story, beautifully written. Dickens' literary masterpiece, some say.* The voice wheedled: *Come Robert, this is your chance. Why not take a closer look?*

Robert saw nothing unusual in being thus addressed; felt no curiosity regarding the voice, lately familiar in times of stress and, more particularly, whenever he needed help. *Go on*, his disembodied mentor urged, adding with precise, reassuring logic: *Where's the harm in looking? They can't lock you up for that can they? What are you waiting for?*

Robert moved nearer the entrance, but stopped. Tempted indeed, but restrained by caution. He looked again in the window where the delectable book seemed to beckon, then back at the entrance to his left. Just then the latch clicked and the door creaked open invitingly. Gosh! Weakening, Robert took two steps sideways and peered warily into the shop.

Surprisingly, the place was devoid of customers; what's more, despite a clear view of the interior, there was nothing to be seen of the shopkeeper either. *What are you waiting for?* the voice repeated. *Go on, nobody's going to bite!*

But still Robert resisted. 'Huh,' he retorted, half under his breath, 'What's the point of looking? I want to buy it, not try it—but I *can't* buy it, I haven't any money. And if you think I'm going to pinch it think again,' he added. 'Do you think me stupid, or what? I'm in trouble enough, thank you very much!' And he subsided, essentially to consider.

This wasn't the public library, where each of the tickets in his pocket would secure the loan of a book for two weeks without charge. Was there *really* any point in going in? For one thing he had only coppers in his pocket, and for another he knew from bitter experience shopkeepers rarely tolerated unaccompanied children. Robert was nobody's fool.

What bookseller wouldn't pounce the instant a boy came

through the door, demand to know what the boy wanted and, if the declared intention was to purchase, insist on seeing the money? Robert *had* no money, and could therefore expect to be told to clear off in no uncertain terms.

But the shopkeeper isn't looking—and there's nobody else around, the voice insisted. *You could read from Oliver Twist—or any other book for that matter.* And further wheedled: *You can, you know you can. You can, can, can if you really want to.*

That did it! Curiosity and compelling, overwhelming desire could no longer be denied. Abandoning caution, Robert entered the premises of 'Henry Plowrite, Bookseller'.

The cathedral-like shop was hushed, the floor heavily carpeted. The smell of printer's ink and the unmistakable, pungent tang of fine leather bindings both tangible and heady. The atmosphere welcomed and enfolded the boy like a warm blanket on a cold winter's night. For all his caution he felt comfortable, at ease—had a curious sense of destiny, as though he'd been here before. When the door closed quietly behind, he scarcely noticed. Even were he captive, so be it. It didn't even occur to him he might need to beat a hasty retreat. Enraptured, determined to take maximum advantage of a splendid opportunity, Robert postponed examining the Dickens classic and wandered the shelves, browsing contentedly. Most books he replaced after cursory inspection, others after a page or so, but if the occasional volume proved outstanding it took conscious effort to return it from whence it came.

Time slipped by unheeded so engrossed was he. Neither did he notice an absence of customers, nor realise that nobody had so much as rattled the door handle since his arrival, nor indeed, that the shopkeeper had yet to appear, much less deliver that half-expected challenge. Nearing the end of the shelving and approaching the counter, Robert's eager gaze was captured by a particularly handsome volume on the topmost shelf. Acting on impulse, he reached up to withdraw the book, but the instant he touched it a surge of power tingled his fingers and shot up his arm like a bolt of electricity. 'Crikey!' he exclaimed, and almost dropped the book. Startled he most certainly was, but massively intrigued and curious too. Whilst holding the book his fingers prickled, but on returning it to the shelf the sensation ceased. 'How very strange!' he muttered and, cautiously, he experimented.

If he touched the book his fingertips tingled—not the least

unpleasant he established, but an extraordinary sensation which persisted until he put it down again. But, try as he might, he was unable to induce the tome to deliver another shock—and even found this a trifle disappointing. Fascinated, Robert took a closer look.

Undoubtedly beautiful, it was bound in dark blue vellum with heavy gold fillets and intricate tooling, the spine reinforced by five raised bands embellished with heavy gold overlay, but only now did he realise neither cover nor spine was entitled or bore the name of the author.

There was evidence of use and a sense of antiquity about the book, but the quality of manufacturing craftsmanship couldn't be denied. Robert supposed it to be hand-finished and must surely therefore represent the very epitome of the bookbinder's art.

Who wrote it? What was it about? Robert didn't know and didn't care. His longing for *Oliver Twist* was eclipsed and superseded by an overwhelming desire to own and cherish *this* book. Permanent acquisition became paramount. This book *had* to be his, above all else!

Totally engrossed, Robert failed to notice a door swing open, but something—instinct perhaps—prompted him to look in time to see a man appear a split-second before the shopkeeper (for it was surely he) elected to greet his one and only customer. 'Good afternoon, Robert,' the newcomer said loudly, in deep, sonorous, sepulchral tones. 'Yes, *you*, Robert William Strudwick,' he boomed, as if to counter the boy's incredulity. 'I am pleased to welcome you to my humble shop,' he added, quaintly old-fashioned.

Book in hand, mouth agape, Robert was rooted to the spot, astonished to be addressed by name. He was equally struck by the way the man moved, a peculiar sort of gliding motion.

The bookseller leered a manic leer, thrust a long, pointed nose across the counter and treated Robert to a fearsome glare. Or was it a smile? Cor, crikey! The fellow was positively *UGLY!* He bore no resemblance to anyone Robert had ever met nor to how he imagined a bookseller might look: narrow, coal-black eyes, jet-black hair slicked back from a central parting and huge thrusting sideboards resembling twin, hairy scimitars. Ugly? No, not ugly. Sort of—*DEVILISH?*

To be thus confronted unnerved Robert, and although his mind and vocal cords made a concerted effort to respond his throat refused to produce even the tiniest of squeaks.

'Well, come on, Robert,' the shopkeeper prompted. 'Aren't you going to say "hello"? Where's your manners, boy? I *have* been expecting you!'

The staring eyes appeared to soften. Grotesquely, there was even the hint of a smile. The man seemed to pose no immediate threat and the resonant voice seemed vaguely familiar. Robert relaxed a little and by dint of effort managed to regain his voice.

'H-hello, Mister P-Plowrite,' he stammered. 'I—I'm v–very pleased to meet you!'

'Yes, and I should think so too!' came the unkind reply. 'You boys of today!' He fell silent, regarding his customer thoughtfully. Long moments passed.

The book in Robert's hands felt warm, comforting—alive, almost. How could he make it his own? He knew he was intelligent—teachers said so. Father expressed doubts, but what did *he* know? It was time to put his brains to work and come up with a solution: *I want this book!*

Bravely, Robert countered the bookseller's stare with a contemplative study of his own. So this was Henry Plowrite, whose name appeared above the door? Appearances notwithstanding, he was probably a typical shopkeeper, in business solely for profit—but perhaps, just perhaps, open to negotiation? Robert certainly hoped so. If anything, his longing intensified. Little money or no, he was more determined than ever to possess the book. Perhaps it was time to go on the offensive—try a touch of subterfuge—but first, a question.

'Er, excuse me Mister Plowrite. How did you know my name?' he asked, hesitantly.

'A-hah,' Plowrite boomed, 'I *knew* you'd ask me that. Well, all you need to know is that I *do* know. *How* I know is *because* I know. *Why* I know is because *you* know *me*.'

'But I've never seen you before—never! But I think I remember your voice from somewhere.'

'Well, there you are then, proof enough,' Plowrite replied, smug but hardly logical. Once again he lapsed into silence, regarding his customer with an even greater intensity.

Robert stared back, wonderingly. It was curious, but although every bit as ugly, the shopkeeper seemed less frightening. Maybe he was becoming used to the man? What had appearance to do with the situation, anyway? Shrugging, Robert decided the man's looks were irrelevant. All that really mattered was finding a way to secure this beautiful book. But he remained suspicious. After all, this shop hadn't been in existence a couple of weeks ago . . .

'I see you've selected a top quality book,' the bookseller eventually observed. 'But don't imagine you can read it, borrow it or keep it without full and proper payment.' From his tone and attitude it was abundantly clear he meant exactly what he said.

'Tell me, which title is it?' he asked. 'Then I shall be pleased to tell you the price.'

Robert held out the book. 'It doesn't say, Mister Plowrite. Look, see for yourself.' He turned the book spine uppermost and thrust it towards the shopkeeper but, glancing down, hastily snatched it back for there, in gold-embossed letters he read:

THE SECRET OF SUCCESS
Pilo Sephten

Rotating the book through forty-five degrees showed the front cover to be similarly inscribed. Robert was both astonished and perplexed.

'That's strange!' he exclaimed, a-flush with embarrassment. 'I'm *sure* it was blank before—the front cover too,' he endeavoured to explain. 'Sorry, I just couldn't have looked properly . . .' Lamely, his voice tailed off.

The bookseller rubbed claw-like hands and shaped his mouth into a tolerant smile—in reality a hideous grimace—and said, ingratiatingly, 'A wise choice, a very special book. One with many titles and, therefore, everything to all men. Look again, boy,' he commanded.

Obediently, Robert looked down and was staggered to find both style and title changed:

YOU *CAN* YOU *MUST* YOU *WILL*
Pilo Sephten

While Robert gaped in astonishment, the original title reappeared briefly before vanishing altogether, leaving both spine and cover completely blank.

It would have been incredible, had not Robert witnessed it with his own eyes! Desire for the book became even more profound.

Think, old son, he told himself. What should he do to gain his objective? He shifted his mind into top gear.

A course of action became apparent in a flash. Well practised, he decided to play the sympathy card for all it was worth. Even if it didn't help, it certainly would do no harm.

He screwed his eyes to make them glisten, puckered his face in anguish and prevailed upon his lower lip to tremble, pathetically ... There now, that should do it! Confident an entreating expression was firmly in place, Robert blinked back a tear and gazed at the bookseller. Taking a deep breath, he launched his campaign.

'I'd like to buy the book, Mr Plowrite,' he began. 'Please, can you tell me how much it is?' (Surely his carefully pitched, plaintive tones deserved *something* in the way of sympathy?) 'But I'm afraid I don't have much money,' he added, hopefully.

'Certainly Robert, of course. Now let me see.'

Henry Plowrite reached beneath the counter. Producing a clipboard, he rifled through typewritten sheets, stopped abruptly and ran a bony forefinger halfway down a page. Emitting a grunt of evident satisfaction, he looked up.

'Ah, yes, here we are,' the apparent bookseller said, with a calculating rub of his beak-like nose. 'This rare and very special book can be yours for'—he paused 'just sixty-six pounds and six pence. And very reasonable too for such a fine volume, as I'm sure you will agree,' he declared, with an unmistakable air of finality.

Robert's heart sank. His dismay must surely be apparent for again his lower lip trembled—this time of its own accord. Realising his back was up against the wall he thought furiously. He had little chance of raising such a large amount, yet felt in his heart the book was worth more. He simply *had* to acquire this exciting treasure; nothing else seemed to matter. Robert's mind raced, calculating assets at top speed.

His newspaper round was worth eight pounds a week. A princely sum, were he not obliged to hand over six pounds towards his keep. An evening round would bring in more, but Father forbade it, saying it would interfere with homework and prevent him from carrying out chores. He was therefore left with two pounds. (A wage-earner no longer qualified for pocket-money.)

'That's an awful lot of money, Mister Plowrite,' Robert eventually brought himself to say. 'I've seven pounds saved. Will it do as a deposit? Can I have the book and pay the rest at two pounds a week? I really want the book and I promise to bring you the money every Friday.'

Slowly, Henry Plowrite shook his head. He even contrived to seem regretful as he said, 'I'm sorry Robert, but the price is a cash price and must be paid in full. Company policy forbids giving credit and I regret there can be no exceptions.'

He extended his hand for the book, but Robert tightened his grasp on the volume, unwilling to give up without a fight. In keeping with generations of youngsters, Robert was no stranger to materialistic aspirations—in his case, mostly frustrated, but no previous acquisitive yearning came within light-years of his desire to possess this wonderful, beautiful book.

'Oh, *please* Mister Plowrite,' he begged, 'I'll do anything. What if I come and work for you after school every day? I'll run errands, sweep up, clean windows—and I won't expect any payment, either.' And when the shopkeeper still seemed unmoved, the boy added, desperately: 'I could come Saturday mornings after papers as well—and *still* give you two pounds a week.'

It was his last shot, his final offer. With bated breath he waited, hoping the bookseller would accept. Rubbing his chin thoughtfully, Henry Plowrite appeared to waver. He knew his 'customer' extremely well, was perfectly aware the boy nurtured a violent dislike for the world in general and a deep, abiding hatred for the majority of his contemporaries.

The boy possessed—even if unaware of it as yet, a deep-rooted capability for cruel, spiteful retaliation towards anyone who crossed his path or frustrated his ambition, together with an innate potential for depravity and evil, rare in anyone regardless of age or circumstances: highly desirable characteristics which had first attracted the attention of Pentophiles, who knew, given the right circumstances, the boy would do anything to further his own ends.

But the being lurking behind the façade of 'Henry Plowrite' still had much to achieve. Gaining trust was an essential step towards the eventual fulfillment of his special ambition. Until the boy was irrevocably committed, the possibility of failure remained, especially should he sense danger and be warned off. The so-called bookseller selected his words with great care.

'We-ll Robert,' he began slowly, 'if you really *are* prepared to do anything—and because you are over the age of thirteen—there is just a possibility I may be able to help you.'

Robert's carefully constructed air of pathos disintegrated in an instant. He listened intently to Plowrite's every word to make sure he didn't miss a single nuance.

'I do *not* require assistance but you might be able to possess the book without actually buying it. However, before I explain, you might find it helpful to open the book and read the dedication.'

'Yes, yes,' Robert cried eagerly, 'of course I will. I said I'd do anything and I meant it!' Excitedly, he put the book down and attempted to raise the cover . . . but the cover wouldn't budge. Tugging simply lifted the volume up from the counter.

Disappointed and angry, Robert threw caution to the winds, glared at Plowrite and yelled, 'What's the game then? The rotten pages must be stuck together. Your stupid book isn't worth coppers. Shove it! I'm off home.'

He slammed down the book and turned away.

'*Wait!*' The bookseller commanded. 'You may not address me thus without forfeit. Atone immediately!'

Inexplicably afraid, Robert's anger abated as swiftly as it had arisen. 'S-sorry, Mister Plowrite,' he stuttered. 'I d-didn't mean to be rude. I thought something must be wrong with the book. W-what's g-going on then? Why *won't* the pages open?'

Without speaking, the counterfeit bookseller reached to his neck, removed a small golden key suspended from a crimson ribbon and offered it to the boy.

Puzzled, Robert deferred acceptance until, with a flash of intuition, he re-examined the book. Turned spine downwards it became clear the volume was fitted with a small clasp and lock.

'Well, I'm blowed!' he exclaimed. 'I didn't notice *that* before. You must think me stupid. I really am truly sorry, Mister Plowrite. I hope you won't hold it against me . . .'

'Of course not my boy, I understand completely. Let that be an end to the matter.' Although the shopkeeper spoke graciously, he didn't sound in the least sincere. 'Now mark me well, Robert William Strudwick,' he continued. 'Not only is this the key to the book, it may also be the key to your future. Only if well prepared should you take the key, open the book and read the dedication therein.'

Robert didn't hesitate. Having scant regard for the import of

Henry Plowrite's words, and with fingers fairly trembling with excitement, he eagerly accepted the proffered key.

Carefully, he inserted it through a tiny escutcheon and into the lock, where a single half-turn rotated the tumblers and released the hasp, allowing the book to open. Lifting the front cover and turning to the title page revealed the dedication.

Robert found it relatively easy to comprehend, despite the quaint script and archaic phraseology. He began to read aloud and before the end of the first line his recently deepened voice reverted to a shaky soprano squeak:

> *This Book was writ for thee, Robert William Strudwick. Follow and obey as counselled, when great power and fortune shall be thine to command, as will the lives of all who cause mischief unto thee or mayhap wish thee ill.*

Robert's voice tailed off. *For me?* He asked himself, wildly, *how can it possibly be?*

Dumbfounded, he read the sentences again, word by word. But the message was unambiguous, incapable of misinterpretation . . . and the gleam of avarice in Robert's eye betrayed his complete and absolute comprehension.

These were critical moments, however, and Henry Plowrite's dark, unblinking gaze never wavered. He watched the boy's jaw drop and, with the advent of dawning realisation, a look of incredulity appear—until enlightenment swept it away the instant his intelligence caught up with his greed. Intelligent the boy most certainly was; his reaction was immediate.

'Hey!' he exclaimed in alarm. 'What the spiff's going on?' His voice rose angrily. 'How come my name's already in the book? Is this some sort of trick? Are you a flipping conjuror?' Without waiting he answered his own question: 'No, that's something you definitely are not.' And, following his own line of reasoning, demanded, 'So who the devil are you, Old Nick?' His eyes widened at the thought. What if . . .? 'Yes, that's who you are,' he declared. '*And I reckon you're after my bloody soul!*'

Robert had once read a book concerning contracts with the devil, when the pledge of a soul would secure for a mortal riches and fame beyond his wildest dreams. At the conclusion of the book, Robert remembered feeling envious and wondering whether *he* might one day receive such an offer, and perhaps thereby escape his own miserable existence. Whether averse to the idea or not, he had no intention of being cheated. Infuriated, thinking how close he might have come to losing his soul with nothing in return, he found himself almost shouting, despite Plowrite's ominous warning—a warning Robert was destined never to forget.

'Have care, Robert William Strudwick,' Plowrite enjoined, with the barest hint of menace. 'Calm yourself, lest you forget to whom you speak. I'm not "Old Nick" nor am I trying to steal your soul. Souls *cannot* be stolen and are *never* accepted unless offered willingly. Have you not guessed that I am Pentophiles, friend and mentor, the voice of your mind?'

Hastily, Robert swallowed his anger, partly in response to the threat in Plowrite's tone.

A tingle from the Book reminded him of what might be at stake and he fell quiet, taking time to digest and analyse the situation and to assess the import of the shopkeeper's words. What if this were true? It would explain why the bookseller's voice sounded remarkably familiar. It would explain everything—might even be the opportunity he had secretly longed for. Still suspicious, unwilling blindly to concede, he decided to probe a little further.

'If you really *are* Pentophiles, the voice of my mind, why are you pretending to be Henry Plowrite, a rotten shopkeeper?' Robert demanded. 'I'm not completely stupid, you know.'

The bogus bookseller leaned on the counter and gazed deep into Robert's eyes.

It was a critical moment—vital to his aspirations to ensnare the best potential intermediary identified in centuries. He *must* convince this boy his suspicions were groundless; enlist and develop his latent talents. Displaying masterful control, the being moderated its voice, added a ring of sincerity and strove to be at its most persuasive.

'You must believe I am but your guide and friend and am sent only to help unite you with the book, so that together you may fulfil your destiny, Robert William Strudwick. My true appearance is not of your world and although my regard for you is sincere, I fear you would find me a little frightening.'

His words, strange as they were, coupled with that deep, soothing voice had an immediate effect. Robert became calm, pliant and receptive. From the deepest recesses of his mind, strange new knowledge became available for recall, gleaned through extensive hypnopaedia over time. This being was positively *not* the devil, out to seize his soul, nor a monster intent on trickery, but a confidante with his best interests at heart and his well-being in mind. He became relaxed, anxious to please his mentor—perhaps his one and only true friend. Robert accepted Pentophiles' revelations without further question, committed henceforth to recognise the shopkeeper for what he claimed to be.

Thanks to careful preparation over a long period of time, through frequent and regular discourse, generally whilst the boy was asleep, Pentophiles knew Robert's proclivities well. He could readily determine, therefore, when his subject's mind was at its most receptive.

Pentophiles' moment was come, and he hastened to press home his advantage. His resonant voice echoed and reverberated with absolute conviction.

'All you have read in the dedication is true, with many wondrous events yet to unfold. Come now, Robert, this is your chance! Let me explain how the Book can be yours; grant you riches untold; rid you of enemies and brilliantly enlighten your future.'

His penetrating stare lessened as he relinquished his influence on Robert's mind. Cognisant of the probable outcome, he waited for his protégé to express himself in words. Patiently, oh, so patiently, Pentophiles watched in silence through Plowrite's eyes—and waited. Robert conversed with his indoctrinated subconscious; reprised his unhappy years; considered those perceived as enemies, and discovered a deep-seated longing for revenge. The satisfaction of retribution; possessing the Book; 'great power, untold riches' — irresistible. These considerations, combined with Pentophiles' persuasive voice and dark, compelling eyes helped him decide—well, almost.

Greed his dominant emotion, animal cunning and caution demanded the best terms possible before agreeing to anything. Maybe he could negotiate. That aside, one important question remained. Taking his courage in both hands, he plunged.

'You said I might be able to have the Book without paying? That's fantastic—but I'm *still* waiting for you to explain, especially if, as you say, you're not trying to steal my soul. You said I'd have to pay the full amount—no exceptions, but turned down my seven pounds. You don't want me to work in your shop or allow me to pay weekly, so what *do* I have to do, *Mister* Plowrite—rob a blinking bank?'

Secure behind the façade of 'Henry Plowrite', Pentophiles was almost confident of victory. The eagerness of the boy, his avaricious demeanour and wry humour virtually clinched it. Plowrite smiled. Pentophiles was delighted! In fact, the smile was more of a grimace. Control of 'Plowrite's' facial expression was never easy, harder still when at pains to ensure that no hint of elation or triumph should become evident in the voice. Continuing to select his words with care, the being from the netherworld set out to explain.

'It really is quite simple, Robert. Because you qualify by virtue of intellect, love of books and are over the age of thirteen—a perfect combination of attributes—I am authorised to offer you a contract granting custodianship of the Book...' He paused to raise an eyebrow and, when Robert nodded to confirm his interest, went on to elaborate.

'To begin with I shall explain the terms of the contract. Whilst perfectly straightforward and unambiguous, you must understand they are inflexible and not subject to negotiation. There will be no coercion, no pressure and you may sign only of your own free will.'

Maintaining the image of Plowrite required effort and Pentophiles took a moment to renew control of the illusion. He dared not allow the features to distort or the limbs to fade during these critical moments. Firm control re-established, the bogus bookseller continued.

'The contract provides that for so long as you solemnly undertake to follow the instructions from time to time made manifest within the Book, you will be invited to sign the contract. Having duly signed you will be granted immediate possession, entitling you to reap the benefits specified throughout the whole of your lifetime, without penalty, financial or otherwise.

'The contract contains four clauses, however, and these, whilst uncomplicated and simple to comply with, are nevertheless extremely important. You will note that some collateral is required, perfectly normal in instances of no deposit. Having your interests always in mind, I can visualise no circumstances in which you would be likely to break the contract and be thus obliged to suffer the terrible consequences. To help you remember and fully understand, I propose to read the details aloud.'

Robert nodded. Rapt, receptive, eager, acquiescent; every word and nuance registered. Spacing his words and phrases with precision, Pentophiles recited:

Firstly: You must *never* allow the Book to pass from your possession unless and until a Transfer Contract be properly executed.
Secondly: No person other than yourself may view *any* part of the contents whilst the Book is under your custodianship.
Thirdly: The Book will reveal each new situation *only* when appropriate and shall always provide instructions for its resolution. You must *swear* to follow such instructions to the letter and *never* attempt to obtain information beyond that which is current.
Finally: Your mortal soul shall remain your own property for as long as these clauses remain inviolate.
Only should a clause be broken shall your life be forfeit and you solemnly declare that in that event the aforementioned soul shall belong to Mephistopheles.

'As I told you at the outset it really is quite simple. Perhaps you would care to see for yourself?'

Busily assimilating and assessing Plowrite's words, Robert didn't answer immediately. Once having weighed advantage versus penalty, however, he inclined his head knowingly.

'I thought as much,' he said. 'I had a feeling my soul would come into the equation somehow. But, as you rightly point out, I'm not stupid enough to renege or run unnecessary risks. What's more, I get to keep two quid a week for spends as well as my seven quid. Right?'

It was Plowrite's turn to acquiesce. He, too, ducked his head.

'Absolutely, Robert,' he said. 'What is your wish, to proceed or to withdraw?'

The boy was no longer in any doubt. Filled with excited anticipation, Robert agreed. 'Yes please,' he said, eagerly. 'Can I have a look?'

The 'bookseller' fished beneath the counter and produced a

furled parchment secured with crimson ribbon. Untying it, he unrolled the document with a flourish and smoothed it flat.

'There you are then, Robert my boy,' he smiled. 'As you can see—exactly as I said. All you need do is sign—I shall witness your signature, and the Book shall be yours to keep.'

Erudite, worldly-wise, Robert would be wary of the small print in any contract, this one certainly no exception. The text was short and concise; even so, he read and reread every word, determined to leave nothing to chance. He found absolutely no ambiguity: every word, sentence and nuance crystal clear, no hidden meaning, no word or phrase capable of more than one interpretation. Satisfied, Robert nevertheless still sought confirmation.

'It *seems* clear enough, Mister Plowrite. I'll be rich and famous but the devil doesn't get my soul—not ever, as long as I obey the Book and don't break any of the clauses, right?'

'Yes Robert, that is precisely so,' Pentophiles replied. He went further: 'But I urge you never to violate the contract lest you suffer the agonies of the damned and writhe in dreadful torment throughout eternity.' He extended five bony digits and patted Robert's arm. 'I have grown fond of you my boy,' he said, 'and have high expectations for your future. Whilst it is undoubtedly in your best interest to sign, I feel it my duty to make sure you fully understand the nature of the consequences a breach of the conditions would bring.'

None of this was at variance with Robert's understanding and he was touched by Plowrite's solicitude—a clever touch from a master manipulator? There seemed no reason to equivocate further.

'Can you lend me a pen, please?' Robert asked.

Again Henry Plowrite smiled.

'Certainly, use mine and I shall witness your signature.' He produced an expensive-looking pen and handed it to Robert: 'Just remember one very important thing, my boy. The Book is for you and you alone. It will ensure your future and gain you ascendancy above other mortals. For these benefits, implicit obedience is but a small price to pay. But only on absolute acceptance of these conditions, and of your own free will should you sign. If you are *certain* you wish to commit yourself, then append your signature now.'

Unhesitatingly, Robert uncapped the pen, signed *Robert William Strudwick*, not with his usual flourish but, thanks to the rather viscous crimson writing fluid, slowly, carefully and laboriously. Pentophiles recovered the pen and used it to witness Robert's signature.

And so the deed was done. A keen-eyed observer would detect a gleam of triumph in Henry Plowrite's eyes, but not so Robert—he had bigger and better fish to fry. For starters, he tucked the Book carefully into his satchel.

Pentophiles picked up the key and signalled his intention to place the vermilion ribbon around Robert's neck. As the boy lowered his head in acceptance, he was too preoccupied to notice the so-called book-merchant's image turn shadowy and begin to lose substance. It was time for 'Henry Plowrite' to bid farewell. 'Goodbye Robert,' he boomed, sonorously, 'I shall doubtless see you again soon.'

'Goodbye Mister Plowrite,' Robert replied. 'And thank you very much,' he added, lamely.

Emerging from the shop, Robert felt vibrant, confident, his former sense of inferiority banished. He knew no-one would dare antagonise him in future – and those who had in the past were likely soon to regret it.

The Book was destined to have a profound effect on his life—just as he expected, of course!

A glance at the town hall clock told him it was 4.15. He did a double-take: What! Less than thirty minutes since he entered the shop? Impossible. Half-an-hour might account for time with the bookseller, but what about the time spent browsing? Robert shivered. Did the power of Pentophiles extend so far beyond the material world he possessed the capability to compress time itself? What other explanation could there be? None Robert could think of! He shrugged and turned his attention to more immediate matters. Grumbling pangs were a reminder of teatime but, despite hunger, the feeling of well-being returned and he strode jauntily along the High Street and across the village green where he broke into an exuberant trot.

Had he delayed, he may possibly have witnessed the bookshop wink from existence and simultaneously be replaced by the hoarding, though passers-by appeared not to notice. He might also have heard a strangely familiar, basso-profundo chuckle, or caught a whiff of a musty, lingering odour, vaguely reminiscent of putrefaction . . .

'The Book is mine, the Book is mine,' his feet seemed to call, as they rhythmically pounded the pavement. Puffing a little, Robert arrived home at 4.30 and went directly to his room.

Concealing his acquisition in the box reserved for personal possessions, he went downstairs and into the kitchen where mother was preparing tea. She smiled as he came through the door.

'Hello dear, how was school today?' she asked, without once mentioning that he was late. Shortly afterwards, she served a heaped plate of his favourite tea – sausage, chips, smoked bacon, mushrooms and grilled tomato, served on crispy, fried bread – *still* without a word of recrimination. And later, his father arrived with a cheery: 'Hello Robert, had a nice day?'

'Yes thanks, Father.'

The boy smiled, knowingly. Much was to change from this day forward . . .

Chapter Two
A Taste of Revenge

After tea, still buzzing from his memorable afternoon, Robert itched to consult the Book but, in order to maintain secrecy and avoid the risk of interruption, opted to wait for the privacy of bedtime. It would take time and experimentation to establish exactly what he could or could not do without exciting attention; therefore Robert pledged to conduct himself with caution from the outset. For this reason he masked his new-found confidence and amazing sense of euphoria by spending the entire evening reading.

Father stipulated that thirteen-year-old boys should retire at 9.30, but they might read for a further thirty minutes – providing bedtime was preceded by satisfactory behaviour. It would raise eyebrows were he to retire earlier, so Robert curbed his impatience until the appointed time, when he put aside his magazine and bade his parents 'goodnight'. He was in and out of the bathroom in minutes.

Repairing to his bedroom, he wedged a chair under the door handle, undressed and pulled on his pyjamas as fast as he was able. Finally, an opportunity properly to consult with the Book. Tingling with excitement and from contact with the treasured volume, Robert climbed into bed. Wriggling himself comfortable, he drew up his knees to form a makeshift lectern, released the clasp and opened the Book. Turning to the flyleaf, the following message fairly leapt from the traditionally plain page:

DO NO DEED UPON THE MORROW –
YET MARK WELL THE FATE THINE ENEMIES

Astounded and delighted, Robert made yet another startling discovery for, even as he watched, fascinated, the script lost substance, shimmered, and simply winked out of existence!

He took stock. Comprehension was certainly no problem; only a fool might fail to understand. No need for notes. Those incredible words would remain imprinted upon his mind. Clearly, he must do nothing the following day. Simply observe whilst retribution, presumably appropriate in nature, was exacted against former adversaries. Brilliant—he could hardly wait! Heeding the warning never to read further, he secured the Book and returned it to his box.

As he pondered the strange events of the day, he fell into a deep, dreamless sleep.

In keeping with normal practice, Robert rose early for papers and was out of the house before six. Towards the end of his round, his rear tyre began losing air and was flat by the time he delivered the last paper. With no alternative but to walk, he arrived home late for breakfast, tired, irritable and extremely hungry.

'If I mess with a puncture now,' he grumbled, 'I'll either miss brekker or be late for school.' As neither appealed, he opted to eat and walk, and defer repairs for later. Decision taken, Robert packed away a hearty breakfast and set off for school on foot.

Prefect Stanley Billham was a bully, a boy who used his fists at the slightest provocation and had a physique to intimidate those of lesser build. He led and dominated a seven-strong band of yobbish lackeys, obliged to comply with orders on threat of physical punishment. High on the list of those targeted was Robert Strudwick, who not only suffered abuse at Stanley's hands, but was endlessly tormented by his cronies, all under instructions to harass wherever and whenever possible. Today was to present just such an opportunity.

Nearing the school on bicycles, three of Stanley's minions spotted Robert ahead. They stopped. 'If Stanley finds out we didn't bother . . .' one shuddered. Another suggested, 'Let's sneak up and grab his cap. Keep to the grass, he won't hear us coming.' The third agreed. 'Good idea, let's make a race of it. One, two, three—go!' And off they went.

Something, instinct perhaps, caused Robert to sense danger and he leapt smartly to one side. With a clatter and screech of metal, intermingled with yells of alarm, thuds and groans, Stanley Billham's over-anxious, fawning yes-men collided, lost control and crashed.

There they were, ignominiously spreadeagled one way, bicycles another, the reason for their downfall obvious. Robert couldn't help but laugh! All were winded and bruised, one sported a cut lip. Nor did the bicycles escape lightly, judging from an awesome jumble of broken spokes, split mudguards and bent handlebars.

'Serves you jolly well right,' Robert chortled, gleefully, and strolled blithely on his way.

Brendon Ford – maths teacher-cum-part-time sports master and stern disciplinarian, a classroom egoist whose sarcasm and inflexible approach was appreciated by few—had taken an instant dislike to Robert when he first set eyes on the youngster. Never slow to miss an opportunity, he was especially sharp where Robert was concerned.

Wednesday was designated 'Sports Day'. After lunch, the class set off for the sports complex at West End, roughly two kilometres from the school and about half-an-hour's walk, the 'volunteers' groaning and humping the heavy bags of cricket gear.

West End facilities comprised three football-cum-rugby pitches, two cricket pitches, a bowling green, pavilions and changing-rooms with en-suite showers, the whole County-maintained for use both by schools and a number of recognised sporting organisations.

Two scratch teams were chosen and took to the field. Side 'B' lost the toss and were put into bat. Officiating as umpire, Mr Ford took up his customary position at square leg. Following some twenty minutes of tumbling bails, Robert – whose inclusion in the team was simply to make up numbers – was called upon to take his place at the wicket. True to form, he slogged wildly at every ball that came within a metre of his bat and, as usual, missed them all except one—the last of the over, a full toss. This delivery floated lazily through the air and curved at the last instant to make contact with the centre of Robert's flailing bat, rocketing with incredible velocity towards square leg. Brendon Ford either failed to see the ball or forgot to duck, for he was struck on the head and fell unconscious. An ambulance was summoned. Robert was a hero – temporarily, at least!

Amid derisive cheers, the unpopular teacher left the field on a stretcher. It was later learned he had had to receive emergency surgery to relieve pressure on the brain, a consequence of a fractured skull. Mr Ford could expect to be away from duty for several months.

Belinda Merriweather and Janice Pearson twittered, giggled and clucked, the way girls do. Walking ahead, they formed part of a group making their way back to school after the accident and the consequent cancellation of activities for the afternoon.

The girls seemed unlikely friends. Pretty, well-developed for her age, twelve-year-old Belinda was five feet four, auburn and something of a flirt. A year older, yet about six inches shorter, dark-haired, brown-eyed Janice was still developing. Puppy-fat was evident at thigh and hip; she padded her brassiere with cotton-wool and dreamed of snaring a boyfriend.

Coming to Moorgate Farm, Janice was first to notice a 'Beware of the Bull' sign prominently displayed on a board beside the gate of what appeared to be an empty field.

'That's new, Lind,' she remarked, pointing, 'but where's the blinking bull?'

'Dunno. I can't see him either,' her best mate replied, 'but I expect he's about somewhere. I know,' she proposed, ever curious, 'let's stop and watch for a bit, we've got plenty of time.'

Janice signalled agreement and the pair left the group and walked to the gate – only to be followed by Stanley Billham and two of his closest cronies.

Billham swaggered up. 'What are you two goggling at? Looking for somewhere to go?' he asked, cockily. (He fancied Belinda, but she couldn't stand the sight of him.) Belinda sniffed and stuck her nose in the air.

Janice was fiercely loyal towards her friend, but considered Stanley quite handsome and leapt at the chance to speak to him.

'Nothing really, Stanley,' she cooed. 'Just wondering if there really *is* a bull. We've had a bit of a look, but there isn't a sign of one anywhere.'

A mildly inquisitive audience gathered, providing an opportunity to show off that Stanley couldn't resist.

'That sign's meant to scare off trespassers,' he pontificated. 'They haven't got a bull.' He grinned, smugly. 'Nosy, soppy, girls. Haven't you anything better to do? Mind you,' he added, 'if you're stuck, I've an idea or two . . .' and he leered at Belinda, suggestively.

'Yes, you would have, wouldn't you,' she retorted, stung by his arrogance. 'But they *have* got a bull, smarty pants—a big brown one. I've seen it myself, so there!'

Stanley shook his head in evident disbelief. Both stooges grinned, knowingly.

'Don't be stupid, Belinda Knickerleg,' Billham told her. 'There isn't a bull. You're talking crap – as usual.'

He was not so much angry at being put down in front of flunkies, but by having his advances rejected out of hand.

'OK then,' she retorted 'If you're so sure, I dare you to run across the field and back but I bet you're too scared. All three of you, for that matter' she taunted, provokingly.

Stanley bridled. Belinda's outburst was not only detrimental to his status, but a direct challenge to his manhood. Maybe there *was* a bull – but, so what? The animal was nowhere in sight and the field no more than two hundred metres across. He could sprint to the far hedgerow and back without so much as working up a sweat.

Any challenge to the male ego might result in the abandonment of caution, more so around the age of puberty, but especially so if you were Stanley Billham, big man, leader of the pack, out to impress a girl. The words were hardly out of Belinda's mouth before he snapped a command to his henchmen and all three were over the gate and running across the field. They made it to the far side and were turning to come back, when a huge Aberdeen Angus lumbered from between two outbuildings where he had been taking an afternoon nap. The bull came to a halt, snorted angrily and paused to confirm that his recently-acquired territory was being violated. He shook his head, pawed the ground twice, let out a bad tempered bellow, and charged. Stanley and his companions were caught mid-field with little hope of escape.

Alerted by the commotion, farm-hands with pitchforks came running to the rescue, but too late to save the boys. All were tossed and trampled, but Stanley was rounded on and fatally gored as he lay injured and helpless on the ground. There was little Robert could do—even had he wanted to—and whilst the watching girls screamed and sobbed in horror and shock, the boys seemed rooted to the spot.

At the height of the furore, two lesser members of Billham's gang happened by on bicycles. Trying to see over the hedge without stopping, the pair—the last of Stanley's minions yet to suffer misfortunate this tragic day—collided, and sailed ignominiously into a wet, muddy ditch. Discounting minor scratches and an odd bruise, however, they escaped relatively unharmed.

Shocked, crying, vulnerable, Belinda was scooped up by one of the boys and skilfully pacified. Janice also seemed comforted, when opportunist Robert insinuated an arm around her waist and walked the flattered, unresisting girl all the way to her front gate.

Robert was more than happy with the manner in which 'justice' was summarily meted to those at whose hands he had suffered. But, concealing his delight and appearing sorrowful, he adopted the universally expressed sentiment: that that particular Wednesday should be remembered as 'Black Wednesday'. Privately ... well, that was another matter!

Arriving home, Robert was gratified to find the puncture repaired, and supposed his father noticed the 'flat' at lunchtime and, presumably, had been unusually disposed to be of service. Allied to the events of the day, the discovery triggered a heady sense of power, and moved Robert to embark on an orgy of gleeful anticipation regarding things that were yet to come. He daydreamed blissfully until teatime.

After the meal, he became impatient for bedtime and further consultation with the Book, anxious to discover what was to happen next and how long he must wait in order to become rich. Once comfortable in bed, he turned to the flyleaf, but it remained stubbornly blank.

The disappointment proved temporary, however. Consulting the Book on a daily basis, he received important instructions on one or more occasions almost every week. But even on days without the benefit of written guidance he was aware that unseen forces were influencing his life and recognised and acknowledged with gratitude the power that lay behind them.

Robert was still thirteen, yet people became increasingly wary of him – a good many openly fearful. Possession of the Book wrought changes to his demeanour he was unable to suppress. Whilst he strove for normality, his newly-discovered self-confidence was plain for all to see.

He learned to influence others and bend them to his will and, beneath his schoolboy facade, he nurtured and developed this ability. Before long, the majority of people could be persuaded to recognise and surrender to his preferences – or risk a displeasure most would prefer to avoid. For others, a few minutes in his presence engendered unease and an anxiety to please.

Improvements in his parents' attitudes continued. Father's former indifference never returned. He went out of his way to avoid friction and became almost obsequious at times. Should Robert complain, Mr Strudwick was apt to cringe, apologise and hurriedly acquiesce.

The monotonous diet once grudgingly produced by an incessantly carping mother was superseded by varied and plentiful meals, well-cooked and tastefully presented. She no longer nagged, but was pleasant, friendly, and careful never to offend.

Thrifty Alfred Strudwick was employed as a cashier at the local branch of the Midland Bank. The position brought salary commensurate with ability, experience and years of dedicated service. It might be supposed Alfred's frugality stemmed from looking after other people's money, but in reality he was simply miserly, a man who hated parting with money except for necessities—unless, of course, it was something he wanted for himself. Robert was deprived of many of the things that most boys took for granted—fishing gear, for example.

Alfred, a keen fisherman, indulged his passion with little regard for cost. He sometimes allowed Robert to accompany him, and might even lend the boy a rod and tackle. But this was on sufferance, and he steadfastly refused to buy Robert equipment of his own.

But Alfred's plaintive 'we can't afford it' seemed latterly abandoned. He took his son to the best fishing-tackle shop in Kingston, where Robert chose two rods – one in steel for pike fishing, and a rosewood beauty for general use, each with a carry-case of its own. Together, they bought a fine selection of tackle: reels, hooks, lines, lures, floats and sinkers, landing and keep nets, waders, oilskins, folding stool, tackle basket—even a fisherman's umbrella. And later, for Robert's fourteenth birthday, he was given a gleaming new bicycle, fitted with drop handlebars, the latest dynamo lighting, leather saddlebag and white-enamelled mudguards.

Youthful contemporaries—once derisive and cruel—displayed remarkable civility in his presence, and took care to be polite and complimentary even when out of earshot. Teachers ceased to ridicule and were at pains to help and assist, particularly Brendon Ford, a changed man since his unfortunate accident, whose attitude towards students generally and to Robert in particular became kindly, helpful and solicitous.

Encouragement and one-to-one tuition advanced Robert's academic prowess, until he became top of the class, not only in Maths, but in English, Business Studies and Science. During this period, he acquired a fascination for Biology, in which he also soon excelled.

The contrast in lifestyle suited the young man admirably and he studied hard, played hard and enjoyed life; perhaps as a consequence, his latent inclinations rarely surfaced. Making the most of his new-found freedom, he spent many useful hours exploring by bicycle.

In time, everything of interest for miles around—buildings, roads, estates, lakes, woods and countryside—were committed to his phenomenal memory. He ceaselessly recruited informers from among those who held him in awe. There were many. These unwitting pawns were encouraged to pass on information—any information—regarding anybody and everybody about whose activities he was the slightest bit curious. Thus were the foundations laid for what was to come.

One afternoon during the summer of 1999, whilst fishing on the River Mole, Robert was obliged to answer a call of nature. During the few minutes he was away from the river, his tackle-box was rifled and a number of items stolen, including a brand-new, red and yellow perch float. It was glaringly obvious the box had been disturbed and cursory inspection pinpointed the losses. With nobody else around, two boys fishing further along the bank seemed to merit investigation. Accordingly, Robert went along to issue a challenge. The pair denied responsibility but, whilst admitting they hadn't noticed anyone else about, each provided the other with an alibi.

'You're nothing but a pair of liars,' Robert told them, grimly. 'If you weren't so cocksure, I could be tempted to believe you, Scaife—except that that's my float; I'd know it anywhere.' And he pointed to the float sticking out of the boy's top pocket.

'Sod off, it's *not* yours, Strudwick,' the accused youth sneered. 'I got it from Kingston on Saturday. That's right, isn't it?' he asked his companion. 'I showed it you yesterday, didn't I?'

The boy flushed. 'Don't drag me into it, Sid. It's nothing to do with me.'

'Come on, Scaife, don't be stupid,' Robert said, holding out his hand: 'Pass it over – *and* my spinner and number twelve hooks, while you're at it, and we'll say no more about the matter.'

A well-built, tallish youth, Sidney rose to his feet. 'Get stuffed, Strudwick! Who do you think you're talking to? Piss off, or I'll shove your teeth down your bloody throat.' He raised his fists threateningly. 'And if you're still not convinced, how do you fancy a boot up the arse?'

'OK, have it your own way—for now,' Robert said, hastily backing away. 'But let me tell you this—and mark my words carefully: One day—one day soon—I promise, you'll be very, very sorry!'

That night, when Robert consulted the Book, the flyleaf conveyed outline instructions for the method by which he was to dispose of a sworn enemy—his very first Mission:

WHOMSOEVER OFFENDS BY WATER
SHALL PERISH BY WATER

Robert sat back to consider the words and how best they might be made effective.

Eagerly, he set about devising a plan appropriate to the crime—clever, foolproof, undetectable. Scaife was to die by water, so why not combine his demise with the recovery of stolen property? It wasn't long before he came up with an ingenious, childishly simple means of being rid of the thieving rat, one that fulfilled essential criteria and seemed entirely fitting.

Sidney boasted for days about his forthcoming fishing trip on the Thames, made no secret of his intention to fish the Middlesex bank near Hampton Court Bridge in the morning and switch to the Surrey side around lunch-time, intending to try out a secluded spot near Hampton Lock. When asked his reason, he said: 'Simple, I can fish all day without getting the sun in me eyes.'

The great day arrived. Prior to tying his tackle-box to the pannier, Sidney airily shoved a can of maggots to one side to make room for a flask of hot tea and a packet of corned beef sandwiches. With nets and rod-cases strapped securely to the crossbar, he waved to his mother watching from the window, and pedalled off gaily to spend the day fishing at Hampton Court.

Among other things, he was anxious to try out a recently acquired, state-of-the-art float.

Sidney, turned fourteen and an excellent swimmer, laughingly dismissed his mother's fears when, before he left home, she cautioned him to be careful and not to fall in the water.

After lunch, Robert pocketed a pair of flesh-coloured house

gloves belonging to his mother and cycled off to the Thames at West Molesey. Coming to a spot where gravel margins sloped gently to the water, he stopped and dismounted. Casting about, he found what he was looking for: a rounded, slightly-flattened stone around half a kilo. Wiping it with grass, he slipped it into his pocket without actually touching it.

About a kilometre from Hampton Lock, he came to a clump of bushes set back from the towpath. Checking that nobody was watching, he pushed his bike well into the bushes out of sight. Slipping on the gloves, he shoved his hand into his pocket to mask the presence of the stone, and set off to cover the remaining distance on foot.

Perched on his fishing stool, Sidney couldn't be seen from the towpath, but Robert knew precisely where to find him. A shallow inlet a few metres upstream from the lock allowed access to the river, otherwise screened from the towpath by thickets of tall bulrushes.

Sidney claimed to have discovered the spot during a bicycle reconnaissance the previous week. It was unlikely to be occupied, having barely enough space for one person and tricky to negotiate, but potentially worth the effort, promising some fine fishing so close to the lock.

Approaching with care, Robert heard the distinctive 'plop' of float hitting water. *There he is!* Just as anticipated, Sidney was too engrossed to hear someone creeping up behind.

Inching through the bulrushes, what little noise Robert made was masked by the rustle of stems, as they swayed in the breezes from off of the river. Robert brought the stone from his pocket and, with one smooth, fluid movement, delivered a single blow to the back of Sidney's head. Sidney toppled into the water with hardly a sound and sank. Robert grabbed the rod as it fell from Sidney's hand and calmly carried on fishing.

He slid the stone into the river and waited, not only to make sure Sidney didn't resurface, but to satisfy himself that nobody was nearby who might have witnessed the 'accident'.

But wait. There came the 'plash' of oars from upstream, followed by the appearance of a skiff some two metres from the bank. The rower, the boat's only occupant, ceased rowing and thoughtfully lifted an oar to avoid snagging Robert's float. As he drifted towards the lock he smiled at Robert in a friendly manner and asked, 'Caught anything, young fellow?' to which Robert replied, 'Not much, just a few tiddlers.'

The rower nodded knowingly and, hearing the blare of the lock-keeper's klaxon for 'gates opening', raised his hand in silent farewell, bent to his oars and pulled away. As soon as he was out of sight, Robert dismantled and packed the fishing gear, climbed aboard Sidney's bicycle and pedalled unhurriedly back to the thicket where his own machine was hidden.

When a man in a track-suit jogged slowly by, Robert went through the motions of pumping an imaginary tyre. Once the coast was clear, it took but an instant to recover the stolen tackle.

Finally, he shoved the remaining gear out of sight, swapped machines and set off for home, arriving in time to replace the gloves before his mother even realised they were missing. Discounting the appearance of the man in the boat, the operation had gone smoothly to plan, heralding the first major act of revenge signalled by the Book but orchestrated by him.

Success had him whistling cheerfully. It had been an interesting, moderately thrilling exercise, an adventure which certainly whetted his appetite for more – much more!

Sidney's parents expected him home by six but the normally reliable boy failed to arrive. At 8.00 p.m., when there was still no sign of Sidney, his father telephoned the police. When the facts were explained, a full-scale search was mounted, but it was Monday before frogmen located Sidney's body, trapped by a sluice beneath the weir adjacent to Hampton Lock.

Some hours after the body was found and identified, a man walking his dog came across a boy's bicycle and a quantity of fishing tackle concealed in bushes about a kilometre from the lock. Identified as Sidney's by Mr Scaife, the grieving father had no means of knowing that items of tackle possessed by his son earlier that day were now missing – a red and yellow perch float, a packet of number twelve hooks and a silver-coloured lure.

Post-mortem examination established death by drowning. No injuries were found on the body: contusions beneath thick hair at the back of the head passed unnoticed.

There seemed nothing to suggest that Sidney's demise was anything other than an unfortunate accident, but the boy's known swimming ability raised doubts and forensic experts were called. At this point, Detective Inspector David Melton from Surbiton CID took charge of the inquiry.

The area surrounding the spot Sidney fished was subjected to a search, but nothing of consequence was found, nor anything to suggest a struggle may have taken place. How and why Sidney's bicycle and fishing gear came to be concealed a kilometre from where he was fishing remained a mystery. Furthermore, the only fingerprints on the bicycle were Sidney's.

Police appealed for witnesses to anything unusual along the Surrey towpath between Hampton Court Bridge and Hampton Lock on 24 July 1999. Any persons who noticed a young man fishing in the vicinity of Hampton Lock during the course of that day were also urged to come forward. The appeal had a measure of success: two witnesses responded; both were duly interviewed.

It transpired that a schoolboy thought to be Sidney had been seen twice, once riding a bicycle along the Surrey towpath near Hampton Court at about 11.00 a.m. when he had stopped to ask an angler 'Caught anything, mister?' and again, just after 2.00 p.m., when fishing some hundred metres up stream from Hampton Lock, where he had exchanged pleasantries with a man rowing a skiff.

Whilst accepting the boy may accidentally have entered the water, neither the police nor Sidney's parents could understand why a strong, healthy lad—an excellent swimmer—failed to regain the bank from a relatively slow-flowing, non-tidal stretch of the Thames. An unanswered question of some concern, but in the absence of any evidence to suggest the possibility of foul play, the coroner recorded a verdict of 'Accidental Death'.

Comfortably ensconced in the library reading-room, Robert Strudwick read the full report and accompanying articles published in the *Surrey Chronicle* with interest and considerable satisfaction. When he eventually replaced the newspaper, he was not only wearing a smug, sardonic grin, he was wondering about the likelihood of a further 'mission' and, he hoped, one considerably more exciting!

It was around this time that Robert befriended Brian Carpenter, a boy about his own age. Brian was not overly bright. He came from a poor family: wore the same stained pullover every day, smelt of perspiration and tended to obesity, owing to an as yet undiagnosed glandular condition. Predictably, he was a target for teacher sarcasm and hurtful taunts from other children—just as Robert himself had been, although in his case for entirely different reasons.

Cornered one day in the playground, Brian was subjected to a series of prods and shoves by three belligerent boys, who fortified needless aggression with hurtful jibes.

'Fatso! Stinker! Lard-arse! Michelin-man!' they jeered—until Robert stepped in. Totally confident, secure in the authority of well-established persona, he barked, 'Pack it in! Clear off, the lot of you. Brian's a friend of mine. Any more and you'll have *me* to deal with,' he threatened, sternly. And when three, ashen-faced youngsters hurried away, Robert not only felt vindicated, he permitted himself a satisfied smirk.

Brian's relentless persecution came to an abrupt end, neither did he suffer further abuse from any of the teachers—no doubt the word had spread!

The boy took Robert's declaration of friendship quite literally and doggedly followed his 'hero' about, seeking an opportunity to perform small services in gratitude. This amused Robert, who set about converting gratitude into obedience and, within a week, simple, gullible Brian was completely under his control. Indeed, Brian Carpenter believed himself forever indebted to his 'friend and protector'. Perhaps he was—but there were also to be times when he would be very much afraid . . .

Chapter Three

Teenagers

At just under five foot, Janice Pearson might be considered suited to Robert Strudwick, at least in one respect. From the day he walked her home following the tragic death of Stanley Billham, she took to following him around, smiling, flirting outrageously, and doing her best to attract his attention. But never once did he condescend so much as to acknowledge her.

For two or three weeks he ignored her covert glances, affected not to hear the flattering remarks when within earshot, and treated the notes she left on his desk with indifferent contempt. Given the slightest encouragement, he would chat animatedly with almost any girl in the school, except Janice—or so it seemed. Eventually, tired of being ignored, yet reluctant to concede defeat, she summoned the courage to approach him directly.

'Excuse me, Robert,' she began, timidly. 'Please, could I have a word with you?'

'I suppose so—what do you want?' was his brusque reply.

'Well, I'm sure you know that I like you,' she blushed, 'but do you think I'm pretty?'

'No, not much!' Robert told her rudely, and walked away, leaving the girl close to tears.

Janice sulked the rest of the day. She tried to put him out of her mind, but without success. No matter what, Robert Strudwick would never be far from her thoughts and, so smitten, she convinced herself his hurtful response wasn't rejection, but a ruse to test her sincerity. Heartened by self-delusion, she resolved to continue her campaign and to bolster the chances of success by adopting an entirely different tactic—but what?

After long and careful consideration, she settled on a plan. That evening, Janice went to bed early. She slept soundly, rose at six and spent the next two and a half hours preparing for battle. She bathed, brushed her teeth until her arm ached, washed and set her hair, and didn't budge from the mirror until her make-up was exactly right. Finally, wearing her best dress and accessories, she set off for school, a very determined gleam in her eye!

At morning break, Janice watched from a distance as Robert strolled across the quadrangle to adopt a favoured position by the far perimeter, something of a sun-trap. Once he seemed settled, she threaded her way through scattered groups across the recreation area and, hips swinging provocatively, sauntered past Robert without so much as a glance. Continuing along the perimeter wall and round to the main building, she went inside. *That'll show him!* she thought—then flushed, feeling a trifle foolish. For not only might the ploy have failed, she may also have appeared rather childish.

But she need not have worried. Robert saw her promenade, of course. He also noticed how nice she looked and wondered why the girl who had lately dogged his every move should suddenly put on a display of calculated indifference. He guessed it was either to repay his snub, or to inform him she was no longer interested. He decided to find out which, and at the same time establish just how far the girl was prepared to go. It could prove entertaining. He would begin by surprising her—simple enough.

First out of class after the bell, he stepped from behind the school gate and intercepted her.

'Hi Janice. Wow, you look nice! Would you like to come for a walk?' he asked, engagingly.

Janice gasped, stopped dead in her tracks and blushed furiously. She seemed startled—but he could tell what her answer was going to be . . . *Talk about easy!*

'Oh, yes Robert, I'd like that!' she blurted out, astonished and delighted.

Bingo, hole in one! With the girl at his side, Robert set off across the village green, heading for the estate road through Waynflete and the private woods which ultimately would take them to Lower Green. Ten minutes later, he steered her into a coppice away from the footpath and they were alone.

Robert put his arms around her, drew her close and they kissed—awkwardly, dry-mouthed. Encouraged, he spread his jacket on the ground and sat down, pulling her down beside him. They kissed again and she submitted to his clumsy attempts to fondle her breasts through her clothing—in fact, it felt quite pleasant, she was surprised to discover. He kissed her, parted her lips with the tip of his tongue—and Janice kissed him back. *Wow!*

Enjoying the experience, Janice made no protest when he sidled his hand up her dress, but was shocked rigid when he roughly insinuated his hand inside her knickers. Outraged, she smacked his hand away and jumped to her feet, cheeks aflame.

'Just what sort of girl do you think I am, Robert Strudwick?' she screeched. Before he could stop her, she was off through the trees heading for home as fast as her legs would carry her, leaving him cursing furiously.

The next day, Janice pointedly avoided Robert. She stuck her nose in the air when he called to her in the quad. Later, in the canteen, she abandoned her lunch and stalked away when he attempted to strike up a conversation.

Robert smirked. He considered rejection an amusing challenge and set about winning her back. Changing strategy, *he* became the pursuer and she the pursued. Throughout several days of unremitting (but flattering) attention, Janice continued to resist his advances, but eventually relented and agreed to walk out with him again.

'Providing you behave yourself, Robert Strudwick,' she stipulated.

'I was only doing what *all* boys do, when they're very fond of a girl,' he protested, a statement she ignored. And when Robert walked her home that afternoon, he made no attempt to invade her privacy, although they kissed and cuddled a great deal.

Janice was delighted and thrilled. At last, the boy she had set her heart on seemed determined to woo her in the manner she imagined all romances ought rightfully to be conducted. In the days and weeks that followed she allowed the association to develop, during which time Robert maximised his formidable powers of persuasion in order to insinuate himself into the girl's affections. Slowly, carefully, he cultivated the association until Janice was completely under his spell. But it wasn't only affection that he sought, he also took control of Janice's emotions and made her his obedient slave.

The moment he judged her sufficiently subservient, he submitted her to a series of sexual acts that began with petting and rapidly extended in scope until no part of her body was safe from his prying eyes and fingers. Yet he frequently abandoned her for a fling elsewhere, returning to resume where he'd left off when—but *only* when—he had tired of the new encounter.

If she protested, he became threatening and abusive, claimed the interlude was only for fun and declared Janice to be the only girl he'd ever really wanted—and each time she forgave him and gladly took him back.

At fifteen, whilst Janice imagined herself in love and was frightened of losing Robert, she was also frightened *of* him, and so emotionally confused she was unable to differentiate between the two states.

She submitted to full sex before she was sixteen, an experience devoid of pleasure for her and which stimulated Robert to enter into a series of experimental, unnatural practices. He treated her with contempt, used her as he saw fit and, following the sex act, would pinch her intimately and make her cry, which apparently afforded him some sort of sadistic pleasure. On the only occasion she tried to put a stop to his deviant behaviour he produced a knife and held it against the terrified girl's throat until, fearing for her life, she tearfully relented. As time passed, she became increasingly nervous and depressed, yet was far too frightened to share her fear and misery with anyone.

Calderwood Clough-Cartwright was self-opinionated, pompous and overweight. He was also manager of the Esher branch of the Midland Bank, a position he had held since his appointment (several stones lighter) in 1991.

He was well-regarded by his seniors, who saw him as a capable, conscientious manager, one who thoroughly understood his duties and responsibilities to company, clients and staff—in that order. To his unfortunate juniors, he was a pompous, overbearing martinet who ruled with military precision, as if they were private soldiers and he the Regimental Sergeant Major. Furthermore, once the branch was running satisfactorily, he shamelessly delegated as much as he could.

The respectful knock on his door came (he consulted his watch) exactly one minute and five seconds after his summons—three full seconds earlier than anticipated.

'Come in, Strudwick!' he boomed, wriggling a corpulent backside a little more comfortably into his leather-upholstered chair.

The door opened. Alfred Strudwick entered and, in obedience to Mr Clough-Cartwright's imperious wave, seated himself gingerly on the lightly upholstered, straight-backed chair in front of the manager's desk, a chair engineered for minimal comfort and to dissuade those who might otherwise be inclined to loiter from outstaying their welcome. Clough-Cartwright began.

'Do you know why I wished to see you, Strudwick?' he asked.

'Yes, sir—well, I think so, sir!' was Strudwick's obsequious reply.

'Yes, I dare say you do, Strudwick'—he hurrumphed—'but I shall explain in detail, nevertheless. It is common knowledge Featherstone is to retire at the end of the year, but not that he applied for a transfer to Cobham in order to complete his service closer to home. I do not object—he is frequently late—due, he says, to delays and congestion on the A3, and I therefore approached 'District' on his behalf and have managed to secure their approval. Rather than prolong the matter, it has been decided to implement his request without delay, which will therefore create a vacancy for a new Chief Clerk. You have the necessary qualifications, experience and seniority Strudwick, so I have recommended you for the post—subject, of course, to a satisfactory interview. I trust you will accept the position should I decide to offer it to you?'

'Yes, sir. Of course, sir. Thank you, sir!'

Alfred knew perfectly well that the interview was a mere formality. Featherstone's transfer was approved at District and his replacement decided. Whispers had reached the branch via the 'grapevine' several days previously, but Alfred turned a deaf ear and waited for the manager's summons. He'd been repeatedly passed over for promotion in the past, and for reasons never fully explained.

Today, however, once the (largely irrelevant) questions had been answered with due deference, Alfred received a congratulatory handshake, an exhortation to work even harder in future and emerged in triumph from the manager's sanctum bearing the long-coveted title, 'Chief Clerk'.

Time passed. The increase in salary proved useful; fringe benefits even more so. For one thing, the Midland Bank operated a generous mortgage scheme for employees.

In August 1999, Alfred and his family vacated their council dwelling and moved to a modern, three-bedroom, semi-detached house in Kenward Crescent, Claygate. This momentous event was followed a year later by another—less spectacular, but certainly no less important—when Alfred traded his second-hand 'banger' for a brand-new family saloon, part-funded by means of a personal loan – again on advantageous terms.

Few dared cross Robert Strudwick; most who did were likely to regret it. Yet Steven Pearce, for years a source of minor irritation remained largely unpunished. Full, proper retribution was inevitable as far as Robert was concerned and he was frequently impatient for the Book to reveal how best it should be exacted. In reality, most of the incidents attributed to Steven were unfounded, the evidence circumstantial. Be that as it may, the earliest irritation (literally) had taken place when Robert was about twelve.

At a compulsory carol service attended by the school, itching powder had been put down Robert's neck by one of two boys sitting behind him. Both denied responsibility, but of the two, Steven Pearce seemed the likelier candidate. Then, only last summer, whilst he was swimming in the Mole at Imber Court, Robert's clothes had been removed from his saddlebag and hidden in the next field, causing him considerable inconvenience. There were no clues as to a possible culprit but, almost inevitably, Robert suspected Steven.

Born in 1984 and a year younger than Robert, Steven was easily his physical equal, which was why Robert had tended to avoid him. But in 1999, when an opportunity to teach the boy a lesson presented itself, Robert scarcely needed the Book in order to recognise it.

Steven was consulting a reference-book inside his desk, hand resting beneath the lid when a shadowy figure crossed his field of vision. Purely on reflex, he tried to snatch his hand away – a fraction of a second late, for the desk-lid slammed down hard across his fingers.

Shocked immobile, his mouth nevertheless opened wide and his lungs filled with air, ready to fuel the anguished roar of pain such injuries demanded, but, with great presence of mind, he managed to stifle the outburst at source. The crashing lid seemed extraordinarily loud in the silent classroom—and didn't go unnoticed. Brendon Ford looked up from the papers he was marking.

'What *is* going on?' he inquired, peering at Steven over the top of his spectacles.

'Nothing sir, sorry sir,' Steven lied. *Bloody hell! A pound to a penny, Robert Strudwick?* 'The lid of my desk slipped. Sorry sir,' he ground out painfully, and stuffed his squashed fingers into his mouth in a desperate attempt to obtain relief. His eyes watered, impairing his vision but, looking left and squinting, he was able to confirm that the blurred figure in the act of sitting down four rows away was indeed Robert Strudwick, back from visiting the lavatory.

Steven had long been wary of Robert, careful to avoid antagonising the boy who never failed to retaliate swiftly and viciously when provoked. The desk-lid was obviously no accident and Steven was at a loss to understand why Robert should behave so spitefully and for no apparent reason. Nobody was likely to admit to having witnessed the 'accident', which simply went to prove that both in and out of the classroom Robert Strudwick could do pretty well as he pleased. Prudently, Steven decided against making a fuss: better to hold his tongue and bide his time.

Steven was a friendly, outgoing boy, well thought of by teachers, popular with schoolmates, girls and boys alike. He had struck up a friendship with Janice long before she had taken up with Robert Strudwick and grown quite fond of her in a brotherly sort of way. When she began going out with Robert, however, he realised his feelings were anything *but* brotherly, but by that time, it was too late to say so. He concealed his dismay, and even though it was the last thing he wanted, respected her right to go out with whomsoever she chose; he studiously avoided her as far as possible, and was careful never to interfere, even when Robert began playing fast and loose. Unhappy, perpetually subdued, Janice seemed resigned to Robert's treachery.   Poor, brave, Janice! She wilted. Yet, unwilling to exhibit distress or cause concern, she strove to maintain an appearance of normality, and might well have succeeded, were it not for Steven, watching from afar.

He had long decided he would keep an eye out for Janice and was devastated when the vivacious girl became dejected, lost weight, lacked colour and was frequently absent from school. Steven ached to take her in his arms and comfort her, yet wasn't prepared to interfere with her relationship, unless and until she signalled a readiness to end it.

Shortly after the desk incident, Janice was making her way to classes, head lowered, her shoulders hunched, when Steven approached from behind, intending only to cheer her up.

'What's the matter Jan?' he asked, gently. 'You don't seem yourself. Have you been ill?'

'It's nothing, Stevie, thanks,' Janice returned, with a wan smile. 'Just a headache. I've had a few recently. But don't worry. It'll pass and I'll be fine, but thanks for asking. Subject closed.' There was a distinct air of weary finality in her voice. What did she mean? *'Subject closed?'*

Steven was having none of it. He grasped her by the arm to bring her plodding feet to a halt, took both her hands in his, turned her gently and looked her straight in the eye. His heart bled with pity at the abject misery he perceived in the pale, lined face and he became tender, protective, and solicitous.

'Come on, Pud, you can't fool me, you know. You've not been yourself for ages. If you won't tell me what's wrong, at least remember we're friends and that I'll help in any way I can.'

'Thanks, Stevie. I'm all right, really. I'll let you know if I need you.'

Steven nodded. Pressing harder might cause further distress—something he wished to avoid. Responding to his concern, Janice moved closer and kissed him on the lips, lightly, gratefully.

It was enough—for now! Holding her hand comfortingly, Steven walked the rest of the way without speaking—until they reached the school, where he stopped and turned to face her.

'Now don't forget, young lady,' he lectured, 'give me a shout if there's anything I can do . . . anything at all. I really can't bear to see you looking so pale and unhappy. Promise me?'

Janice nodded. Unshed tears glistened her eye and his enraptured heart lurched a second time. She smiled, disengaged her hand and hurried into school, leaving Steven to follow.

They weren't to know that their walk together, that innocent kiss, the holding of hands, were all reported to Robert Strudwick.

The brightly-lit, open-fronted establishment—boasting a full-length, chromium-plated counter, matching stools and stainless-steel drinks-dispensers—was designed to attract passing trade and, more specifically, the younger generation: a place to meet, enjoy a snack, a soft drink . . . All of these things it did admirably.

Kingston's Black & White Milk Bar, prominently situated opposite the bus station, had been refurbished and modernised during the late nineteen-forties. The attraction quickly 'caught on' and became practically an institution for teenagers for miles around, one of the few places they could meet freely, refresh themselves, gossip and generally 'put the world to rights'.

Although the establishment had changed ownership several times, it retained a successful format, and continued to flourish throughout the decades into the nineties, despite competition.

For differing reasons and independently of one another, five teenagers travelled to Kingston one Saturday. They were Calvin Smith, Caroline Lucas, Francis Bridgwater, Malandra Pennington and Robert Strudwick. By chance, all five visited the milk bar around the same time and met, though none were close friends.

Malandra was sixteen, the others something beyond their fifteenth birthdays, an age when the opposite sex starts to become increasingly important, yet no serious relationship existed for any of them yet.

Of the girls, Malandra was easily the most attractive. Blonde, petite, with flawless complexion and beautiful hair, her near-perfect figure would be the envy of thousands. She dressed fashionably and wore just a trace of make-up, effectively applied. Malandra had no shortage of suitors.

Caroline wore her straight, light-brown hair pageboy style. She played basketball and netball, sewed, knitted and embroidered—and still took her teddy to bed. Her figure tended to the dumpy, and she dressed to disguise the embarrassing lumps on her chest. Unsure of her feelings towards boys—strange, unpleasant creatures—Caroline became confused and uncomfortable whenever one ventured close or appeared overly attentive.

At five foot ten, Calvin Smith would probably top six foot in a year or so. A popular boy, especially with girls, fair-haired, fresh-faced and freckled, he was an outstanding athlete. Calvin wasn't the least bothered whether fair sex conquests were due to luck, looks or personality, or were simply the fringe benefits of sporting success—dammit, he simply enjoyed girls!

When it came to girls, classic looks put Francis Bridgwater in a league of his own. Well-travelled and worldly-wise, five foot seven and still growing, brown-eyed and handsome, Francis broke hearts regularly as he fell in and out of love: he was a 'love 'em and leave 'em' exponent.

Robert Strudwick assumed an ambitious, patronising attitude

THE FLYLEAF KILLER

towards girls. He was inclined, sooner or later, to make overtures to practically every pretty female he met. Despite his reputation and general unpopularity, he achieved considerable success.

By 3.00 p.m. all three Kingston cinemas were in the throes of feature films, which explained the number of empty tables in the milk bar. Caroline was perched on a stool sipping coffee when Robert walked though the doorway. He spotted her at once and exchanged greetings as he climbed aboard the vacant seat at her side. He ordered an iced orange squash.

Caroline immediately became ill at ease and fiddled nervously with the handle of her cup; she was much too close to a boy whose reputation where girls were concerned left much to be desired. Noting her discomfort, Robert placed a reassuring hand on her arm, but she pulled away in alarm.

'Keep your hands to yourself, Robert Strudwick!' she ordered, with an angry toss of her head. 'My name isn't Janice. I'm not a twopenny tart you can pick up and dump as you please.' She was clearly outraged; it was a public place; Robert apologised at once.

'Sorry Caroline,' he said, 'I didn't mean to offend you, but you seemed rather edgy and I was trying to be friendly . . .' He seemed genuinely sincere.

'Well, all right,' she said, mollified. 'But just remember, *I don't like being mauled*!' She took a sip or two of coffee, apparently to steady her nerves. Robert's drink arrived. He paid, took a swallow and returned the glass to the counter, then turned towards Caroline as if to speak, just as Francis and Malandra strolled in and made straight for the bar. Hard on their heels came Calvin Smith. Their arrival presented an opportunity for Robert to reassure Caroline further. He seized it.

'Very well, Caroline,' he said quietly. 'Don't worry, I've got the message. But look, there's Malandra—and, oh, Calvin Smith. I vote we take our drinks and ask them to join us. There are loads of tables available and we could make up a party.'

Caroline nodded, whereupon Robert picked up his glass and headed for the newcomers, leaving the girl to follow. All five seated themselves around two tables pushed together, and fell into animated conversation. Nobody seemed to consider their meeting up in any way remarkable, which said a great deal for the popularity of the place.

Ignoring Caroline, Robert contrived to sit beside Malandra and attempted to monopolise her.

'Hi Malandra, how are you doing? Wow, you look lovely, as usual, good enough to eat. Tell me, you tasty little thing,' he smirked, 'What are you doing in Kingston?'

Malandra giggled nervously, flattered despite herself.

'I'm fine thanks, Robert,' she replied. 'Just shopping for odds and ends. I ran into Frank in Bentalls. He was kind enough to offer me coffee, so here we are.'

On more than one occasion in recent weeks, Robert had unsuccessfully propositioned Malandra, and each time accepted her gentle evasion with a nonchalant smile, as though rejection wasn't particularly important. It seemed strange, therefore, that he should make a play for her in public, and she was uncomfortably aware of the cold, compelling stare behind his thick, pebble lens glasses. She shivered, involuntarily. Strudwick seemed not to notice.

Lowering his voice, he murmured, 'You *know* how I feel about you, gorgeous. I'm lonesome, I'm flush, so how about the pictures, my treat? There's a cracking film at the Odeon . . .'

He placed a possessive hand on her arm. Malandra pushed him away. She wanted nothing to do with boys right now—especially Robert Strudwick; he was beginning to frighten her. Instinct told her to finish her coffee and catch the next bus home. *Bother rotten, conceited, one track-minded boys. God's gift? Pooh, I hate the lot of them!* Maybe it was time *somebody* put arrogant, creepy Robert Strudwick in his place.

'Thanks, but no thanks and *especially* no thanks,' Malandra sneered, in obvious disgust. Her annoyance intensified as she went on, 'You're nothing but a weirdo, but in any case, you know perfectly well I came in with Frank, so what makes you think I'm likely to dump him for the likes of you?' and she gave Francis a beseeching look.

'Come off it, Malandra,' Robert sneered. 'Maybe you *did* come in with him, but so what? You're not his girlfriend; never have been. So how about coming out with me? I fancy you rotten—always have—*and* you jolly-well know it!'

Again, his hand went to her arm and this time she flinched and drew away sharply.

'Come *on*,' he insisted. 'Don't play hard to get. I'm offering you a front seat on the balcony. Look, I've got plenty of cash!' He flashed his wallet, stuffed with notes.

Malandra gave Francis another imploring look and this time he responded gallantly. He half rose from his seat and leaned across the table.

'Why don't you get stuffed, Strudwick?' he snarled. 'You heard what Malandra said. Keep your dirty paws off. She came with me and she's leaving with me, just as she says.'

His look of contempt spoke volumes. Robert flushed angrily. He also started to rise.

'Watch it, Bridgwater. Mind you're own business,' he growled, but hurriedly sat down again when Francis raised his fists.

Caroline said nothing, hoping Robert would collect a well-deserved punch on the nose. Calvin looked uncomfortable—but it wasn't his quarrel so he also said nothing. He feared Robert and decided Frank would have to finish whatever it was he'd started by himself.

Romantic opportunist, Francis spotted an opening far too good to miss. Malandra was extremely pretty and in need of help; she might be grateful, so why not? He grabbed the initiative.

'Come on, darling,' he said cheerfully. 'Let's get out of here!'

Malandra hesitated. Francis was nice-looking and seemed safe, but she didn't *really* want to go out with him—or any other boy, for that matter. She continued to dither and, misinterpreting her indecision, Francis rounded the table, elbowed Robert away, and lifted the girl to her feet.

'Don't worry about *him* sweetheart,' he said reassuringly. 'I'll see you safely home, and make *certain* the obnoxious, four-eyed little twit doesn't bother you any more today.' Abruptly, Malandra decided. Frank must surely be the lesser of two evils?

'OK Frank,' she agreed. 'I'll finish my drink and we'll go . . .'

Her words were cut short when Robert leapt to his feet, spilling his remaining squash down the front of his trousers. Dabbing uselessly with his handkerchief, voice thick with rage, he almost lost control. 'If you two leave together, you've had it,' he snarled. 'I'll get even one day, just see if I don't.'

It was more than Malandra could swallow. 'Don't you *dare* threaten me, Robert Strudwick,' she gasped, indignantly. 'Who do you think you are? Tyrone Power? You wish! Fact is you're nothing but an obnoxious, conceited, goggle-eyed pillock. Yuk, I wouldn't go out with *you* if you were the last boy on earth!'

Her contempt was plain for all to see.

'Yeah, she's right, so shut your stupid face,' Frank said rudely, and took Malandra's hand. Turning to lead her away, he hissed in Robert's ear, 'Arsehole!' and delivered a surreptitious, but remarkably accurate kick to the shins. He was rewarded with an anguished grunt of pain.

Francis and Malandra left the milk bar hand-in-hand without looking back. Neither could have registered the incandescent fury that flashed across Robert Strudwick's face. It would have made little difference if they had. Despite his anger, he was amazingly cautious, cunning and scheming.

'You stinking, lousy bastards! You're as good as dead—both of you,' he hissed, deliberately *sotto voce*...

The following year, taking advantage of father's car, father's tuition, private roads and common-land tracks, Robert learned to drive and, with the benefit of three professional driving lessons (a seventeenth birthday present), passed his driving test. Success behind the wheel coincided with another milestone—he landed a job!

At interview, Robert seemed just the young man they sought: willing, presentable, intelligent, with impressive GCSE grades, and his father a senior employee of the Midland Bank.

'Can you start next Monday?' Mr Hathaway asked. Robert most certainly could.

On Monday, 22 April 2002 Robert became a management trainee at the Long Ditton offices of Gaston Hathaway, a notable firm of estate agents with branches throughout Surrey.

Chapter Four
Noises

It was Sunday, 14 July, a little before midnight. For the third time since retiring, Daphne Frasier slipped into mules, shrugged into a dressing gown and padded uneasily out of the room. She crossed the landing and into the rear bedroom, where the sounds seemed more distinct, and listened. *There it goes again!*

Nervously, she peered from the darkened room through a slit in the curtains. A pale, crescent moon added little to a glimmer of reflected street lighting and, strain as she might, she saw nothing more than outlined shrubs and the garden fencing.

Daphne was by no means nervous. Her natural self-reliance had stood her in good stead after the death of her husband three years earlier. Although she missed him terribly, social work, visits from her daughter, her son-in-law and baby grandson helped heal the hurt and render the loss more bearable; they fostered a determination to get on with her life.

Knowing the neighbours were away for the weekend, she wondered whether the noises might be a scavenging animal of some description. The clatter of a falling dustbin often heralded the presence of a marauding fox, seeking an easy meal. But the more she listened, the more certain she became the sounds were not those of an animal. She hesitated a moment longer, tempted to go back to bed, and this time to stay there. Might there, after all, be a perfectly innocent explanation?

She frowned into the darkness, annoyed with herself for dithering, but instinct told her something was definitely amiss. At the risk of being labelled a busybody, she returned to her bedroom, picked up the telephone and dialled 999.

A brisk, female voice responded. 'Emergency! Which service?'

'Police,' Daphne replied.

'Connecting you,' the operator said, and after a single 'brrr brrr', a pleasant, baritone voice came on the line.

'Police! How can I help?' 'Emergency call from an Esher number 01372 448721;' the operator interjected, then: 'You're through, caller.'

'I want to report unusual noises from the garden next door—eleven, Rodene Close, Lower Green,' Daphne began, excitedly. 'The owners—the Pearces—are away for the weekend.'

'Just one moment, madam. Please confirm your telephone number, and state your full name and address.'

The quiet, authoritative voice again. Daphne became impatient. 'The noises, I keep hearing them. Someone's trespassing; if you hurry you might catch them. Hurry, please hurry. If you waste time asking questions, whoever it is will be gone.'

'Perhaps so, madam,' the officer said, 'but we still need details in order to take action.' *Keep calm*, Daphne told herself. Struggling for composure, she took another deep breath.

'01372 448721; Frasier, Daphne—Mrs. Thirteen, Rodene Close, Lower Green, Esher,' she managed, this time articulating slowly and deliberately.

'Right, got that. Please describe the noises; explain exactly why you called.'

'I'd gone to bed,' she said, 'when I heard unusual sounds. When I listened carefully, they appeared to be coming from round the back, so I got up and went into the rear bedroom, where the noises seemed louder. There were scraping sounds, and a sort of *thud, thud*, every now and then,' she went on. 'At first, I thought something was in my garden—an animal, perhaps. But when I listened again—I went back two or three times—I realised the sounds were coming from the next door garden. I mightn't have thought much about it,' she added, 'except that I know the Pearces are away until tomorrow, so that's when I decided to call.'

'That's fine, Mrs Frasier, thank you. You did the right thing. But I need to be clear about one or two things. Are you alone in the house?'

'Yes, my husband died three years ago.'

'I see, I'm sorry to hear that.' There was a pause, then: 'Tell me, you looked from the rear bedroom but saw nothing. Is that correct?'

'Yes.'

'Did you switch on the light?'

'No—well, yes—but only in my bedroom. I came back here in order to ring you.'

'Your bedroom—it's at the *front* of the house, presumably?'

'Yes.'

'Then it probably doesn't matter—unless the intruder spots it from the rear. Could he?'

'No, he couldn't. Definitely not.'

'That's fine. Now, don't worry. Leave everything to us. We'll send a patrol car to investigate.'

'Thank you,' Daphne said, 'I'm sorry to be a nuisance.'

'You're certainly not a nuisance. Thank you for calling—someone will be along shortly.'

'Goodbye, thank you again.'

With considerable relief, Daphne replaced the receiver. The call had lasted barely a minute. Quick, and nowhere as difficult as she had imagined.

Police mobile 'Zebra Two'—manned by PCs Gordon Bennett and Samuel Edmunds—To investigate a reported prowler at the rear of eleven, Rodene Close, Lower Green. Owners believed to be away for the weekend. Informant, Mrs Daphne Frasier, number thirteen.

At 12.22 a.m. the patrol car entered Rodene Close, PC Bennett at the wheel. He slowed to check house numbers, continued for some twenty metres or so, killed the engine and coasted to a halt, some way short of number eleven.

Vacating the car, the officers walked up the path of eleven and tested the front door and ground floor windows. Moving to the rear, they repeated the process. All seemed secure. When a cursory inspection of the garden revealed nothing untoward, they made their way back to the front, where PC Edmunds took it upon himself to comment.

'There weren't nobody lurking, Gordon,' he grumbled, 'Quiet as the grave—another bloody wild goose chase?'

'More than likely,' his partner agreed, 'we get plenty of 'em, these days ... oh, well. Anyway, we're here, so we'd better have a word with the lady next door.'

Edmunds grunted.

The policemen regained the pavement and made their way to number thirteen. Light showed at a first-floor window, the rest of the house was in darkness. As senior, Bennett took it upon himself to tap gently on the front door. The hall light snapped on and the door opened, framing a slightly-built, grey-haired woman in mules and a floral dressing-gown.

'Good evening, Mrs Frasier?' Bennett inquired, and when she nodded, went on, 'I'm Police Constable Bennett from Surbiton, this is Police Constable Edmunds.'

'Good evening, I've been expecting you. Won't you come in?' She moved back a step, opening the door invitingly.

'Not for the moment, thank you. We won't keep you long.' He produced his notebook. 'Now then, about fifteen minutes ago you reported hearing noises next door, number eleven, yet the owners—I need their name—are away for the weekend. Is that correct?'

'Yes, that's right. The owners are called Pearce. They went to Brighton.'

'Thank you. Can you describe the noises?'

Daphne sighed. 'Just after I went to bed, I heard scraping and thudding sounds somewhere behind the house. It was difficult to pinpoint the source, so I got up, went to the rear and listened—I went back a couple of times—and concluded the noises were coming from the neighbours' back garden. I knew the Pearces were away, so I dialled nine, nine, nine. I've heard nothing since. The noises seem to have stopped.'

Bennett scribbled briefly, and cleared his throat. 'I see,' he said. 'As you probably know, we've already checked next door, front and back.' (Daphne looked at him suspiciously: he seemed not to notice.) 'All doors and windows are secure and there's no sign of a break-in. We also checked the garden. Did you notice anyone hanging about?'

'No, it's too dark. With all the shrubs, I couldn't see beyond the fence anyway, even in daylight.' *Why the inquisition?* She felt a flush of indignation. 'But *somebody* was there, make no mistake—and it wasn't an animal, either!'

Silent until now, PC Edmunds decided to 'pour oil on troubled waters'.

'Nobody doubts you, Mrs Frasier,' he intervened, reassuringly. 'You make an excellent witness. What we *are* saying is that nobody's about now and nothing appears to have been disturbed. There's nothing more we can do, as I'm sure you appreciate.'

What does he mean? 'I hope you don't think I've wasted your time,' Daphne countered.

'Not at all,' Bennett said, 'you were right to call, and if you hear or see anything else unusual, please ring again. Rest assured, whoever was prowling has gone – probably legged it before we got here.' Sliding his pencil into the spine, Bennett returned his notebook to his breast pocket. 'Play safe. Make sure your doors and windows are locked, and try to get a good night's sleep.'

Daphne couldn't shake off a singularly uneasy feeling and sought to delay their departure.

'Would you like a cup of tea before you go? It wouldn't take a minute.'

Bennett shook his head. 'No, thank you. That's very kind, but we're still on duty and with considerable ground still to cover. Good night, Mrs Frasier.'

Turning, he started towards the road, closely followed by PC Edmunds.

'Good night—and thank you,' Daphne called.

They heard the door close, a rattle of bolts, and the rasp of a key in the lock. Bennett slid behind the wheel and closed the door. Edmunds reached for the microphone.

'Zebra Two—receiving?'

'Zebra Two, go ahead.' (The unmistakable voice of the station Duty Sergeant.)

'Nothing to report figures one-one Rodene, Sarge. No sign of break-in, all doors and windows secure. Nobody hanging about, nothing apparently disturbed.'

'Roger. What about the neighbour?'

'Confirms she didn't actually see anything, says noises stopped right after she phoned.'

'OK, carry on with your patrol. Keep an eye for anything suspicious—nip back once in a while, and make a further inspection in daylight before you knock off.'

'Roger Sarge, will do. Zebra Two, out.'

Edmunds replaced the microphone. Bennett returned the notebook to his pocket and started the engine.

7.40 a.m. Nearing the end of an otherwise uneventful shift, the officers returned to Rodene Close. They checked the doors and windows again. Everything seemed secure.

'Waste of bloody time,' Edmunds muttered, and headed for the gate.

Ever cautious, Bennett touched his sleeve. 'Hang on. We'd best check the garden . . .' (he yawned) '. . . in case somebody's nicked the roses.'

Edmunds reacted ungraciously by thumbing his nose, but nevertheless accompanied his fellow officer to the patio. Bennett glanced down the garden, suddenly alert. He took three paces and spun on his heel to confront his colleague.

'Hey, Sam, look!' he exclaimed. 'Someone *was* here last night, look at the grass. See those marks in the dew? Footprints—and neither of us strayed from the path.'

Edmund's eyes followed his colleague's finger. 'Crikey, you're right!' he exclaimed.

'Look, over there on the ground as well.'

'Where?'

'Over by the bushes—rhododendrons, or whatever.' He moved forward. 'Come on, let's take a closer look.'

He turned, side-stepped the washing-line and was about to cross the lawn, only to be restrained by his more-experienced colleague. Bennett grabbed his sleeve.

'Whoa. Not so fast, Sam. Something's up! Better steer clear of the grass, just in case.' Bennett's wisdom, born of sound training and years of experience, took him a step further. 'Tell you what,' he suggested. 'Nip next door and take a shufti over the fence. I'll wait here.'

Edmunds frowned. 'What for?'

'Someone could be watching us,' his partner sighed. 'We can't risk anyone coming in and poking about while our backs are turned.'

'Just what I was thinking,' he returned, a tad too hastily to carry conviction. 'But before I go tramping across Mrs Frasier's garden, oughtn't I to get her permission?'

'Yes. Tell her we've found *something*, but it's too early to say whether or not it's important. Suggest she keeps the matter confidential for the time being. Say: "Pending investigation".'

With permission granted, Edmunds traversed Daphne's neat borders and peered over the fence. Staring down at freshly disturbed earth, he whistled softly between his teeth.

'Better come and look, Gordon,' he called. 'Something's been buried—recently, by the looks of it. Come round and see for yourself.'

Crikey, that's all we need! Bennett thought.

'Come back first, Sam,' he ordered. 'Make sure nobody gets anywhere near this little lot, or we'll be in hot water.'

Edmunds returned as ordered. Finding things just as his partner had described, Bennett keyed his personal radio.

'Zebra Two.' No response. 'Damn,' he muttered. 'Out of range!' Leaving his partner to prevent unauthorised access, Bennett returned to the patrol car. He reached for the microphone, thinking *Daytime. Network relay. Stick to procedure!* 'Zebra Two, receiving?'

'Zebra Two, go ahead. Where are you?' Again the night-shift sergeant, sounding weary. Bennett knew the feeling, poor sod: eyes prickly from lack of sleep—just like his own.

'Back at figures one-one Rodene, Sarge. Found some marks on the grass, not visible earlier—might be footprints. More near a clump of rhododendrons. We've taken a look from next door's garden—figures one-three—to find freshly disturbed ground behind the shrubbery. Zebra Two, over.'

'OK, Gordon. Stay put, both of you. Make sure nothing's disturbed. A squad will relieve. I'll stick around until you get back. See you later, Zebra Two—over.'

'Roger, Sarge. Thanks. Zebra Two—out.'

Thoughtfully, Bennett replaced the mike. In circumstances as suspicious as these nothing, but nothing, would be left to chance. In the light of Mrs Frasier's call and subsequent reports, referral to CID became mandatory. Bennett rejoined PC Edmunds.

'Sorry Sam, seems we're stuck here a while. Squad coming out to relieve—CID most probably, but don't hold your breath—could be an hour or two before they get here. Sergeant Glinksky is none too thrilled, either. He's due to stand down, but says he'll hang on till we get back. Maybe we've stumbled on something important. He certainly thinks so, by the looks of it.'

'Oh, sod! Who'd be a bleedin' copper? Mark my words. It'll turn out to be a dead cat! Oh, hell! I'm knackered, thirsty, starving, overdue a crap—and I want my bloody bed!'

'Can it, Sam. You're not the only one. Just think of that lovely big plate of canteen bacon and eggs, with gallons of tea and piles of hot buttered toast!' He grinned, impishly. 'And I'll bet you a fiver it's no dead cat—are you on?'

Edmunds shook his head, hastily.

'Not bloody likely. Since when did *you* bet on *anything* except a stonking certainty?'

Bennett's eyes twinkled—but immediately he became serious again.

'To save time, I'll go back to the car and get the report started. You carry on here.'

Edmunds glanced at his watch – 7.55 a.m. He shrugged.

'OK, Gordon.' His reluctance was obvious. 'I hope Glinks gets his finger out. Stuff being stuck here half the bloody morning.'

Bennett, wisely perhaps, made no reply.

'Glinks' did get his finger out, however. At eight thirty on the dot – contrary to Bennett's forecast and coinciding with the completion of his draft report—the 'cavalry' arrived: a formidable, professional squad, comprising plainclothes CID officers Detective Sergeant Ben O'Connor, Detective Constables Harry Slade and Graham Gibson and, for security duties, a uniformed bobby. Swiftly debriefed, Bennett and Edmunds were finally relieved—their shift was at an end.

Back at the station at 8.45, Bennett finalised the report and submitted it to a bog-eyed Sergeant Glinksky, who had awaited their return as promised, riven with curiosity. Stuffed with breakfast, the officers chatted a while, speculating as to what might or might not be recovered from the garden, Edmunds steadfastly refusing to bet on his pussycat assertion. By 9.15, over a third mug of tea, however, both men began to nod. It was time to call it a day.

Meanwhile, at Rodene Close, Mrs Frasier was interviewed and her statement taken. The task of identifying and preserving clues began; the investigation was under way.

At 10.30, DS O'Connor, in the interests of confidentiality, contacted headquarters using Daphne's hallway telephone and asked to be put through to Detective Inspector Melton.

'Melton,' the familiar voice announced.

'Good morning, sir. O'Connor. I'm calling from Rodene Close.'

'Good morning, Ben,' his senior responded—then started firing questions: 'What's up? Why phone? What's wrong with your personal radio—well?'

'Flat spot, sir. Lower Green's well named, it suits. Mobile's OK, but networked. This is a sensitive matter, so I thought it better to land line. OK sir?' *What's eating the old grump?*

DI Melton hesitated before he replied.

'OK. What's the position? Anything important? Incidentally, I've already seen Bennett and Edmunds' report.'

O'Connor was also silent for a moment, gathering his thoughts.

'Well, Guv'nor,' he finally said, 'keep your wool on. It's bad news, I'm afraid. We've a murder on our hands—a nasty one at that. I'll try to be brief, although there's quite a bit to report. The footprints on the grass didn't amount to much, but Slade spotted a fairly distinct impression behind the shrubs. We took a *Quickcast* there and then, in case it got trodden on. I roped in Slade and Gibson as you suggested—good job I did. Before you could say 'Knife', Gibson found cloth fibres on a fence post—he must have eyes like a hawk. While the ground was much as the late-night visitor left it, Slade took soil samples. He also shot the photos. With that out of the way, they set-to with spades and discovered the body. Shocking!

Crudely butchered, dismembered, wrapped in plastic sheeting and shoved in dustbin liners, four in all, each tied at the neck with string. One contained the head and arms of what appears to be a young woman—not a pretty sight, I might add. I came close to throwing-up. The rest of the body divided between the other three bags. In a word, sir, gruesome!

We've a bobby minding the pavement; the gardens are taped front and rear. There's no space for an awning, so I've organised a tent for the lawn, due shortly.' O'Connor paused, thought for a moment, and asked, 'I wonder sir, would you mind alerting the pathologist? I don't want to use Mrs Frasier's phone more than absolutely necessary.'

'Certainly Ben, will do—and thanks. Give me half an hour. I'll be on my way.'

Chapter Five

The Body in the Garden

Detective Inspector David Melton, CID, arrived at 11 Rodene Close, Lower Green, Esher at 11.30. Unaccompanied, driving his official Rover, he drew to a halt behind two other cars, carefully locked his vehicle and made directly for the gate.

He was recognised, saluted and waved inside by the uniformed officer on duty. Ducking beneath the blue and white tape proclaiming *POLICE. DO NOT ENTER.* he acknowledged the greeting with a smile.

As if on cue, Detective Sergeant Benjamin O'Connor, CID, appeared from the direction of the rear and neatly intercepted his superior. 'Morning again, Guv'nor. Nasty business!'

'Yes,' the DI replied, grimly, 'Headline news—but the way the cookie crumbles, I suppose.'

'One way of looking at it,' his assistant remarked, adding, 'but we can't pick and choose, more's the pity.'

'Would that we could,' Melton replied, drily. 'Would that we could.' He shrugged. 'But, enough of the chitchat. Where are we up to?'

'Nothing new, Guv'nor—except that Doctor Matthews arrived ten minutes ago and is conducting a preliminary examination right now.'

'OK Ben,' Melton said. 'Thanks. I'll catch up with him directly. Meanwhile I'd like to inspect the spot where the body was found. You've spoken with Mrs Frasier?'

'Yes sir, she's already made a statement.'

'Good, I'd like to see it. But before I do, I want you to have another word with her. Ask her if she can add anything to her statement, and warn her not to speak to anyone just yet. It won't be long before the press gets wind of our presence, and we don't need reporters milling about and getting under our feet—at least until we're good and ready.'

'Right sir.'

O'Connor left, leaving Melton to find his own way to the rear.

The garden was typically suburban: patio, lawn, shrub borders, vegetable plot, garden shed. Already erected, the tent was positioned to the right of the lawn, tight to the shrubbery—mainly rhododendrons—close to a pair of bamboo canes pushed into the ground, supporting blue and white ribbon on either side of a half-metre gap, positioned to allow access to the shrubbery.

Melton waited as two barrier-suited, spade-bearing officers emerged; then he squeezed through. Behind the shrubbery, he found himself in a half-metre wide space, which extended about six metres up to the house. Other than freshly-turned earth, there seemed little else of significance. Melton stood still in order to register the scene, then emerged from the shrubbery and entered the tent.

In relief against the glare of portable lighting, a white-coated, stooped figure with his back to the doorway straightened up, and a dapper, grey-haired man in his fifties turned to greet the newcomer. He smiled gravely.

'Good morning, Detective Inspector. I saw no point in leaving the remains in situ, so I asked your forensic chaps to transfer the bags out here. It fitted in nicely—they were more or less finished, and with the 'body bags' out of the way, were able to get on with back-filling. I believe they've finished, in point of fact.'

Melton nodded, impressed. Doctor Matthews had an ability to take charge without offending.

'As you see,' the professor was saying, with a twinkle, 'they brought me the corpse in bits, still wrapped and more or less as it was unearthed.' He wrinkled his nose. 'I've not quite finished my initial examination, but I won't be long—if you'd care to hang on a minute . . .'

Melton nodded, and Professor Stephen Matthews bent to resume. He straightened again after a minute or so.

'Come and look,' he invited, 'but brace yourself. This isn't particularly pleasant.'

The pathologist stepped to one side. He snapped off his gloves, dropped them into a bag, produced a notebook from an inside pocket and proceeded to make notes.

Melton bent for a closer look. His stomach heaved. Here lay the pathetic bloodied remains of a cruelly dismembered body. Forcing himself to examine the grisly remains, he swore softly.

Spread on the grass were several sheets of opened-up, black plastic bin-liners, on which lay the pitiful remains of what was still recognisably a naked girl. Fair, matted hair framed a decapitated head; remnants of youthful breasts clung to a lacerated torso.

Little more than a child, her face had been slashed, battered and ripped, the few remaining features scarcely recognisable as human. Melton shuddered. It wasn't a sight for the squeamish.

A transparent specimen sack adjacent to the tent wall caught the detective's eye. It contained several plastic bags, similar to the sheets beneath the remains. All were soil-encrusted and heavily stained with blood.

Melton was sickened and appalled. 'If it would help, David,' Matthews said, 'I've a spot of brandy . . .'

He reached inside the valise, produced a hip-flask and proffered it sympathetically. Gratefully, the DI accepted.

'Thank you Stephen,' Melton said, returning the flask. 'That certainly helped.'

'You're entirely welcome, my friend. By the way, Sergeant O'Connor organised that large specimen sack. He wants the bin-bags and string preserved for forensics, leaving plenty of room for the sheets after I've finished. Incidentally, it was my idea to spread them to prevent staining the grass.'

It was stating the obvious, but Melton realised the professor was prompting a return to reality. Pulling himself together, he said, 'We cannot afford to be maudlin, but I make no excuses for being affected when obliged to look closely at something like *that*, the poor soul!' He shuddered. Then: 'What have you established so far, Doctor Matthews?' he asked, formally.

'Not a great deal at this stage, I'm afraid, Inspector. Death probably occurred some eighteen to twenty-four hours ago, although I cannot be specific. Female of course. Young—late teens I should think—a little over five foot, somewhere around seven stones. Killed elsewhere, transported here almost certainly, and not long dead before dismemberment, judging by the amount of blood. Cause of death? It's impossible to say until after post-mortem.'

Melton nodded, thoughtfully. He knew the pathologist well.

The regard each held for the other had rapidly developed into friendship—but a friendship neither permitted to interfere with professionalism. Both observed the formalities demanded by position, more especially in the presence of others.

'I appreciate what you say. But can you give me something more? Anything that might help identify the animal responsible for this ... atrocity?' He gestured. Again, Matthews shook his head.

'Sorry Inspector, I've told you as much as I can. Anything more would be speculative. I prefer to wait until the post-mortem.'

Melton hesitated. Stephen was unlikely to be drawn further, but the pathologist's intuition was legendary. His thesis, 'The Workings of the Criminal Mind' was a well-respected study. Might he therefore be persuaded to speculate? Suggest what type of person could be capable of this sort of crime? His train of thought was interrupted by the sound of nearby voices. *Damn, what's going on?* He decided to postpone quizzing the professor until later. Doctor Matthews was right. Better await the post-mortem and hard facts. Time enough for theory, should nothing tangible emerge on which to build. The voices were louder, more heated. Irritated, Melton turned to the exit, pulled back the flap and stepped outside.

Standing on the patio, whilst a well-built youth looked on and the uniformed officer from the gate stood by, a middle-aged couple were haranguing O'Connor. The man gesticulated angrily, and blustered.

'I'll tell you just once more, copper. This is our house and you've no right to stop us coming and going as we damn-well please. I don't care *what* you've found in the bloody garden. Who the hell gave you permission to poke around out there in the first place? And what's that sodding great tent doing on my lawn?'

Patiently, O'Connor set out to explain.

'Calm down, Mr Pearce. As I've already told you, a serious crime has been committed and we've been obliged to close the garden to preserve vital evidence . . .' He broke off. DI Melton was emerging from the tent and starting across the lawn. Evidently relieved, DS O'Connor gestured with his thumb. 'Here's Detective Inspector Melton, the officer in charge, perhaps you'll listen to *him*, Mr Pearce.'

Perhaps awed by the appearance of a senior police officer, the man allowed his anger to subside. Ben O'Connor stepped to one side: the uniformed the bobby discreetly returned to his post. It required but a single pertinent question to establish that George and Nancy Pearce—accompanied by Steven, their sixteen-year-old-son—were back from a weekend trip.

Mr Pearce had not taken too kindly to being accosted at his front gate by a uniformed policeman. He had refused to accept that he and his family were to remain in the house until further notice, and was objecting vehemently to the blanket appropriation of his garden. Brushing past the officer, he had bulldozed his way to the rear until intercepted by DS O'Connor. He was still, understandably, perhaps, indignant.

'After all,' he protested, 'Nancy wants to go shopping: we've nothing in for dinner.'

'Well, Mr Pearce,' soothed Melton, 'I understand your point of view, but it is important you co-operate with Detective Sergeant O'Connor. If you just answer his questions, there will be no further restrictions on your movements or those of your family.

'You must understand, however, this a murder inquiry and important evidence has been found in your garden which must remain closed until further notice. Carry on please, Sergeant!'

Melton turned on his heel and strode back to the tent, effectively terminating the conversation, giving DS O'Connor an opportunity to recover his lost initiative.

'Shall we go inside, Mr Pearce?' he suggested. 'Perhaps you'd care to lead the way?'

But, even now, George Pearce was determined to have the last word. 'What about Steven? Surely, you don't need him as well? He's due back in school at twelve to start his exams.'

O'Connor sighed. 'In that case he's free to go. No doubt you and Mrs Pearce will be able to provide us with sufficient information for the time being.' He turned to the youth. 'It seems you've something better to do, young fellow. You can cut along if you like. If we find we need to talk to you again, we'll let you know.'

Back across the lawn, Melton re-entered the tent.

'Sorry to keep you, Doctor. House-owner problem.'

The pathologist smiled.

'Not at all, David—gave me time to finish. I'd like to get on with the post-mortem, and the sooner the remains get to the mortuary the sooner I can get started. Um—did you happen to notice whether the ambulance has arrived? I asked your Sergeant to call one half an hour ago?'

'It arrived five minutes ago—sorry, I should have mentioned it. While I was talking to Mr Pearce—the house owner—the driver came round the corner, probably realised it wasn't a good moment and hightailed it back outside.'

'Tactful of him,' Matthews commented, adding crisply, 'I've all but finished here. I'll give them the go-ahead on my way out.'

DI Melton glanced at the corpse, snapped his fingers and exclaimed, 'I almost forgot. Sergeant O'Connor. Would you mind hanging on while I fetch him? I think he should view the remains properly, having had only the briefest of glimpses earlier. I doubt whether he fully comprehends what was done to that poor girl. It would take but a couple of minutes.'

'By all means. I'll grab a spot of lunch and go straight to the mortuary. I should be through with the post-mortem by four. Will you call, or shall I give you a ring?'

'Thank you. I'll be there at four. I'll just fetch O'Connor.'

Detective Sergeant O'Connor accepted it was his duty to see for himself the full extent of the atrocities perpetrated on the young woman. He entered the tent and, like Melton—despite having glimpsed the severed head and arms earlier—turned pale at the sight of grisly body-parts lying like pieces of a macabre jigsaw puzzle where the pathologist had positioned head, limbs and torso for the purpose of taking measurements. He gulped and turned away.

'Thank you, Doctor,' he said, shakily. 'We can't afford *not* to catch the bastard responsible for this, can we?'

It was a rhetorical question. Matthews grunted. 'I'll see you later Inspector,' he said, and duly departed.

Gloved hands placed six pieces of corpse into a body bag—sparing the pathetic remains the indignity of further exposure—transferred the misshapen bag onto a stretcher, and covered it respectfully with a blanket. The officers followed the stretcher to the waiting vehicle, and watched while it was carefully loaded and driven away.

Returning to the garden, O'Connor signalled to the waiting detectives who recovered the sheeting from the grass and placed it into the specimen sack, which was duly sealed and labelled for forensic examination. David Melton had a question.

'I presume Mrs Frasier had nothing further to add, Sergeant?'

'No sir, not a sausage,' his right-hand man replied. Melton went for a walk.

Keeping to paths, keen eyes missing nothing, hands clasped characteristically behind his back, the DI prowled the garden, committing details to memory, taking in atmosphere, a technique which had led to the successful resolution of his first investigation as a Detective Inspector and paid dividends on numerous occasions since.

Several days of forensic testing would ensue before the garden could be returned to its owners, and Melton wanted to get the feel of the place before fingertip examination began, centimetre by centimetre.

The house itself was in no way connected with the crime, so the search for evidence need not extend beyond the garden. The owner and his family were, therefore, free to come and go as they pleased. Local inquiries were in hand, and incident-room facilities permanently in place at Police Headquarters—minutes away by road—were preferable to a cumbersome caravan at the scene. Rodene Close was not a 'through road' and the body had been buried at night, rendering the likelihood of obtaining witnesses slender. But an appeal would be launched, nevertheless.

Melton spent ten minutes in the garden, returning again to the space behind the shrubbery. Here, he contemplated the disturbed ground thoughtfully, finding it hard to believe a spade or similar implement could be so effectively wielded in such confined space and in almost total darkness. Melton knew with absolute certainty that whosoever had buried the bags in such an unlikely place had planned carefully in advance: they could never have stumbled across the spot by chance.

When Melton finally left the garden, O'Connor was waiting to buttonhole him.

'Mr Pearce co-operated like a lamb, Guv'nor; says he'll call at Esher 'Nick' around four to make a statement. The ground search is organised, which means I've finished here for now. If you're through, I thought we might grab a bite on the way back to headquarters—if you fancy lunch, that is.'

THE FLYLEAF KILLER

The DI glanced at his watch. 'Twelve o'clock, already? My, doesn't time fly! I'm not particularly hungry, but we're in for a late one and I'm not overly keen on canteen sandwiches—they generally taste of cardboard. That being so, a decent cup of coffee and a ham roll wouldn't go amiss—and I'd like to compare notes, anyway, preferably uninterrupted. Come on, we'll use my car. You can pick yours up later.'

The two lunched on chicken sandwiches and some of the excellent coffee for which the small restaurant in Surbiton was noted. They arrived back at HQ just before 2.00 p.m. O'Connor went to check progress on the house-to-house and other inquiries under way. These would systematically proceed until every adult in the area had been interviewed or accounted for, passers-by quizzed, nearby gardens checked, every outbuilding searched.

Prior to dealing with accumulated reports and correspondence, Melton updated his superior, Detective Chief Superintendent Jarvis, while O'Connor took the opportunity to collect his car.

Back in his office, Melton fielded an appeal for help from the Desk Sergeant, who was under siege by reporters, who had somehow caught wind of 'unusual police activities' and were pestering him for information.

'Dammit,' grumbled Melton. 'Stall 'em for a bit, I'll be right down.'

Shortly afterwards he walked straight into bedlam.

'Dangerfield, Evening News. What's this about a murder, Inspector?'

'Surrey Chronicle. What can you tell us, Mr Melton?'

'Benjamin Jopney, Thames Television' (complete with cameraman) . . .

'Gentlemen, gentlemen, quiet, please!' They hushed. 'Thank you.'

'We are in the early stages of a murder inquiry. A body has been found, as yet unidentified. I am unable to release any further information at present. Some progress has been made, however, and I shall be pleased to brief you this afternoon at seventeen hundred hours. For the moment, please disperse quietly. Thank you, and good day.'

With that Melton walked away. He summoned his secretary and dictated a draft press release. It was typed and back on his desk within minutes ready for approval and signature.

SURREY CONSTABULARY—SURBITON DIVISION
PRESS RELEASE No. 6721
Monday 15 JULY 2002

Acting on information received, the body of a young woman was discovered earlier today, buried in a garden at Rodene Close, Esher.

The deceased has not yet been identified and any member of the public who has any information regarding missing persons which might assist the police should contact Surbiton Police Headquarters or their nearest police station as soon as possible. Anyone who may have noticed anything unusual in the vicinity of Rodene Close or either of the access roads—Cobham Street and Methodist Way—between the hours of 10.30 p.m. and midnight on Sunday 14 July 2002 are also asked either to come forward, or ring the incident room free on 0801 661 7788. All information received will be treated as confidential.

Melton made no mention of the atrocities perpetrated on the unfortunate victim. To do so at this stage might not only prejudice the inquiry, but precipitate a flood of crank telephone calls. Neither was there any point in referring to the post-mortem. He would need to digest the findings before deciding to what extent he would recommend the media be informed.

The DI cleared the release with the 'Chief', arranged for photostat copies to be made and returned to his office to finish clearing his desk.

That done, he took a service lift to the ground floor and, skirting reception, left the building via a rear door to reach the car park unchallenged. Ten minutes later he was seated in a small anteroom at the mortuary, waiting for Professor Matthews.

It was not quite four and Melton fidgeted. He thought about his relationship with Stephen. Incredibly, nine years had passed since David Melton was a newly-promoted, ambitious Detective Sergeant and it was about this time that Professor Matthews retired from a London Teaching Hospital to take up a pathology post for the county of Surrey, based at Surbiton. It was his home town: a very convenient appointment. He later told Melton he expected the appointment to be less demanding and, with the need to commute abolished, at last have time to write the book he had had planned for years. They had met professionally several times before a chance encounter at Claremont disclosed an interest that had nothing to do with work—more about irons, putters and swing! Working encounters increased, following his promotion to Detective Inspector. Appreciation of each other's professionalism and an occasional round of golf led to their becoming firm friends, despite their widely differing backgrounds.

David sighed, picked up a dog-eared copy of *The Reader's Digest* and began to read about the Eskimos—how civilisation had intervened, changing a once hard but happy existence into one of comparative wealth but, sadly, one which encouraged indolence and alcoholism. As he was nearing the end of the article, he heard a door slam and the sound of approaching footsteps. He put the magazine down as Professor Matthews came into the room.

Still in shirtsleeves—though fortunately minus rubber boots, apron, gown and gloves—the pathologist smiled gravely and sat down to face Melton across the table.

The DI half rose in greeting, but Matthews gestured him to remain seated.

'Don't get up on my account, Inspector,' he said. 'Shall we get on?' And he proceeded to read from notes, without preamble:

'The deceased was female, slightly-built, aged between sixteen and eighteen years: a natural blonde with no distinguishing marks. Height: five foot three inches. Calculated body weight seven stones three, taking blood-loss and missing tissue into account.

Death occurred sometime between 9.00 p.m. and 11.00 p.m. yesterday—some fourteen hours before I examined the body, as a result of massive bleeding from the neck.

Both the jugular vein and the carotid artery were severed. When life ceased, decapitation and dismemberment quickly followed. Extensive contusions, rope-burns and other injuries indicate extreme violence whilst the victim was still alive.

First impressions that parts of the cadaver were missing are confirmed. Fifty per cent of the right breast, some twenty per cent of the left; sections of tissue from upper arms together with the right earlobe, were ripped off and are missing. The woman was not a virgin, but there was no evidence of recent sexual penetration.

Dismemberment and decapitation was crude, carried out by someone with rudimentary anatomical knowledge by means of a hacksaw and a moderately sharp knife. Surgically-sharp instruments were not in evidence.

Most facial and cranial damage was inflicted by multiple blows by a blunt instrument—a hammer, perhaps; slashing was inflicted by knife, most probably the same used for dismemberment. Bite marks on breasts and arms are consistent with human teeth, as were similar lesions elsewhere.

The deceased did not eat immediately prior to death. The stomach contained uncooked vegetable matter in the latter stages of digestion, which indicates the final meal was predominantly salad, consumed some nine hours before life became extinct—say, around 1.00 p.m.

The teeth were sound—apart from two small fillings—and complete except for wisdom teeth. These were at an advanced stage of development within the gums and corroborate the estimated age of the deceased arrived at by other means.'

The quiet, precise voice fell silent and Matthews placed his clipboard on the table and looked up. He raised an eyebrow and lapsed into informality.

'That about sums it up, David. Do you have any questions?'

Melton had remained motionless whilst the pathologist was speaking, his memory sufficiently good as to render note-taking unnecessary. Still concentrating, however, he strove to digest and analyse the pathologist's findings, and eventually replied, 'I don't think so Stephen, but I need a few moments to soak it all in. Please bear with me.'

Matthews understood.

'Don't worry too much now,' he said. 'Although I've covered the salient points and omitted only the finer details and technical jargon, the full findings will be in your hands by noon tomorrow.'

'I'm obliged,' Melton replied, gratefully, and then asked, thoughtfully, 'I wouldn't dream of challenging what you say, but I take it there's no doubt about the bite marks—they were definitely made by human teeth?'

'No doubt at all, David. No doubt whatsoever.'

'I see.' His warm, brown eyes darkened and his voice was grim.

'I need pointers, Stephen. I suspect we'll need more than luck in order to wrap *this* one up.'

'Only time will tell. I'd say dismemberment had much to do with getting rid of the body. But it would be messy and almost certain to leave evidence lying around.' He paused. 'Perhaps it was carried out in isolation somewhere; where a more conventional means of disposal wasn't available—no nearby common-land, gravel-pit, or even a river, for example. Maybe the murderer wanted to draw attention away from the place—or felt it dangerous to leave the intact body in situ, positively crawling with clues. Consider: dividing the body between bags would hardly render transportation easier— a girl that size would fit readily in the boot of a car. Maybe a car formed only part of his plans. He may have needed to disguise the body in order to move it in a public place, where use of bin bags might render that possible without arousing much in the way of suspicion—depending on the circumstances and time of day. It would also be far more manageable.' He paused again.

'Are you with me so far, David?'

Absorbed with the professor's theory, Melton simply inclined his head.

'In that case,' the pathologist went on, 'let us consider the killer's mentality.' He rubbed his chin, thoughtfully, 'Without benefit of expert psychological evaluation or close study over time, it's virtually impossible to draw conclusions—at least none we could safely rely on. But to venture an opinion—and it *is* only an opinion—I conclude the killer to be clever, organised and self-reliant. He will be fit, strong and comparatively young—I say 'he', because I'm pretty certain the murderer is a man. The damage to the body and the manner in which it was dismembered calls for considerable strength; what's more, those bags would prove awkward and difficult to carry.

'If in his own mind, the man has justifiable reasons for his crime, which seems likely, it means—again in my opinion—he's compulsively psychopathic: therefore completely and utterly mad.' Inspector Melton nodded, but frowned, seemingly puzzled.

'What's troubling you?' Matthews asked. 'You seem a little . . . unsure?'

'Sorry,' Melton apologised, 'but I confess to feeling confused.

You say you believe the killer clever, yet seem convinced he's a psychopath. I was wondering how both characteristics could apply to the same person. Is he schizophrenic then—a split personality?'

'I don't think so. But he *is* clever *and* a good organiser—he must be. He killed somewhere, unseen and unheard, so far as we know, and contrived to find unoccupied premises in order to plant a body at night in a spot where it was unlikely to be discovered. He arrived undetected, carried out a physically demanding task in almost total darkness, then melted away like a shadow. In a sense, we were lucky. If Mrs Frasier hadn't heard noises, or hadn't felt inclined to report them, then the poor girl's body might never have been found. Does that answer your question?'

'Yes, it does. You've been more than helpful. Thank you.'

'You are entirely welcome,' the pathologist replied.

Melton got to his feet. 'I'd better get back to HQ. I'm meeting reporters at five. A press release is already in draft, but requires alteration in the light of the post-mortem result. Incidentally,' he added, 'I've included witness appeals, so media support is essential.'

'Good. I wish you luck. Let me know if there's anything I can do to help. Small comfort that a depraved killer is at large. The sooner he's caught and locked up the better.'

The two men shook hands and David Melton departed, deep in thought.

DI Melton had risen through the ranks, not by virtue of intellect or good luck—although he had had his share of both—but by dogged, methodical application of long-established methods and procedures which form the foundation upon which all police work is based. Becoming a police cadet at eighteen, he wangled his way onto courses covering most aspects of crime prevention, departing the 'Beat' at twenty-six to become a Detective Constable.

Promotion followed: Detective Sergeant at thirty-six, Detective Inspector three years later.

It is an unfortunate fact that up and down the country many crimes remain unsolved and Surbiton was no exception. Modestly discounting years of hard work, David considered himself fortunate to have fewer such cases to his account than most of similar age and experience.

*

1645, Tuesday 16th July, 2002: Police HQ, Surbiton.

En route to his office, Melton buttonholed his assistant.

O'Connor looked up. 'Hello sir, how did it go?'

'Much as expected. I'll brief you later. Are there any developments?'

'Yes sir. Seems as if the search is paying off. Rogers and Connelly found a brown-paper parcel tied with string inside the bin at seven, Rodene Close. It seemed odd so they unwrapped it to find an almost new anorak and a muddy pair of trainers. The owners of the house—people by the name of Beswick—deny all knowledge and say it wasn't there yesterday. I believe them. Nice old couple—wouldn't say "boo" to a goose. The trainers appeared similar in size to the impression near the shrubs, so I took them and the anorak to Forensics about twenty minutes ago. Mr Ferguson was very busy—as usual. Apparently he's got three cases on the go and a whole raft of samples waiting to be dealt with. He said analysis of the fibres is well in hand, however, and agreed to check the trainers against the *Quickcast* as soon as he gets time. We'll have to be patient, I suppose, but he's working late tonight and promised to get the reports to us first thing in the morning. I'd say it's coming together nicely, Guv'nor. Could be we're on the trail of the killer already.'

Melton seemed suitably heartened, if not wildly enthusiastic.

'Good work, Sergeant,' he said. 'Well done. Give Rogers and Connelly my compliments—but, to be honest, I'm more concerned about that poor girl. Any clue as to her identity yet?'

'No, bugger all,' came the reply.

The journalists earlier dispersed were now back, numbers more than doubled. Too many to fit comfortably in reception, the pressmen were ushered into interview rooms and told to wait.

Already dubbed 'Body in the Garden' by an unimaginative reporter, the murder sparked a flurry of speculation among the waiting newsmen. Rumour was tempered by fact, however. It was common knowledge Surbiton police were in the throes of a murder inquiry.

A babble of voices greeted DI Melton when he walked into the briefing-room, and not until he took his position on the podium and raised his hand did the hum of conversation fully die away. As he sat down, a glare of portable lighting at the rear intensified and television cameras began recording the proceedings, whilst remote-switched microphones became 'live', in readiness to capture every word.

'Good evening, gentlemen and lady,' he began, for there was a lone female present. 'For those of you who do not know, I am Detective Inspector David Melton and the officer on my right, here to take notes, is Detective Constable Martin Edwards. First of all, thank you for your patience and for sparing me your time. I have here a prepared statement which I propose to read before endeavouring to answer your questions—and to spare us the screeching of pens, the officer at the door will provide you all with a copy.'

Speaking in measured tones, Melton read the release aloud and when he had finished, his response to the inevitable barrage of questions was simple: he would point to the owner of an upraised hand and wait for silence.

'Christopher Dangerfield, *Evening News.*'

With a gesture, the reporter was duly acknowledged. 'Can you reveal the victim's name, where she comes from and the probable cause of death?'

'Not yet. The body was badly mutilated, the face battered beyond recognition and up to now we know of no missing person who might correspond with what little we have to go on.

'To answer your second question, the post-mortem results will not be available until tomorrow but preliminary findings suggest death was caused by massive bleeding from the neck. Next!'

'Benjamin Jopney, *Thames Television.* Can you tell us something about the murdered girl?'

'As you already know, the deceased was a young female—I can reveal that she was a natural blonde, aged between sixteen and eighteen, slightly built and around seven stone in weight.'

'Can you confirm the body was found buried in the garden of the Pearce family at eleven, Rodene Close, Lower Green, Esher?'

'Yes.'

'Can you also confirm the body was dismembered and in plastic bags when found?'

Melton hesitated. 'Well, yes—but where did you get that information from, Mr Jopney?'

'Just an informed guess, Inspector!'

A smile creased the reporter's face. He wouldn't reveal his

source, but it wasn't difficult to guess that it was probably the ambulance driver, who would have had little reason for refusing a couple of simple questions, not having been sworn to secrecy.

'Next question.'

'Robin Prendergast, *Surrey Chronicle*.' The reporter smirked. His was a minor newspaper. 'Was the deceased sexually assaulted and if so, could that be the motive behind the killing?'

Melton hesitated before answering, then decided to accept the question. 'There was no evidence of sexual interference prior to death. Sex has, therefore, been ruled out as a possible motive ... Yes, Mr Dangerfield.' Melton turned to the reporter from the *Evening News*.

'Have the police any leads and, if so, along what lines are inquiries being pursued?'

'Certain evidence was found near to where the body was concealed which may prove helpful, but I cannot as yet be more specific. Until the victim is positively identified and her family and friends, movements and so on, are discovered, it will be difficult to establish motive. Without which,' he added, 'we have little chance of flushing out the murderer.'

'You mentioned evidence—what evidence?' Dangerfield demanded to know.

Others immediately jumped to their feet and chorused the same question.

Melton gestured for silence and spoke firmly.

'I'm sorry. I cannot release further information. It is confidential.'

Benjamin Jopney was next on his feet:

'What comment *can* you make for the benefit of viewers?'

Here was Melton's opportunity, and he needed little prompting.

'This was a brutal murder perpetrated on a young woman in a particularly horrifying manner. It is vital that the killer be apprehended as quickly as possible before he has a chance to strike again.

'I appeal to anyone who knows of a young girl missing either from home or her normal place of work to come forward. We also wish to hear from anybody who witnessed anything unusual in Rodene Close, Lower Green—including Cobham Street and Methodist Way—on 14th July.

'Information can be given at any police station or free of charge by telephone to the special incident room on 0801 661 7788. Informants will not be required to disclose their identity and all information will be treated as strictly confidential. Thank you!'

With absolute finality, Melton closed the file and stood up. As he made for the exit, the television lights dimmed: filming had ceased.

Benjamin Jopney moved swiftly, intercepting DI Melton before he could reach the door. He expressed his appreciation and shook Melton's hand.

'Thank you, Detective Inspector. I hope we can include your appeal on both early evening and ten o'clock news programmes. Limited slot-time will prevent the entire recording on either, but an edited version should make the latter. Good luck! If there's anything I can do which might help to nail the killer, don't hesitate to get in touch. Here's my card!'

'Thank you, Mr Jopney; we'll keep you informed.'

Before anyone else could stop him, Melton slipped through the door and headed for his office. O'Connor was deeply engrossed when the 'Guv'nor' came through the door. He glanced up, but resumed his study of a report when the DI passed without speaking and entered his office.

Melton dropped his clipboard and sat down. Then he rang his wife and told her to expect him by 7.30 and, with the receiver still in his hand, tapped on the glass partition. O'Connor looked up; Melton beckoned to him to come in. Over coffee, the two went over the case in detail and agreed strategy for the following day. They left headquarters at 6.30, with O'Connor at the wheel of Melton's official Rover, and drove to the Railway Arms—a 'free-house' watering-hole adjacent to Surbiton station—for a well-earned half of Worthington 'E', a beverage to which both were partial. It was 7.30 precisely when O'Connor delivered his superior officer to his Hinchley Wood home—but the day wasn't over for either man.

At 9.30 the DI's enjoyment of his post-prandial malt whisky was interrupted by the telephone.

'Melton,' he announced, and listened intently, from time to time interjecting 'Oh', Yes', or 'Right'. He visibly brightened and, after a minute or so, said, 'He's willing to call and make a statement then? Tomorrow, you say? Yes, first thing in the morning would be fine. Can you arrange it for nine? He will? Good. Thank you, yes, that's fine.'

'Sorry darling, work,' David said, in response to his wife's inquiring look.

She smiled. The principle of not bringing work home was well-established, but she knew the odd phone call couldn't be avoided; she neither expected nor wanted details.

George Taite proved helpful, articulate and sure of his facts—an ideal witness—and lived at 16 Cobham Street, Lower Green, opposite the 'T' junction connecting with Rodene Close.

At about 11.15 on Sunday night, fifteenth July, Taite was returning from the 'take-away' at Thames Ditton with supper for himself and his wife, when he saw in his headlights someone wearing an anorak with a yellow fluorescent stripe down each sleeve. This person—he was sure it was a man—turned left into Rodene Close just as Taite rounded the corner, but there was time to notice the fellow was carrying what appeared to be bags of laundry. Taite didn't see the man's face nor could he give a description, other than that he seemed fairly young, wasn't very tall and had shortish hair—possibly light to medium brown, it was hard to tell.

Taite remembered thinking it odd that someone should be bringing washing from the launderette that late, but it seemed a trivial matter and went out of his mind as he reversed into his drive to park for the night. He was positive about the time, however, having arrived at the 'take-away' at 10.50, with just minutes to spare before closing. They had locked the door after he went in as he was the last customer of the evening. He noticed the clock on the wall showed ten-past eleven as he left, the assistant having to let him out. The drive home was uneventful and couldn't have taken more than five or six minutes.

George had rung the incident room after the television appeal on the nine o'clock news, which he had watched out of curiosity, because his wife was agog about the earlier mention of a murder.

'Right on our doorstep, George,' she had informed him, excitedly.

While Melton was reading the signed statement, there came a knock on the door and Albert Ferguson from the forensic lab stuck his head in. He seemed flustered.

'Good morning Mr Melton,' he said, a brace of folders

extended. 'The reports I promised. Can't stop, I've piles to do.' And without waiting, he spun on his heel and scurried from the room.

'Old fuss-pot,' O'Connor muttered. 'Always cracks on he's busy, but a brilliant technician.'

Still reading, Melton affected not to hear, but a few minutes later, he exclaimed, 'No doubt about it, Ben, you were right, there *is* a connection!' He tapped the reports. 'It seems there was a bloodstain on the anorak which checks out 'O' Rhesus Positive, the same blood-group and type as the deceased, and the fibres from the fence appear to match the blue anorak. On top of that, the *Quickcast* tallies with the trainers in size and shape. Unfortunately, the impression was shallow, suggesting someone not particularly heavy. But the cast showed hardly any tread, which rules out a positive ID, more's the pity. It *is* promising,' he added, hurrying on. 'Whilst the footprint isn't conclusive, the anorak fibres match those from the fence which, with the bloodstain, leads to a fairly positive conclusion. As the anorak tallies with George Tait's description, the time factor and the man with the laundry bags ties in neatly. The noises Mrs Frasier heard add weight. If that lot taken together isn't sufficient to secure a conviction, I'll eat my hat.'

Melton jabbed the documents with an emphatic forefinger. 'Yes,' he said, 'ten to one the man carrying those bags of so-called laundry on Sunday night is owner of the anorak and trainers, and the sooner he's under lock and key the better.'

Bingo! They had a trail to the killer, it seemed. But these were early days. In order to 'feel the collar', so to speak, they must first identify the owner of the anorak and trainers.

O'Connor ran five fingers through short, sandy hair, a sure sign he was thinking. Then he brightened, and his neatly-clipped moustache positively bristled.

'I wonder, Guv'nor,' he ventured, 'as trainers and anoraks are popular with teenagers, some local youngster might know of someone who wears similar gear—might even come up with a name. How about the Pearce boy, the one who was away for the weekend with his parents? He might be able to help. He probably expects to be interviewed, anyway.'

'Nice one, Sergeant,' responded the DI, 'An excellent suggestion. Let's have a word with Steven Pearce.'

En route to Esher, Melton's mobile warbled: Chief Superintendent Jarvis required a word. O'Connor took over the wheel and steered the Rover to a halt outside 11 Rodene Close at 11.45.

Whilst Melton was on the blower, O'Connor collected a package from the boot. Approaching the house, the DI was spotted immediately. Several reporters surged forward. Ignoring their questions, Melton brushed past.

'Watch out for this lot, constable,' he warned the policeman on duty. 'Keep them back, well out of the way. Those two especially,' he said, indicating the cameraman and his companion.

'Yes sir,' the officer replied. 'I'll take care of it.'

As he preceded his assistant up the path, a curtain twitched. Melton knocked. They waited.

Understandably overwrought, Mrs Pearce peeked from the lounge suspiciously. She then opened the door.

'Mr Pearce is at work,' she snapped.

'Good morning, Mrs Pearce,' Melton quietly rejoined, raising his hat, politely. 'I'm sure you recognise us: DI Melton and DS O'Connor. But it isn't Mr Pearce we've come to see, it's young Steven. We'd like a word, if possible. He may be able to help in our inquiries and his assistance might prove invaluable. Can you tell us which school he attends, please? Time is of the essence. It's important we speak to him at the earliest opportunity.'

Mrs Pearce glared. 'Steven's not at school, he's in bed. He's having a day or two off after exams. All this hassle and excitement,' she ranted. 'It's very upsetting, you understand.'

'Yes, Mrs Pearce. Of course we understand. But I hardly need remind you of the importance of this inquiry. It's a question of murder, madam—and the body was found in *your* back garden. Please fetch Steven, Mrs Pearce. You won't mind if we come in and wait, will you?'

He stepped forward and, annoyed though she obviously was, she meekly opened the door.

'All right, you'd better come in. I'll go and fetch Steven.'

She led them to the lounge, indicated chairs and left the room. A couple of minutes later she returned with a tousled, sleepy-looking Steven. Melton smiled, reassuringly.

'Hello Steven, sorry to disturb you, but this is important. I'm Detective Inspector Melton, and this is Detective Sergeant O'Connor. We think you may be able to help with our inquiries.'

Steven's eyes widened.

'You don't have to say anything, darling,' his mother twittered, anxiously. 'I'll ring Daddy to come home...' Almost brusquely, Melton intervened. 'Just a moment, Mrs Pearce. Steven may have information which could help apprehend a murderer. We cannot afford a moment's delay.' Dismissive, he returned to the youth, making it obvious he would brook no argument. 'Now Steven, I want you to look carefully at some items which you may be able to help identify. Sergeant, if you please.'

The DS unwrapped the parcel and displayed the contents.

Wide awake now, Steven went pale and began to tremble. He looked wildly from side to side as if seeking an avenue of escape, and shook his head in disbelief. His mother shrieked. '*Steven—oh, my God!*' she wailed. 'That's *your* anorak—*and* your trainers!' Angrily, protectively, she rounded on Melton. 'Where did you get them? What's going on? Why are you accusing my Steven?'

Recognising signs of mounting hysteria, Melton rose to his feet. 'Nobody is accusing your son of anything,' he said, sharply. 'I must ask you to keep quiet while we question him—unless you'd prefer we went to the station?'

She paled, bit her lip, and shook her head.

Melton resumed. 'Now Steven, this anorak, these trainers. *Are* they yours, as your mother seems to think?'

The youth shifted from foot to foot, then muttered, 'Yes, they're mine. I lost them a couple of weeks ago—from the pavilion at West End, I think.'

He caught his mother's eye, appealingly. But now *she* seemed confused and unsure.

Retaining the initiative, Melton said sternly, 'Steven Pearce. I would like you to go now with Detective Sergeant O'Connor and get dressed, then accompany us to Surbiton Police Station where further questions will be put to you.'

DS O'Connor took Steven by the elbow and propelled him from the room.

'Are you arresting Steven?' his mother asked tremulously.

Melton shook his head. 'Mrs Pearce, Steven is *not* being arrested. He is needed urgently in pursuit of our inquiries. Telephone your husband if you wish, of course, but I must insist your son comes to the station. As a minor, you may accompany him, but are not entitled to be present while he is interviewed. You may advise your solicitor, if you prefer, although it isn't really necessary for the moment.'

The search of the garden continued. Although further samples from differing locations were taken for analysis, nothing was found to add to the evidence already collected, but traces of earth *were* discovered on a spade in the shed. George Pearce insisted the tool hadn't been used recently and a lack of fingerprints supported his assertion that, when gardening, he invariably wore gloves.

Laboratory tests failed to identify any traces of blood, and the implement being regarded as of no further consequence was returned to its owner. Steven Pearce was interviewed for three successive days but stuck resolutely to his story, added nothing and couldn't be shaken. Cautioned about deliberately witholding evidence, he was eventually released without charge. Evidence to link him with the murder remained, but his arrival in Brighton and subsequent departure the following Monday morning was well documented, and the movements of both him and his parents during the intervening period were fully accounted for.

Steven Pearce had no involvement in either the murder or the subsequent disposal of the body. Nor could Steven be persuaded to say anything further about the circumstances surrounding the disappearance of his anorak and trainers, nor explain why he had failed to mention their loss, which left investigators unable to determine how and when the items had come into the murderer's possession.

But Robert Strudwick knew well enough—and much more besides. Not least about the activities of the police in connection with the murder . . .

Lack of progress caused media interest to slacken, and whilst the team as a whole gained respite from persistent, news-hungry reporters, Melton and O'Connor agreed to be profiled so as to keep the investigation before the public eye and focus attention on the appeal.

Chapter Six

Beast

There *was* no precise moment to define the beginning of his 2002 adventure. As far as Robert was concerned, everything of consequence related to when he had become custodian of the Book. He was far too engrossed with his career and the acquisition of material possessions to waste time on unproductive reminiscence, and whilst grateful for what *had* been thus far granted, knew *real* wealth would not be forthcoming until he proved himself completely and utterly worthy.

He did, however, permit himself an occasional, self-congratulatory reflection. His salary was low, but so what? Excellent commission tripled his income in the very first month. For this was Surrey, heart of the stockbroker belt, where ceaseless demand for property of all types and values rendered virtually anything standing a saleable commodity, and one which could generally be expected to sell in a matter of weeks.

With parental assistance, Robert bought his first car a week after starting with Gaston Hathaway, having learned that generous mileage allowance was paid when tidy, well-kept private cars were used on business. It was an arrangement preferred by Mr Hathaway, who believed the system more cost-effective than buying and maintaining a fleet of company vehicles.

Apart from his career, the year would differ vastly from those preceding and Robert knew it. Pentophiles' visitations became far more frequent; his inner voice was rarely silent. Robert welcomed both. Instinct told him a mission was due; months of relative inactivity were nearing an end; long-promised riches would soon become reality.

There were side-effects following Pentophiles' manifestations, however, of which Robert remained unaware. Had it been otherwise, he would most certainly have taken such unworldly peculiarities into consideration when formulating his plans and conducting his daily affairs.

To the casual observer, Kenward Crescent, Claygate was as unremarkable as many hundreds of residential streets within commuting distance of London. Number seven was a fairly typical three-bedroom semi towards the end of the cul-de-sac.

Occasionally, however, and lately with increasing frequency, an eerie, indefinable aura seemed to surround the property, setting it strangely apart from other nearby dwellings. This tenuous, miasmic atmosphere was readily apparent to those whose sensitivities were sufficiently attuned; others, less sensitive, experienced only a vague disquiet. Apart from this sense of unease, a faint, barely discernible odour of putrefaction, reminiscent of bad drains, would sometimes linger, and noses of passers-by might wrinkle in distaste. Since the new family had taken up residence, neighbours no longer called to pass the time of day, borrow a cup of sugar or ask for the loan of a tool, and those who were obliged to pass did so hurriedly and with averted gaze. Wildlife shunned the garden. Neighbourhood cats rarely trespassed and birds were likely to nest, feed and sing elsewhere. Dogs out walking were apt to pull on the leash without stopping, whilst passing strays invariably favoured the opposite pavement. This was the house that door-to-door salesmen contrived to overlook and to which few window-cleaners willingly returned. It was home to Albert Strudwick and his wife; equally home, lair and headquarters to their son Robert.

And then, one evening in early June when Robert routinely opened the Book, a message leapt from the flyleaf, scintillating as a display of fireworks:

BY THY KEENE BLADE SHALL PERISH FAIR MAID
SHE WHO DIDST SPURN AND REVILE THEE

His lips moved involuntarily as he mouthed the words he knew he must interpret correctly and obey unquestioningly. Yet, as he silently recited the script intended for his eyes alone, the fiery letters writhed, blurred and faded until the page became, as before, utterly blank.

Emitting a sigh, he closed the book thoughtfully, locked it and replaced the key around his neck. Here were concise instructions for his first major mission in almost three years, instructions to be rid of the bitch who had rejected his advances and exposed him to ridicule. She was to die by the knife, of course—but what about strategy? Nothing at all had been specified.

Then it dawned on him that the omission was intentional—he was to devise a plan of his own. It was a sobering thought. What if he should fail? He could hardly bear to think about it. Instead of the elation which normally accompanied a successful consultation, he felt subdued, apprehensive even, and he shivered a little at the thought of what must be done and how best it could be achieved—or was it in fear of the terrible consequences of failure? He wasn't sure which.

Robert remained in bed, book rested against his knees, searching for the beginnings of a plan. Then he chuckled—a mirthless, inhuman sound from deep within his throat—and an expression of utter bestiality momentarily contorted his face. But the moment passed and the manic chortle ceased. An idea coalesced in his mind.

Without further ado, Robert went into action.

Although late in the evening, he made several telephone calls and listened without comment to what he was told in response to carefully-worded, ambiguous, but highly pertinent questions. He considered and recalled everything relevant from the mass of information stored within his prodigious memory. Bridgwater's name sprang to mind. And oh, how he wished that snivelling arsehole could be included in the scheme! Perhaps it was feasible, even now, but instructions from the Book held sway and dared not be tampered with. He consoled himself with the thought that Bridgwater's day would inevitably come, and must surely merit some rather special attention—all to himself!

Part of the strategy was to confuse the police and he came up with a way of not only achieving that, but also of being avenged on girlfriend-thieving Steven Pearce as something of a private bonus. Robert rubbed his hands gleefully, and set about developing the idea.

Wednesday 19 June dawned warm and sunny, the day Esher Secondary Modern were to play Hinchley Wood Grammar in the County Senior Cricket League at West End.

It was a key match and maximum possible support for Esher was essential.

The entire school was required to attend by order of the

headmaster, who let it be known that he personally would deal with instances of unauthorised absenteeism the following morning.

The match was due to start at 2.15 p.m., but seating was limited; the ground filled rapidly and few spectator places were left by two o'clock.

Among those fortunate enough to secure a seat on the benches in front of the pavilion was Janice Pearson, intent on cheering on a special young man, one she had started to view rather differently once her traumatic affair with Robert Strudwick had finally come to an end.

The openers emerged from the pavilion at 2.10 and Janice grabbed the sleeve of one, threw her arms around his neck and gave him a resounding kiss for luck. This was the last school match in which he expected to play.

At 2.20, one of several 'old boys' watching from the pavilion, a latecomer, wriggled as if in some discomfort, excused himself and headed for the men's toilets—via the changing rooms. He located what he was looking for almost immediately, checked to make sure he remained unobserved and stuffed into his empty briefcase a pair of canvas trainers and a dark-blue anorak bearing a yellow stripe down each sleeve—items he knew to be the property of one of the two stalwarts currently opening the batting—and was back on the veranda in a couple of minutes.

Malandra Pennington rose early, left a note for the milkman and went to the office to tie up a few loose ends. Whilst there, she cancelled her newspapers over the telephone, leaving again at 11.30 in plenty of time to deal with remaining, outstanding matters—and there were several: call at the shops, suntan lotion, camera check, supply of films, pick up traveller's cheques, hairdressers at 12.15, home again by 1.30. Lunch—convenience prepack from larder; refrigerator—empty, switch off; pass leftovers to neighbour ... and oh, leave a spare latchkey in case of any problems.

Thrilled at the prospect of her first holiday abroad, Malandra hummed happily as she packed. It was Friday, the day before departure and she crossed each item off her list as she filled two suitcases with neatly-folded clothes and a plethora of other holiday essentials. Check: passport, entry visa, hotel booking, tickets for train, theatre and plane—all correct! As planned, she would lunch out somewhere, take a train to Waterloo and taxi to Knightsbridge, dine at the hotel and spend an evening at the theatre.

Her friend Jennifer was visiting parents at Wimbledon—she was probably on her way by now. They were to meet Sunday afternoon at the Britair terminal in Kensington, spend an hour or two sightseeing, returning to catch the coach to Heathrow in readiness to fly out later that night.

And now, with preparations finally out of the way, Saturday morning could be spend trying to replace her ageing Mini, forever breaking down and costing a small fortune to keep on the road. The search had begun weeks ago. Malandra had heard about two potentially interesting cars for sale and, though neither was of the type she really wanted, intended to look at them in the morning. She went to bed early; slept fitfully.

On Saturday morning, at 7.55 a bleary-eyed Malandra crawled from between the sheets. She showered, dressed and applied her usual touch of make-up before eating breakfast—two slices of toast engineered from elderly bread, garnished with the last scrapings of butter from the tub. She glanced at the clock—8.58—and, tempted to have a few words with Jennifer, she reached out for the telephone—just as it began to ring.

'Miss Pennington?'

'Yes.'

'Good morning. Tobias Charlesworth from Charlesworth's garage. Sorry if I've disturbed you, but you were asking about a good, second-hand Astra? Well, we have a real beauty in emerald green coming in this morning which might well suit you. It's a one-point-three, under two years old—first registered August 2000, to be precise. Loads of extras—power steering, driver's airbag, stereo-cassette radio, wheel-trims and head-restraints, genuine low mileage; one owner and an absolute snip at four thousand two hundred and ninety-five pounds. I thought I'd better ring you immediately before someone else snaps it up.'

Charlesworth was in full flow. 'This little cracker is coming in at the right price, so we can offer two thousand pounds in part-exchange for the Mini—double its actual worth . . .'

Her silence told him the bait had been taken.

'Can you call in tomorrow morning?' he asked. 'We open at ten-thirty, so how would eleven o'clock suit you?'

Malandra had set her heart on an Astra. A new vehicle was beyond her means and good, second-hand examples of the popular car were rarely offered for sale. The opportunity seemed just too good to miss.

'I'm certainly interested, Mr Charlesworth—but what about today? I'd planned to spend the morning looking at cars, anyway.'

'I'm sorry, Miss Pennington, but there's a full service to be carried out—oil change, filters and so on, and we valet every vehicle before offering it for sale. There's absolutely no chance of having it ready before this evening, and we close for the day at five o'clock, I'm afraid.'

'Well, I was intending to stay overnight in London—I'm going on holiday tomorrow. Getting a new car sorted is something of a priority though, so I suppose it's a good enough reason for stopping another night. Look, I'll be pressed for time tomorrow and I've practically emptied my current account. If I decide to buy the Astra, will you accept a small deposit and hold it for me? I'll be back in a fortnight.'

'No problem.'

'All right then, eleven tomorrow it is. Thank you very much, Mr Charlesworth.' Malandra had barely replaced the receiver when the phone rang again.

'Hi Landra, how's the packing?' Jennifer inquired breezily. 'Mum and I are going shopping in a minute, but I thought I'd give you a quick bell to see where you're up to.'

'I finished packing last night, Jen, but guess what? There's a nearly-new Astra coming in today at Charlesworth's—it sounds brilliant, and I'm going to look at it tomorrow morning ... Oh, crikey, that reminds me—I must ring the hotel and cancel my room for tonight!'

'What about your trip to the theatre then—knocking it on the head?'

'Yes, getting a car sorted is far more important.'

George Pearce and his family, meanwhile, were on their way to Brighton. Elsewhere, final touches were being made to plans for which the Pearce's absence was absolutely critical.

The next morning Malandra looked stunning. Uncluttered by accessories and empty-handed apart from her latchkey, her pale-lemon summer frock flattering her superb figure and flawless complexion, she collected several appreciative looks as she walked to town. She reached Charlesworth's a trifle early, at 10.55.

'Good morning, Miss Pennington.'

Hand outstretched in greeting, Tobias rose from his chair but seemed rather flustered for such an experienced salesman.

'I'm so sorry,' he apologised, 'but I've two more customers coming in at any moment—managed to get myself double-booked, I'm afraid. Did you bring your car with you?'

'No, I walked round. The Mini is locked in the garage until after my holiday—and no bumps or scratches since you last saw it, either,' she assured him.

He smiled. 'Well, I'm sure we can take your word for that—we know you pretty well—so much so, I wonder whether you'd mind looking at the Astra by yourself? It's parked in the driveway leading to the car park at the rear, fully serviced, ready and waiting to go.'

Malandra knew exactly where he meant. Set behind the main showroom was a small enclosed area of hard-standing, reserved specifically as overflow parking when the front was full.

'No, I don't mind a bit—but what about a test drive?'

'Please feel free Miss Pennington. Take it out for as long a run as you like. There's plenty of fuel in the tank, it's taxed, your own insurance will suffice and it's a beautiful runner, as I think you'll agree. Drop the key off when you return and let me know whether or not we have a deal.' He proffered a fob bearing a single key. 'Doors, ignition, boot and fuel tank—all rolled into one.'

'Thank you, but I won't be gone long. I need to collect my cases and handbag—and I'd better come back to pay the deposit—assuming I like the Astra, that is,' she added, hastily.

'You will, Miss Pennington, you will. But, as I said before, take as long as you like—but be back before five or we'll send out a search-party.'

He leered.

What in heaven does he mean by that?

'I've no intention of being that late. I need to be at the station in time to catch the one-thirty. I've already told you I'm going away on holiday.'

Charlesworth paled. Everything running like clockwork and he came close to alarming the girl. He placed the key in Malandra's hand and she turned to leave, just as a middle-aged couple were entering. Charlesworth's 'double booking', she supposed.

She crossed the forecourt and made her way round the showroom to the rear car park access-way. She spotted it immediately—a beautiful Astra, in emerald green. It looked pristine, paintwork gleaming like new. Malandra fell in love with the car there and then. A glance round told her it was free from major dents or scratches. She unlocked the door and slid behind the wheel. Surprisingly, the driving position suited her perfectly. A good omen!

She placed her front-door key on the passenger seat, fastened the seat belt and turned the key in the ignition. The engine purred into life.

'Don't turn round—and don't scream!'

Malandra froze. A hand came over her shoulder clutching a fearsome-looking knife; razor-sharp steel was pressed menacingly against her throat. Strong fingers gripped her shoulder; there was little chance of escape. Malandra was utterly petrified. She risked a glance in the rear-view mirror but it was in the tilted position, set for night driving.

'Do exactly as I say. Keep the engine running and listen carefully. When I say "go", drive off slowly without attracting attention and turn left up the High Street. When you get to The Bear, turn left at the lights and head for Leatherhead—have you got that?'

She inclined her head slightly, terrified of the knife, not trusting herself to speak.

'All right then. I'll take the knife away—but remember what I said: just one false move . . .'

Malandra trembled anew—the threat was unmistakable. He gripped her shoulder hard.

'I'll tell you what to do once we're heading towards Leatherhead—*go!*'

The Astra moved smoothly away. The hand left her shoulder and the knife withdrew, but the presence behind was overpowering.

'Don't do anything foolish—I've got a knife, remember.'

She reached the end of the access road and stopped, numb with fear.

'Get going, you bitch, or I'll slit your throat right here and now.'

Maintaining a steady thirty miles per hour, the frightened girl continued along the A13 until she neared The Bear, where she turned left onto the A244 as instructed.

'We're on the Leatherhead road,' she managed to quaver. 'What do I do now?'

'Keep driving until I say different,' he rasped, and the knife was back at her throat in an instant. She instinctively flinched, and the blade nicked her tender skin. But she felt no pain, unaware that a trickle of blood was slowly staining her collar crimson.

After a mile or two, the winding road straightened and they passed out of the restricted zone. Two cars passed, both travelling in the opposite direction. The first part of the operation had gone precisely to plan, but Strudwick knew he had much to achieve in order to complete his most difficult mission to date.

'Slow down—now! Take the next right—yes, down there,' he ordered tersely, and as Malandra complied, he tightened his grip on her shoulder—brutally hard—but she bit her lip and somehow managed to remain silent. *Oh dear God, does he have to be so cruel?*

There followed some twenty minutes of complicated manoeuvring, when Malandra drove along tortuous narrow lanes, crossing and re-crossing a seemingly familiar track that she thought might lead to the exit route across Oxshott Heath, but she was wrong. She did not realise they were scouring the area for signs of people rather than heading for a specific destination.

But once her captor was satisfied the scrubland was deserted, he directed her into much deeper woodland where they bumped along a barely discernible track until he said, 'Right, that clearing ahead to the left, pull into it, stop, switch off the engine but leave the key in the ignition.'

She hadn't glimpsed a soul since turning off the main road and the empty woodland engendered a terrible feeling of isolation. Her bladder signalled an oncoming need for relief. She began to feel uncomfortable. *Does he intend to rape me? If so, please God make it quick so I can get out of here! But who is he? Have I heard that voice somewhere before? Damn, I need to go the loo!*

His voice cut across her thoughts.

'There are two sandwich boxes in the glove-box. Get them out—yes, that's right. Pass me the white one—no, don't look round. The other one's for you. Go ahead, open it and have your lunch—but keep your seat belt on—*and don't turn around*!'

THE FLYLEAF KILLER

Malandra was hungry, having eaten nothing since lunch the previous day, and when she heard the snap of a plastic lid followed by the sounds of eating, she almost sighed with relief. An extraordinarily bizarre situation seemed suddenly less ominous.

'Excuse me. I'm extremely sorry, but I need to go to the loo,' she ventured, timidly.

'OK—but eat your lunch first,' he ordered.

She opened her box: beef salad, an apple, and a plastic knife and fork neatly wrapped in a paper serviette.

Immediately she felt better. *He doesn't intend me harm – if he did, why would he give me lunch?*

She began to eat, hesitantly at first. But appetite improved with each mouthful and the food rapidly disappeared, leaving her feeling considerably more confident.

'Excuse me, but I really must spend a penny. Can I go into the bushes, please?'

'Wait a moment. Don't move—keep your seat belt fastened.'

There came fumbling sounds. Then a length of nylon cord looped swiftly over her head and tightened around her neck. It bit deep into her skin. She gasped for air. Burning pain! Fear returned. *The bastard, he had a rope all ready – he actually* expected *this!*

'Undo your seat belt and open the door—slowly, mind. Right, get out—*but don't turn around!*'

The cord slackened and Malandra climbed out of the car. She heard the driver's seat move forward and sensed him close behind as she started towards the bushes.

'I'll release enough line to allow you to go, but if you try to get loose, I'll pull it—like this!'

The cord jerked savagely and she gurgled and snatched in an attempt to ease the pain, but it was tight, too slippery to grasp. When she pulled her hands away there was blood on her fingers. Strudwick noticed too. He shoved her roughly towards the nearest tree where she stumbled and fell, crying with pain and gasping from lack of oxygen.

'Now you can go,' he said, and when she hesitated, confused, he jerked the cord viciously. 'You said you wanted to go, so *go!*' he roared, angrily. 'Are you bloody stupid, or what?' Rather than wet herself, Malandra slipped down her panties and squatted against the bole of a tree, acutely aware that her tormentor was standing close behind, no doubt watching her every move.

As she started to straighten up, he moved closer and tugged again. Trying to ease the pain and relieve the pressure on her neck forced her in his direction, causing her to trip over the panties around her ankles and fall awkwardly, completely exposing herself. Cheeks aflame she scrambled to her feet and hastily pulled the skimpy garment back into place. So indignant was she that she ignored the tether around her neck and turned to confront her captor.

'Robert Strudwick,' she gasped. 'You rotten bastard!' *No wonder the voice had seemed familiar!* Strudwick's face filled with rage. He raised a clenched fist and drew it back.

'Go on then, you filthy disgusting swine,' she taunted. 'Hit a girl, would you? How dare you! I'm not frightened of you. Once a pig, always a p—!'

Her words ceased abruptly as iron-hard knuckles crashed into her face. She didn't seem so pretty, lying in a crumpled heap at his feet. He watched, fascinated, as the knuckle-marks on her cheek turned livid and licked his lips at the sight of a scarlet trickle meandering slowly towards her ear.

'Sod it,' he snarled, frustrated. He ought to have fitted a blindfold before letting her out of the car, but the bandage intended for the job was still in the boot with the other gear. Too late! Now she knew who he was, the ungrateful whore would forego the joy of anonymous sex.

He loosened the cord and after a while she stirred, gave a little gasp and opened her eyes. She looked appealingly into his face, but he hauled savagely on the cord.

'Bloody trollop, don't try the glad-eye on me. I can't easily be fooled, you stinking little bitch. I'm no bloody gigolo, either. Someone you can pick up for a quick screw then dump again.'

With the girl completely at his mercy, Strudwick decided to experiment. He dragged her to her feet and, watching her face dispassionately, passed a second loop of cord around her neck and viciously twisted it tight. Malandra began to suffocate. Her pallid face changed colour—first red then purple. Her tongue began to protrude, her eyes bulged horribly and, suddenly, she went limp. Curiosity satisfied, he dropped her to the ground, untied the cord and removed it completely.

It took two or three minutes, but, after several rasping breaths, Malandra started to breathe again. She opened her eyes and some semblance of colour returned to her cheeks. Rolling her over, he manhandled the slender figure into a sitting position against a nearby sapling and secured her by tying her wrists together behind her back.

Knowing that she watched, Strudwick fished in his pocket and produced a key, crossed to the car, unlocked and raised the hatchback door. Inside were items of clothing, brown paper, a large valise, a plastic bucket, a sponge; a filled ten-litre plastic water-container, a garden trowel, a ball of string and an eight-pack roll of rubbish bags.

He took off his clothes, including his shoes and socks, and placed them all in the boot. Stark naked, he turned to face his victim, then walked slowly across and stood over her.

'Time you knew what a *real* man looks like,' he sneered. 'What do you think—do you like me?' Malandra let out an anguished shriek. He smacked her face, twice in quick succession. She sobbed once, then fell quiet.

'Don't scream again,' he warned. 'For one thing I don't like it, and for another, no-one out here is likely to hear you.' *You're wasting time. Stop messing. You know what to do so get on with it!*

He bent and pulled her dress clear of one shoulder, then deliberately ripped the garment to the hem, to reveal she wore nothing beneath except a matching half-cup brassiere and tiny briefs.

'Aren't you going to show me the rest, Malandra?' he mocked. 'Especially now you see what you've been missing. Surely you don't mind a handsome, loving friend taking a proper look?'

She made no reply, but her expression of loathing, revulsion and contempt was surely answer enough.

He grasped her brassiere by the connecting strap between each cup and, with one pull, ripped the garment completely off, exposing her pert young breasts. He then grabbed the front of her panties and pulled hard – but the silken material proved surprisingly resilient and held firm. Cursing, he retrieved his knife from the car and slit the minuscule garment on each slender hip, leaving it hanging between her legs. He replaced the knife, unfastened her corded wrist and wound the surplus around his hand. Moving in front, he hauled savagely and forced her to her feet, ignoring her gasps of pain. He was rapidly becoming aroused but, as yet, was far from satisfied.

'Let's take a *proper* look at you,' he snarled, and pulled the skimpy cloth from her crotch, leaving the poor girl completely naked except for her sandals. Keeping hold of the cord, her tormentor stepped back to drink in her beauty, while she strove desperately with her free hand to thwart his lascivious gaze, though to little effect.

Strudwick came closer and, starting with her breasts, moved his hands slowly and intimately across most of her beautiful body. And when Malandra closed her eyes, Strudwick stepped back angrily and struck her a vicious, open-handed blow across the cheek. Shocked and startled, her eyes snapped open.

'Look at me!' he shouted. He frothed at the mouth as if possessed. 'Don't close your eyes, I *want* you to look. Look at *this*,' he insisted, gesturing obscenely. 'Look what you've missed. I'd have made love to you years ago. Don't you wish you'd let me?'

Fully aroused, he rubbed against her suggestively, while she tried desperately to push him away.

Malandra had had many would-be suitors. Few got beyond first base; only two ever got her into bed. In fact she disliked being fondled and considered the mechanics of intimacy embarrassing. Finding herself tethered, naked and in the power of a man long feared was an ordeal in itself; severe physical abuse rendered it infinitely more distressing. When the ordeal was compounded by salacious advances, however, Malandra could contain herself no longer.

'Stop it! Leave me alone, you filthy beast. Haven't you done enough already?' she shouted, sobbing. 'Wh-whatever did I do to make you treat me like this?'

In an instant, his face darkened with fury.

'Don't pretend you don't know, you slag. What about the times you turned me down? Dumping me and going off with Bridgwater, the slimy arsehole. Did you think I wouldn't care? You know exactly what you've done, you bitch. Just try and deny it—if you dare!'

Thinking hard, she vaguely recalled the incident. *Is that really what this is all about? God, have pity! He's mad—stark, raving mad!*

Enraged by the recollection, he raised his fist as if to strike, but when she flinched, he dropped his hand to her inner thigh, and began to rub her intimately with his fingers.

'How do you like that?' he leered. 'Nice, eh? Or would you prefer a smack in the mouth?' He pressed closer—perilously so, and thrust at her body, suggestively.

'Come on, you cow, stop pretending. It wouldn't be your first length of dick, now would it?'

Malandra's head throbbed and ached. Strudwick's malevolent presence and invasive attack filled her with nausea. She tried again to repel his advances, pushing weakly with her one free hand. Contemptuously, he brushed her arm aside. Utterly convinced she was about to be violated, she used the last remaining weapon in her meagre armoury—she spat directly into his face!

Was Pentophiles' moment come? *Dirty bitch! . . . Kill! . . . Kill! . . . Kill!*

Outraged, Robert roared with fury. Adrenaline surged; his brain pounded; dark-red mist obscured his vision. Triggered by frustrated lust, driven by hate and goaded by the voice in his mind, he knocked her to the ground and threw himself on top, growling, snarling and slavering like a wild animal. Her resistance inflamed him further, and he punched, bit, scratched and kicked almost every part of her body.

She screamed piteously but he silenced her with a punch in the face. Mindlessly, he gripped an earlobe between his teeth and ripped it off then threw back his head and howled like a dog. Eventually, the onslaught proved too much. Malandra lost consciousness and lay still, yet still he continued to beat her. For timeless minutes the assault continued until it dawned on him that she was unconscious.

No longer masquerading as a man, a dreadful shadowy being approached the clearing in Oxshott Woods. The fulfilment of pent-up demonic lust was surely imminent, but his protégé must hurry: *KILL HER! . . . KILL HER!*

Strudwick, however, lay still. He waited for his head to clear, then sat up and gazed dispassionately at his handiwork.

Malandra's injuries were horrendous: her once-beautiful face was a featureless mask of split skin, cartilage and ruptured flesh, her body a mass of abrasions, bruises and cuts and she was blooded, quite literally, from the top of her head to the tips of her toes.

He too was covered with blood, Strudwick noted, casually. He felt no remorse and watched for a while as she lay crumpled on the ground like a rag doll wondering how such a useless pile of meat had ever taken his fancy. He was calmer now, more receptive to the voice in his mind: *The whore, serves the bitch right!* She stirred, groaned, peered through pain-filled eyes and reached upwards towards the sapling. Strudwick grinned, sardonically. He released the cord and watched as she struggled to regain her feet. Eventually, through sheer tenacity and effort, she raised herself enough to look directly at him. Speaking through split and bruised lips her every word was agony.

'You bastard! You stinking lousy bastard! I hope you rot in hell.'

Exhausted by the effort, she sagged against the tree and again lost consciousness.

He stared at her, incurious, but made no move. The lust to inflict pain was sated, and nothing would now be allowed to prevent him from following his carefully-constructed strategy to the letter. To do otherwise would not only increase the risk of failure, but be a gross betrayal of the one person whose brilliant intellect he esteemed above all others—himself!

Although late afternoon it remained comfortably warm. Remaining naked formed an essential part of the plan. He rose without haste and re-secured Malandra to the tree, then lay down and calmly fell asleep.

Flies appeared, as if from nowhere, drawn by the sickly stench of blood and he stirred from time to time, irritated by the insects.

His victim remained slumped against the tree, barely conscious. Her breathing was shallow and she groaned from time to time. It was late evening before he awoke. Somewhat chilled, he got to his feet, stretched, and covered the short distance to the Astra in two or three strides. Taking care to touch nothing, he peered through the driver's side-window to consult the dashboard clock, noting with satisfaction that it was nine o'clock—perfect.

Moving purposefully, he pulled on cotton gloves, earlier placed in readiness and strode to the boot, where he filled the bucket with three or four litres of water. He pulled four refuse sacks from the roll and placed them on the ground about two metres from the girl. Returning to the boot, he took the towel from the valise and draped it over the bumper. Lastly, he slit the remaining rubbish bags and spread the resulting sheets in front of his victim. He was ready.

Strudwick took his knife in one hand, strode across to Malandra and grasped a handful of hair with the other. He lifted her head and peered into her face, but detected no signs of awareness.

'Wake up, you bitch,' he snarled angrily, and shook her head from side to side. Failing to elicit response, he began to slap her bruised and battered cheeks back and forth, alternating between his palm and the back of his hand. Eventually she emitted a feeble groan, and he eagerly redoubled his efforts... *Kill her, but make sure the bitch is awake!*

Slowly, she began to regain consciousness. By and by, she raised her head and opened dull slits of eyes.

Pentophiles drew ever closer. *NOW! NOW! NOW!*

'Oh good, you snotty little cow. Awake at last,' Strudwick jeered. 'Now you've had a nice, long restful sleep, the time has come to say 'goodbye'—so goodbye, you stinking bitch!'

To prevent her moving, he grasped her hair and passed the knife to and fro in front of her face, watching, fascinated, as comprehension dawned. Mercilessly, employing a technique of his own devising, he slit her throat with one vicious, slashing stroke, starting from under one ear, continuing across and under the chin almost to the other. Blood fountained from the severed neck but her assassin made no attempt to avoid it. He allowed the warm, crimson fluid to pump freely over his hands and trickle down his body.

He watched and waited until her eyes glazed over and the flow of life-blood ceased.

Using the trowel, he dug a substantial hole in soft, sandy soil inside a clump of bushes beyond the clearing, into which he tossed the bonds from her wrists, the trowel, her sandals and the remnants of her clothes. Then Strudwick stood over the body, threw back his head and emitted a peal of demonic laughter. Pentophiles triumphant—*AT LAST! AT LAST!* In a manic frenzy, he bit, tore and ripped at what little was left of her features; he took and ingested mouthfuls of flesh from the breasts and upper arms. Not until sated did his rage subside; he rested a while.

Once refreshed and back in control, Strudwick worked swiftly. He spread the prepared plastic sheets and heaved the body on top, severed the head, sawed and hacked to separate arms and legs and wrapped the parts to form four parcels—the torso in one, head and arms in another and a leg in each of the two remaining. Shoving the parcels into plastic bags, he secured the necks with string and loaded all four into the boot.

He removed the gloves, rinsed and dried the knife and returned it to its sheath, threw the hacksaw and soiled gloves into the hole. Then he sponged himself from head to toe and poured away the water, repeating the process until every trace of blood was gone. He dried himself and tossed both towel and sponge into the hole, which he carefully back-filled and smoothed by hand.

Despite a thorough douching with the remaining water, traces of blood persisted around the sapling, but these would be flushed away by the next shower of rain. Donning fresh gloves, he wiped the can and bucket handles and everything on the car he might accidentally have touched.

He returned the bucket to the boot, latched it and, after carefully checking the clearing, started the engine and manoeuvred the car back on to the track. Leaving the engine running, he returned to the clearing in his bare feet. He used a dead branch to sweep the area clear of tyre-marks and footprints and, once satisfied, went back to the car to dress. Strudwick left the woods by the shortest and most direct route.

The Marquis of Granby—a well-known hotel near the Scilly Isles roundabout—was a convenient place to stop for sandwiches and a soft drink. Strudwick left his gloves in the car whilst making his purchase and put them back on when he returned. He ate and drank in the car, disposing of the bottle and wrappings in a handy rubbish bin, and at the same time taking the opportunity to be rid of two plastic sandwich boxes he had wiped clean of fingerprints.

At ten minutes past eleven, he parked the Astra behind Lower Green Post Office, switched off the engine and extinguished the lights. Slipping on the anorak and trainers, he took the bags from the boot and walked openly to Rodene Close via Cobham Street and through the side entrance of number eleven.

Strudwick was entirely familiar with the garden, having reconnoitred thoroughly in advance. He used a spade from the shed to bury the bags, taking no particular trouble to work quietly. Interment was completed in under ten minutes, the hole filled and the spade returned to the shed. *There, Steven Pearce. Let's see you wriggle your way out of* that. If the police were smart enough, his toe-rag rival might spend the next twenty years in jail. He grinned happily at the thought.

But, excellent though his intelligence-gathering had been, Strudwick was not aware that Steven's ticket had failed to arrive, nor that at the eleventh hour he had accepted his father's offer of a free weekend, assured that Manchester United would undoubtedly survive, even without his support.

THE FLYLEAF KILLER

Robert returned to the car, where it was the work of a few minutes to make a parcel of the trainers and anorak, run silently in his socks to a nearby house and dump the package in a dustbin where, with a bit of luck, it might reasonably be found.

Five minutes later, he was en route for a quarter-past midnight rendezvous with a hard-up mechanic from an Isleworth garage (a useful contact through his father, who managed Charlesworth's finances) to return the Astra borrowed for the weekend on an unofficial 'sale or return' arrangement. He stopped beside the Thames at Hampton near the A311 turn-off for Twickenham and threw the bucket, water-container and latchkey into the river. In a back street close to the garage, the car was checked and £200 paid over in cash, the agreed 'sweetener' should the vehicle fail to sell. No names were mentioned: no questions asked. Strudwick summoned a taxi from a nearby call box, was picked up in minutes and back in Esher High Street by 12.50, barely a couple of minutes walk from where he had left his car. An hour later, he was home, bathed and fast asleep in bed.

Sparkling and pristine, the Astra was back on the Isleworth forecourt by nine and purchased by an elderly couple from Osterley before midday for £5,000—a very reasonable price for a highly sought-after, low-mileage car in extremely nice condition.

Chapter Seven
Investigation

Police work relies on information, whether communicated electronically, verbally or via the traditional piece of paper—without information, few crimes would ever be solved. Modern information technology, infinitely capacious and a thousand times faster than the data transmission of yesteryear, would contribute little to efficiency were this vast reservoir of available information not prioritised. The humble copper must therefore be selective and turn to the computer only when absolutely necessary.

There are basically two species of policeman: the 'beat bobby' (a rarity, these days) whose brief is to uphold the law and prevent crime, and the detective, who must concentrate on tracking down and bringing miscreants to justice. Enter the Criminal Investigation Department. Be assured, the modern detective is simply an old-fashioned detective with electronic additions.

And what, you may ask, constitutes a successful detective?

Take intuition, attention to detail and sheer, hard grind—mostly the latter—plus, if you like, the dogged application of crime-detection methods devised, applied and proven over the years and you have the makings of a solid, dependable CID officer.

Detective Inspector David Melton was essentially an old-fashioned type of policeman. Keenly intuitive, his attention to detail regularly pinpointed clues that might otherwise be overlooked, and therefore he probed and prodded at every snippet purely as a matter of course. In common with most successful officers, he never ignored memoranda—routine or otherwise. He simply worked longer hours when necessary.

Monday, 20 July 2002
    Week three into the investigation—The *Body in the Garden* murder.

Following the release without charge of Steven Pearce, the area covered by house-to-house inquiries and the search of gardens and outbuildings were twice extended, yet nothing further emerged to suggest a possible suspect, or provide a clue which might help establish the murdered girl's identity, nor uncover anything to indicate a possible motive for the crime. Even though the blood on the anorak matched that of the corpse, it was necessary to establish beyond doubt they were from the same person. Samples were therefore sent for genetic analysis. Missing person reports from all over the country were checked, but none stood up to scrutiny and after a week with little or no progress to report, media interest waned.

But, on July 31, nineteen-year-old Jennifer Montague arrived home after ten miserable days in Tangiers. For some unknown reason, her close friend Malandra Pennington had failed to keep their rendezvous at the Britair departure terminal in Kensington on Sunday July 14.

Jennifer dialled Malandra's number—no reply; tried her mobile—switched off. *Strange!* She went round to Malandra's flat, knocked the door and rang the doorbell—no response.

What if Malandra's change of heart had been unintentional? Might she have fallen ill—been taken to hospital, perhaps? *And whose so-called friend went on holiday without first finding out?* Jennifer almost ran to the garages behind the flats. She stood on tiptoe to peer through a window and there in Malandra's lockup stood a car, unmistakably her ancient Mini. Something was definitely wrong.

She returned to Malandra's flat and hammered on the door. Again there was no response, but the next-door neighbour came out.

'What's going on? Oh, hello Jennifer. What's the matter?'

'I can't locate Malandra. She doesn't answer the phone, she's not at home, but her car is still in the garage.'

'I thought she was away on holiday—with you!'

'She didn't turn up at the air terminal. I kept ringing her but couldn't get an answer. I thought she'd changed her mind—she often does—so I went on holiday without her. What else could I do?'

Phyllis Gleave—Malandra's neighbour—turned deathly white. She swayed, seemed likely to faint, and may even have fallen, had not Jennifer grabbed her arm.

'Whatever is the matter, Phyllis? You look as though you've seen a ghost!'

'Oh my God, Jennifer. It's Malandra—it must be! The police found the body of a girl in a garden at Lower Green a fortnight ago . . . and she was a blonde. It was on telly and in all the papers.' Jennifer blanched. 'Do you really think . . .?' she whispered. 'Oh, no!' She burst into tears.

It was Phyllis' turn to be supportive. 'Steady on love, don't cry. I've got a key—shall we take a look? Maybe it's all a mistake.'

Jennifer nodded and wiped her eyes. 'Yes, we'd better make sure, I suppose.'

Mrs Gleave ran for the key. Nervously, she turned it in the lock and pushed back the door. Behind it lay a scattering of mail. There were two suitcases and beyond, lying on the hall table beside a vase of dead flowers, stood Malandra's handbag. Jennifer shrieked.

'Shut the door Phyllis and come away. I'm calling the police. Can I use your phone?'

'Of course you can. There's a special number to ring—it's been in all the papers. It was in the *Sunday Mirror*. I've still got my copy, somewhere—hang on, I'll go and find it.'

Scaled-down incident-room staff were doggedly 'plodding', but soon after Jennifer Montague telephoned the special number, the atmosphere became dramatically transformed. Her call was taken by a civilian telephone operator, who immediately alerted DS O'Connor.

'Hey Sarge, there's a Miss Jennifer Montague on the line, from Esher. Says she's a friend of an eighteen-year-old girl named Malandra Pennington—a blonde. Seems they were going away on holiday on July fourteenth, but when Miss Pennington didn't show up as arranged, she went to Tangiers on her own. She got back from holiday an hour ago. Tried to phone her friend, but there was no reply. She checked Miss Pennington's flat to find nobody at home, yet her car is still in the garage. Miss Montague is ringing from the flat next door. Apparently the neighbour heard knocking, came out, told her about the murder and our appeal. Do you want to speak to her?'

'Yes George, put her through. I'd very much like a word!'

Minutes later, he reported the text of the conversation to DS Melton.

'It seems the neighbour had a key to Miss Pennington's flat. They checked inside, but didn't enter. One look was enough to convince them Malandra had gone missing. Her holiday suitcases and her handbag were still in the hall as she left them, together with a pile of unopened mail. Not surprisingly, Miss Montague is distraught, but she's still perfectly coherent.'

'Get her to come in—better still, go and see her,' Melton said. 'Turn her story over and take a statement. Get a description of Miss Pennington and a photo, if possible—you know the form. Action stations, Ben. Give me a ring. If everything checks out, there'll be buttons to push!'

Melton was visibly brighter. After two weeks without progress and a cold trail on this callous, well-planned killing, there were signs of despondency in the team. Everybody needed a breakthrough. For the first time in more than a fortnight, Melton actually smiled.

'The more I think about it the surer I am. We're on to the girl's identity.'

DS O'Connor also seemed confident. Half an hour later he came on the line.

'We may have a match sir, the description fits. I'm at Miss Montague's home—16 Stretton Mews, two minutes' walk from Miss Pennington's flat. I'll explain why I'm here in a minute. I gave the neighbour a receipt for the key and advised Mrs Gleave not to jump to conclusions, to stay calm and not assume the worst until positive identification is established. I pointed out there could be a perfectly reasonable explanation for Miss Pennington's absence.

'I also suggested it would be wiser not to discuss the matter with anyone, at least for the moment. It was impossible to question Miss Montague—Mrs Gleave was parroting ten to the dozen—so I escorted her home to talk to her and pick up a photograph of Miss Pennington. She produced several and I picked out a couple taken last year. What a pretty little thing she was too—an orphan, so Miss Montague says.

'She seems convinced the girl is dead and is extremely upset. She and Miss Pennington have been close friends for years—they went to school together, apparently. When I asked her if she knew of anyone who might wish to see Miss Pennington dead, or might have a motive for wanting to harm her, she said she hadn't the remotest idea—and burst into tears. It's too soon to try for a statement, but she might have more to say once she's calmed down . . .' He went quiet for a couple of seconds, then asked, 'Do you want to get in on this, Guv'nor?'

'No, you're doing well enough, Ben. Too much pressure and she might clam up. Our first priority is to secure positive ID. If the body turns out to be Miss Pennington and her friend was as close to Malandra as she claims, then Miss Montague may be the key to this whole business, even if she doesn't realise it.' He thought for a moment. 'Are you happy to carry on dealing with Miss Montague yourself?'

'Yes sir, I am. She's likely to be relaxed and more talkative in her own home. I'll see if I can draw her out over a cup of tea. There is just one thing, sir.'

'What's that, Sergeant?'

'There's a killer loose somewhere out there and Miss Montague might therefore be in danger. Do you think . . . ?' He left the question suspended, and Melton was quick to respond.

'Yes, I do—and you only just managed to beat me to it. She'll be in danger from the moment this gets out. But let me correct you, Sergeant. He's not "somewhere out there", he's nearby—a local man—someone who knows the area thoroughly.

'Explain to Miss Montague how things work, but try not to frighten her unduly. I'll arrange for round-the-clock protection. I'll also get Slade and Gibson to collect the key to Miss Pennington's flat so they can get started—oh, and before you get back to Miss Montague, it would be cruel to ask her to formally identify the body—I doubt whether it's even possible. Keep off the radio, Sergeant. And what's the number there, in case I need to get back to you?'

By late afternoon, DI Melton had consulted the 'Chief', issued instructions and made a number of important telephone calls. A much heartened, reinvigorated police unit swung back into action. Within the hour, barrier-suited DCs Gibson and Slade began work in Malandra Pennington's flat. Gibson dusted for fingerprints, whilst Slade searched for strands of hair. When examination of the girl's brushes, combs and toiletries failed to produce results, he promptly dismantled the shower waste and recovered enough hair for both identification and DNA purposes.

Slade joined in the hunt for fingerprints, but the flat was spotless, leading the officers to assume it had had a thorough cleaning by someone wearing gloves, prior to being closed for a fortnight. They checked around, and Slade (the junior of the two) wondered about the handbag and luggage.

'Have you checked the suitcases, Graham?' Gibson shook his head. 'I didn't give them a thought, to tell the truth.'

Slade regarded his colleague solemnly: 'Never mind, let's *both* take a shufti, shall we?'

A light dusting of power produced two sets of prints, one on each suitcase handle.

'Thank goodness for that,' Gibson remarked, not the least bit put out. 'Go get the digicam, Harry, old son. I put it in the kitchen behind the door.'

With the prints photographed, the pair locked and sealed the flat and returned to headquarters. Gibson downloaded camera to diskette, made back-up copies and ran for a print comparison with the computer database. In less than a minute it came up with a match.

'Come on, Harry,' Gibson said, 'we'd better go see the Guv'nor!'

DS O'Connor, meanwhile, returned to Jennifer's flat and succeeded in persuading the tearful girl to talk, particularly about Malandra and their long-standing relationship. At first, Jennifer 'pooh-poohed' fears for her own safety and insisted nothing mattered except finding out what happened to her dearest friend—and catching her killer, if she really was dead. But she relented, agreed to be protected, and promptly resumed sobbing. DS O'Connor succeeded in calming her and she agreed to make a statement the following morning.

O'Connor took his leave, returned to HQ and reported to Melton.

'Sorry I took so long Guv'nor,' he said, 'but it's quite a story.' He handed over the photographs. 'That's her, Malandra Pennington—the murder victim, I reckon. What a pretty girl! Look at her figure, that gorgeous hair . . . pretty distinctive, wouldn't you say?'

Melton studied the prints carefully.

'It looks that way,' he agreed, 'But the corpse's hair was tangled and matted, which makes it difficult to be sure. We'll know for certain soon enough, so for the moment, let's keep an open mind.'

'Yes sir. Can I bring you up to speed regarding Miss Montague?'

'Yes, Sergeant. I take it she's added to her earlier information?'

'With a bit of prompting and the help of umpteen cups of tea, yes sir, she has.'

Melton tilted his chair until his head rested against the wall, placed his fingertips together and raised an inquisitive eyebrow.

'Well sir, Miss Montague would make a credible witness,' O'Connor began. 'Although distressed, she was lucid and a good communicator. She didn't deviate one iota from what she told me previously, even though I gave her plenty of opportunity. I took notes, of course, and I'll write my report as soon as I can.' He took a deep breath. 'Sir, I consider Miss Montague's information to be reliable and I expect her statement tomorrow to corroborate every word.'

'That's encouraging,' Melton said. 'But what else did she tell you?'

'I was coming to that sir. Concise as Miss Montague was, there were important omissions. Apparently she and Miss Pennington spoke on the phone just after 9.00 a.m. on the Saturday, the day before they were due to meet. They chatted about this and that, but Miss Pennington said she'd changed her mind about going to London that afternoon, intended to cancel her hotel booking and stay another night at her flat. It was because a nearly-new Vauxhall Astra was due in at Charlesworth's and she was intending to look at it on Sunday morning. I asked why that was important and she said Malandra had been after an Astra for some time and her current car, a Mini, was almost ready for the breakers.

'She needed a reliable vehicle for work and didn't relish returning to (and I quote) "a clapped-out old banger that probably wouldn't go" (unquote). She had intended to go to the theatre but decided to give it a miss.' He looked up. 'And that's about it sir.'

Melton was impressed. It took skill to extract pertinent information from an upset witness.

'Well done, Ben,' he said. 'I'll have to watch out. You'll be after *my* job next. That information could be crucial. It narrows the time-scale during which Miss Pennington disappeared to within a few hours. Regretfully, owing to the state of the corpse, formal ID is a non-starter, but in the light of this evidence I think we'll get by without. I intend approaching the 'Chief' about staging a reconstruction, although it might pay to hold back on the event itself until after we've spoken with Charlesworth's. At last we're getting somewhere.'

There came a tap on the door and DC Harry Slade appeared on the threshold.

'Come in, Slade,' said Melton. 'Did you have any luck?'

'Yes sir, we've established positive fingerprint ID. Do you want details?'

'I most certainly do.'

'Well sir, the flat was remarkably spotless, but Graham recovered hair from the shower waste. The only prints we could find were on the suitcase handles—which I photographed, naturally. Realising it might turn out to be important, we locked and sealed the flat and came back here. To save time, we downloaded, ran for a computer match and got a result in next-to-no time. Here's the printout sir. As you can see, sir, the prints match those taken from the body before it went to the mortuary.'

'Well done, Harry. Now we really *can* get cracking. Providing there's nothing pressing, I suggest you and Graham call it a day . . .' he turned questioningly towards DS O'Connor, who nodded '. . . and carry on at the flat in the morning.'

'Yes sir, thank you. I'll go and tell Graham,' said Slade and started towards the door.

'Hold on a second. Before you knock off, take the hair to Forensics and tell Ferguson I want it compared immediately with the sample from the body. He'll tell you he's too busy, most likely, so tell him if I don't hear from him within thirty minutes, I'll come over there and confiscate his bloody microscope!'

It was 6.40 p.m. when Albert Ferguson knocked on Melton's door.

'The hair samples, Inspector—they seem absolutely identical. The microscope rarely lies, but to be absolutely certain I recommend DNA profiling. Would you like me to do the necessary?'

'Yes please, Albert.' Melton smiled to himself. Ferguson *loved* his microscope. On August 1st, just after 9.00 a.m. Melton briefed Detective Chief Superintendent Jarvis. Press policy was agreed, discretionary authority for overtime was granted and, later that morning, Melton organised a brief statement:

INVESTIGATION

SURREY CONSTABULARY—SURBITON DIVISION
PRESS RELEASE No. 6729
Thursday, 01 AUGUST 2002

Acting on information received, investigating officers made progress towards establishing the identity of the young woman whose body was unearthed at Rodene Close, Esher, sixteen days ago.

Details of the injuries inflicted on the victim cannot be revealed without risk of compromising the investigation, but were of such a nature as to render formal identification difficult, if not impossible.

For this and other legal reasons and pending the outcome of further tests, the victim's name cannot yet be released, but may be made known shortly. A reconstruction of the murdered woman's last known movements is planned, at which time media publicity will be sought and gratefully acknowledged.

The statement was issued at 11.00 a.m. Newsmen pressed for further information, but were refused.

Moves to secure legal waiving of formal identification began. Having demonstrated a rapport with key witness Jennifer Montague, it became DS O'Connor's brief to take her formal statement and establish Malandra Pennington's known acquaintances to the best of Miss Montague's knowledge and recollection. He was to set up a register and arrange for each to be traced, and to update the register as and when further names emerged. The objective was to interview every single one of Malandra's work mates, friends, neighours and acquaintances.

Later still, Robert Strudwick was brought up to date. He made a number of telephone calls . . .

04 August: DNA tests proved positive. Tissue from the corpse, blood from the anorak, hair from the cadaver and Malandra Pennington's flat, all matched and were therefore from the same person. The *Body in the Garden* was, without question, Malandra Pennington, aged eighteen.

Formal identification no longer seemed necessary—much to DS O'Connor's relief. But the ultimate legal responsibility rested with the coroner. The matter must therefore wait for a decision at the Coroner's Inquest when convened.

Unannounced (but not unexpected) DI Melton called at Charlesworth's sales office. He introduced himself and asked to speak to the salesperson on duty over the weekend of the thirteenth and fourteenth of July.

'That would be me, Detective Inspector. I'm Tobias Charlesworth, Sales Manager.'

'You seem very sure, Mr Charlesworth. Haven't you any other sales staff?'

'Yes Inspector—part-timers, weekdays only. Our regular salesman walked out at the end of June—and left us in the lurch. Experienced staff are difficult to find, so I cover weekends myself.'

'I see—but *every* weekend Mr Charlesworth? That seems rather hard—your wife must be very understanding. Let's hope you find someone suitable in the very near future.'

'Thank you, but it's not a problem—I'm not married. Now, what can I do for you, Inspector?'

Melton looked meaningfully towards an office at the rear. 'Can we talk in private?'

'Certainly. This way, Inspector.'

Preceding Melton into the office, Charlesworth cleared a space on the desk and sat down, indicating a chair directly opposite. Melton observed Charlesworth carefully.

'We are investigating the disappearance of Miss Malandra Pennington who, we have reason to believe, is a client of yours. Is that correct, Mr Charlesworth?'

The salesman didn't turn a hair.

'Not exactly, Inspector. we haven't sold her a car—yet. But I certainly remember her—a very pretty girl. She came in—let me see—' (he turned the pages of a desk diary)—'ah, yes, June eleventh—oh, and again on the twenty-sixth. She was looking for a 1300 Astra under three years old and wanted to part-exchange a worn-out 1988 Mini Traveller which, quite frankly, we wouldn't touch although I couldn't hurt her feelings by saying so. Recent one point threes are like gold-dust, Inspector. We haven't handled one in months.'

Melton's dislike of the man deepened. He bridled.

'I had better warn you, Mr Charlesworth, this is a murder investigation. Miss Pennington disappeared on Sunday the fourteenth of July and her body was found buried in a local garden the following day. The case has been particularly well publicised. Am I to believe you've heard nothing about it?'

'Oh, was that the same Miss Pennington? I didn't realise. Yes, I did read something about it now you come to mention it. Terrible shame, lovely girl. But what's all this to do with me?'

The man's expression revealed nothing. *Salesman—or consummate liar and gifted actor?* Melton decided to put on pressure.

'Mr Charlesworth,' he said, sternly, 'we have every reason to believe Miss Pennington called at these premises the day she disappeared—Sunday fourteenth July, to look at a Vauxhall Astra . . .'

How the hell did they find out? He said no-one would ever know!

'. . . and I'm not satisfied you are telling me the complete truth. Perhaps we should continue this interview at the station.'

'If you like, Inspector.' Charlesworth shrugged, apparently unconcerned. 'But as I've already told you, we don't have an Astra—and you're perfectly welcome to look at the books.' *So piss off, copper!*

Charlesworth downloaded stock printouts for May, June and July and gave them to Melton, produced the sales ledger from the safe and placed it on the desk.

'There you are, Detective Inspector . . . see for yourself—and *then* can I get on with my work?'

Melton checked. No Astras. Stalemate! He put the printouts in his briefcase and stood up.

'Thank you for your time, Mr Charlesworth. You've been most helpful. But hold yourself in readiness,' he warned, 'we may wish to talk with you further.'

Tobias Charlesworth also rose, and smiled. 'Any time, Detective Inspector, any time.'

As Melton drove away, Charlesworth slumped in his chair, drained. *God, what a mess. Why did I let him talk me into it? He wanted to 'surprise the girl', he said: Christ, some surprise! I'll have to stick it out—it would kill Dad if he knew the business was in hock because of me. What's more, one wrong word from me and I'll also be dead. I know that bastard of old!*

Back at Surbiton, DI Melton and DS O'Connor conferred and

THE FLYLEAF KILLER

reluctantly concluded they were no further forward, despite Jennifer Montague's revelation.

'I thought we were on to something,' Melton said, disappointed. 'Charlesworth admits knowing Malandra Pennington and that she visited his premises on two occasions in June, confirms she was looking for an Astra, but denies seeing her on July fourteenth. He swears he hasn't retailed an Astra 1300 in months and I couldn't shake his story. When he produced computer stock-records *and* sales-ledger to back his assertion, I had no alternative other than to let the matter drop—at least for the time being.'

'Do you believe him, Guv'nor?'

Melton rubbed his chin.

'I'm not sure; he's a cool customer. If we pressure him without any sort of evidence to suggest he's lying, we might find ourselves facing a writ for unfounded harassment.'

'What about Miss Montague? Her statement confirms everything she said yesterday. It's on file, sir, there on your desk. You don't think she invented that conversation with Malandra, surely? She's far too level-headed and sensible—I'd stake my life on it.' O'Connor was unusually vehement.

Absently, Melton picked up the file and put it down again. 'I'm sure you're right, but even so, we'll keep Tobias on ice for the time being. Don't worry, Ben, our Mr Charlesworth hasn't heard the last of this—not by a long shot.'

O'Connor frowned, unconvinced.

'Now listen, Sergeant. Miss Montague's integrity is not in question, but we must remember the conversation took place *before* the event and we've no proof Miss Pennington actually carried out her intention. I'm sorry, Ben, but in the absence of compelling evidence to the contrary, we're obliged to give Charlesworth the benefit of the doubt.'

O'Connor was obliged to concede—for the moment. *Oh well*, he thought, ruefully, *another day, perhaps!*

Melton picked up the file and began reading. O'Connor waited for him to finish before handing across a typewritten sheet.

'There you are sir, a list of the murdered girl's acquaintances, male and female, to the best of Miss Montague's recollection. Two are middle-aged neighbours, the remainder from the deceased's and Miss Montague's age-group—and we've two men out interviewing already. Miss Montague also named several children she believes attended school about the same time as Jennifer and mentioned some teachers who might also be able to help.

'As far as background is concerned, Malandra was an only child. She lost her father as a toddler and her mother died from cancer two years ago. She grew up in Lower Green—incidentally, I suggest we extend house-to-house to cover the whole area, while we're at it.'

Melton nodded.

'That's fine. Do it a.s.a.p. but first, park your tail. I'd like to summarise what we have so far.'

'Hang on sir, there's something else. Other than hair and fingerprints, the search of the flat produced little, except mouldering food in a plastic food box inside one of the suitcases which turned out to be the remains of ham salad. I wonder sir,' he suggested, 'whether it was intended for Miss Pennington's lunch, in which case where did the salad found in her stomach come from?'

'Bought elsewhere, most likely,' Melton said, absently, and continued with his line of thought. 'I see from the statement that Miss Pennington planned to travel to Waterloo by train then take a taxi to Kensington. If so, in order to keep a three p.m. rendezvous with Miss Montague, she would need to have left Esher station around one-thirty. Check Sunday train timings, please, Sergeant. It follows that if she actually *did* call at the garage, it must have been between ten-thirty—the time the place opens, I checked—and twelve forty-five.

'This narrows the period of her probable disappearance and strengthens my argument for reconstructing her last known movements—I'll have another word with the Chief. And if somebody in the area just happened to see Malandra anywhere between those times, we'll have another little chat with Mr Charlesworth and this time, we'll haul him in.'

'Good, I'd like to be in on that, sir.' O'Connor responded, then added, 'There was one other thing. It may not be important, but Miss Montague happened to mention that Miss Pennington was shy and had few boyfriends. She was extremely attractive—Miss Montague was not a little envious—and although there were plenty of admirers sniffing around, few got further than a trip to the pictures and a quick snog.'

'That's interesting—might even come in useful,' Melton

remarked, thoughtfully. He rose and checked his watch. 'Four-thirty,' he said. 'Press briefing at five. Coming?'

'No sir, not unless you need me. I've still a mountain of paperwork to plough through.'

'OK, you carry on. I'll go to see the Chief and catch up with you later.'

During a major investigation, *every* day was a working day. The press-briefing did more than simply revive media interest, it brought it to life with a vengeance. There came a flurry of sightings and demands for information on a scale unprecedented, keeping telephone operators busy until well after midnight.

Melton stopped for a newspaper on his way to headquarters and picked up a copy of *Mail on Saturday*, struck by the double headline which thundered across the front page. He returned to his car, and read:

BODY IN GARDEN MURDER – MYSTERY GIRL IDENTIFIED!
TRAGIC VICTIM MALANDRA PENNINGTON, EIGHTEEN

Last known movements of beautiful blonde—re-enactment planned.
Police hunting killer to seek witnesses

Following yesterday's dramatic announcement naming the *Body in the Garden* victim, the last-known movements of beautiful blonde Malandra Pennington of Esher are to be re-enacted on Sunday 11th August, four weeks to the day the attractive young woman disappeared.

Detective Inspector Melton, CID, the officer heading the investigation, revealed that a friend of Miss Pennington returned from holiday on 31st July and reported Malandra missing.

Asked to name the mystery witness, Inspector Melton refused to be drawn, raising the possibility police fear for the safety of Miss Pennington's friend, who may unwittingly hold the key to the killer's identity.

It is further believed injuries to the girl's body were so horrendous as to render identification impossible. Exhaustive tests, including DNA profiling, were carried out to establish beyond doubt the body recovered from Rodene Close in July was Miss Pennington.

Full details regarding the re-enactment will be made public in due course, but in the meantime, anyone who saw Malandra Pennington in Esher on Sunday 14th July should contact the police immediately. Police would also like to hear from anyone who knows of someone who may have had reason to harm Miss Pennington or wish to see her dead.

'Flaming reporters!' O'Connor remarked, returning the newspaper. 'They always manage to print more than is actually said.' He tapped the paper. 'I'd bet a pound to a penny you didn't even *mention* the girl's injuries, much less anything about formal identification.'

Melton merely shrugged, resignedly.

'It's the nature of their business, Ben. They become expert at reading between the lines. It *can* be irritating but they do have their uses, so we learn to live with it.'

He folded and returned the newspaper to his briefcase, effectively closing the subject.

Response to the appeal was remarkable. Lines into police headquarters came alive a little after 8.00: Malandra Pennington, it seemed, had been spotted in places from as far afield as Aberdeen, Norwich and Exeter. Five sightings were logged before ten and a further six were to follow, bringing the day's total to eleven. Each would be checked, none dismissed out of hand.

Disappointingly, just two informants claimed to have seen Malandra Pennington in Esher on Sunday July 14, and arrangements were put in place for interviews to be conducted forthwith.

Detective Chief Superintendent Jarvis stormed in and buttonholed Melton. He tossed *Weekend Guardian* on the desk, its front page remarkably similar to Melton's paper. Angrily, Jarvis singled out two particular paragraphs that read:

> Detective Inspector Melton, CID—the officer heading the investigation, told our reporter that a friend of Miss Pennington returned from holiday to find Miss Pennington missing, heard about the *Body in the Garden* murder and called the police.
>
> Although Inspector Melton seemed reluctant to name the witness, it subsequently became known that the person was Miss Jennifer Montague, aged nineteen, also of Esher.

Jarvis positively fumed. 'Exactly how do you suppose the press got hold of *that* little snippet, Inspector?'

Melton reddened. 'I'm sorry sir, I really don't know,' he said, 'but it certainly didn't come from me. I can only assume somebody informed the reporter of Miss Montague's round-the-clock protection.'

'Oh,' grunted Jarvis, 'suppose I should have realised...' He subsided, but with very bad grace.

A few minutes later, the Chief Superintendent left for his Saturday round of golf. With him safely out of the way, Melton and his assistant put their heads together. They went over the forthcoming reconstruction in detail and agreed that O'Connor should invite Jennifer Montague to stand in for her murdered friend rather than enlist the services of a policewoman. Dark-haired Jennifer would need a wig, but she resembled Malandra in build and would be familiar with both her walk and her mannerisms.

Shortly afterwards, Melton tilted his chair backwards and rested his head against the wall.

'I'm hopeful the re-enactment will jog a few memories, Ben, but we have to be realistic. Three weeks have elapsed since the girl was killed and whatever trail the killer left behind will long since be cold.' Pausing to collect his thoughts, he went on, 'We've made progress, but too many questions remain unanswered—not least, the sort of man we're up against. Doctor Matthews' analysis may prove useful; just how remains to be seen. The killer seems to have disappeared like a puff of smoke, yet he was a local man—he has to be! I can't help but wonder about the combination of circumstances which allowed the girl's absence to go unnoticed, and I ask myself, "Did luck favour the killer or was the killing the end-product of masterful planning?" Witness the false trail, the blood-stained anorak, the footprint, the trainers. But whichever way you look at it,' he concluded, 'nothing we do can make up for the fortnight we lost between Malandra's death and Jennifer's return from holiday.'

Later that evening DS O'Connor rang his superior at home. The news wasn't good.

'You asked me to ring, Guv'nor,' he said. 'Well, neither of those sightings was worth a fig. But it's getting late,' he complained. 'Can I give you the details first-thing Monday?'

'Damn!' Melton exclaimed. 'I hoped we'd find out what Malandra was wearing, at least. Oh well, never mind. Thanks for ringing, Ben. I'll see you Monday—goodnight.'

August 5: Melton dumped his briefcase on the desk and sat down. He sighed. The start of another week, destined, he feared, to end much as the last. It wasn't like him to be discouraged. Usually, the more difficult a case the harder he strove and the cheerier he became. But this was altogether different.

DS O'Connor tapped the door, entered at Melton's bidding and sat down. He duly reported. The first interviewee—a Mrs Mavis Green—had peered short-sightedly at Malandra's photo and shaken her head. 'I'm sorry, officer,' she had said, 'that's not her. The girl I saw had much darker hair. She was the other side of the road, but I think her nose was more pointed than this. I hope I haven't put you to too much trouble.'

Edward Newnes, a retired gardener, was positive he'd seen Miss Pennington—the girl in the snapshot—when he was going for his Sunday pint. 'She was walking down the High Street towards the council offices,' he had said, 'wearing a yellow summer frock. She was pretty as a picture. But me memory ain't all that it was, and I can't be sure of the date, either. It might've been the second or third Sunday in June—or maybe even the last!'

Apart from the information provided by Jennifer Montague, little was known of the murdered girl's background and it seemed extraordinarily difficult to unearth anything about her social life.

A blank was drawn at Malandra's place of work. She was the only female who worked at the place and studiously avoided social contact with any of her colleagues. Nor could Jennifer Montague help, having never been Malandra's confidante where matters of the opposite sex were concerned. All that remained was the list of acquaintances supplied by Jennifer, several incomplete or missing addresses established—eventually, thanks to DS O'Connor's diligent researcher.

Melton and his assistant left headquarters at 10.30, determined to question all nine before the day was out. Listed in alphabetical order, they were:

Bridgwater, Francis	37 Poplar Causeway, West End
Carpenter, Brian	27 Gaston Avenue, Esher
Gleave, Phyllis	21 Penfold Mews, Esher
Lucas, Caroline	24 Rombole Crescent, Long Ditton

THE FLYLEAF KILLER

    Pearce, Steven Vincent   11 Rodene Close, Lower Green
    Pearson, Janice Anne   11 Douglas Lane, Lower Green
    Roberts, Fletcher   25 Penfold Mews, Esher
    Smith, Calvin   14 Lombard Road, Lower Green
    Strudwick, Robert William 7 Kenward Crescent, Claygate

Only three were at home, obliging them to ascertain, not without difficulty, the workplaces of as many of the remainder as possible, following which they set about conducting interviews in situ. Pressed for time, Melton and O'Connor made do with sandwiches and coffee around 1.00.

It transpired, to their dismay, that none interviewed knew the deceased girl intimately and Malandra's neighbours were simply neighbours—friendly when encountered, but not in any way privy to Malandra's private life. With one exception, the question, 'Do you know of anyone who may have wished to harm Malandra or who might benefit from her death?' the answer was 'No'.

The one exception was Robert Strudwick.

At first it seemed nobody was in, but they persevered and after repeated knocking, listening and bell pressing, a thin, flustered, middle-aged woman came to the door.

'Good afternoon, madam,' Melton began, displaying his warrant card. 'We are police officers. I am Detective Inspector Melton from Surbiton and this is Detective Sergeant O'Connor. Are you Mrs Strudwick?'

She became agitated and wrung her hands.

'Yes, I'm Mrs Strudwick, and I'm in the kitchen busy getting dinner. What do you want?'

'We won't keep you, but we're investigating a serious crime and would like a word with Robert William Strudwick who may be able to assist with our inquiries. Would Robert be your son?'

'Yes—but he's not here. He's at work and he won't be home before six.'

Melton glanced at his watch: three forty-five—too long to wait. He pressed harder. 'The matter is important,' he insisted. 'Where does your son work?'

'I'm not sure whether I should . . .'

Melton frowned.

'I don't suppose it matters, you'll find out anyway. All right then—but I hope he isn't cross. Gaston Hathaway, Long Ditton,' she said. 'Estate agents. Robert is a management trainee.' DI Melton thanked her and with O'Connor at the wheel, they departed.

Presently, the DS remarked, 'Rum sort of house, Guv'nor. Seemed ordinary enough, but fair gave me the creeps.'

'Oh, you noticed too? Lived in but a sort of "fustinesss" about the place. Lack of maintenance, do you suppose? Dodgy drains, maybe? They ought to get the council in.'

'Yes, something like that,' O'Connor grunted, and fell quiet. Unusually for O'Connor, he remained preoccupied for the remainder of the journey.

Reaching Ditton, he parked in front of Gaston Hathaway; Melton led the way inside. A smartly-dressed youth seated at a desk by the entrance looked up and rose to his feet.

'Good afternoon, gentlemen. How may I help?' he asked.

Melton flashed his warrant card.

'We're police officers. Would you happen to be Robert William Strudwick, by any chance?'

The lad shook his head. 'Not flipping likely I'm not; he's out with a client. I'm Roger Tattler. Would you care to leave a message?'

'No, we need to speak privately with Mr Strudwick. Is he likely to be long?'

'Sorry, I don't know'. He looked at the clock. 'Mr Robert went on a three o'clock appointment and it's well after four. I don't expect he'll be very much longer. Would you care to wait?'

'If you don't mind . . .' Melton glanced about.

'No problem. Mr Hathaway is out all day. I'm here by myself. Have a chair.'

The youth resumed addressing envelopes, leaving Melton and O'Connor to settle down and wait.

Time passed. At four fifty-five, Roger Tattler got to his feet.

'I'm sorry,' he said. 'I can't think where he's got to. We close at five and I must start locking up. Could you could come back tomorrow? If you'll excuse me . . .'

The policemen exchanged glances, then rose to their feet. Melton cleared his throat.

'All right, Mr Tattler, you weren't to know. Thanks anyway. We may call again tomorrow.'

The investigators returned to Melton's car:

'What a waste of bloody time,' Melton grumbled, with a rare

display of ill-temper. 'I wonder if Strudwick's mother tipped him off and the artful sod deliberately avoided us.'

O'Connor held his peace. It was not until they were at HQ, negotiating the entrance to the underground car park, that he voiced his thoughts. 'If Strudwick purposely dodged us, maybe he's something to hide?'

DI Melton hesitated. 'I don't know, but it's a thought. But I'll tell you what *is* important, Sergeant. Discovering something of the murdered girl's background, that's what. Somebody either knows who the killer is or has a pretty good idea of who he might be. A hint would help. And I keep thinking about Steven Pearce—*he* could be that somebody.

'The theft of the anorak and trainers two weeks before the murder—if Steven's story is to be believed—means the killing was planned at least that far ahead. If nothing else, the gear was planted in the garden to deliberately implicate the boy, added to which the body was buried with little or no attempt to do so quietly or avoid being seen. Had the murderer deferred dumping the corpse until, say, two or three in the morning, those bags might still be buried behind the rhododendrons with no-one the wiser.

'Steven is no killer, but the fact he denies knowing anyone capable of planting evidence sufficient to have him convicted just doesn't ring true. Had he not gone to Brighton with his family, Steven Pearce would be facing arrest, trial and imprisonment for abduction, bestiality and murder. He's either naive, stupid, or a very frightened young man—and I think the latter is the most likely.'

He turned to retrieve his briefcase, giving O'Connor an opportunity to air his own views.

'I think we ought to pull him in again, sir. I'm not too happy about him either. OK, we know he didn't carry out the murder but, as you rightly say, he knows much more than he pretends. Despite denials, I think he was "fitted up" by someone bearing a grudge—and that someone could only be the murderer, or at the very least an accomplice.'

Back in his office, Melton dumped his briefcase and dropped into his chair.

'You know, Ben,' he said, thoughtfully, 'you've a habit of going over the same ground twice, but that remark back there in the car set me thinking—and you're right, Steven *could* hold the key to the killer's identity, even if he doesn't realise it, although I very much doubt that. We went over it, time and again, but he refused to be drawn and stuck resolutely to his story—you were there, don't forget. Unfortunately, there's nothing further we can do. However—and this is the point I think you were trying to make—if he *does* have knowledge of the killer's probable identity, then his life is in very grave danger.'

Vindicated, O'Connor nodded. 'I've been trying to point that out almost since day one.'

'OK,' Melton said. 'It's well worth following up. I'll see what the Chief thinks about appealing to Steven Pearce again, and I've little doubt he'll agree. Incidentally—and this is my final word on the subject for the time being—the killer of Malandra Pennington takes size seven shoes. No larger, but maybe a size smaller.'

O'Connor winced but, wisely, made no reply.

'Meanwhile,' Melton went on, 'there could be an absolute mine of information out there waiting to be tapped and, rather than settle for a wasted day, what say we sort things out here then go get ourselves a chat with that damned, elusive Robert Strudwick? Are you on, Pimpernel?'

At 6.45 p.m. Melton's car swung into Kenward Close and drew to a halt at number seven. The officers walked up the driveway together.

It is they but have no fear. Your cause was just, your plan supreme. They do not know, they shall not know. Send them away!

Melton depressed the bell-push and rapped hard on the door. There was no immediate response, and he shuddered uneasily, as if chilled.

'I'm glad I don't live here, Ben,' he remarked. 'What a dismal dump. I'm not superstitious nor the least bit sensitive, as far as I know, but I swear I felt the hairs on the back of my neck rise as we came through the gates. And whew, that awful pong. Maybe it's not the drains. Could be a septic tank needs emptying.'

O'Connor pulled a face. 'Dunno, Guv'nor, but it's worse than this afternoon, if you ask me. Like I said before, the bloody place gives me the creeps!'

There came the rasp of a key followed by a rattle of bolts. The door opened and they were confronted by a sallow youth wearing bulbous glasses, through which he glared belligerently.

'Yes, what do you want?' he demanded. 'We're in the middle of dinner.'

'Sorry to disturb you,' Melton apologised, displaying his warrant card. 'We're police officers. I'm Detective Inspector Melton from Surbiton and this is Detective Sergeant O'Connor—we called earlier, but you were out. We're investigating a serious crime and it's a matter of some urgency that we speak to Mr Robert Strudwick. Am I correct in assuming that you are he?'

'Oh, it's you again. My mother said the police had been here. Yes, I'm Robert Strudwick and again, what do you want? You'd better make it snappy or my dinner will get cold.'

'I've already apologised but, as I said, the matter is urgent. May we come in?'

'No, you may not. You can talk to me here. I'll give you two minutes.'

The policemen exchanged glances. Each sensed the commanding, compelling presence radiated by this self-assured young man. Melton tried to take the initiative.

'I think I'd better warn you, Mr Strudwick,' he cautioned, 'we are conducting a murder inquiry and understand you were acquainted with the victim, Miss Malandra Pennington. I'm sure you will have heard something of the tragic case. As part of our enquiries it is essential we establish as much of her background as possible and, in that connection, there are a number of questions we wish to put to you. To begin with, how long have you known the deceased?'

'You're wasting your time—and mine. A right snooty bitch, if ever there was one! I've only seen her a couple of times since leaving school. Next. You've another minute and a half.'

'Do you know of anyone who might wish her harm or might benefit from her death in any way?'

The young man's attitude abruptly changed. He became derisive and sneered, 'No, I don't. It must surely be obvious, even to you, that I hardly knew the woman. Any further questions would be pointless. Now, I really would like to get back to my dinner, goodnight!'

The door closed. 'Goodnight, Mr Strudwick,' Melton said softly, swallowing his disappointment.

He turned and headed for the gates. He could almost sense his colleague's moustache bristle with frustration as O'Connor stumped along at his side.

'What a nasty, arrogant little swine!' O'Connor declared, as he piloted Melton's car towards Hinchley Wood. 'Strewth, I almost felt like flattening him.'

'Wouldn't have done either of us any good, Sergeant,' Melton responded, wearily. 'I didn't think he'd be able to help, but it was worth a try. He was far too sure of himself to be hiding something. Sorry Ben, we've met with another dead end, so we might just as well accept it.'

O'Connor drove in silence. He wanted his dinner and a good night's sleep. *Something* told him that the Guv'nor was right. Pursuing Strudwick further would be pointless.

August 8, Thursday

Of similar build and also size ten, Jennifer Montague agreed to wear one of Malandra's dresses and take part in the forthcoming reconstruction. Having no idea what Malandra actually wore that fateful Sunday, Jennifer chose a pale-blue, sleeveless frock from her late friend's wardrobe, one of her favourites, a style Malandra would be likely to favour for a warm, summer's day. Jennifer must obviously pose as blonde and was therefore fitted with a wig at public expense.

With interest on the wane, the fickle reporters had largely abandoned police headquarters in favour of more newsworthy subjects elsewhere. The widest possible publicity would maximise the chances of someone coming forward who remembered seeing Malandra the day she disappeared.

With this uppermost in mind, Melton organised a further press briefing for later that afternoon. During that briefing, on the understanding that nothing would be published in advance of the event, details and timings of the planned reconstruction were released but, for security reasons, Jennifer Montague's intended participation was withheld. Asked whether a policewoman lookalike would stand in for the murdered teenager, Melton had answered, 'Well, what else do you suppose?'

The forecast for Sunday, 11 August 2002 was accurate. The day promised to be fine and warm. Looking uncannily like the Malandra in the photographs, Jennifer emerged from her friend's flat at 10.45 and walked briskly towards the town centre. She was filmed

THE FLYLEAF KILLER

from a safe distance and shadowed discreetly by a team of plain-clothes officers.

Reaching the High Street, Jennifer adjusted her pace, ostensibly in order to window-shop whilst still on the move, as Malandra might have done, yet headed directly for Charlesworth's Garage. In addition to those keeping a watchful eye on Jennifer, further officers intercepted and questioned early-morning strollers in an attempt to jog memories, but met with little success.

At 10.55, Jennifer reached Charlesworth's. She traversed the forecourt, scanning the dozen or so cars on display, then paused at one for a closer inspection.

Aware he was clutching at straws, Melton also monitored Jennifer's progress with some anxiety. Except for Steven Pearce, perhaps, the entire investigation might well depend on a satisfactory outcome to today's re-enactment. Witnesses were vital. No other viable line of inquiry remained. As matters stood, the only challenge to Charlesworth's statement was the word of an elderly, rather unreliable witness.

When Jennifer was briefed, it was explained she must appear unaccompanied. She was alarmed at first, but accepted Melton's assurance that help would be on hand should she appear threatened.

She looked about nervously, but nobody appeared to be paying much attention. Following her mandate, she entered the main doors and made her way to the sales office. Inside, a man was talking on the telephone, to all intents and purposes oblivious to her arrival. Spared the need to ask for directions to Kingston—her intended ploy—she turned about, walked out of the showrooms and retraced her steps to the town centre.

DS O'Connor intercepted Jennifer in front of the Odeon. 'Well done, Jennifer,' he said, warmly. 'That was absolutely brilliant. I'll see you home and hand you over to your minder. Then, if you'd care to change, I'll relieve you of the wig and return the dress to Miss Pennington's flat.'

Reminded of the uncomfortably warm hairpiece, Jennifer's hand started towards her head.

'No,' O'Connor warned, 'leave it alone. Don't take it off here; you might be identified.'

'Sorry,' she apologised. 'I wasn't thinking. OK, what happens next?'

'Nothing as far as you're concerned. We're hoping your performance will lead us to the killer. But it was a "one-off", you know. It probably represents our last hope of finding somebody who can remember seeing Malandra on Sunday the fourteenth of July.'

August 12, Monday

Keeping their collective word, pressmen and television journalists gave the *Body in the Garden* reconstruction an extensive airing, a photograph of Malandra prominently displayed. The reason for the reconstruction was explained, with a further appeal for witnesses.

Public response was disappointing, although incident-room telephones began ringing around nine. From a total of eight would-be informers, six failed initial scrutiny and were discounted. The two remaining, Arthur and Mildred Jupp, were logged for subsequent interview.

On Tuesday August fourteenth, the couple were interviewed jointly by Melton and O'Connor. They stated that they visited Charlesworth's garage just after 11.00 a.m. on the fourteenth July, a few minutes late for an appointment to inspect a Ford Fiesta advertised in *Esher News* that week. They had entered in something of a hurry, almost bumping into a young woman on her way out. They had caught the briefest of glimpses, but thought she resembled the photo in Monday's newspaper. Arthur Jupp had been struck by her beauty and obvious youth, whereas Mildred remembered how well her hair seemed to complement her rather daring, lemon-coloured dress. Invited by Melton to look carefully at the original photograph, however, neither could swear it was *definitely* the same girl.

August 14, Wednesday

Melton and O'Connor called on Tobias Charlesworth. Melton proffered his warrant card and introduced his assistant. Charlesworth made no move to shake hands and remained seated.

'Oh, it's you again, Detective Inspector,' he sighed. 'What on earth do you want this time?'

Melton trod warily.

'Since my last visit, Mr Charlesworth, two witnesses claim to have seen a young woman leaving these premises just after eleven on Sunday fourteenth July, wearing a yellow summer dress. Both are of the opinion she strongly resembled Malandra Pennington. I am obliged, therefore, to ask you again: Did Miss Pennington call at these showrooms on the day in question?'

Call their bluff; sit tight. He says they're guessing, haven't got a clue.

Pre-warned, DS O'Connor watched for the slightest unease, as did Melton. Far from looking guilty, however, Charlesworth put on a masterful display of exasperation. He rose to his feet.

'Listen, Detective Inspector—you too, Sergeant O'Connor. I've had just about enough of this. I've already made it perfectly clear. I haven't seen Miss Pennington since June, but if you come back with a warrant, I'll gladly make my appointments diary available. I cannot in all conscience say the woman *hasn't* checked our forecourt stock since June, she may well have done—perhaps on a number of occasions. After all, she was seeking to replace her car. But whether she did so or not is immaterial. We do not keep tabs on every pedestrian in the street. If there's nothing further, gentlemen, I've plenty to do. You won't mind seeing yourselves out?'

Steven Pearce again found himself in a Surbiton interview room. He sat facing the same two officers across the same, bare, coffee-stained table. DS O'Connor spoke into a microphone.

'Interview timed at fourteen-thirty hours August fourteenth two thousand and two. Persons present: Detective Inspector David Melton, Detective Sergeant Benjamin O'Connor, Surrey Police, and Steven Pearce, aged sixteen. Say 'Yes', Steven, if that is correct.'

'Yes.'

'You live at number eleven Rodene Close, Lower Green, Esher. Is that also correct?'

'Yes, you know I do.'

'Now Steven, I'd like you to cast your mind back to June nineteenth of this year—the day of the league cricket match at West End in which you participated. At a previous interview, you identified as your property a blue anorak with yellow-striped sleeves and a pair of canvas trainers sized seven and claimed that these were removed during the course of the match, entirely without your knowledge or consent. Is that correct?'

'Yes.'

'You are aware that the same anorak and trainers were scientifically linked with the murder of Malandra Pennington on the fourteenth of July—whose body was discovered in your garden the following day—and that the very same items were subsequently recovered from a nearby dustbin?'

'Yes . . . but we've been through all this before, over and over.'

'I know, but these points have to be confirmed for the record. Now, bearing in mind that whoever stole your property may also have murdered Miss Pennington, I have to ask you once again to tell us the name of anyone you suspect might be the thief—no matter how remote the possibility. Somebody tried to frame you for a crime you didn't commit. Surely you've *some* idea who that somebody might be? Come on, Steven, who dislikes you enough to have you convicted for murder? Take your time—think hard. This is extremely important.'

Melton waited.

Steven sighed, appeared to consider, but nothing was changed: *Do they really expect a cheap, sneak-thief, maybe-killer, to be handed them on a plate? They are the detectives, why don't they go out and do some detecting? On the other hand, whom* do *I know who might fit the bill?— Nobody, really—except, perhaps . . . no, not even him. A two-faced rat certainly, a nasty little shit who once made Jan's life a misery, but a killer? No way! How could he have nicked my gear, he wasn't even at the match, was he? OK, suppose I did give his name and they pulled him in for questioning, what then? They'd get nowhere and have to let him go, that's what. Pretty soon he'd find out who grassed him up—and* then *who would he take it out on? Yes, poor Janice again. Then it'd be my bloody turn—no chance! She's happy. I love her and I reckon she loves me. I can't risk getting up his nose just to shift a couple of lousy coppers off of my back . . .*

'Sorry Mr Melton,' Steven said, 'but as I've already told you, I haven't the remotest.'

DI Melton wrote: 'Steven Pearce, re-interviewed, nothing to add. Dead end, again!'

August 23, Friday

Lacking justification for its continuance, the incident room was closed. The case, however, was anything but closed, and Detective Inspector David Melton resolved to keep the *Body in the Garden* file current, and to bring the killer to justice, no matter how long it took.

Much good that'll *do them,* Strudwick sniggered, derisively.

December, 2002.

Four months into the investigation the police were no nearer solving the crime. Robert Strudwick felt no sense of relief, however. Why would he? Supremely confident his masterful scheme would remain detection-proof, backed by the Book and the powers of his mentor, how could it be otherwise?

But he wasn't complacent. There *had* been flaws: gambler Toby Charlesworth—always a weak link, though he'd never dare talk; and Steven Pearce's last-minute change of plan, without which the police would long since have declared the case closed. The girlfriend-stealing rat ought to be staring a life-sentence in the face, instead of which (he was reliably informed) he was to remain free, despite a well-justified suspicion that he knew far more than he cared to admit. Steven Pearce's turn would come but first, Francis Bridgwater, Robert promised himself, grimly.

It had been a wonderful year, for all that. With personal sales rapidly approaching those of millionaire Gaston Hathaway, Robert's income, investments and assets grew month on month. His future seemed assured. Safe, unassailable, confident his mentor was sated for the time being, he nevertheless consulted the Book each and every day.

Chapter Eight

Preparation

Just about everybody knew about it, read about it, talked about it, worried about it, lived in fear and dread of it: the *Body in the Garden* murder . . . yes, *MURDER!* Right here, in the quiet, normal, everyday, workaday town of Esher. And whilst the nature of the atrocities to which Malandra Pennington's body had been subjected were never fully made public, just about everybody knew there was a depraved killer living somewhere in their midst—a *local* man! Even so, what *had* been revealed about the crime was so monstrous as almost to defy imagination.

But time is indeed a great healer and, as the weeks and months passed, the frequency with which the subject cropped up steadily diminished, until the day came when young women no longer thought it necessary to seek safety in numbers and began to venture out alone once more.

All was duly noted by Robert Strudwick, who maintained and expanded his local knowledge as a matter of course, keeping tabs on persons of particular interest through a network of craven informants, subjugated puppets recruited over time since the Book had come into his possession.

Nor did he neglect his other skills. Apart from almost effortless success as a young, up-and-coming estate agent, he amused himself exploring and developing a wide range of possibilities for obtaining revenge on those earmarked for further attention—and there were several. But one in particular was never far from his thoughts: that arrogant, womanising creep Francis Bridgwater. Well-rid of the Pennington bitch, Robert ached for the signal to repay Francis too—and painfully.

One potential plan called for the use of disguise. This prompted a visit to the library to learn more and he became fascinated by the subject. Reading that no disguise was infinitely preferable to a poor one—more likely to attract rather than divert attention—he put the theory into practice and developed a simple but entertaining means of gaining unchallenged access to protected premises in locations spread across half of Surrey.

On his first outing, he discovered a natural talent for blending into the background, and learned to transform his appearance by wearing contact lenses instead of spectacles; by adopting a small mannerism—a stoop, a slight limp perhaps; or simply by wearing clothes appropriate to the venue. Robert practised under a variety of guises in widely differing circumstances and places without ever once raising a single, questioning eyebrow.

For all his success with women, however, Robert seemed unable to sustain a relationship for any length of time and continued to indulge in brief, spasmodic affairs. When at a loose end, he tried occasionally to force his attentions on Janice, cynically ignoring her protests that she and Steven were very much in love. Although fearful of the consequences, she steadfastly kept him at arm's length, which further exacerbated his dislike of Steven. Eventually, tired of being rebuffed, Robert decided not to bother with her again, but to be avenged on them both, given a suitable opportunity. Meanwhile, he decided to amplify Steven Pearce's fear as a reminder to keep his mouth shut.

Happening across Steven in the High Street a day or so later, Robert took him to one side.

'Listen, Pearce,' he said, ominously, 'just in case you suspect *me* of nicking your gear at that bloody cricket match . . .'

It was both threat and accusation. Steven hastily defended himself.

'Why on earth should I?' he protested. 'You weren't even at the match, as far as I know.'

'That's right, I wasn't—and make sure you remember it!' was Robert's swift rejoinder. Then: 'And another thing. You enticed Janice away from me and I won't forget that in a hurry, either!'

It was an unfair assertion, delivered with menace. Suddenly fearful, Steven shook his head.

'I didn't entice her; I didn't need to. She was finished with you long before I asked her for a date.'

'Bullshit! She was still my girlfriend when you snogged her on the way to school—and don't bother denying it either. A friend of mine saw the pair of you canoodling and holding hands.'

Steven paled. He recalled both the incident and the mitigating circumstances, but it would be futile to try and explain it away to Robert. Realising that to say more might only make matters worse, he made as if to walk away, but Strudwick wasn't allowing that. Gripping Steven roughly by his arm and in a voice heavy with menace, he snarled, 'Yes, Pearce, I've known all along what you were up to and, what's more, you'll pay for it, one of these days!

'But about your anorak and trainers. If you breathe a word to the police—or anybody else, for that matter, I'll treat you to a razor-job—Janice too. Will you still fancy her with a ripped cake hole? And what will she say when she finds out it's all down to you? Do you get my drift—arsehole?'

Steven was no coward, but Robert scared him. He was even more frightened for Janice's safety.

'But I love Janice and she loves me. Just leave us alone—I swear I'll keep out of your way . . .' His plea fell on deaf ears. Robert strode away without so much as a backward glance.

Janice and Steven's childhood friendship—resumed out of sympathy towards the end of her unhappy relationship with Robert—blossomed from the day she told him her affair was at an end, whereupon he had confessed his true feelings. Janice was astonished at first, but his ardour, sincerity and manliness couldn't be denied, and it wasn't long before she eagerly reciprocated his advances . . .

But what of Francis Bridgwater, so often the subject of Robert Strudwick's malevolent thoughts? Francis, an only child, never knew his mother, who had died from complications following his birth. He was brought up virtually single-handed by his father, whose main concern was to ensure that the boy enjoyed a normal childhood, despite the lack of a mother's love and attention—and he had succeeded. Francis (or Frank, as he was popularly known) not only did most of the things boys generally did, he also coped well at school, excelling in languages, especially French and Italian.

Slender resources or no, Kenneth Bridgwater financed a continental holiday each year for the boy, something Frank hugely enjoyed, and he worked tirelessly to improve his colloquial fluency in order to repay his father's generosity.

Nowadays, Kenneth owned a neat, semi-detached bungalow at West End, but it had not always been so. At one time, he had made a good living as a travelling-salesman, but when his wife died, he gave it up to become a part-time window-cleaner, an occupation which didn't pay very well, but allowed him to regulate his hours, in order to care for his son. Even so, he was grateful for the kindness shown by a motherly neighbour, without whose help Francis might well have been taken into care.

In 2002, the year Francis left school to begin work, the mortgage was repaid and the resultant increase in family disposable income, coupled with a modest bank-loan, made it possible for Kenneth to buy a milk round of some 300 customers, which he promptly set about increasing. After years of toil for scant reward, and despite the unsociable hours, Kenneth was in his element.

On leaving school, Francis worked on the production line of an automotive factory, but after a year of boredom, he decided his future lay elsewhere and sought a vocation where his linguistic talents could be usefully employed. He checked out a number of possibilities, none of which fired his imagination but eventually, after several disappointments, he was offered a position as a trainee holiday courier with a travel company based at Hounslow, a job he gladly accepted.

As part of his training, he accompanied an experienced courier on a number of trips and, like most newcomers, was expected to be competent enough to tour unaided by the end of the season. A brilliant linguist, already a seasoned traveller, he took to the business like a duck to water, and became a courier in his own right within three months.

The work suited Frank admirably; not only did he travel around Europe, he got paid into the bargain.

The rewards were high: a fair basic salary, tips, free food and accommodation—not bad, for an eighteen-year-old. But there were other benefits too. Many of the single ladies in his parties—and some who obviously were married—fell madly in love and the handsome six-footer was usually happy to oblige. Trip-end tips could be astronomical, gratuities from grateful hoteliers and restaurateurs frequent and generous. Oh, yes, Frank loved his work all right but, unfortunately, it was seasonal.

After idly kicking his heels for an entire winter, he cast around for something to occupy his time from November to March, and found it—as a freelance airline steward for Air France, working out of Toulouse Airport. It would mean being away from home most of the year, but Frank promised to telephone his father regularly and return for a break as often as he could. He attended a twelve-week training course in order to qualify. Air France rewarded his efforts by keeping him continuously employed for the remainder of that winter—and beyond . . .

The romance between Janice and Steven deepened with the passage of time and, after two blissful years together, the happy couple chose April 15, 2004—Janice's nineteenth birthday—to reveal to the world their commitment each to the other by announcing their engagement. Towards the end of the evening, at a wonderful party to mark the occasion, Steven and Janice were still dancing.

'That's it, old lady,' he said, putting his arms around her and giving her a kiss, 'first a house, next the church—then we can think about starting a family. Come to think of it, what about finding somewhere quiet for a spot of practice right now,' he murmured seductively, noting with delight how easily she blushed.

Janice looked at him adoringly.

'Not so much of the old,' she retorted (he was a year younger than she). Come on then.'

August 1 2004. To celebrate his recent appointment as senior negotiator with Gaston Hathaway, Robert Strudwick took delivery of a brand-new Jaguar XJS in white—and paid cash!

On October 31, after an interval of more than two years, came the long-awaited message:

WITH KEENE STEEL BE AVENGED, HIS TIME IS NIGH, HE WHO DIDST STEAL FAIR MAID

Robert's heart lurched and a familiar surge of adrenaline caused his pulse to quicken. Word by word, he studied the archaic prose, determined to assimilate each and every character. Again he watched, awestruck, as the words shimmered and faded, just as he knew they would. Their import was crystal clear—Francis Bridgwater was to be the subject of his next mission: *Keene steel? I'll cut the bastard's head off!*

Once more he was to devise his own plan, set his own agenda, taking care never to deviate from steel as the designated weapon. A number of interesting possibilities crossed his mind and he licked his lips, thinking about the pain he would inflict before dispatching the snivelling bastard. But where was Bridgwater? He would find out tomorrow. Robert put away the book.

It promised to be a demanding mission, yet he relished the challenge and began to apply his intellect to the task of creating an outstanding strategy, not merely to dispense with a physically superior enemy and baffle the police, but to enhance his standing with Pentophiles, giving his mentor no reason whatever to withhold the material wealth Robert so desperately craved. He wanted to be a millionaire—he *expected* to be a millionaire. He wouldn't fail, he couldn't fail, for he was the chosen one. Had he not willingly conceded metamorphosis to Pentophiles, making it possible for his nether-region guru to satisfy a long-denied craving for human flesh and blood?

Robert continued to deliberate. Bridgwater's movements must be monitored from the moment he arrived home; that much was obvious. Equally obvious was the fact that Robert must stay in the background well out of sight, or the cleverest of plans might fail. To succeed, he would need help.

No longer willing to risk the likes of Charlesworth, he would restrict his informants to two, neither of whom must know the other, or be bright enough to connect him with subsequent events. But before Robert could decide who to employ and how, something—was it fate?—intervened...

Proud father Kenneth told several of his customers about Francis' impending arrival for a two week vacation and was overheard by the son of one of them, who promptly made a telephone call. The caller lived opposite the Bridgwaters; he also knew a great deal about Frank—including his activities the last time home. Even as he spoke—and whilst Robert listened intently—a plan began to form.

Besides the current informant, the services of another trustworthy person would be needed to act as intermediary, and Brian Carpenter was exactly the man for the task. Carefully briefed, Brian would follow instructions to the letter—and never dare to reveal his involvement afterwards. By the time the connection was broken, the complete strategy had been decided—simple, but brilliant.

The next day Robert visited Kingston Hospital, venue of two successful disguise experiments. Parking unobtrusively, he put on a white coat and, wearing contact lenses and horn-rimmed spectacles fitted with plain glass, he strode purposefully through the main entrance doors.

Briefcase in hand, he made his way towards the operating theatre, but slowed his pace when a scrub-nurse bearing a pile of folded laundry emerged from a sterile store a few metres ahead. She elbowed her way through the swing-doors of the theatre and disappeared from view, giving Robert precisely the opportunity he'd hoped for. Unchallenged, with a complete set of green operating clothes tucked inside his briefcase, he was halfway down the corridor before the nurse remedied her omission and returned to lock the door.

Before he left Kingston, Robert bought a folding wheelchair and a second-hand surgical scalpel in a leather case from a market bric-a-brac stall. Highly-prized by model-makers, these fine Victorian instruments are sharper than modelling-knives, even when no longer fit for surgery, remaining keen-edged almost indefinitely, providing they are not abused.

Frank Bridgwater's brief vacation drew to a close. On Monday November 15, two days in advance of his scheduled return to France, he visited Esher railway station to purchase his train ticket. Once he was gone, the booking clerk earned his £20: he dialled the number scribbled on a scrap of paper by a charming, rather elderly gentleman who had called at the station earlier that morning.

'Hello, I'm ringing to confirm Mr Bridgwater's reserved seat on Eurostar Express, departing Waterloo International at 10.30 a.m. on November 17, just as you expected, sir. By the way, I hope the farewell-party goes well, but don't get him *too* drunk—he might miss his train.'

The first phase of the plan concluded, Robert relaxed, smiled with satisfaction and chuckled.

'Thanks, but don't worry. I expect he'll have a nasty headache—but I've plenty of aspirin!'

Ten minutes later, Robert rang Brian Carpenter.

'Hello Brian, it's me. Are you at home?'

'Yes, Robert.'

'How much petrol have you got in your tank?'

'Not much—about two gallons.'

'Good, that's enough for the moment. You can fill up later—my treat. Now, listen carefully, I've an important job lined up for tomorrow evening and I need your help. Let's see what the time is—um . . . just after five. Right. Leave at six and drive to Esher station. Go to the rear of the car park, switch off your lights and wait for me there. I'll be along shortly to explain exactly what I want you to do. Have you got that?'

'Yes, Robert. Leave at six, go to Esher station and wait for you at the back of the car park.'

'That's right. I'll see you there at six-fifteen. Don't forget, turn off your lights—and be there!'

En route to the station, Robert made a detour to surreptitiously borrow a key . . .

Kenneth went to work long before Frank fancied getting up. Eight o'clock was plenty early enough.
Providing he left by nine, he could bus to Esher station and catch the 9.45 for Waterloo—perfect. It was becoming routine. Packed, ready to leave by teatime on the eve of departure, he would round his holiday off with a trip to the cinema.

For safety's sake, Frank zipped his wallet and passport into the side-pocket of his valise. He shrugged into his overcoat, closed the bedroom door and went in the living-room where the 'old fellow' was working. Promising to telephone by month end, Frank hugged his father good-bye and caught the 6.05 bus for Kingston.

Robert's mobile rang—he grinned. True to form, just as on the last two occasions, Francis Bridgwater was heading for the cinema. But which one? Robert dialled another mobile number and a similar instrument warbled in the Black and White Milk Bar, adjacent to the 218 bus stop.

'He's on the bus, Brian. Watch for him. Ring me back when you see which cinema he goes to.'

Diagonally opposite stood the Odeon cinema, some seventy metres from its Granada rival on the next corner, the entrances to both clearly visible from the Milk Bar. *The Milk Bar!* Justice demanded that it should figure in this retribution-seeking scheme. Robert grinned sardonically.

The 218 from Staines drew up at 7.10. Twenty or so passengers alighted and dispersed. Some headed towards the Granada cinema, others to the Odeon, among them Frank Bridgwater.

Fearful, yet obedient and fully-briefed, Brian Carpenter made his return phone call.

'He's going to the Odeon, Robert,' he said.

Strudwick smirked, all was going well.

'OK Brian. Thanks. Don't forget why I gave you that fifty. Sit near him, then bump into him as if by accident when the film finishes. Be pleased to see him. Get him to the bar. Buy him a pint or two and keep him talking. It shouldn't be difficult—he loves his beer. Remember, he mustn't catch the bus. It would spoil his surprise. Offer him a ride home—anything. Don't forget, if he doesn't want a drink or refuses a lift, go to the toilets and ring me, but I doubt that'll be necessary.

'Leave at ten thirty-five exactly. I'll be watching, don't forget. As soon as you clear Kingston, mention the coffee in the glove-box and tell him to help himself, but don't be too pushy—and don't drink any yourself—it's full of knockout drops. He'll be easier to handle if he takes a drink, but it's not vital.

'Pull into the lay-by on Littleworth Common. Tell him you're bursting for a piddle if he's still awake and, if there's anybody about, you'd better pretend to have one. I'll park right close behind. As soon as he's in my car, you can go home. I shan't need you any more tonight.'

Kingston was about twenty minutes drive away. Robert completed his preparations and took stock: key, bell wire, wheelchair, surgical clothing and impedimenta in the boot, cosh under his seat, a second flask of coffee in one glove-box, cagoule and knife (for emergencies) in the other. Elated, confident, fully prepared for any eventuality, Robert left Claygate at nine-fifty . . .

Kenneth experienced some unease when November drew to a close without the promised phone call. On the night of December 1st, two full weeks after Francis' departure, Kenneth hardly slept in case the phone should ring and he might not wake to answer it. Morning found him edgy, fearful that something was wrong. Francis was always as good as his word, never broke a solemn promise or intentionally caused anyone needless anxiety. Yes, something was definitely amiss with the boy—but what? An accident of some sort? A plane crash? Surely not. He would have been notified immediately.

Kenneth vacillated. What should he do? He couldn't think straight any more. By December 3, tired, irritable and frantic with worry, he muddled deliveries—even missed some out altogether—

and, by the afternoon, almost out of his mind with anxiety, he disregarded Air France company rules and telephoned Toulouse airport.

Unlike Frank, Kenneth's command of French was limited and he had difficulty making himself understood. But he persevered, and was eventually connected with the cabin-crew manager.

'I must speak urgently with Francis Bridgwater, please. I am his father, Kenneth Bridgwater.'

'But 'e is not 'ere, M'sieur Bridgwater!' the Frenchman exclaimed. 'François was engaged as acting senior cabin steward for Flight G8 for Toronto, but 'e did not report for duty. The plane 'ad to leave Toulouse on November the nineteenth understaffed as a consequence. Passengers were inconvenienced, M'sieur. I was inconvenienced. It was inconsiderate of 'im. I am still very angry!'

Horrified, Kenneth protested, 'You must be mistaken. Francis left for Paris on November the seventeenth—he *must* have arrived.'

'I am sorry M'sieur, but there is no mistake. François did not report for duty. 'E did not even take trouble to telephone me and explain 'imself...' Fearful, trembling, Kenneth mumbled his thanks. Without replacing the receiver, he broke the connection and telephoned the police...

Chapter Nine

Assassin

During the 1920s, the expanding village of Esher became a parish within the diocese of Guildford and, to reflect this enhanced status, a new church was commissioned and built on a dominant position overlooking ancient common land, earmarked to become the village green. Designed to reflect Early English architecture, the new structure took full advantage of twentieth-century materials and techniques and the scaled-down cathedral-like edifice had the capacity to cope with whatever size congregation might conceivably develop in the future.

The consecration of Esher Parish Church was generally welcomed, but a surprising number of residents complained that its presence rendered the tiny chapel of Saint George—the village place of worship since the twelfth century—virtually redundant. Bowing to pressure, the church authorities agreed that St. George's—known locally thereafter as the 'Old Church'—should be maintained in good repair in perpetuity, but stipulated that a minimum of two services must be conducted on the premises each year.

The chapel is open daily and visitors are free to worship, to inspect the artefacts or to visit the ancient graveyard, where monuments to the long-departed still stand, many of historical interest. The Old Church is set behind the original village green, two minutes' walk from the present-day town centre. Its imposing main entrance door is of oak. The entrance is approached over a cobbled pathway through a rather splendid lychgate. The graveyard is enclosed by substantial stone walls and a second, rarely-used gate opens to a service area behind a parade of High Street shops. Two ladies from a church-sponsored charity spend a morning each week cleaning the interior, whilst staff from the parish church look after the building, graveyard and the surrounds.

Beneath the main body of the church lies the crypt, abandoned and sealed for over two hundred years. At the foot of a short flight of steps, a single, solid-oak door provides access to an anteroom, thence to a side-vault, once privately owned.

Nothing in church records gives any indication of the former owner, nor whether at one time the space was employed as a burial-chamber.

The tall, wrought iron gates guarding the crypt have remained chained and padlocked for longer than anyone can remember, and years have elapsed since the vault was last used. Few are aware that access can be gained by means of a key hanging from a nail in the vestry.

In the days when St. George's was in regular use, limited storage probably prompted an enterprising verger to press the vault into service. Nothing was stored there currently, however, except a pair of wooden trestles, a rickety old stepladder and a couple of decrepit, cane-bottomed chairs.

St. George's was converted from gas to electricity in 1934 and whilst it was thought unnecessary to have electricity wired to the disused crypt, the side-vault and anteroom were included in the interests of safety and supplied via a separate, fused lighting-spur.

Robert Strudwick knew more about St George's than most, having explored the place during his early teens and realised its potential. It became immediately obvious that it was rarely used and he was particularly intrigued to discover that it could be entered covertly from the rear. It didn't take long to establish which door could be opened by means of the key in the vestry, but a hacksaw would be needed in order to get into the crypt. However, its use would simply advertise a break-in and neutralise an otherwise potentially first-rate entrapment venue. Eventually, Robert's caution paid off. The vault beneath St. George's represented the perfect place wherein to exact long-awaited vengeance on smarmy, oh-so-cocky Francis Bridgwater . . .

Bridgwater eagerly accepted Brian Carpenter's offer of a pint and a lift home. He drank two full cups of drug-laced coffee and was out to the world in minutes. As expected, the Littleworth Common lay-by was deserted. Here, Bridgwater was speedily bundled into the boot of the Jag and the conspirators went their separate ways, completely unobserved.

Screened from the High Street and by means of the wheelchair, the ease with which he was able single-handedly to transfer Bridgwater into the vault seemed something of an anticlimax and the lack of excitement left Strudwick vaguely disappointed . . .

Emerging slowly from a drugged stupor, he had no awareness of danger, merely a vague sense of discomfort coupled with a pounding headache. As the level of consciousness improved, however, Francis attempted to move, only to realise he was secured to a hard wooden seat of some description with his wrists tied securely behind his back.

It was deathly quiet, the only discernible sound the beating of his heart as the muscle thumped in sympathy with a synchronous throbbing somewhere inside his head. A blindfold covered his eyes and the blackness beyond suggested he was confined in a place of darkness. A gag was jammed firmly between his teeth making it difficult to breathe.

Where the hell am I? What's going on? He winced with pain.

The effort of trying to think simply magnified his headache. Barely conscious, he tried shifting his legs, but they were tied tightly together and strapped securely to the chair, making it impossible for his feet to touch the floor. To say he was uncomfortable would be something of an understatement. As time passed and the effects of restricted circulation worsened, discomfort turned first to pain and thence into sheer agony. Eventually, and paradoxically, he reached a stage when paralysed nerve-endings and numbness allowed exhaustion to take precedence and he dozed fitfully, scarcely aware of his predicament.

After an hour or so of fragmented slumber, however, this anaesthetising insensibility wore off, and the pain from his tortured buttocks alone destroyed any possibility of sleep.

With the return of full consciousness, the eerie silence seemed to intensify. No sound disturbed the deathly hush, yet he gradually became aware of a faint, continuous whistling noise, equally audible in both ears. He did not know it but profound silence, coupled with extreme discomfort, had triggered the onset of a hearing condition known medically as tinnitus.

Increasingly desperate and disregarding the likelihood of bruising himself, he rocked the seat from side to side, trying to topple over and thereby relieve the excruciating pain at the base of his spine, but was thwarted when his shoulders came into contact with solid walling on either side. It was almost if he were entombed, or

THE FLYLEAF KILLER

penned in some kind of narrow tunnel or enclosure. He regretted the discovery. For the first time in his life he was overwhelmed by claustrophobic panic. Fear of close confinement magnified his pain and he tried to scream, but the gag between his teeth was tied tightly at the back of his neck and he could manage little more than a gurgle.

He could breathe only through his nose and, as he struggled, his lungs became seriously starved of oxygen, causing his heart to thump violently.

It took a monumental effort of will but, eventually, he managed to calm himself sufficiently to restore his breathing to its former, barely adequate level.

The atmosphere was dank and musty, which suggested his prison was underground. It was bitterly cold and Francis shivered; he realised for the first time that his overcoat was missing. His remaining clothes were chilly and damp. Tears of self-pity began to well up in his eyes. They were absorbed in an instant by the blindfold. *Sod it, I can't even bloody-well cry!* He was racked with misery.

Returned to full awareness, he cursed his crass stupidity at having been gullible enough to fall into what he now recognised was a carefully-prepared trap. *Brian Carpenter, of all people, but why? The coffee, it must have been drugged—again why? Perhaps it's all a joke. He'll turn up any moment and let me go, pissing himself with laughter—or will he?*

Despite his pain he strove to establish a reason for his predicament. Brian Carpenter—fat, smelly Brian, one of Robert Strudwick's crazy minions. What was he playing at? But wait! What if Strudwick himself was behind this? And if so, what were his intentions? Revenge for an imagined insult or what? The penny dropped; his heart sank.

Strudwick. He struggled frantically. *Oh no, not Strudwick. Not that vindictive bastard, surely!*

Time passed. After battling with his bladder for what seemed an eternity, he was forced to succumb to nature. The resultant flow of urine added sore thighs and a stinging crotch to his catalogue of woes.

Desperately thirsty, he was tortured by images of countless glasses of ice-cold lager lined up on the bar. He blamed his present predicament on his weakness for the beverage, and vowed on his late mother's memory that, once free, he would never touch the stuff again . . .

He had no way of judging the passage of time. It may have been twenty-four hours after he first awoke, or even forty-eight, when he heard the rattle of a bolt and the rasp of a key. Light showed dimly through the blindfold. At last! His heart leapt. His spirits revived at the prospect of imminent rescue. A creak of hinges and a barely perceptible waft of air told him someone had entered his prison, but no other sound reached his ears, although he tilted his head and listened intently.

Suddenly, without warning, a vicious blow to the forehead sent his seat rocking backwards and he cracked his head painfully against a wall: *A wall! There's another wall behind me?*
At once claustrophobia returned; this and the combination of facial and cranial impact produced blinding flashes of lights, agonising pains and a terrible feeling of nausea. Mercilessly, the assailant struck again, this time full in the face—another crack of the head.

His nose was broken, the pain almost unbearable. Blood poured down his face and soaked the gag. He couldn't breathe. For long moments he was gripped by panic; only willpower and a strong sense of self-preservation kept him from inhaling and drowning in his own blood. He forced himself to exhale slowly through his shattered nose and, by dint of careful control, managed to take in sufficient life-giving air until, eventually, his breathing returned to something approaching normal. The roaring in his ears persisted.

He failed to hear the door open and close, nor the key turn in the lock. Eventually, a sense of isolation swept over him and he knew he was alone once more. As the pain lessened he began to recover a little and realised for the first time that his assailant hadn't uttered a word. *It's that bastard Strudwick—it has to be.* His heart sank. Far from being a rescuer, the visitor had been his gaoler and tormentor.

During the assault, his control of bodily functions all but lost, he had defecated from shock. His damaged olfactory senses were incapable of confirming the fact, but the physical discomfort was unmistakable. *Robert Strudwick, the evil sod. It's him, it's got to be him, no doubt about it!*

Frank knew of his captor's dislike, had known it for years. The antagonism, begun over some long-forgotten trifle when they were schoolboys, had persisted in a minor sort of way but hadn't really surfaced until he had managed to date that pretty girl (he could scarcely remember her name) in the Black and White Milk Bar, and she had told Strudwick exactly what she thought of him. Ironically, that one and only date had begun with a walk in the park and ended two hours later when, having seen her safely home as he had promised, she had refused him a kiss at her front gate.

Strudwick's motives became suddenly overwhelmingly important. *What harm did I ever do him?* he agonised. *Oh! dear God, I hurt. Christ. I can't stand much more of this. What does he mean to do? When will he let me go? I hate the lousy shitbag—hate! hate! hate!*

The borderline between sanity and madness is fragile and easily breached, it is said. By the time the pathetic, stinking creature had reached what he supposed to be his third day of incarceration he was praying desperately for insanity to release him from reality.

Consciousness ebbed and waned. His head drooped lower each time he started to slip away until, eventually, he slumped forward, limp and lifeless. The rickety chair overbalanced. Accelerated by the weight of his entire body, his forehead struck the floor with concussive force and he remained in a state of blessed oblivion for well over an hour.

But, bruised and sore, suffering excruciating pain from pinioned arms and legs, with the terrible roaring inside his skull beating time with an intense, throbbing headache, he finally ascended through successive levels of consciousness, summoned by strange, persistent keening sounds. When he eventually returned to full consciousness, however, he realised the anguished mewling was coming from his own throat.

The scrape of the key crashed into his awareness like a thunderclap. He lay motionless and when minutes passed with no further sound he shivered, uncontrollably. Then came the 'click' of a switch and light gleamed once more through the blindfold, seeming extraordinarily bright after so long in total darkness. A rustle of clothing was followed by two distinct thuds—not unlike shoes being dropped. Soft, shuffling steps approached him and he froze, holding his breath in agonised anticipation. There were sharp, slapping sounds—elastic? A catapult? Rubber gloves? Gloves? *For what?*

He felt no touch but, suddenly and roughly, was hauled upright and returned to a sitting position. It dawned on him that he had been lifted bodily by the back of the chair.

The covering over his eyes was snatched away. Blinding agony! The brilliance of a naked bulb shone directly into his face and his senses reeled. After hours in Stygian blackness, his eyes reacted violently. Tears flowed, sharply astringent against the rawness of his facial contusions. As his eyes grew accustomed to the light, he was able to make out a shadowy shape standing before him. Gradually, imperceptibly, the silent, motionless figure became clearer until, quite suddenly, Frank was able to see again.

A scalpel glinted centimetres in front of his face, held in an unwavering, rubber-gloved hand. Forcing himself to focus beyond the blade he saw, to his horror, that his captor was clad in a green surgical gown, cap and mask. Green, rubber surgeon's boots protruded from beneath the gown.

The hand flashed forward and back like a striking snake. He felt an impact and knew his left cheek had been laid open. Warm blood gushed down his face. Pain followed, fierce as flame.

The scalpel again thrust towards his face and he threw his head frantically from side to side, seeking to avoid the flashing blade.

'Keep still, you bastard,' his captor hissed and grasped a handful of hair to hold his victim still.

Francis saw the blade for a second time as the scalding pain of another bone-deep incision caused him to shriek in anguish.

The blood-soaked gag fell away, cut in two by the second strike of the blade.

The 'surgeon' stepped back to inspect his work and grunted with satisfaction.

'There, you arrogant shit,' he snarled. 'That's "V" for victory, pig-arse, and the victory is mine!'

Francis screamed—an awesome, heart-rending howl, made possible only by the removal of the gag. It sounded incredibly loud and he wondered, curiously, where the sound came from. Weakened by hunger, dehydration, blood-loss and physical suffering, the terrified youth relapsed into unconsciousness.

Kill the bastard, kill, kill, kill! But Strudwick had no such intention. To be properly avenged, Bridgwater must suffer further—*and* be aware that he was about to die. The prisoner stirred and groaned. The watcher tensed, ready to strike again, but there was no further movement. *Damn!* It was getting late. Strudwick decided to return a night or so later. Bridgwater would still be alive; he could be revived sufficiently to recognise what he had coming.

When eventually the unfortunate man did recover, it was to discover both gag and blindfold had been replaced, the dungeon was once again in darkness and his assailant long gone.

Mercifully perhaps, he was unaware that most of his organs were failing and that even if rescued immediately, he was already beyond the help of medical science. It would require a miracle now to save him from certain death.

Further long hours dragged by, during which he alternated between consciousness and oblivion. When the door was unlocked for a third time he scarcely noticed.

After a time, he became vaguely aware of the blindfold being removed and kept his eyes screwed tight against the light. Contemptuously the watcher waited. More time passed. Eventually the captive's eyelids fluttered and his eyes slowly opened. He squinted and watched as the outline behind the light slowly resolved into the menacing, green-garbed figure. Without doubt, it was Robert Strudwick. Once again the apparition stood silent and unmoving.

Strudwick peered balefully over his mask, impatient for at least a flicker of reaction. But Bridgwater seemed irritatingly oblivious, both to his situation and his surroundings. Vacant eyes showed no sign of awareness, no readable emotion, no fear, no hate, no despair. Pain had etched deep lines across a once-youthful brow and suppurating wounds rendered the countenance gaunt and macabre.

Strudwick's throat constricted, but not from pity. He would wait. *Too late, too late—you've left it too late!*

But he would not be cheated. He stepped forward and splashed water into Bridgwater's face.

Gradually, the features began to re-animate. Slowly, memory returned. Francis attempted to beg for mercy, but the gag—now thick with coagulated blood—effectively thwarted the attempt and he barely managed to groan. Indifferent to any sort of plea, Strudwick's only concern was the return of his subject to full awareness. It was time!

He stood directly beneath the lamp and produced a large, sheathed knife from inside his gown. Ensuring the terrified eyes of his victim were following every move, he held the protective cover in one hand and withdrew the blade with the other, taunting his captive by rotating the shining steel in front of his eyes.

Placing himself an arm's length from the wretch, he lowered his mask and watched as recognition dawned, leaning forward until his eyes were a few centimetres from those of his captive.

He shoved the knife hard against the hapless man's neck, just below his right ear, and hissed, 'At last, you stinking shitbag, at last. I told you I'd get even one day. Now it's *my* turn to take the fucking piss. So die, you filthy, scum-bagging bastard—die!'

He stabbed the cutting edge deep into soft flesh and drew it rapidly across and under the chin, stepping back when blood spurted from the severed arteries. For one brief instant, horror and understanding registered on that pallid, bloodied face; then the head fell forward when his neck could no longer support its own weight. Agony departed, unseeing eyes dimmed and glazed over. Blessed oblivion finally released nineteen-year-old Francis Bridgwater from his ordeal. Merciful death followed a short while afterwards.

Strudwick shrugged, disappointed. The climax had proved nowhere as exciting as he'd hoped. It was time, however, to remove any possible evidence. Having disposed of the wheelchair on day one, he now wiped the knife on the gown and returned it to its sheath, slipped out of the protective garments and tied the lot into a bundle by means of the apron straps, rubber boots and gloves innermost. He would return to Kingston hospital tomorrow and dump the lot in a laundry-trolley.

The gag and blindfold had been formed from doubled-over 75 millimetre bandage and the bonds from common bell wire—both problem-free, untraceable. He left the corpse in the niche, exactly as it was.

After a careful look around he used his handkerchief to wipe the light switches and door latches clean, retrieved his hand-torch from the steps and locked the outer door on the way out. It was late at night and nobody was about—nor would they be until the sexton unlocked the church at 8.00 a.m. the following morning...

Ten minutes later, Strudwick strolled into the Old Church and glanced around—it was empty. Treading warily, nevertheless, he stealthily replaced the key in the vestry...

Chapter Ten
The Old Church

Impatient for news of his most recent mission to feature on television and be reported in the newspapers, Robert Strudwick nevertheless continued to apply himself both diligently and successfully to the business of property marketing. Throughout December and for the whole of January 2005 he worked and waited, whilst the remains of Francis Bridgwater lay mouldering in the vault beneath Esher Old Church.

Busy or no, Robert kept the lives of those in whom he was especially interested under constant review, and reserved sufficient time each day to maintain contact with each and every one of his informants. Access to police intelligence had already proven its worth and in case he might have further need of inside information, Strudwick took care to hone and nurture his covert contact at Surbiton.

Bridgwater's fate and that of the girl had been sealed from the moment they had ignored his warning and left the Milk Bar together. Now he wanted the satisfaction of observing the puerile scampering of the police, as they set about trying to identify an unknown, clever assailant, one able to emerge at will, strike with impunity and vanish without trace. Certain that inspired planning and meticulous attention to detail had left no possible clue as to his identity, he craved publicity for the latest insoluble mystery to his credit—press and public alike would be suitably impressed by yet another remarkable achievement and they would ridicule another pathetic failure on the part of the police.

Francis Bridgwater *did* receive mention, however, when, in early December, an article reporting the young man's disappearance appeared in *Esher News*. 'Francis mysteriously vanished whilst en route to France', the paper said, 'to resume work after a short holiday in the UK.'

Police appealed for anyone who had seen Francis between November 16th and December 1st to come forward but, in the absence of evidence to the contrary, a spokesman ruled out any suggestion of foul play—much to Robert Strudwick's amusement. As with the Pennington girl, the master tactician's strategy for disposing of Francis Bridgwater had been designed to defer involvement of the police long enough for memories to fade and reduce the effectiveness of the inevitable witness appeals.

By early February, however, the assassin's patience was wearing thin and he considered making an anonymous call to the police from an outlying phone box, suggesting they search St. George's Church where there was reason to believe the body of a murdered man was concealed.

Considering the idea at dinner one evening, his thoughts were abruptly interrupted. *Come to your room this instant, I wish to speak with you*, a fearsome voice commanded. Strudwick blanched, and almost choked on a mouthful of fish. His knife and fork clattered noisily onto his plate. It was unprecedented. Pentophiles *never* approached unless he was alone—nor, as yet, had he done so in such an intrusive manner. His father looked up, bemused, and his mother twittered anxiously.

'Are you all right, Robert darling? You look as if you've seen a ghost.' Something was seriously amiss to merit such a peremptory summons. Robert rose shakily.

'Sorry, I don't feel very well,' he said. 'Excuse me, I'm going to my room . . .'

Since becoming custodian of the Book, he frequently sensed the presence of Pentophiles—usually as a prelude to communication—but following the fantastically exciting adventure which had culminated in the annihilation of the Pennington bitch in Oxshott Woods, the demonic emissary revealed himself once only, when, gloating over the mission's success, he had delivered personal congratulations for the girl's highly-satisfactory demise. Her soul-wrenching anguish had provided precisely the catalyst Pentophiles needed to exchange personalities temporarily with Robert, enabling him to savour human flesh and blood for the first time in several hundreds of years.

'Henry Plowrite' materialised the moment Robert entered his bedroom and closed the door. The patently hostile demeanour of the nether-being did nothing to counter Robert's apprehension.

Indeed, there was far more of the demon in those pseudo-human features than before. 'Henry Plowrite' fixed red-flecked, gleaming black eyes firmly on those of his young protégé.

'I come deliver thee warning,' he intoned, formally and without preamble. 'Mark well thy contract, Robert William Strudwick, for no other reminder shalt thou have, ere thy soul be instantly forfeit.' The apparition vanished, leaving the barest suggestion of putrescence in its wake.

As if to underline his displeasure, Pentophiles had made no attempt to transpose his formalised, archaic prose into modern English and it took a while for his words to fully register, but when they did, Robert feared he had inadvertently violated the contract in some way; but logic prevailed. Should such a calamitous eventuality already have taken place, it was unlikely his mentor would content himself with a mere verbal warning. Clearly, Robert was in mortal danger but he was intelligent enough to recognise an opportunity to identify and address the problem.

The contract—in what way did he risk violation? Six years after the conditions had been expounded by Pentophiles, he was able to recall every word and nuance as though it were only yesterday:

Firstly: You must *never* allow the book to pass from your possession unless and until a Transfer Contract be properly executed.

Secondly: No person other than yourself may view *any* part of the contents whilst the book is under your custodianship.

Thirdly: The book will reveal each new situation *only* when appropriate and shall always provide precise details for its resolution. You must *swear* to follow these instructions to the letter and *never* attempt to obtain information beyond that which is current.

Finally: Your mortal soul shall remain your own property for as long as these clauses remain inviolate.

Only should a clause be broken shall your life be forfeit and you solemnly declare that in that event the aforementioned soul shall belong to Mephistopheles.

Robert considered: Clause I—The book was secure in its accustomed place (he checked, to make sure) which automatically took care of Clause II. The final clause spelled the consequences of a breach of any of those preceding. Therefore he must be in imminent risk of violating the third. Robert took heart. Clearly, he was destined for matters of greater importance, or his mentor would not have bothered to intervene. Mephistopheles would *never* reprieve a soul already forfeit.

A moment's thought and it became obvious. *Never attempt to obtain information beyond that which is current.* Of course, that was it! It was so simple he almost blushed: Pentophiles *knew* he was planning to telephone the police. Had he done so, information connected with the mission would have become public before the preordained time and Robert would thereby gain foreknowledge— a clear violation of Clause III.

It was a narrow escape; he breathed a sigh of relief. But for Pentophiles's intervention, his impatience might well have cost him his life, and his soul would have become the property of Mephistopheles, thereafter to suffer the agonies of eternal damnation. He abandoned the idea of ringing the police and resolved to allow matters to follow their natural course. In fact, fate was already conspiring to set in motion a chain of events that were destined to lead to the discovery of the body—and with it the publicity he so desperately craved.

As custom decreed, St. George's chapel was the venue for the Royal British Legion annual Church Parade—but for some reason the fact wasn't announced until a few days before the event. Fully committed at the Parish Church and elsewhere, and by agreement with the vicar, the lady cleaners opted to defer their visit to St. George's until Saturday, when they would have ample time to clean thoroughly in addition to taking care of the floral arrangements.

Early on the day in question, Saturday 12 February, the ladies were enjoying a quiet cup of tea before starting work, when James Billows came into the vestry and unceremoniously thrust a piece of paper under the senior cleaning lady's nose.

''Ere,' the sexton grumbled irritably, 'just take a look at this blinkin' note from the vicar. Shoved it through me flamin' letter-box last night 'e did. Just 'cos it's the British Legion service tomorrow, 'e wants me to clean bat-muck off the organ-loft balcony this morning.'

Matronly, prim and proper, Edna considered it her duty to put Master Billows in his place.

'Don't come moaning to me,' she said, sharply. 'If Vicar wants it done, why don't you just get on and do it instead of whinging. Really Mr Billows, if you carry on like this at home it's no wonder your poor wife always looks harassed. How on earth she manages to put up with you . . .?'

Billows' mouth opened—and closed again. Edna sniffed, waved a dismissive duster and winked covertly at Gladys, her cleaning colleague, who hurriedly turned away to hide her amusement.

The sexton flushed and shuffled his feet uncomfortably.

'Well, what are you waiting for?' Edna demanded of the discomfited man. 'Come on, we ladies have a lot to do this morning.'

Untypically, Billows, stood his ground.

'I wasn't whinging really,' he protested, mildly. 'It's just that the curate borrowed the steps on Friday and 'asn't brought 'em back—and there's no way I can reach up there without 'em.'

'Fiddlesticks!' she retorted, sarcastically. 'If that's all that's troubling you, it's a pity you didn't say so in the first place instead of moaning and groaning. I might've been able to help. As it happens, there used to be a pair of steps and a couple of trestles down in the crypt—still there, I shouldn't wonder. They might be a bit rickety by this time but still usable, with care. I suggest you go and take a look, Mr Billows—there's the key, over there look, on the wall!'

Perfectly aware Billows was hen-pecked unmercifully by his wife, Edna felt a twinge of remorse as, with arms akimbo, she watched the inoffensive little man hasten to collect the vault key from the nail on the wall, then scuttle out of the vestry without so much as a word of protest.

'Oh, you are awful, Edna,' Gladys giggled. 'Poor James. He didn't expect a flea in his ear, I'll be bound. You fair frightened the life out of him—he must've thought he was still at home.'

James stumped down the crypt steps, turned the key in the lock and creaked open the heavy, oak door.

'Cor, blimey Moses!' he gasped, close to gagging. 'What a bloody awful pong!'

Holding his nose, the sexton pushed wide the door and depressed the light switch. A single bulb suspended from the lobby ceiling came on, revealing a small inner chamber. He saw nothing at first, but when a second switch produced much brighter light within, he edged forward nervously a couple of paces—then stopped dead in his tracks.

'Good God Almighty! It's a bloody stiff. Jesus, I'm out of here!' Despite his shock, Billows closed and re-locked the vault door, before rushing back to the vestry as fast as his shaking legs would allow. He reappeared, wide-eyed and panting.

'Don't go down there. There's a dead body in a chair!' he yelled, gesturing dramatically. He threw the vault key onto the table. 'I've locked the door. There's the key. I'm going to fetch the police!' he shouted over his shoulder, already halfway out of the door.

'Good gracious!' Gladys exclaimed 'Poor Jim's gone off his rocker—it's either that or he's pulling our legs, trying to get his own back. Personally, I don't believe a word of it.'

Edna Burstow crossed to the open door and looked out. There was no sign of the sexton, nor was his bicycle propped against the vestry wall in its accustomed place—so it wasn't a joke.

'I'm not so sure,' she cautioned. 'It's not James' style. His bike's gone—and look at the way he shot out of the door as if his britches were on fire. If he says there's a body, then there *is* a body. I've known Jim for years. He's no liar—and I've never seen him run anywhere, before today.'

Gladys sniffed, picked up her cup and swallowed the last of her tea.

'Dead bodies in church cellars—pooh, whatever next? I think I'll get on with the dusting—but do be sure to call me if dear Mr Billows comes rushing back with a policeman,' she sneered.

Meanwhile, having pedalled furiously up the High Street to the police station, the terrified sexton threw the machine against the front wall, and, fighting to recover his breath, buttonholed the duty policeman.

'It's in the—the Old Church' he eventually wheezed. 'In the vault—a dead body in a chair . . .'

'Whoa, steady on sir,' the young constable interjected. Just hang on till you get your breath back, then start at the beginning.

'A body—in the vault, you say? All right, Mr Billows, you'd

THE FLYLEAF KILLER

better give me the details. Take your time. The body you saw won't go anywhere. We'll sort your statement out when we've established the facts.'

One look in the vault was sufficient. Police Sergeant Stapleton retreated, ashen-faced, and DCs Gibson and Slade took charge of the key, and re-locked the door. Back in their car, Gibson radioed HQ to confirm the discovery while Slade unloaded a reel of blue and white tape and set about cordoning off the church entrances.

Although unnerved by the horrific scene, Sgt Stapleton deferred going off duty and returned to Esher police station where he telephoned headquarters for instructions.

With promotion in mind, and knowing the importance of keeping the discovery under wraps until the officer-in-charge decided otherwise, Stapleton skilfully parried the Duty Sergeant's questions and waited instead to be connected with DS O'Connor. Pre-warned, case-file opened, presence of a corpse confirmed, O'Connor was expecting his call.

'Two beat-bobbies are already on their way from here, George,' he said briskly, 'but the DI reckons we'll need four to secure the site properly. Do you think you can get two of your chaps round there reasonably quickly?'

'No problem, Ben, I'll organise that before I go off duty. Would fifteen to twenty minutes be soon enough?'

'Sounds fine to me—but listen. The DI and I are coming over—he's in a meeting right now, but we're leaving the moment he comes out. It might be as well if you went back to the church. Hang on until we arrive. Mr Melton wants to view the scene before calling the pathologist, so make sure nobody gets into that cellar until he says so—and that includes Gibson and Slade. Keep the media outside the gates, no matter what, and have the sexton and the cleaners on hand ready for the DI to talk to—you know the form. Can I leave it with you, George?'

Duty, duty, duty. 'OK Ben, see you later.'

At St. George's, meanwhile, taping-off complete, Gibson and Slade were ferrying equipment from the car to the head of the crypt steps in readiness to begin work inside. Whilst they toiled passers-by stopped to stare, for the most part ignored by the detectives, who preferred to leave moving-on of spectators to the 'uniforms' who were due almost at any time.

At this juncture, whilst Slade was returning from the car, Billows rounded the corner from the direction of the vestry, pushing his bike. DC Slade looked up.

'Oi!' he exclaimed. 'Just where d'you think you're going?'

'Just goin' for a packet of fags, that's where. And just what's wrong with that, may I ask?'

'Nothing, I suppose,' the officer conceded, 'so long as you're coming straight back. One of our senior officers will be along shortly and as you were the one to discover the body, you'll probably be the first person he'll want to speak to. You're a very important witness, Mr Billows.'

Such flattering words were music to Billows' ears.

'Don't worry your 'ead on that score, young feller. I'll be back in a jiffy, no sweat,' the sexton declared and, without further ado, he placed one foot on a pedal and scooted towards the gate—just as DC Gibson was coming up the path. Craftily, Billows pre-empted a second challenge.

'Just goin' for some fags,' he shouted, as he whizzed past. 'Yer mate back there says it's OK.'

Short of throwing himself in front of the bike, there was no way Gibson could have stopped the sexton and he quickened his step, determined to put his partner in his place, once and for all.

'That sexton chap,' Gibson began, 'Why did you let him loose? Lost your marbles or what?'

'You know perfectly well we've no authority to detain him,' Slade protested. 'So why are you making so much fuss? The silly old bath-brick will probably be back in five minutes, anyway.'

'It's not whether he comes back or not that bothers me,' Gibson retorted. 'It's whether he keeps his flaming mouth shut once he's out of sight. You know as well as I do the DI dislikes premature publicity and if he arrives to find a mob of reporters lying in wait . . .' He drew a finger across his throat.

Harry shrugged, offhandedly. 'If the old chap talks, he talks. There's sod-all we can do about it. Like I said, there's nothing to prevent him from coming and going as he pleases—and if I *had* told him to keep his mouth shut, most likely he'd be on the phone to the *Mirror* right now.' Feeling he'd said all that there was to be said, Slade turned away and began unpacking camera gear.

'I *still* think you should have checked with me first. After all I am in charge,' Gibson muttered.

Meanwhile, as a consequence of a telephone tip-off, a modest saloon drew up behind Gibson and Slade's car and two men emerged, one carrying an elderly Speed Graphic.

Fortunately, James Billows returned. As he dismounted, an astute reporter stepped forward with a smile—and a twenty-pound note between the fingers of his extended right hand.

'Excuse me sir,' he began, politely, 'I wonder whether you'd mind telling me what's going on? I'm Robin Prendergast, by the way, crime reporter for the *Surrey Chronicle*. I also freelance for the *Esher News* and it's at their request we're here. Somebody local rang in, apparently.'

'Yes, course I will,' James Billows replied, astutely persuading the twenty-pound note into his top pocket. Oh, yes, Billows was *more* than willing to introduce himself. 'I'm James Billows, parish church sexton, 'ere at St George's too. Wished I wasn't, sometimes, especially today, what with finding a dead body down in the vault and rotten coppers everywhere . . .'

Once started, with scarcely a pause for breath, the sexton blurted out the whole story. Scribbling furiously, Prendergast took down the sexton's gabbled information. The flash gun attached to the Speed Graphic popped, and James Billows' claim to fame seemed assured.

DC Gibson came hurrying down the path, too late to prevent his fears from being realised. A wave of his hand was sufficient. The pressmen retreated.

'Come on, Mr Billows,' he said, trying to keep his cool, 'I rather expected this to happen. You shouldn't have spoken to the press just yet; the investigation has hardly begun. My Guv'nor won't be best pleased, I can tell you. Might be better if you go back to the vestry and wait there.' Billows sniffed, pointedly, but heeded the instruction and headed for the church.

Sgt Stapleton and two uniformed bobbies arrived and the officers set about dispersing a crowd of curious spectators.

Robin Prendergast spoke urgently and at length into his mobile telephone. Within minutes, the story was on the wire and an armada of media representatives set out for Esher.

Detective Inspector Melton and his assistant arrived at 11.45, expecting to find the entrance cordoned and uniformed men restraining and dispersing onlookers, but the rush of waiting reporters as Melton's car drew to a halt rather took them by surprise. Ignoring a babble of shouted questions, they pushed through the throng and on through the lychgate.

Approaching the church, the two were intercepted by DC Gibson as senior man, whilst Slade craftily distanced himself by taking a position slightly to the rear and at one side of his colleague.

'Good morning, sir—Sergeant,' Gibson began. 'Nasty business. If you'd care to come this way, the sexton who found the body is waiting in the vestry—and the cleaners are working inside somewhere, should you wish to see them.' Turning to his colleague he went on, briskly, 'You'd better get back to the vault, Harry. Don't let anyone down those steps.'

An icy glance from Melton stopped both men dead in their tracks.

'How come the press is here in force? Which of you two charmers do we have to thank, I wonder?'

'Neither sir, it was James Billows—the sexton—actually,' Gibson explained. 'He insisted on going out for some cigarettes and, legally sir, there was nothing we could do to prevent him.'

'I see, but I presume you tried?'

'Yes sir.

'That *still* doesn't explain the army of reporters.'

'No sir. At first, there was only Robin Prendergast and his cameraman—until Billows spilled the beans the moment he got back from the shops. That mob turned up about half an hour ago.'

'OK,' said Melton, 'enough said.' He changed the subject. 'First of all, I'd like to see the body and then we'll talk to the sexton—I take it you've already questioned him?'

'Yes sir,' Gibson nodded.

'Have you also spoken to the cleaners?'

Again, Gibson nodded.

'Good. I'd like to hear their side of the story. You can tell us about it on the way to the vault.'

Gibson produced his notebook and began to turn the pages. The DI turned to Slade. 'I take it the vault is secured?'

The constable nodded.

'Then perhaps you should go and keep Billows company,' Melton suggested, with a twinkle. 'He might be short of matches and we don't want him nipping out again, now do we?'

'No sir,' Slade said—and quickly hurried away.

'Lead on, Gibson,' Melton said. 'Ben and I can hear the gory details on the way.'

Referring to his notebook, Gibson recounted Billows' version of events that morning. Still speaking as they arrived at a flight of steps, Gibson stopped, and concluded, 'When Billows went to report his discovery, it seems the ladies were too frightened to look for themselves, so the vault remained locked until Sergeant Stapleton arrived. Nothing's been disturbed, sir. Everything is exactly as Mr Billows found it.' He looked up, anxiously.

'That's quite a story, Gibson,' Melton said. 'Would you care to lead the way? Let's take a look in that vault.'

Gibson produced a key from within his briefcase and preceded Melton and O'Connor down the steps.

As he opened the door a stench, foul beyond description, belched from within. A couple of bluebottles buzzed angrily past. Melton grimly squared his shoulders.

'Detective Sergeant O'Connor and I will go inside,' he told Gibson. 'You'd better wait here by the door—we won't be more than a couple of minutes.'

O'Connor switched on the lights. Approximately three metres by two, the vault included a half-metre recess at roughly the centre of the rear wall, wherein a macabre, hunched figure sat lashed to a rickety, old-fashioned cane chair. The stench brought the officers to the brink of throwing up. Breathing as little of the disgusting atmosphere as possible, Melton and O'Connor moved nearer the seated cadaver and viewed the gruesome remains with pity and revulsion.

The head lolled grotesquely, but remained attached to the body. There was a gaping wound across the neck, extending from beneath one ear almost to the other and vicious, bone-deep gashes plummeted from sideburn to chin on both cheeks. The body was in poor condition and would require careful handling if it were to remain intact. There were no signs of maggot infestation, however, much to Melton's relief.

'Damn good job we haven't had lunch yet,' the DI murmured wryly.

'Yes sir. Poor sod must've been dead for weeks!'

Neither ventured closer. Whilst forensic examination would take care of the vault and contents, detailed examination of the remains remained the prerogative of the pathologist. Far better to await his findings than attempt to draw conclusions of their own. Melton had seen enough and so, he suspected, had O'Connor. The prospect of fresh air seemed extraordinarily attractive.

'Come on Sergeant, let's get out of here before we both honk up!'

'Right with you, sir,' O'Connor said, and shot out of the door and up the steps two at a time.

'I haven't seen you move that fast lately, Sergeant,' Melton remarked when they were both outside. 'Have the vault guarded until the pathologist gets here. Oh, by the way, I don't think we need trouble Billows further at this stage. He obviously touched nothing down there and I don't see what else he could add to what he's already told Gibson. Tell him to finish what he's doing and go home—the cleaners too, but ask them to say as little as possible to reporters for the time being. The less media speculation the better, and I dare say Billows has said more than enough already.'

'Yes sir—er, do you want me to call the pathologist?'

'No thanks, I'll get hold of Doctor Matthews myself. I'm hoping he'll deal with this personally. But there's no way we can allow a service here tomorrow and I'd be obliged if you'd contact the church authorities. No promises. Tell them we'll give them back their church as soon as we can.'

Avidly scanning the newspapers spread across his desk, Strudwick grinned sardonically. *BODY IN THE VAULT* one headline screamed. *HUNT INTENSIFIES FOR SLASHER; SURREY RIPPER SOUGHT; KNIFE-FIEND STRIKES IN SURREY CHURCH* yelled others.

The story in every paper began with a graphic description of the scene in the vault as given to Robin Prendergast by James Billows and went on to quote the sexton: 'The corpse was tied to a bloody chair, stinking rotten. Been there ages, I reckon. The poor bugger had both cheeks slashed and his bloody throat was slit from ear to ear.'

As Strudwick recalled in delicious detail the cycle of events which had led to those injuries, his grin broadened—and when he remembered the pleasure derived from inflicting them, he laughed until his sides hurt. Yet still he considered the mission nowhere as exciting as the Pennington adventure.

Pentophiles' lapdog closed his eyes and tried to visualise what form his next task might take. When nothing came to mind, he

153

returned briskly to reality and resumed drafting particulars for a property newly entrusted to Gaston Hathaway.

Melton put down the post-mortem report, tilted his chair until his head rested against the wall, wedged one knee under the desk and focused his eyes somewhere above his assistant's head—a posture adopted as an aid to concentration. Challenging his memory, he began to recite.

> The deceased was male, aged between eighteen and twenty. Height, five foot eleven. Estimated weight, eleven stone ten pounds. Fresh complexion, brown hair, hazel eyes. There were no distinguishing marks on the body.
> Advanced decomposition was consistent with the man having been dead for ten or eleven weeks. Ambient temperature and relative humidity inside the vault were recorded on twelfth February, from which adjustments were made to arrive at an average for the preceding twelve weeks. During this period, the weather was predominantly cold and dry, which undoubtedly delayed bacterial action quite significantly.
> Life became extinct around November thirtieth—with an error probability of plus or minus four days—within ninety seconds of the throat having been cut and was due to massive bleeding from the carotid artery and jugular vein.
> The stomach, intestines and bladder were empty at the time of death and extremely low blood-sugar levels, coupled with severe liver damage, suggests no food or water were taken for at least ten days prior to that event.
> Kidney function had already ceased, however, and the heart was failing rapidly through dehydration, blood-loss, malnutrition and general debilitation.
> Cardiac arrest and/or renal failure were inevitable, probably within forty-eight hours. Assuming food and water intake ceased simultaneously, the man was placed in the vault about the fourteenth to sixteenth November, some two weeks before he died. Prior to that date, the deceased was free of disease but wasn't particularly fit which—coupled with an absence of hand calluses—is indicative of a sedentary occupation. The wrists and ankles were tied tightly with white,

plastic-covered bell-wire of the type readily obtainable in most DIY stores. The gag was simply a bandage.

Clothing is normally removed on arrival at the morgue, but it was left to the discretion of the pathologist in this instance because of the cadaver's condition.

The body was fully-dressed when discovered and the clothes, although badly soiled and mildewed, were of good quality. The man wore a cotton singlet and matching X-front underpants, a cream Van Heusen open-neck shirt, a grey pullover, grey flannel trousers and a fawn jacket, two-tone grey sports socks and brown leather walking shoes. No identification or laundry-marks were noted, but all items of clothing were sealed in specimen bags and transferred to the forensic laboratory, together with the bell-wire.

Melton removed his knee and allowed gravity to return his chair to an upright position.

The post-mortem report brought vividly to mind the decomposing remains viewed at the morgue, his second sighting of the rotting corpse, more revolting than the first when, despite the horrible gagging smell, the body had at least been decently covered and more or less intact. Little in Melton's experience had ever affected him more deeply. He nudged the file towards O'Connor.

'Take a look,' he invited, adding, 'what a terrible way to die! The poor sod must have been in agony for days before the sadistic bastard finally cut his throat.'

Melton shook his head dispiritedly. The killer was cold, merciless, and inherently evil—or was he? Melton simply didn't know. He tried to imagine how the man might look like. Was he tall, short, fat—or what? Would he in any way stand out from the crowd? Probably not. Life would certainly be easier were he to wear horns and stroll around hatless—perish the facetious thought. Professor Matthews' theories were all very well, but how do you search for an invisible man? Was this another detective's nightmare? Another Pennington case? He hoped not.

Watching his assistant leaf through the file, Melton decided to pose the question to O'Connor.

'What do you make of it, Ben? What sort of fiend would do that to a fellow human?' The DS hesitated. Unsure what Melton was really getting, he replied, somewhat evasively.

'Dunno sir. A raving lunatic, maybe!'

He turned a few more pages and wrinkled his nose. He too had visited the morgue and, like Melton, gained Professor Matthews' 'off the record' opinion in advance of the post-mortem. Apart from technicalities, probable dates and details concerned with internal organs, blood type and so on, the paperwork appeared to confirm much they already knew or suspected.

Knowing he was closely observed, O'Connor continued to shy away from a considered reply.

'It's poor Doc Matthews *I* feel sorry for,' he grimaced. 'I wouldn't have his job for a gold watch. Fancy having to poke around in a smelly, rotten stiff—what a way to make a living!'

Melton treated his assistant to a withering look. Crime detection owed a great deal to pathology—vital work required by law which had to be carried out by someone.

'That's as maybe, Ben. But someone has to do it and the professor is one of the best in his field. If it's a question of pathology and he states that something is so, then you can bet your last shilling that ninety-nine times out of a hundred he'll be correct. Now then, what do you *really* think?'

O'Connor slid meaty fingers through his sandy thatch, whilst Melton waited, expectantly. Encouraging juniors to think was an essential part of training, as vital to the 'Job' as obeying orders and feeling a few collars. Thinking was essential for every copper with ambition. Melton knew that a little patient prodding would often persuade Ben to open up.

'I've been wondering,' O'Connor at last ventured, 'do you think the killer could be the same man who butchered the Pennington girl? Doctor Matthews made no such inference, but his description of the way the poor chap's throat was cut matches to a tee, right down to the type of knife.'

He shuddered, involuntarily.

The Pennington murder was no nearer resolution more than two years after the event, a fact which constantly irked two career detectives whose detection record rated among the best in the Force. The coroner had brought in a verdict of 'Murder' and found that Malandra Pennington was unlawfully killed on 14 July 2002 by person or persons unknown, and formally declared the inquest closed.

'Yes, that has also occurred to me,' Melton replied, 'but, more importantly, the man must live somewhere in the area. He knows Esher extremely well. How else could he have pinpointed the Pearce's back garden or even know of the vault's existence, much less how to gain access?

'There's little doubt that on both occasions he operated after dark, but the church is locked at night. He must therefore have taken the key from the vestry in advance, contriving to return it without its absence being noticed. He must also have known the vault was virtually soundproof, so his captive was unlikely to be heard, even if he managed to be rid of the gag and shouted for help.

'It's a worst-case scenario, Ben. A vicious, cold-blooded murder, carefully planned and ruthlessly carried out by a local man, who is currently walking free, undetected. I'm totally convinced that neither this killing—nor, indeed that of Malandra Pennington—would have been feasible without extensive local knowledge. That said, I can see few other similarities between the two killings, can you?'

O'Connor shook his head. 'No sir. Apart from the knifing strokes—and that the killer must have local knowledge they appear entirely dissimilar.

'The first victim was female, the second male; the girl was dismembered and transported from the murder site whereas the second remained in situ; the girl's remains were subjected to bestiality and the male's were not.'

He subsided. Melton was impressed by what seemed a well-reasoned evaluation.

'Spot on, Ben, but there might be a similarity we've overlooked—tenuous perhaps, but in both cases there was a significant delay between the murder and the discovery of the remains. The periods were different, but that could be down to luck and choice of location.'

'W-ell Guv'nor, I suppose that *could* be a similarity of sorts,' O'Connor conceded. 'But how that might help track down the killer I'm blessed if I know. If anything, it makes our task more difficult.' He scratched his head. 'People tend to forget; witness appeals become less effective. It's a cliché but nevertheless true. Whatever trail was left by the *Body in the Vault* killer has already gone cold, and in the case of the Pennington girl it must be frozen—rock, bloody solid. Chummy must be laughing his socks off.'

O'Connor shoved the file back across the desk.

Melton merely grunted and leafed through it again. The salient points were already committed to memory but had he overlooked some small snippet that might help identify the deceased, or point to a possible motive for the killing, perhaps?

O'Connor had a fair idea of what was going through the Guv'nor's mind. But would he consider another go at Tobias Charlesworth? And what about that nasty piece of work, Robert Strudwick?

Hold it, Ben, he told himself, firmly. Having spoken his mind regarding both men before, he didn't relish being put in his place again. The Guv'nor was wary of Charlesworth and shied away from the subject whenever Strudwick's name cropped up, almost as if he were somehow frightened of the man. Ben sighed and sat quietly, deeming it prudent not to interrupt the DI's train of thought.

After deliberating a while, Melton became brisk and businesslike.

'Right Sergeant,' he said, crisply, 'let's get cracking. Our first priority is to identify the body. Get your backside over to Forensics. I want to know whether the clothes have been under the microscope yet—and if not, why not? Any form of identification or laundry mark would be helpful, no matter how indistinct.' He tapped the file. 'Doctor Matthews' observations regarding the post-mortem, whilst helpful, go nowhere near far enough. Next, I want on my desk pronto a list of every male disappearance both locally and throughout Greater London from the first November until . . . say, fifteenth December.'

He waited for O'Connor to finish writing, then went on.

'Then get hold of Brendan Curtis—the artist fellow we've used before for missing person inquiries, and see about getting a sketch made of the dead man's likely appearance. It'll be neither easy nor pleasant, but speed is essential.' He thought for a moment. 'I imagine Professor Matthews will help regarding skin, features, hairstyle and so on—I'll have a word beforehand to make sure. Oh, and you'd better warn Curtis the face looks ghastly. Buy him a stiff brandy before he goes into the morgue if you like. Despite those terrible slashes, I'd say the features are more or less intact and we should end up with a reasonable likeness.'

Again he waited for O'Connor to catch up.

'When I meet the press later on,' Melton continued, 'I'll mention that we're thinking of using an artist's impression to help establish identity.' He looked up. 'Have you got that, Sergeant?'

THE OLD CHURCH

'Noted sir, will do. But isn't publishing a *guesswork* murder-victim likeness a bit unorthodox?'

'So it might be, but I don't recall seeing a missing persons report likely to fit the bill, do you? Let's face it, with nothing whatever to go on, it's the obvious thing to do when you think about it. Of course,' he went on, 'it's always possible we mightn't need that sketch, but I want one up my sleeve in readiness, just the same.'

'Fair enough, Guv'nor,' he said. 'I'm on my way.'

Routine formed a substantial part of Melton's workload, for which his basic establishment was adequate, and in the event of a major inquiry, he could readily muster additional resources. DS O'Connor's departure marked the moment Melton effectively 'pushed the button' on the Old Church murder inquiry, when an expanded team slipped smoothly and efficiently into top gear.

A computer-generated schedule detailing thirty-two male persons reported missing throughout London and the Home Counties during November and December arrived on his desk in an hour. Running a practised eye down the list, Melton struck through all but four with a black marker pen.

One stuck out like a sore thumb. Melton cursed under his breath. *Stapleton, the pompous prat.* A corpse on his doorstep, and he didn't have the nous to check his own 'missing persons'? There it was, like a carbuncle on a parson's nose. December 3rd, 2004: Mr Kenneth Bridgwater of West End reported his son Francis, aged nineteen missing—at ESHER police station, no less!

Incandescent, Melton opened his door, button-holed the nearest officer and roared, 'Get on the blower to Esher. I want full details regarding Francis Bridgwater, reported missing on third December by his father, Kenneth Bridgwater—and I want them NOW! And should you be unfortunate enough to have Sergeant Stapleton come on the line, you'd better warn him to keep out of my way or I might just be tempted to recommend him for demotion and retraining.'

Still fuming, he strode across to the nearest copper and tossed him the list.

'Deal with it,' was all that he said, and stumped back to his office.

Academic perhaps, but within twenty-four hours, three out of the remaining four culled from the missing persons' register by DI

Melton had been accounted for. Two days after one man had gone missing, a body recovered from Brent reservoir was positively identified. Another turned out to be of Asian origin and a third had returned to the bosom of his family after a week—but nobody had thought to inform the police.

Late on the morning of February 16th, forty-eight hours after O'Connor had approached Brendan Curtis, a charcoal sketch suggesting the murdered man's likely appearance arrived.

Events were shortly to render the drawing unnecessary, but it was, nevertheless, to prove a remarkably accurate likeness . . .

Chapter Eleven

Francis, R.I.P.

The day Kenneth Bridgwater reported his son missing marked a turning point in his life. As day succeeded day and days became weeks, he became increasingly morose and withdrawn. Long accustomed to unsociable hours and physically demanding work, his general level of fitness remained unchanged, but long weeks of worry for his son were taking their toll. Work that once brought pleasure turned to drudgery. He lost weight, and his weather-beaten face seemed permanently creased with anxiety. Fearing the worst, yet hoping against hope, Kenneth suffered an agonising wait for news. So far he had waited in vain and when February arrived with still no word, poor Kenneth scarcely noticed.

It was getting on for 10.30 by the time he arrived home. He was irritable and in need of sleep. Within minutes, the telephone shrilled.

'Hello,' he grumbled. 'Who is it and what do you want?'

'Good morning. Mr Bridgwater?' a baritone voice inquired.

'Yes, who want's to know?'

'Detective Inspector Melton, Surbiton police. I wonder if I might call. It's regarding your son, Francis. I understand you reported him missing in early December.' Kenneth's heart lurched. *Francis!* He gulped.

'Yes, of course but what's happened? Is Frank in hospital? Was he in an accident or something?'

'Nothing like that, I'm afraid,' Melton responded gently. 'Perhaps I should explain when I see you. I could be there in about twenty minutes, if that is convenient?'

'Y-es, I suppose so,' Ken agreed, reluctant on the one hand, yet anxious for news on the other. 'I'm just in from work, and I need a couple of hours sleep. But I *must* know what it is you've discovered. Come on over. I'll put the kettle on—I could do with a cuppa myself.'

THE FLYLEAF KILLER

Ken managed to make a pot of tea, but then forgot about it. He made some toast, burnt it, threw it away. He started to pace up and down, waiting for the knock on the door. *There he is!* He tripped on a rug and fumbled with the door handle. When he opened it he didn't know what to say.

'Mr Bridgwater? Detective Inspector Melton.' He showed his warrant card. 'I rang a short time ago. May I come in?'

Leading the way to the kitchen, Ken ushered the policeman inside.

'Excuse the mess, but I'm a milkman, as you probably know. Not much sleep—up early and not long home. I'm absolutely bushed. What's happened to my son?'

'How about that tea, Mr Bridgwater—and can we sit down?'

Kenneth poured; they sat.

Melton collected his thoughts.

'I hardly know how to explain, so it might be better if I came directly to the point.'

Ken nodded, not trusting himself to speak, and the policeman began.

'Last Saturday, a body was discovered in a locked vault beneath Esher Old Church.'

Observing the milkman intently, Melton continued.

'As yet, we have no means of identification, but the probable age of the deceased matches that of your son and the approximate time of death—around the end of November—appears to tally with the date your son went missing.'

Kenneth paled and clutched at his throat.

'You probably suspected something to be seriously amiss,' Melton continued, after a pause.

Ken gave Melton an anguished look. 'Yes, I suppose I did. I've been worried sick ever since Frank failed to ring. You see, Inspector, he promised, and my boy never broke a promise to me—not once in the whole of his life.'

Kenneth's face crumpled; he was dangerously close to tears. The policeman nodded. Hard though it was, he had to get over a very important point.

'I understand and sympathise. The evidence is flimsy and circumstantial and we cannot simply assume the body to be that of your son. Mr Bridgwater!' Melton exclaimed sharply, noticing tears

162

welling in the man's eyes, 'It might turn out *not* to be Francis, in which case the sooner that identity can be established the better.'

Kenneth shook his head, not trusting himself to speak.

'I don't wish to trouble you with too many questions, but I wonder if you'd mind clearing up one rather important point?'

Kenneth drew himself up, took a deep breath and nodded.

'Thank you.' Melton resumed. 'It's my understanding Francis left for France on November seventeenth, yet it was the third of December before you reported him missing. Tell me, what was the reason for such a long delay?'

Kenneth was fatigued, but he distinctly remembered the same question having been put before, when he had reported his son's absence. Perhaps the dopey copper hadn't bothered to record his answer? He blinked and knuckled his eyes. 'In season, Frank works as a courier for a holiday company and fills in as a cabin steward with Air France, Toulouse, during the winter.' He paused, collecting his thoughts. 'Frank goes all over the world on long-haul trips, and picks up work for other airlines whenever there's a scheduled delay. But he *always* keeps in touch and *promised* he'd ring by the end of November. I waited a few days in case he'd met with difficulties, then rang his manager at Toulouse. When he insisted Francis hadn't reported for work, I knew for certain something was wrong.'

Reliving the memory and the agony suffered since, Kenneth found his lower lip trembling. Melton grasped the milkman's arm, reassuringly.

'Bear up, sir; we desperately need your help. Do you have a recent photo of Francis?'

'Yes, a couple, taken last year—in France, I think. They're in the album in my bedroom. Wait here, and I'll fetch it.' He got up and started towards the door. 'I wish I didn't feel so tired,' he added.

When he returned, Melton propped the album on his knee. He had a gut-feeling that the smiling young man indicated by his father and the rotting corpse in Kingston morgue would prove to be one and the same. *Who'd want to be a bloody copper?* Melton asked himself.

'I can only say how sorry I am,' he began, placing a hand on Kenneth's arm, 'but these seem sufficient reason to ask for your

THE FLYLEAF KILLER

help with formal identification. It involves visiting the morgue, but that can wait till later when I shall accompany you. You need to prepare yourself. Better get your head down for an hour or two, if you can.

'Before I go—with your permission, of course, I'd appreciate a look at your son's bedroom. It could be important—there may be something to help our inquiries. Would you mind? And may I borrow these photographs?'

Mr Bridgwater stood up and bravely squared his shoulders. 'By all means, Inspector Melton,' he said. 'Frank's room is just down there (he pointed). 'I haven't been inside—apart from shoving the vacuum cleaner round—or touched anything. Couldn't bring myself to somehow . . . and yes, you can borrow the photos, but I'd like them back when you've finished. My boy, Frank, you see . . .'

He stifled the beginnings of a sob, strode purposefully along the hallway and stopped. Turning, he said proudly, 'This is Frank's room, Mr Melton.'

Reaching the threshold, Melton stopped, motioned Kenneth to remain where he was and stood still for a moment, taking in something of the atmosphere. Casting around the bedroom, he saw nothing out of the ordinary, nothing caught his attention. The room was neat and tidy. No sign of a hurried departure, no note in a prominent position, no towel, clothes or dressing-gown, no shoes beneath the bed—nothing!

'Are you *certain* you've disturbed nothing?' he asked.

'Yes, quite sure.'

'Would you mind if I look in the wardrobe? I'll be careful not to disturb anything.'

'No, go right ahead.'

Melton took a pair of latex gloves from an inside pocket and snapped them on. Gingerly, he opened both doors and leaned forward for a closer look.

There were two, well-stocked hanging rails. Two pairs of walking shoes strode cheek-by-jowl with a battered pair of trainers, behind which stood a hiker's rucksack and a canvas travelling valise, partially obscured by clothes. He straightened and turned to Kenneth.

'Come and take a look Mr Bridgwater. What was Francis wearing the day of his departure? Do you know what luggage he took?' He broke off as Kenneth slowly entered the room and added, 'Sorry to press you, but I really do need to know.'

'I'm afraid I've no idea. Frank said "good-bye" around six the evening before he left—that's when he promised to ring.' He thought for a moment. 'Then he went out—to the pictures, I think—and I went to bed. I'd have been asleep when he came home and long gone when he awoke in the morning. I think he intended to bus to Esher station then train to Waterloo, but I can't be sure. Chances are he did, however. He did the last time he was home, I'm absolutely certain.'

'I see.' Melton was disappointed. Pursuing the same line of thought, he asked, 'If you didn't know what he wore the morning of his departure, then what about the evening before, when he was going to the cinema?'

Again Ken pondered.

'Sorry Inspector,' he replied regretfully. 'I really can't remember. Frank has loads of clothes, and changes frequently—sometimes twice in one day. I never could keep up with him. I'm truly sorry; I really wish I could help.'

'What about luggage? What would he normally take on a trip?'

Bridgwater bent to peer into the wardrobe. Fear sent shivers down his spine. Distressed, he clutched at Melton's arm.

'Wh-at?—I don't understand,' he quavered. 'Francis' rucksack—and his valise. It's—it's Frank's luggage, Inspector. It's all he has—it's what he takes, every trip. What does it mean? It's not like Francis to be forgetful. He'd *never* go off without his gear.'

Melton took Kenneth by the arm and steered him towards the bed.

'Sit down for a minute,' he soothed. 'It doesn't pay to jump to conclusions. We need to consider carefully. There could be a perfectly simple explanation.'

But for Melton, another possibility arose: *What if young Bridgwater never left for France?* Supposing he *did* visit the cinema that evening but never returned home—was waylaid, mugged and robbed, taken by force to the Old Church, incarcerated and subsequently murdered? Robbery could form part of the motive: nothing had been found on the body. But what if the young man took just enough cash for the evening and left everything of value at home?

Melton was all but convinced. If Francis Bridgwater's passport, travel tickets and cash were somewhere within this room, it only could mean one thing—the body lying in Kingston morgue was that of Francis Bridgwater, and his disappearance and murder had been deliberate and premeditated. But, to satisfy the requirement of law, the identity of dead persons must formally be established.

'If you feel up to it, Mr Bridgwater,' Melton said, gently, 'I'd like to ask another question.'

'I'm OK really, so go ahead. You probably think me an old fool but I still don't understand.'

'Nor do I sir—not yet, anyway. It would be foolish to assume anything at this stage.'

'I'm trying to work out why Frank's luggage is still in the wardrobe, Detective Inspector. I mustn't jump to conclusions. You might think otherwise, but you know,' he said, sorrowfully, 'I've the strangest feeling I'm unlikely ever to see Francis again—alive, that is.' The look on his face said it all.

'You may well be right Mr Bridgwater, but we've a long way to go in order to be sure. With your permission, I'd like to examine Francis' luggage.'

'Would you mind explaining why, Mr Melton?'

'Not at all,' he said. 'Nothing was found on the body: no cash, no means of identification, nothing. Should Francis have left his passport, cash and travel documents at home that evening—perhaps for reasons of security, then the body found in the vault may well be his. Should that be so—but remember, until positively identified we cannot be sure—he may have been waylaid, forcibly abducted, taken to the church, held prisoner and eventually killed. In any event, Mr Bridgwater, we have a ruthless killer somewhere within the community, one who must be caught and brought to justice before he finds an opportunity to strike again. Even if the victim proves not to be your son, I've no doubt you'll assist in any way you can to help apprehend the murderer. Now sir, if you don't mind, may I please look inside Francis' luggage?'

Kenneth nodded.

'If it turns out my son *has* been murdered, then rest assured I'll do anything and everything within my power to help nail the bastard responsible.'

Ken placed the rucksack and the valise on the bed:

'There you are, Mr Melton,' he said, firmly, 'go ahead and help yourself.'

A bulging pocket on the valise stood out like a sore thumb. Still gloved, Melton slid back the zip and fished out the contents: a wallet, a passport—and an envelope containing railway tickets.

Gingerly unhinging the wallet, taking care that nothing should become disturbed, he whistled through his teeth and invited Kenneth to view the contents. There were traveller's cheques and a NatWest Visa card, clearly visible through the transparent window of a dedicated card pocket.

For all his courage Kenneth's face was a picture of despair; his last vestige of hope had been destroyed.

'Come on, sir,' the DI said gently, replacing the luggage for forensic examination later. 'Try to get some sleep. It won't change anything, but it might help a little. I'll go back to the station and return around three this afternoon, when I'd like you to accompany me to the morgue—and, believe me, it's a duty I'd willingly postpone if I thought it would do any good. But, in my experience, the sooner something like this can be got out of the way the better. We none of us move forward, otherwise.'

Kenneth managed a wan smile.

'Thank you, Inspector. You've been very kind and I'm grateful . . .' He broke off. 'I wonder, can you tell me what to expect, assuming the body does turn out to be Francis?'

Melton paused before replying.

'For you, sadly, a coroner's inquest, a funeral and getting your life back together—which won't be easy. I'm told your wife died soon after childbirth and you brought Francis up yourself. For my colleagues and me, we've a killer to track down whatever happens.

'If you *do* confirm your son was his victim, then we shall have a name to go on and can begin exploring his background, checking friends, habits and so on and, hopefully, establish a motive which may eventually lead to an arrest. But more of that another time. First things first.'

Kenneth no longer seemed fatigued. Long weeks of uncertainty were almost at an end, and this helped him discover an inner strength. Melton regarded him with admiration.

As a prelude to departure, Melton shook hands with Kenneth at his front door.

'Good-bye for now, Mr Bridgwater—and thank you for your invaluable help. I'll see you around three this afternoon. In the meantime, do try and get some rest.'

Kenneth smiled ruefully. 'Au revoir, Mr Melton.'

Back at HQ, the DI brought his assistant up to date over a plate of lethargic sandwiches with a pot of the usual coffee—seldom hot, of dubious origin, frequently undrinkable.

'Plucky chap,' he remarked, eventually, 'been through hell, poor devil. I reckon he knew in his heart all along his son was dead but wouldn't admit it, even to himself, long before the boy's luggage turned up.

'I'm as sure as I can be that before the end of the day the morgue will have a name to attach to their corpse.'

'I hope you're right, sir,' O'Connor murmured. 'We need a bloody break. What are those, Guv'nor?' he asked, pointing to two photographs lying on Melton's desk.

'Sorry, Ben,' he said sheepishly, 'I forgot: Francis Bridgwater, borrowed from his father.' He slid the prints across the desk.

O'Connor gave his chief a peculiar look and rummaged 'sans permission' in Melton's 'In' tray for an envelope. Triumphantly he withdrew a charcoal sketch.

'Delivered less than an hour ago, Guv'nor,' he announced. 'Brendon Curtis' "John Doe". Look for yourself, sir. If they're not one and the same person, then I'm a Dutchman.'

Taken in sunshine against a lakeland background, the snapshots were fairly good. Viewed alongside the sketch, they showed similarities so far as head, ears and jaw line were concerned, but precious little else. Whilst computer enhancement was possible, image detail might suffer as a consequence.

Melton by no means shared the conviction so enthusiastically displayed by his assistant, preferring to defer judgement until the evidence was corroborated beyond all possible doubt.

'You might just find yourself learning a new language, Ben,' he observed, drily. 'Yes, there are similarities, I'll grant, but I'd rather wait for a positive ID to be absolutely sure.'

Melton collected Kenneth Bridgwater himself and they drove in silence to Kingston morgue. Arriving just after 3.30, Melton parked his car and led the way to Reception. As soon as the preliminary formalities were completed, the DI took Kenneth to one side.

'Are you sure you're up to this, Mr Bridgwater?'

'Yes, quite sure thank you. I'll be OK. Now please—can we get on with it?'

'Then brace yourself,' Melton advised gently. 'I feel it my duty to warn you what to expect. You will be taken to a sheeted figure and asked whether you recognise the person. The sheet will then be lifted. Remember, the body is in a state of decomposition. On top of that, some rather nasty injuries were inflicted prior to death.

'You must look at the face, but I advise you not to linger—it's not a sight for the squeamish. Furthermore, morgues tend to be smelly—formaldehyde, you know. You're sure you're OK?'

Kenneth nodded grimly.

'Then let's go,' Melton said, simply.

No stranger to the place or what went on within its white-tiled walls, the hardened policeman led the way.

They were intercepted in a vestibule by a white-coated, wellington-booted attendant, clutching a stainless-steel clipboard, who conducted them through plastic, double swing doors into a long, dank, chilly chamber, lit by ranks of bright fluorescent tubes and flanked by rows of stainless-steel, tiered cabinets.

Halfway on the left, the attendant stopped, referred to his clipboard and grasped a handle.

On silent wheels, a trolley bearing a sheeted body emerged. He checked the label, glanced again at his clipboard and asked, 'Mr Kenneth Bridgwater?'

'Yes.'

'There is reason to believe you may have personal knowledge of the deceased?'

'Yes.'

'Then you are required by law to look upon the person displayed to you and state clearly whether you recognise the person. Do you understand?'

Kenneth nodded.

'Then do you recognise this person?' The attendant raised a corner of the sheet.

Kenneth recoiled and covered his eyes in horror.

'No, no,' he croaked. 'That's not Francis, that's not my son.'

Melton's heart sank; he had been sure, so very, very sure. He grasped Kenneth firmly by the arm.

THE FLYLEAF KILLER

'Hold on, Mr Bridgwater. I warned you it wouldn't be pleasant. Take a minute to compose yourself.'

He waited, and after a while, Ken whispered, 'I'm sorry Inspector—the shock . . .'

'Never mind,' Melton soothed, 'perfectly understandable. Come sir, brace yourself and take another look—and this time, try to look beyond the injuries; the head, hair, ears, nose and chin.'

He signalled to the attendant, who raised the sheet and said for a second time, 'I have to asked you again, sir: do you recognise this person?'

Kenneth stepped bravely forward. He forced himself to follow Melton's advice and looked carefully at the cadaver. Shortly, recognition dawned, and for a full minute he stood in silence, remembering the years of joy, sometimes laced with heartache: how a tiny baby first began to toddle, then went to school and developed into a young man of whom any parent might justly be proud. And as he stood and gazed at what remained of his once handsome son, tears filled his eyes and he wept copiously and without shame.

'Yes,' he whispered, eventually and, 'Yes,' louder still, then 'Yes!' firmly and emphatically. 'That's my son—that *was* my son. Francis Bridgwater, definitely—and God help the bastard who did this if ever I lay hands on him!'

Back in Melton's car, Kenneth Bridgwater fastened his seat-belt and heaved a great sigh.

'I must say, Mr Melton, I feel better with that awful business over and done with.'

Melton heartily agreed. 'You and me both, Mr Bridgwater,' he said.

Kenneth lapsed into silence, no doubt busy with his thoughts. The journey back to West End took barely twenty minutes.

Although his motives for acting as personal chauffeur to a member of the public were never likely to be questioned, Melton had a perfectly valid reason for failing to delegate. Put simply, the result achieved would have been unlikely, had he not won the confidence of the witness and afforded him sympathetic guidance throughout the unfortunate man's harrowing ordeal.

But, off the record, it was a way of paying tribute to an honest, hardworking and extremely courageous man, to whom he had taken a liking almost from the moment they first met.

On reaching Bridgwater's bungalow, the detective checked his watch: four oh five—already? He turned to his passenger and proffered his hand.

'May I offer my condolences, Mr Bridgwater? I wish there was more I could do to help.'

'Thank you,' Kenneth said. 'You've been more than helpful already, extremely kind, in fact. I doubt I'd have survived the afternoon without your support.'

'You're entirely welcome, I can assure you,' Melton responded, warmly. 'I must get back to headquarters, but we need as much information as possible regarding Francis's past acquaintances to help build a background picture. May I call again tomorrow? About ten-thirty? I'd like you to meet my assistant, Detective Sergeant Ben O'Connor.'

'Not in the least. I look forward to seeing you both—and the kettle will be on, you may be sure.'

Now that the victim was formally identified, the investigation proper could get under way, and there was a great deal more to be accomplished before Melton and O'Connor dare call it a day.

Chief Superintendent Jarvis was briefed and, on his authority, Melton and his assistant combined forces to issue a short but credible press-release. This was accomplished in time for inclusion in mid-evening television news programmes and to feature in national newspapers destined for the streets the following morning. Additionally, acting on a hunch of O'Connor's, they sifted through the Pennington file and confirmed Ben's suspicion that Francis Bridgwater, then seventeen, was one of seven teenagers interviewed almost three years previously during the *Body in the Garden* investigation.

'I bloody-well knew it Guv'nor,' Ben O'Connor felt entitled to crow. 'Eight of them—if you include Malandra Pennington, and they all went to the same local school. That's no coincidence, surely, nor the fact that both victim's throats were cut in the same way and with a similar type of instrument. There isn't any doubt. We're looking for a man with extensive local knowledge. What's more, the killer of Francis Bridgwater and Miss Pennington are one and the same.'

'Hold it, Ben,' Melton snorted, impatiently. 'What the hell are you rabbiting on about? We've been over this already; try something a bit more original. You've added nothing to what we already know—and what's so unusual about eight local youngsters going to the same local school, anyway? Where the hell else would you expect local children of local parents to go?'

Chastened, his assistant came down to earth.

'Sorry sir,' he mumbled, 'I got carried away.'

Melton grinned. 'No problem—so long as you stick to facts and don't jump to conclusions. Although in one respect I do agree: the more we compare cases, the more likely it seems the two murders *are* connected.'

Returning to the Pennington file, he shuffled through a sheaf of interview reports, checked each against an abridged summation and came to a decision.

'All right Ben,' he allowed. 'It might be as well to re-interview those youngsters. Set it up for tomorrow—except for Pearce and Robert Strudwick. We'll deal with those two ourselves.'

No sooner were the words out than Melton was regretting his decision. Not for the first time, any suggestion that Strudwick might not be all that he seemed brought a rush of irrational irritability. What was the point of pursuing a perfectly innocent, forthright, upright citizen? Had it been within Robert Strudwick's power to assist, he surely would have done. *Damn!* These re-interviews would stand, however, if only to stop his assistant's incessant badgering.

Abruptly, he selected a hand-written sheet, shoved it towards O'Connor and ordered, sharply, 'Do three photostat copies—and put the original back in the file before it ends up in the bin.'

His tone was peremptory, unexpected and out of character. O'Connor frowned, but held his tongue. When he was halfway to the copier, Melton issued an afterthought.

'But before you do, delete Phyllis Gleave and Fletcher Roberts—they're no longer relevant.'

Melton glanced at the wall clock: 6.15. His grumpiness subsided as quickly as it had arisen. He whistled in surprise and tidied his desk.

'Time we weren't here Ben,' he remarked, in a return to his normal, easy-going manner. 'I'll cop it if I'm late for dinner again,' he explained, lamely. 'See you in the morning . . . Incidentally, I've made an appointment, ten-thirty, to visit Kenneth Bridgwater and I'd like you along. The sooner we delve into his son's background, the sooner we might unearth something to indicate a motive which could lead us to the killer. Keep an hour or so free; we ought to be back by midday. Goodnight, Sergeant.'

'G'night sir.' *Miserable sod. Didn't so much as suggest a pint,* Ben thought gloomily . . .

Hungry for information and hoping to repeat the success born of James Billows' indiscretions—and retain credibility with editors demanding follow-on articles—Robin Prendergast pounded his typewriter furiously. Waste-bin awash with discarded material and faced with a 10.00 p.m. deadline, he strove for acceptable copy; with only a miserly police press-release to go on, he came close to giving up.

Desperately seeking a snippet of some sort, he tentatively telephoned a contact, and gleaned an unexpected disclosure, sufficient to transform an indifferent item into a juicy report. He redoubled his efforts at the keyboard and ten minutes later pronounced himself satisfied. Not an eye-catching, full-page article, perhaps, but sufficient to keep the story 'live' another day. Robin dictated copy to three news desk editors, patted his elderly 'Imperial' (he maintained it aided concentration), sneered at the blank screen of his computer and strolled out of the house to the local watering-hole, bent on rounding off the day with a pint or two of Guinness.

His reward came the following morning with front-page headlines in the *Surrey Chronicle* and second-feature status in several national dailies. Thursday, 17 February 2005:

INSPECTOR MELTON HUNTS THE SLASHER
BODY IN THE VAULT IDENTIFIED

A report from our special correspondent Robin Prendergast.

Detective Inspector David Melton, CID, the officer conducting the *Body in the Vault* inquiry, today launches a full-scale murder investigation following formal identification of the deceased late yesterday afternoon.

The decomposed remains discovered by sexton James Billows in a little-known vault beneath the historic church of St. George at Esher on Saturday February 12 were positively identified as those of Francis Bridgwater aged 19, formerly of West End, Esher, by his father Kenneth, a popular local milkman. It is understood post-mortem examination established that death took place during late November, about two weeks after Francis disappeared. The body was discovered, quite by chance, by Mr Billows. Twelfth century St. George's remained cordoned off until Tuesday afternoon when Forensic specialists withdrew and the church reopened to the public. Detective Inspector Melton was not available for comment, but is expected to release further details at a press conference later today.

David Melton pushed a copy of a daily tabloid across the desk.

'Read that Ben—factual and accurate,' he remarked without rancour. 'Where do you reckon Prendergast got his information?'

O'Connor scanned the item and grunted.

'Easy, Guv'nor—has to be the morgue. Just the place for an ambitious young crime reporter to invest a sweetener now and then.'

He handed the paper back.

'Oiling the wheels, they call it,' Melton grumbled. 'Buying confidential information, more like. Not easily preventable, however, more's the pity—nor illegal, so far as I'm aware. He's wrong about the press conference though. I intend to release a prepared statement later on, and he'll get a copy just like the rest of them. If he doesn't like it, he can lump it.'

'Egg on his face, Guv'nor? Maybe he'll think twice before trying to second-guess you in future.'

'I doubt it. Reporters are thick-skinned—have to be to be successful, I suppose . . . Come in,' Melton called, in response to a knock on the door, effectively closing the subject. The door opened and a constable entered, bearing an assortment of papers, envelopes and files:

'Post, sir,' he announced, dumping a pile on the desk. 'Rather a lot and that one on top is regarding Bridgwater, sir, from Forensics. Came by messenger, about five minutes ago.'

Melton grabbed the envelope, tugged open the flap, withdrew a sheaf of papers and began to read. O'Connor sorted the remaining reports and memos, placing everything for immediate attention in Melton's 'In' tray and the remainder in 'Pending'. Nothing escaped the Guv'nor, however; he'd plough through the lot in an hour.

O'Connor completed his self-imposed task as Melton looked up.

'Interesting reading,' he remarked, 'if not particularly enlightening. Good job the body's been identified. There were no laundry or other marks on any item of clothing. Nothing of consequence came from the fingertip search, and the sweepings from the cellar floor were mainly dust and dirt, with minute quantities of pollen—none recent—either blown by wind or carried in on footwear over the years.

'On top of that, samples taken from the vault walls and ledges were similar to ordinary household dust: soil particles, dead skin cells and mites and, once again, nothing of recent origin. In short, almost a complete blank.

'However—and this is the interesting bit—out of more than a dozen hairs found on the cadaver, one differed from the rest. As soon as Mr Ferguson realised the significance, he had it packaged, labelled and sent it for DNA profiling, requesting comparison with DNA from tissue routinely sent by the mortuary.' Melton tapped the desk with an emphatic forefinger. 'That single hair could prove significant.'

'It just might, sir. Presumably all the other hairs belong to Francis Bridgwater?'

'We'll have the answer to that quite soon, I hope—but yes, I should think they probably do.'

He returned the papers to the envelope and passed it to his assistant.

'Shove it in the file for now, Ben. Read it later if you've a mind to.' Dismissive, the DI removed the contents of his 'In' tray, bent his head and began to read. The message was clear. O'Connor withdrew.

At 09.40, Melton visited the forensic lab for a word with Mr Ferguson, the senior technician.

At 10.00, with O'Connor driving, the policemen left Surbiton and headed for West End. The easiest and most direct route took them via Long Ditton, the A3 to Esher and Lammas Lane.

At 10.25, Ken Bridgwater left his partially-loaded washing-machine in order to answer the door. Melton introduced his companion. The DS stepped forward and offered his hand.

'Glad to meet you, sir. I'm sorry to hear about your son. Please accept my condolences.'

THE FLYLEAF KILLER

'Thank you.'

Formalities out of the way, the milkman led the way to his kitchen and indicated chairs.

'I rarely use the living room and was in the middle of putting the washing on,' he explained. 'Excuse me, I won't be a moment.' Kenneth loaded a few more items into the machine and switched it on.

'Which would you prefer, tea or coffee? The kettle has already boiled.' Both chose tea and with his visitors comfortably seated, Kenneth opened the conversation.

'You said yesterday you needed information about Francis' background, Inspector. What exactly would you like to know?'

'We'd like to know where Francis went to school, and the names of as many of his teachers and classmates as you can recall. Also friends and companions since leaving school. A résumé of his career would be helpful—names of employers and colleagues and, finally, an insight into his hobbies, social and sporting interests. Any incident, however trivial or apparently unrelated, might eventually lead us to the murderer.'

Needing no further prompting, Kenneth began to speak. Melton listened; O'Connor took notes. Francis had certainly lived his short life to the full. Even though his father spoke concisely, it took over half an hour for him to exhaust his fund of information, all of which was relevant.

'That was certainly comprehensive, Mr Bridgwater,' Melton declared, 'and you put it across extremely well, given the circumstances. Thank you! That information may well prove invaluable. I very much doubt whether we shall need to trouble you further.'

'But should there be anything further you need to know,' Kenneth added, 'please don't hesitate to call me—at any time.'

'We'll bear that in mind. I'm sorry we have to rush, but duty calls.'

The officers got up to go, but Bridgwater gripped Melton's arm.

'I want to see Francis' killer behind bars. It's a pity the death penalty has been abolished; I'd like the bastard to swing.' He sighed. 'Be that as it may . . . I'm sure you're always busy, but would it be possible to keep me informed of progress?'

'Of course, it's the least we can do—and, in confidence, may I ask *you* a final question?'

'By all means, Inspector. Fire away.'

'Can you think of anyone—male, female, young or old—who may at any time have had reason to think ill of Francis or who bore him a grudge in any way? Please think carefully before you answer.'

'No, Inspector. Frank didn't have an enemy in the whole, wide world, I'm absolutely positive.'

'We'll add "so far as you're aware" to that Mr Bridgwater,' Melton suggested. 'Your son had the misfortune to acquire *one* enemy at least, and a deadly enemy at that, as events have shown.'

En route back to Surbiton, Melton referred to his watch and remarked, 'No time for lunch, we're running late. We'd better head straight back to headquarters.'

'Ooh, lovely! Cardboard wedgies—again!'

DS O'Connor spent half an hour clearing accumulated correspondence, and it was 1.00 p.m. when he tapped the inner sanctum door and waited for an invitation to enter.

'Come in, Sergeant,' Melton called. 'Park your tail, Ben. I won't be a minute.'

O'Connor duly sat and watched in silence whilst reports were read, initialled and tossed into the 'Out' tray. Melton stood up, yawned, stretched—and sat down again.

'I won't ask whether you enjoyed your lunch,' he chuckled, 'but I take it you're all sorted?'

'Yes sir.'

'Anything I ought to know?'

'Not much really, except the information from the former school chums interviewed so far. Calvin Smith vaguely recalled a Frank Bridgwater at school, but couldn't remember what he looked like, and Brian Carpenter locked himself in the toilet and refused to come out. Waste of time going to see him again, sir—he's not quite all there, you know. The others were equally dismayed by the untimely death of Francis, who was popular, and all expressed regret at being unable to help.'

'More or less as expected,' the DI remarked. 'Maybe we'll do better with Pearce or Strudwick.'

'Hopefully, Guv'nor,' O'Connor sounded dubious. 'What's the plan of action?'

'Long Ditton first,' Melton replied, 'then Pearce. He is at home—I've checked with his mother.'

*

THE FLYLEAF KILLER

Arriving at Gaston Hathaway, O'Connor trundled the Rover into the car park at the rear and whistled appreciatively at the gleaming white Jaguar XJ6 standing alone in a marked-off space labelled 'Mr R.W.Strudwick'. He pulled up tight behind the beautiful car, effectively blocking its exit.

They are here! They know nothing, they shall know nothing. Send them away!

'Over there, Guv'nor,' O'Connor observed, gesturing with his chin, 'rear entrance—shall we?'

'No, better use the front. We'll do things properly and announce ourselves to the receptionist.'

The policemen made their way back to the high street on foot, and entered by the front door. As if expected, they were intercepted by Strudwick in an otherwise empty reception area. He immediately issued a challenge. 'If it isn't dear Inspector Melton—and his faithful lackey, Sergeant O'Connor. Well, well, what a surprise! And what exactly do you mean by bothering me at work?'

When roused, O'Connor's face was apt to mimic the colour of his flaming hair. A hand restrained him from rising to the bait. Apparently unruffled, Melton took the insult in his stride.

'Good afternoon, Mr Strudwick. Our apologies for calling without prior appointment, but we are investigating the brutal murder of Francis Bridgwater—a young man we believe you are acquainted with, and would like you to assist in our inquiries by answering a few questions. Can we use your office?'

Strudwick shook his head.

'No, you damn well can't,' he snarled. 'I'm far too busy to waste time pandering to your stupid whims.'

Addressing himself equally to Melton and O'Connor, his eyes gleamed darkly behind pebble-lens spectacles as he strove to impose his will upon the luckless policemen. In seconds, both were rendered impotent, transfixed by the satanic gaze. Each detective stood as if mesmerised while Strudwick ranted on.

'For your information, yes, I knew Bridgwater—went to school with him as you doubtless know. But I've neither seen nor heard of him since he cleared off to Spain—or somewhere. I never did like the man. I know *nothing* about him. I don't *want* to know anything about him and, if somebody upped and killed him—and I heard recently that somebody did—then that's a matter between you, the killer and his conscience. I don't *care* what questions you were going to ask; I wouldn't know the answers. Now, if you don't mind, I've an appointment with an important client in ten minutes.'

Abruptly, his attitude changed. He smiled and ushered the officers out of the door.

'I'm sorry you've had a wasted journey, gentlemen. I almost wish I was able to help.'

'What the hell was that all about Guv'nor?' O'Connor gasped, safely back on the pavement. 'I had an eerie sense of foreboding in there—the same as at Strudwick's house that night—and the strangest impression he was speaking, but I'm damned if I can remember what he said. Is the man a bloody hypnotist sir—or am I losing my marbles?'

What on earth was the man raving about? Melton gaped uncomprehendingly, then remembered his own sense of unreality in Strudwick's presence. Shrugging away his own profound unease, he puzzled furiously for a rational explanation, anxious to reassure his obviously shaken assistant.

The answer came in a flash. Astonishingly, he found himself laughing—if not in amusement, at least with considerable relief.

'Don't look so worried Ben,' he chortled, 'you're every bit as sane as I am. I'm afraid Strudwick may have been tipped off—he was certainly expecting us. Didn't you notice a faint smell in there? Some kind of mesmeric gas, I should think.' O'Connor looked dubious. 'I believe he hates everybody in authority, coppers in particular, and will stop at nothing to make fools of us. I also believe he knows absolutely nothing about Francis Bridgwater or the murder. But he's clever, our Mr Strudwick, and a more compelling personality would be difficult to find.

'Come on, let's go and spend ten minutes with Steven Pearce. *He* might be able to help. Then we'll hightail it back to HQ. I've an important press release waiting to be compiled.'

At 14.02 O'Connor swung the Rover into Rodene Drive and drew to a halt at number eleven. Melton got out and made for the gate, forcing his assistant to step lively in order to catch up. As they walked up the path, a twitching curtain suggested their arrival was already noted. Mrs Pearce answered Melton's knock almost before the echoes had had time to fade.

THE FLYLEAF KILLER

'Come in, Inspector—you too Sergeant,' she bustled. 'I've been expecting you. Steven's upstairs. Please wait in the living-room. I'll go and fetch him.'

'Hello, Steven, nice to see you again,' Melton said, pleasantly, when the young man came into the room.

'What am I supposed to have done this time?'

'Nothing. We're investigating the unfortunate death of Francis Bridgwater, and badly need background information. You do know his body was found last Saturday?'

'Yes, I read about it in the papers—in the Old Church, wasn't it? How awful. I knew Frank pretty well, although I haven't seen much of him since he went off working abroad.'

'Can you remember when you *did* last see him?'

'Not for sure. Around this time last year, I think, when he was home on leave. Yes, that's right—he was having a week off before going back to France for the start of the new season.'

'Not since then? Are you sure?'

'Quite sure. But why are you questioning me?'

'Because you knew Frank and we want to learn as much about him as possible. The unusual circumstances surrounding his death suggest he was killed by somebody local, someone who knows Esher extremely well. A murder of this nature would not have been perpetrated without reason, and if the motive can be established, we'll be well on the way to catching the killer.'

'I see. What else do you want to know?'

'Do you know of anyone—young or old, recently or at any time in the past—who may have had reason to wish Francis harm or bore him a grudge of any sort?'

Don't dare say a bloody word! 'No sir, I never heard Frank say a bad word about anyone. Just about everybody liked him.'

Surrey County Police Headquarters, Surbiton: 1600. Time for Detective Inspector Melton's prearranged meeting with Chief Superintendent Jarvis. Melton tapped on the door and entered. The incumbent, busily scanning a document of some description, paused to look up.

'Hello David. Dead on time as usual. Come and sit down, I'll be right with you.'

Jarvis bent his head, ran a forefinger down a column of figures, scrawled his initials and closed the file.

'Appropriation summary,' he grunted, by way of explanation. 'A nuisance, but necessary. Right,' he said, briskly, 'time is short so we'd better get down to business—but before we look at your draft statement, I'd appreciate an update on developments.'

'Certainly sir,' Melton replied and, omitting minor details, swiftly brought his superior up to date. DCS Jarvis listened without comment until Melton had finished. Then he positively exploded.

'Am I to understand that not one of those former friends of Francis Bridgwater crossed swords with him in some way before, during or since school—or knew of anyone who did?' Melton was taken aback.

'Unfortunately, sir, that is exactly so,' he protested. 'I admit it's unfortunate that none of the interviewees could remember a past protagonist nor hint at a possible enemy, but every interview was conducted in accordance with proper procedure.'

Logic prevailed. Jarvis' wrath subsided as rapidly as it had arisen.

'Sorry if I upset you, David, but I can't for the life of me imagine what to say to the DACC. He's pushing hard for an early result—and *still* asks about the Pennington case almost every week.' Such a feeble, half-hearted apology did little to extinguish Melton's controlled indignation:

'But surely he must realise a body discovered a few short days ago has already been identified. Getting on for three months went by between the murder and discovery of the corpse. Consequently whatever trail the murderer may have left is long since cold. Let's face it, sir, only last Saturday we were saddled with a decomposing corpse with absolutely no means of identification. That's progress, surely?'

'I'll grant you that—but will the DACC? He's under pressure himself. I can just hear him asking: "What sort of man was he, this Bridgwater chap, some sort of saint? No minor playground squabble? Never nicked another chap's girlfriend or slept with another man's wife? Not a single enemy in the world? Rubbish!" Your men had better believe he had an enemy, David—the poor chap wouldn't be lying in the morgue otherwise. Come on, Inspector Melton. He expects results and so do I. Without going into detail, what *is* your strategy for trying to establish some sort of motive?'

THE FLYLEAF KILLER

'Well sir, with the exception of one officer on telephone and radio liaison and six tied up with routine and other matters, the remaining eight are out seeking a lead on anyone who may have had a difference of opinion with the deceased sometime in the past. Two are calling house-to-house in West End, two are tracking down former employers and colleagues and the other four are canvassing local tradespeople, pubs, clubs and the like, anywhere he may have frequented, not necessarily with his father's knowledge. I really don't see what more we can do.'

The Chief Superintendent snorted.

'That's fine, but former friends of Francis Bridgwater must still represent the best chance of a lead to the killer and therefore—except for the two you've already questioned—they are to be interviewed again, and by you personally this time—and no "ifs" or "buts" about it. I don't doubt the interrogatory skills of your men, but none can match your experience or perception.

'You're an excellent policeman, David, and I've come to rely on your judgement. Under your leadership we've built a team the equal of any in the Force, and I'd like to be sure my confidence isn't misplaced so, please, root out something that might conceivably point to a motive, OK?'

'Yes sir.'

'Right, subject closed. Let's have a look at this draft bulletin of yours.'

At 16.25 Melton left the 'Chief Super's' office and conveyed an amended draft to the data office. The route back to his own office took him through front Reception where he was accosted by excited news reporters.

'Dangerfield, *Evening News!*' the nearest announced.

Melton acknowledged the crime reporter.

'Wire Services E-mail Inspector. *Body in the Vault* inquiry. Press Conference this afternoon—but your desk sergeant says it's the first he's heard of it. What the hell is going on?'

'Well, I did hear a rumour to that effect, but it didn't come from me. I suggest you ask Robin Prendergast for an explanation, Mr Dangerfield. I'm told he's an absolute mine of information.'

'Oh, *him* was it?' snorted another reporter. 'I read his article in the *Surrey Chronicle* this morning.'

Several eager faces surrounding Melton darkened in annoyance. One fellow scowled and muttered, 'I'll have his guts for garters, just see if I don't. I've travelled miles to get here this afternoon.'

Having lit a bonfire, so to speak, Melton decided to apply a bucketful of water.

'Now gentlemen,' he soothed, 'it may not be entirely his fault; try blaming his crystal ball. In any event, none of you have had an entirely wasted journey. A special press release will be issued at 1700 hours.'

An edited version of the bulletin gained inclusion in the mid-evening and main television news programmes that evening and was fully reported in national dailies the following morning: 18 February, 2005:

POLICE STEP UP HUNT FOR KILLER
BODY IN THE VAULT LATEST

In a statement issued by police hunting the killer of nineteen-year-old Francis Bridgwater, Detective Inspector David Melton, CID—the officer heading the investigation—had little to add to what he told reporters yesterday. 'Details of the circumstances surrounding the way in which Francis Bridgwater met with an untimely end are being withheld so as not to prejudice the investigation,' he said, and went on to reveal that detectives are 'actively pursuing certain lines of inquiry' which it is hoped will help establish a motive for the brutal killing and eventually lead to the murderer being apprehended.

It can also be disclosed that Francis—seasonally employed as a courier for a national holiday company—disappeared last November after failing to arrive in southern France where he was contracted to work as an airline steward.

08.30: Police HQ, Surbiton

'Stone the perishing crows,' DS O'Connor snorted, vehemently. He prodded the newspaper.

'Have you read the last paragraph, Guv'nor? Francis Bridgwater's employment wasn't even *mentioned* in that release.'

'Yes, I know, I wrote it,' Melton said angrily. 'And that's what I think of *that*!' he added, sweeping the newspaper from the desk directly into the waste bin.

Between 9.00 and 9.15, all officers currently working on the Bridgwater investigation received instructions to report to the briefing room to attend a case conference commencing at 10.00 sharp.

After preliminaries, DI Melton delivered a concise summation of the investigation to date. He expressed his disappointment at the lack of progress since identification of the body, and invited comment, but after fifteen minutes of general discussion little of value had emerged.

With continued pressure from higher authority and the prospect of another unsolved murder, Melton decided the time had come to place the bulk of routine on hold and commit all available resources. The Chief Superintendent was right. It was crucial a motive be established without delay. He rapped his desk for order.

'Right, ladies and gentlemen,' he resumed, 'as you all know, almost three months have elapsed since Francis Bridgwater was murdered. That fact alone substantially reduces detection possibilities. Whatever trail that may once have existed will have long since disappeared. To stand any chance of apprehending the killer, we must first establish a motive.

'The deceased man's father—his only living relative apart from a distant cousin, has bravely set aside his grief to provide a comprehensive résumé of his dead son's former friends and associates. Unfortunately for this investigation, he knew of no-one with whom Francis had had any kind of disagreement; he was confident his son hadn't an enemy in the world. Clearly that was not the case.

'It is neither desirable nor operationally acceptable for this inquiry to drag on indefinitely. The longer the file remains on my desk, the less the chance of ever apprehending the killer. To this end, all routine and other matters not of an urgent nature are to be placed on the back burner with immediate effect, allowing us to concentrate every effort on seeking a breakthrough.

'The following measures will be implemented forthwith:

'Door-to-door inquiries in West End will be extended to include all residents over the age of twelve—a brief word with the householder will no longer suffice. To achieve this without prolonging the investigation unduly, the number of officers detailed will increase to six.

'Similarly, to speed the task of trawling through local business people, shops, pubs and the like, the existing complement of two is to be doubled.

'Finally, two additional officers will help locate and interview all Francis Bridgwater's former employers and workmates everywhere he worked since leaving school—in the UK, that is. Anyone who smells an excuse for a continental holiday might as well forget it.

'Few people are at home during the day, so those on house-to-house inquiries will work flexitime up to a maximum of ten hours a day. Excess overtime will *not* be authorised.

'A word of warning to anyone who fancies skiving off sick over the next couple of weeks. He—or she—will find themselves referred to a medical board for absences exceeding twenty-four hours.

'Your brief: To persevere, to exhaust every possibility, but winkle out some form of altercation in which Francis Bridgwater almost certainly became engaged at some time during his short life, no matter how trivial and that, I might add, includes a playground tiff or sports-field disagreement. The lead we so desperately need is out there somewhere. Go and find it! Detective Sergeant O'Connor will detail and organise to suit operational convenience. Remember—no enemy equals no motive equals no killer in the dock. Good hunting!'

After a trying afternoon, Melton returned to HQ at 6.00 p.m. to find DS O'Connor still at work. To avoid upsetting the original interviewing officers, his itinerary remained confidential to all except his assistant. Tired, grumpy and despondent, Melton dropped into his chair.

'Hello, Guv'nor. How did it go? Any luck?'

'Not really,' Melton sighed. 'Caroline Lucas—last of the three. Lady minicab driver—sans radio. Finally ran her to earth half-an-hour ago. Says she was saddened by Frank Bridgwater's death, would love to help, but couldn't recall him falling out with anyone. I might as well have gone to Sandown, or sneaked home for the afternoon to put my feet up.'

He fished out his car keys and tossed them on the desk.

'Here, partner, take my car tonight and drop me off. I'll buy you a half on the way.'

0915, 19th February, 2005, County Police Headquarters, Surbiton

Mufti-clad, on what was supposedly his Saturday off, Detective Chief Superintendent Jarvis arrived, stomped through reception and continued noisily towards his office. He went in and slammed

THE FLYLEAF KILLER

the door. Seconds later, an unmistakable voice issued from Melton's office intercom.

'Inspector Melton?' *What the blazes . . . ? It's supposed to be his Saturday off!* 'Yes sir.'

'Oh good, you *are* in. Can you spare a minute?'

'Certainly sir. Right away sir?'

'Yes please.'

A 'click' from the speaker and the intercom fell silent. Melton made his way to the Chief Super's office.

'Come and sit down, David,' Jarvis said. 'Sorry to trouble you, but I'm meeting the DACC at ten for golf. He's bound to ask about the Bridgwater case and I wonder if you'd mind telling where we're up to.'

'Well sir,' Melton began, 'I'll be as brief as possible. Should I start to digress, please tell me. I wouldn't want to make you late for your appointment.'

Suspecting sarcasm, Jarvis looked up, but Melton seemed intent only on delivering his report.

'You were absolutely right, sir. Success or failure depends almost entirely on our ability to establish a motive. When it became clear at yesterday's forum we were in danger of stalemate—even at this early stage—I decided, prompted by your remarks, to set routine to one side in order to concentrate all the available resources. Time is of the essence, sir. Whatever trail once existed grows fainter by the day.

'Forgive me for being dramatic, but now I've committed, it's vital I have your full backing. As from today—apart from telephone and radio liaison duties at headquarters—all officers are devoting themselves to finding a connection, however tenuous, between the deceased and the man who clearly had powerful enough reason to plan and execute an extremely heinous crime.

'Every West End resident over the age of twelve is to be questioned, all tradespeople canvassed, every staff member identified and visited—similarly with pubs, clubs and bars throughout the area. Furthermore, we shall seek out former school friends and teachers, UK employers and colleagues and follow through every item of information gleaned—all in all, sir, a formidable undertaking.

'Few people are home during the day. Therefore officers on

house-to-house inquiries will work flexitime up to a maximum of ten hours spread across the day. I see no need to seek authority for excess overtime. Can I take it these measures meet with your approval sir?'

'Exactly what I hoped to hear you say, David. I trust your efforts will speedily be rewarded. By the way, the former school friends, did you learn anything?'

Damn, I knew *he'd ask me that!* 'No sir. All expressed regret about the tragic death and wanted to help, but not one could recall a single instance when Francis Bridgwater openly disagreed with anybody.'

'Pity,' Jarvis remarked. He looked at his watch. 'Better dash; mustn't keep the Deputy Assistant waiting.'

The moment Melton was back in his office, O'Connor popped his head round the door.

'How did you get on, Guv'nor?' he asked.

Melton rubbed his nose conspiratorially.

'Don't ask silly questions, you nosy sod. Get on with your work,' he replied, mischievously.

'That's the trouble with this bloody place,' retorted O'Connor. 'Nobody tells me anything.' Melton failed to rise to the bait, and both men turned their attention to a substantial amount of paperwork left over from the previous day.

Each bent to his task and made steady progress but, nearing midday, Melton was interrupted.

Not by any means for the first time—and probably not for the last—the hapless Desk Sergeant found himself under siege from a quartet of newsmen. These were demanding full and proper information regarding the investigation, without which they refused to go away. In desperation, he rang DI Melton to ask for help.

'I'm sorry to have to trouble you sir, but they're kicking up a hell of a fuss. They won't leave without finding out what's going on, and demand to hear it from you. I've told them you're busy, but they won't take "no" for an answer.'

Melton sighed. 'OK Sergeant, I'll see what I can do. Tell them I'll be down in a few minutes.'

Five minutes later. Melton walked into a noisy reception.

'Hush, gentlemen,' he pleaded. 'Statements have been issued twice already this week and there's nothing further to tell.

'The investigation has been stepped up, and fifteen officers are now working flat out.'

With this the journalists had to be content.

The investigation intensified, as police sought anyone even *suspected* of having shown the slightest degree of animosity towards the dead man at some time in the past. It roared ahead throughout Monday and Tuesday, but without uncovering a single useful lead.

1100, Wednesday 23rd February 2005: Police HQ, Surbiton

DI Melton began working through the contents of his 'In' tray. Several files and memos later, he came to a brown manila envelope inscribed: CONFIDENTIAL: Detective Inspector Melton CID.

'Funny,' he remarked, to no-one in particular, 'I didn't notice that. Wonder when it arrived?'

'Seen this before, Ben?' he asked his assistant, sitting opposite.

'No sir. It wasn't there last night. Must have arrived with the post. But it does seem important. Oughtn't you take a look.'

Melton opened the envelope, withdrew a foolscap sheet and began to read.

Affecting indifference, O'Connor studiously returned to his file. Suddenly, Melton slapped the desk. 'Eureka! The first piece of real evidence.'

'Those hairs recovered from the deceased man's clothing, all but one belonged to Francis Bridgwater. DNA was extracted and the profile checked against the computer database at Central Criminal Records. *There was no match.* When we find the man whose DNA *does* match, we shall have our murderer.'

'That's good news sir—up to a point. There'd be an outcry if we attempted to saliva-test every local male and if it were done voluntarily, it's unlikely our man would be daft enough to come forward. We'd only catch the blighter if he was arrested and tested for a totally unrelated reason.

'What defines "local" anyway? To be certain of netting the killer, we'd need a swab from every male over the age of sixteen within a radius of, say, five miles of Esher? That takes in Twickenham, Hounslow and Isleworth, Kingston and Teddington, as far south as Leatherhead, Weybridge in the west, across to Epsom and Ewell in the east. I'm no population expert, sir, but I'd guess we're talking in excess of a million.'

'I'm sure you're right, Sergeant, but blanket DNA census isn't *quite* what I had in mind.'

Thoughtfully, he returned the paper to its envelope and tucked it into his inside pocket. He gestured towards the outer office. 'I'll acquaint the Chief Super and explain my reasons in due course, but in the meantime I want the existence of this document kept strictly between ourselves. Unless you disapprove, I intend to take this home and lock it in my safe.

'One day—hopefully soon—we will have reason to bring in a suspect in connection with the murder of Francis Bridgwater. When we do, I shall propose a simple saliva test, which could free an innocent party of all suspicion.' He looked his assistant squarely in the eye. 'Do you have any such objection, Detective Sergeant O'Connor?' he asked.

O'Connor did not. Ben rubbed his chin, thought for a moment, then asked, curiously, 'How come that result came directly to you instead of through usual channels?'

Melton tapped his nose.

'Why do you suppose? I arranged it of course, right after we learned of the hair's existence.'

0945, Friday 25th February 2005: Police HQ, Surbiton

The office intercom sprang into life.

'Inspector Melton!' the all-too-familiar voice snapped.

'Yes sir.'

'I dare say you're busy, (*How* did *he guess?*) but I'd appreciate a word.'

'Right away, sir.'

'I'll give you one guess what *he* wants,' O'Connor ventured.

Melton didn't even bother to reply. He got to his feet and left immediately, to return some ten minutes later, grim faced.

'That's it, Ben,' he said, morosely, 'we wind the inquiry down to a maximum of just two men. One continues sniffing pubs, clubs and so on, the other following up former employers. All others come off the investigation as of today and we revert to standard manning forthwith.'

'I wish there was something I could say, Guv'nor. All that effort for damn-all. But I suppose the Chief Super didn't really have much choice.'

'No, the investigation has cost a bomb already and couldn't possibly continue indefinitely. We have to be realistic. Reduced maybe, but the inquiry goes on. We *will* nab that murderer.'

At 1.30 p.m. reporters arrived.

With a practice born of long experience, Melton ignored their barrage of questions, gaining attention with nothing more potent than a smile and a raised eyebrow.

'Well gentlemen,' he began, 'I presume you've picked up another of those dreadful rumours. You've probably heard the Bridgwater investigation is to be scaled down. I have here a prepared statement which I propose to read aloud . . .'

Elsewhere, later that evening, Robert Strudwick's eyes glinted with satisfaction as he listened to an informed voice explain that, despite intense effort, the 'Bridgwater' investigation had been scaled down owing to lack of progress. The woman rang off. Robert replaced the receiver with a satisfied smirk.

Saturday 26 February 2005

BODY IN THE VAULT DEVELOPMENT
HUNT FOR KILLER SCALED DOWN

Reading from a prepared statement, Detective Inspector David Melton CID, the officer heading the Francis Bridgwater murder inquiry, yesterday confirmed that the wide-ranging investigation was to be scaled-down with immediate effect. The inquiry, which began in earnest on February 14 following the accidental discovery of nineteen-year-old Francis' decomposing body in a locked vault beneath Esher's Old Church, was dramatically intensified just seven days ago. 'The first and most important part of an ongoing investigation has been speedily concluded and, as a consequence, certain lines of inquiry have been eliminated. This will enable other elements to proceed unimpeded,' Inspector Melton said. The Inspector paid tribute to a dedicated team of detectives who worked tirelessly for long hours under difficult conditions to produce a satisfactory result in record time. 'I am confident the continuing investigation will culminate with the apprehension of a vicious, ruthless and unbelievably sadistic killer,' he concluded.

Robert Strudwick folded his newspaper, yawned—and pondered the nature of his next mission.

Chapter Twelve

Abducted

Although engaged for almost a year, Steven and Janice had yet to spend a full night together. That apart, 'quality time' together was always at a premium, due largely to Janice's quaintly old-fashioned mother, who knew perfectly well what young lovers got up to—having been there herself—yet didn't consider it 'proper' for her daughter to sleep with Steven 'under her own roof'. A potential solution presented itself early in their relationship—a 'just the two of us' holiday. The subject cropped up often enough, but even though the balance in their joint account grew steadily, a great deal more would be needed if they were to get married and set up home together, and the idea of plundering their savings for the sake of a holiday never entered their heads.

One Saturday in February, however, Janice chanced across a holiday advertisement:

Weekend Mini-hols in London for two!
All-inclusive.
Two nights' overnight luxury hotel accommodation.
Afternoon sightseeing coach tour.
Tickets to a Saturday-night show, choice of three theatres.
Return coach fare: Croydon/Malden/Surbiton/Kingston/Twickenham
Depart 6 p.m. Friday—return 5 p.m. Sunday
Why not treat yourselves? Send for a brochure—now!

Surbiton was awkward to get to by bus, but easy by taxi, and relatively cheap. Janice tore out the page.

'Ace Cars', the only taxi company of substance within the Esher urban district, was based at Long Ditton and, discounting a couple of 'rogue' minicabs, enjoyed a virtual monopoly within the area.

The cars were radio-controlled from a small office on Portsmouth Road by Sylvia Fairweather, a thirty-five-year-old spinster and owner of a business inherited from her father. She soon discovered it barely 'broke even' with a fleet of just three vehicles. Two were somewhat decrepit ex-London taxis and the newest at ten years old was still on extended contract hire.

In a matter of weeks, however, thanks to substantial backing from the Midland Bank, negotiated through their Esher branch, the revitalised business ran a fleet of five modern taxicabs operated by self-employed drivers, whose remuneration was determined as a percentage of their own takings. With commission set at ten per cent of turnover, Sylvia's financial security seemed assured. But, convinced the business would fail should the bank ever decide to call-in her loan, Sylvia was at pains never to offend Calderwood Clough-Cartwright the manager nor, more particularly, his chief clerk, Alfred Strudwick, the man with whom she was normally expected to deal.

Poor gullible Sylvia. She did not realise that most reputable banks would consider financial support for a company such as hers, and although putting up her home as security would be the norm, few would demand she second-mortgage the office premises, garage and workshops, much less insist on retaining the deeds pending full repayment of the loan plus interest. Neither was she aware that, apart from the setting-up and administrative fee, standard interest on outstanding monthly balances was probably the only reward that most would seek to impose.

Her introduction to the Midland came about when she sought advice from local Estate Agent, Gaston Hathaway, when she was considering mortgaging her house in order to raise capital. Naively, she attributed her change of fortune to the kindness of Robert Strudwick, who took trouble to introduce her personally to his father, something for which, she made clear, she would always be grateful. From this a friendship of sorts developed—a friendship Strudwick would use to his advantage.

During June 2001, Strudwick heard that one of Sylvia's drivers reputedly nurtured an unnatural interest in children, and had the man discreetly investigated by a private detective from Richmond. The sleuth earned his fee by discovering that the man, a resident of Gravesend at the time, had been convicted at Maidstone Crown Court in August 1998 on two charges of indecent assault against children, for which he had been fined heavily and sentenced to three months in prison.

Confronted with the evidence that he was a convicted paedophile, who must therefore have falsified references when applying for a Surrey hackney licence, the former felon was easily recruited into Strudwick's ever-expanding informer network. In addition to keeping his 'employer' acquainted with the activities of Sylvia and the other drivers, the man was coerced into the occasional covert trip, without recording details, and, should his cab happen to be 'borrowed' for the odd evening, knew better than to ask questions.

Robert Strudwick was firmly ensconced as a successful estate agent, but fast becoming bored. Since learning that the police had all but abandoned hope of establishing a connection between Bridgwater and an unknown enemy, his interest in that particular investigation had evaporated. Whilst aware Steven Pearce was probably the only medium through which he might be linked with Bridgwater's death, Robert was confident the 'slimy arsehole' would never dare mention his one-time altercations with 'poor departed Francis'—to the police or anybody else. Or was he? For the first time, Strudwick pondered the question and, for a while, felt distinctly uneasy.

But any lingering doubt was dispelled by cold, hard logic. His first major mission had been carefully devised and meticulously carried out and, by their own admission, the police hadn't a single clue. Yet still he craved excitement. Months had passed since the last mission and he longed to be called upon to fulfil another—Steven Pearce and Janice Pearson, perhaps? His wishes were granted when he opened the Book that very evening. Even as he watched, fascinated, the flyleaf shimmered and a message sprang into being:

SEEK VENGEANCE ON THINE ENEMY
AND SHE WHO SPURNED THEE FOR HIM

As on previous occasions, the script blurred, faded and rapidly disappeared.

Strudwick stared unseeing at the blank page whilst he evaluated the message and applied it to the mortal world and the people he most had reason to dislike. It really was quite simple; his fondest hopes were to be fulfilled. Pearce and Pearson were to be the subjects of his next mission.

Although gratified, he nevertheless felt a pang of disappointment. There was nothing in the message to suggest he was to dispose of the hated couple permanently—but wait! In the absence of specific instructions, he was surely free to take revenge in any way he chose. *Janice and Steven*, he mused. It was common knowledge Janice had booked a weekend break in London for Steven and herself; she never tired of talking about it. Might that form part of a plan?

Robert Strudwick smiled. He applied his superior intellect to the question and it wasn't long before Sylvia and her taxis came to mind; he swiftly devised an appropriate and interesting solution. That plan came to fruition at 5.25 p.m. on Friday, 18 March 2005 when a cabdriver tooted his horn outside Janice's house. Excitedly, Janice kissed her mother at the front door.

''Bye Mum, see you Sunday,' she chirruped, and tripped gaily down the path, making light of her suitcase and overnight bag.

'Have a lovely time dear—mind you take care now,' Mrs Pearson called after her daughter. It was the first time her precious Janice would be away from home, and she watched, anxiously, as the driver received the girl's luggage and placed it on the back seat. She nodded her approval when he held the door open for his passenger, before resuming his position at the wheel. With another 'toot' of the horn and a waving of hands, the taxi sped swiftly away.

For the security of the driver—standard equipment in most modern taxicabs—the vehicle was fitted with an electrically-operated, toughened-glass screen, enabling the cabby to isolate at will the rear passenger compartment and passengers. Additionally, a flick of a switch would remotely lock both rear doors for the safety of child passengers, with the added advantage of preventing dodgy fares from trying to abscond without first making payment.

Steven was obliged to work that day and had been refused permission to leave early. But a colleague had promised him a lift to Surbiton and, on the strength of this, he and Janice agreed to meet under the clock at 5.45 p.m. He dealt with the problem of luggage by simply taking it to work with him.

'You won't be late, Stevie darling?' she entreated anxiously. 'We mustn't miss the coach.'

'No worries, Jan,' he replied. 'George won't let me down. I'll be there, have no fear.'

The taxi trundled along Lower Green Road, giving way to oncoming traffic on Station Road before heading across the common towards Hampton Court Way. The driver should have crossed the dual carriageway heading for the Dittons, but turned right, towards the Scilly Isles. Despite the onset of dusk, the girl was quick to notice.

'Why are you going the wrong way?' she demanded. 'This isn't the way to Surbiton station and I have to be there before six. What the heck do you think you're playing at?'

'S'orl right miss, just a slight detour,' the man replied, reassuringly. 'I bin tole there's a burst water-main jus' along Victoria Road, so I'm finkin' it'd be better 'f we go the bypass way.'

'First I've heard of it, and anyway, there isn't time. Our coach leaves dead on six. Take the next left onto Portsmouth Road,' she ordered. 'Go through Long Ditton. Take the second right past the reservoir. Turn left,' she shouted, 'left, left—now!'

But instead of turning onto the A308, the driver made for the second roundabout and took the first exit right across Littleworth Common, accelerating hard in the direction of Claygate.

'What do you think you're doing? Where are you taking me?' she cried, becoming alarmed.

He made no reply. The girl heard the whine of an electric motor and the glass screen dividing the passenger compartment from that of the driver slid upwards and thudded into the closed position. Frightened, Janice tugged the door handles—locked. She felt for a window-winder—there were none. *Electrically-operated windows and doors! God, I've got to get out. The bastard means to rape me!*

Their headlights illuminated the road ahead; it was becoming dark. If only she could attract someone's attention. But the gorse-fringed road didn't even have a footpath. What's more, whilst the tinted windows allowed her to see out, they were designed to ensure the passenger's privacy, rendering it unlikely she would attract attention, even in full daylight.

There was no means of escape, even if the cab should stop. Janice realised she was trapped! She fought back an impulse to scream—nobody but the driver would hear her anyway. What should she do? What *could* she do? Much afraid, the girl nevertheless pressed her nose to the glass and tried to identify their whereabouts and route, but it was already too dark so see much.

Abruptly, the cab left the main road, and twisted and turned so much she was forced to concede she was hopelessly lost. *Oh, Stevie darling, what about our holiday?* Janice fought back her tears. She peered at the luminous dial of her watch: 5.35. They had been travelling for barely ten minutes.

They passed through a series of unfamiliar lanes, until the driver slowed and swung into a winding, tree-lined driveway. After some eighty metres, a house came within range of the headlights. There were no welcoming lights, no sign of life—the place seemed deserted. The vehicle slowed to a crawl. *Where are we? Why has he brought me here?*

There came a crunch of gravel, whereupon the driver swung the cab round in little more than it's own length, coming to a halt facing the way they had come. She scarcely noticed that the engine was still running.

'Where is this? What are you going to do?' she shouted, banging the screen with her fist.

Ignoring her, the driver pulled his cap down over his eyes and got out. *God, he's coming for me!* Menacingly—or so it seemed—he opened the rear passenger door. Janice couldn't help but cringe.

'You get out here,' he ordered. 'Come on, hurry up!'

I'm frightened! What is he going to do? Fearing she was about to be raped—killed, possibly—Janice remained seated, too petrified to move.

'Get out, you stupid cow,' he growled, 'I ain't got all bleedin' night!'

Janice recovered her voice. 'What for? Where are you taking me? Why are you doing this?'

Ignoring her protests, he dragged her out of the vehicle and pushed her roughly to one side. Without speaking, he snatched her cases from the back seat and threw them to the ground, got back behind the wheel and drove away, leaving the terrified girl alone in almost total darkness.

Casting about, Janice located the house, vaguely outlined against a leaden sky. Hurriedly picking up her luggage, she set off towards the road, feeling her way by means of the gravel underfoot, but after a few faltering paces, she was violently grabbed from behind. Her bags went flying and, unable to resist, she was forcibly propelled in the direction of the house.

Janice could hardly breathe. A powerful arm encircled her neck in a vicious half-nelson and a brutal hand clamped firmly over her mouth preventing her from screaming. She was shoved roughly through a door into a dank interior, poorly lit by a paraffin lantern.

A voice snarled hoarsely in her ear, 'I'm going to take my hands away and when I do, put your hands behind your back—quietly, or I'll slit your throat right here and now.'

His voice seemed vaguely familiar. The sincerity of the threat, however, was unmistakable.

Janice obeyed, and her hands were promptly secured.

'In case you decide to scream . . .'

A gag was shoved across her mouth and tied behind her neck. A blindfold swiftly followed and Janice was manhandled across the room, down steep steps and shoved ignominiously to the floor and into a sitting position. Sensing his proximity, she cringed when her captor bent to fasten her ankles together.

'That's you fixed nicely,' the man said. 'Just keep still—and remember, I'll be watching!'

Meanwhile, at Surbiton station, Steven fidgeted. It was 5.43 p.m. and Janice had yet to arrive. Their coach was due to depart in a little over ten minutes. Assuming she had left home as arranged, she should surely have arrived by now, so where was she? After all, the journey was relatively short—no more than six or seven minutes, ten at the most. Anxiously, he checked his watch against the station clock.

Five more minutes ticked inexorably by with still no sign of Janice. Steven began to pace to and fro anxiously—six steps this way, six that, keeping within metres of the rendezvous. *Damn, if only I had my mobile with me.*

There were public telephones the other side of the concourse, however. *If she's not here soon I'll ring her Mum and ask what's happened.* But at 5.48, a taxi drew into the forecourt.

'Thank goodness!' Steven exclaimed aloud.

He picked up his luggage, crossed to the vehicle and peered through the tinted glass windows. His heart sank: there were no passengers on board.

'You Steven Pearce?' the driver inquired gruffly, through a partially lowered window.

'Yes. Where's Miss Pearson? What's going on?' Steven demanded in agitation. 'Where's my fiancée?'

'Calm down sir—please! I've bin sent ter collect yer. Miss Pearson met with a haccident an needs yer hurgently. Jump in, I'll take yer.'

'What's happened to Janice? Where is she?' Steven repeated, anger forgotten.

'Don' know no more than wot I've already tole yer,' the driver answered. 'I'm jus' takin' yer to where she's bein' looked arter till the hambulance arrives.'

Unhesitatingly, he scrambled aboard the vehicle, which moved smartly away the instant he slammed the door. The journey lasted around ten minutes and was conducted in silence, Steven accepting that the driver was simply following instructions. Such was his anxiety, he was not in the least suspicious and took no particular notice of the route by which they travelled.

'Nearly there, guv,' the driver ventured, as they entered a long gravelled driveway leading to a rather ramshackle house, although Steven scarcely noticed.

The cabbie gestured towards the front door, starkly illuminated by the glare of his headlights.

'She's bin took inside out of the cold, guv. I was told to tell yer it's OK ter go straight in.'

'Thanks. Wait for me please,' Steven said, and leapt from the cab. The vehicle moved forward and started to turn—in readiness to depart, Steven supposed—and plunged the house into darkness, forcing him to moderate his headlong dash. Picking his way, Steven reached the entrance without incident and pushed wide the unlatched door. Hesitantly, not bothering to knock, he fumbled his way inside.

The hallway smelt musty and was in pitch darkness. He heard no sound, other than the beat of his own heart. *Where could Janice be?* The hairs at the nape of his neck stiffened. Beside himself with concern, confused and bewildered, he simply couldn't understand.

'Janice! Janice! Where are you?' he called.

His only answer was the muffled echo of his own voice. Yet still he had no inkling of danger. Cautiously, Steven shuffled forward a couple of paces. Suddenly, there came a brilliant flash of light, a loud roaring in his ears, a violent pain inside his head and he knew no more. Steven slumped to the floor unconscious, felled by a single blow to the back of the skull, delivered by the man who had waited behind the door, truncheon raised in readiness.

Muffled footsteps somewhere above her head preceded the thud of a door, followed by silence for perhaps fifteen or twenty minutes. It was difficult to assess the passage of time in total darkness.

The sounds from overhead were different now. There was an indistinct 'thud', shuffling footsteps and slithery noises that sounded like a bag of potatoes being dragged across a floor. Unmistakably, a door opened and, much louder, came a series of hollow bumping sounds, as if that same sack of potatoes was being manhandled down a flight of stairs—in her direction. She heard grunts of exertion, scraping sounds, another thud, a groan and a long, drawn-out sigh. The footsteps retreated, a door slammed, more footsteps and a second door thudded—distant, less distinct. Then silence once more—except that if she held her breath and listened carefully, she could just make out the soft, steady sound of someone breathing. Janice was not alone! Petrified, she kept as still as a mouse, hardly daring to breathe. *What if. . .?* But her captor was gone.

Time passed and were it not for the need to shift regularly to ease discomfort Janice may well have drifted into sleep. She had no idea whether two hours or twenty had passed since she had been abducted. But the poor girl was obliged to relieve herself—twice, maybe three times. In all probability, the period of incarceration had already exceeded twenty-four hours.

Throbbing pain rose and fell in intensity, each peak serving to bring consciousness a little closer. The process was gradual, for the mind will always prolong the comatose state in the event of serious head injury, giving nature's healing processes sufficient time to effect repairs.

The girl's companion in confinement groaned softly. Janice stiffened. It sounded as if it was Steven! The groan came again, and this time she was almost certain. Cursing the gag, Janice tried to speak, but 'Mmmm! Mmmm!' was all she could manage. Janice abandoned the effort. Taking strength from the thought that it really might be Steven whose breath she could hear, she thereafter contented herself with listening. Time passed and Steven gradually regained his senses.

At first, he found himself the victim of a thundering headache which seemed to alternate in potency, the pain tending to fall away then increase in intensity until it became almost unbearable. He remained still, shrewdly suspecting that to do otherwise would make matters worse. Eventually, he tried to open his eyes, but saw nothing but blackness. Exhausted, he decided to rest for a while, vaguely aware he was propped against a wall. The headache persisted, but the longer he waited, the less intense it became. As time passed, he came to realise his arms and legs were numb, his backside sore and he positively ached all over.

Seeking relief, Steven wriggled painfully, and managed to relieve the pressure on his lower spine. But attempts to coax movement from lifeless arms and legs failed, and only now did it register that both his wrists and ankles were securely pinioned. Dammit! He was trussed up like a chicken. Another revelation followed. In attempting to take a deep breath, he discovered he was gagged.

Slowly, memory returned. Surbiton bus station ... taxi ... accident ... Janice? ... *Janice!* He struggled to free himself—get up—find Janice—anything! But, giddy and weakened he desisted. He groaned, panted through his nose and, after a while, felt a little better. *Sit still, you silly pillock*, he told himself. *Save your bloody energy.*

What was that? Janice pricked up her ears. After ages and ages, that sound again—*Steven?*

'Mmmm—Mmmm—Mmmm.' She did her best to articulate—and, amazingly, Steven heard her.

'Glur—Nind?' He tried desperately to respond. *Jan, Janice!* he shouted, but only inside his head. *It's no use. Even if it* is *Jan, I can't make her understand.* He slumped against the wall, defeated.

Was it Steven? Perhaps! Janice recognised the futility of struggling and didn't try again. The hours drifted painfully by.

2100, Saturday 19th March 2005

A white XJS left Kenward Close and headed for a secluded, five-bedroomed house standing in seven acres of woodland on the outskirts of Claygate. The house, formerly the home of an elderly recluse, had been bought covertly by Strudwick the previous year when Gaston Hathaway were invited by the executors to market the property 'For Sale and Renovation'. Undoubtedly a sound investment, it would make a tidy profit when put to rights and re-marketed, but in the meantime would provide an excellent mission venue, with ample disposal opportunities right on the doorstep and well away from prying eyes.

Nearing his destination, Strudwick killed the headlights, negotiated the driveway on head and tail only and parked well out of sight to the side and rear of the house. Armed with a flashlight, he patted his jacket to confirm an essential item of equipment was in place, vacated the car, remotely locked the doors and set the alarm system. After a careful reconnaissance to make sure nothing had been disturbed in his absence, he let himself in through the front door.

After interminable hours with only the rhythmic sigh of breathing for company, there came the 'thud' of a distant door, muffled footsteps overhead—then, for a little while, silence again. The securely trussed prisoners, each gagged and one wearing a blindfold, confined in darkness within a dank cellar for over twenty-four hours, cold, filthy, hungry, thirsty, stiffened at the sound, before lapsing again into dreamlike apathy. But when the door opened and someone came down the steps, both instantly became alert.

Steven closed his eyes to avoid the dazzle of a lantern, while Janice sat as upright as she could and wondered hopefully whether rescue was at hand. The newcomer suspended the lantern from a convenient nail and turned to face Steven.

'Hello arsehole,' he drawled. 'Fancy seeing *you* here—sucker!' Janice froze. That voice—Why hadn't she recognised it before? *Robert Strudwick!* She shivered. Steven's eyes bulged: *Robert Strudwick!* The taxi, this cellar; it all made sense. *Janice!*

Even though his eyes had become accustomed to the light, the poor illumination barely reached the other side of the dingy cellar, but the instant his eyes encountered the figure seated almost directly opposite, he had no difficulty in recognising the slender, adorable girl he'd known and loved almost from the moment he'd first clapped eyes on her.

Steven reasoned furiously. Why abduct them both? He realised he represented a threat to Strudwick's freedom, but the bastard knew he'd never breathe a word. *Does the evil swine mean to silence me after all, even though he knows I'd never grass? But what about Janice? She knows nothing!*

His mouth was covered, but perhaps his eyes were too expressive. Strudwick grinned knowingly.

'You may well wonder, shit-features,' he mocked. 'You've been a pain in the arse for years, and now I'm going to fix you once and for all, you *and* your bloody tart. But first—a little fun.'

He turned up the lantern-wick for maximum illumination, looked around the cellar and spotted an old wooden bench adjacent to the rear wall.

'Ah,' he grunted in evident satisfaction and, righting it, he dragged it nearer the centre beneath the lantern. He took off his jacket, folded it and placed it on the end of the bench, unbuckled the sheath beneath his armpit and withdrew a fearsome-looking cook's knife.

Steven watched with horror. Long convinced that Strudwick was crazy and probably capable of murder, he was already half out of his mind with fear—not only for himself, but for Janice. Strudwick tested the keenness of the weapon with his thumb, turning it this way and that so as to reflect the lantern-light directly into his prisoner's eyes.

He laid both knife and sheath side by side on top of the coat, and moved across to Janice.

Janice! What does the bastard want with Janice? Steven struggled furiously, but his bonds were cruelly tight, and he was obliged to desist.

Sensing Steven's disquiet, Strudwick turned. 'Huff, puff and fart till you shit yourself for all I care,' he ground out, scornfully. '*You're* going nowhere, you miserable arsehole, but before I slit your fucking throat I've some unfinished business with *this* bloody trollop!'

He kicked at Janice's foot, angrily. His violent words filled the girl with terror and she too struggled to get free.

'Oho!' Strudwick exclaimed. 'Unhappy with the way I've tied you up, is that it? Well, what a shame. Perhaps I'd better do something about it.'

He reached for the knife, waved it at Steven—who almost choked behind his gag, stooped, and with a single stroke, sliced cleanly through the bonds securing Janice's ankles. Strudwick stood back expectantly, but the girl didn't move. She either failed to comprehend or didn't even realise her legs had been freed.

'Shift your arse, you silly cow,' he barked impatiently. 'Stand up. Your feet are untied. Come on, you bitch, get up and turn around and I'll undo your hands.'

Behind the gag, Janice bit her lip. *What does he want? What does he mean to do? Stevie, help me, darling. I'm frightened!*

'Hurry up, sod you. I've got a knife. Get a bloody move on or I'll stick it up your boyfriend's arse.'

Bravely, Janice tried to comply. With her back pressed against the wall, she pushed with her feet and managed to lift herself a little, but having precious little feeling below her waist, she flopped painfully back to the floor, close to tears and even more terrified.

Exasperated, Strudwick snorted, but restoring her to full mobility was essential to the plan, so he reached out and hauled her to her feet. Effortlessly, he spun her round and severed the bonds securing her wrists. Propping her against the wall, he waited to make sure she wasn't about to lose her footing.

'Rub your wrists hard, then your legs,' he commanded. 'I want you in decent working order!'

He stood back and watched impassively as the frightened girl hastened to obey. Satisfied, for the moment at least, he turned his attention to Steven.

'Now do you get the drift, shit-features?' he asked, with a dreadful, meaningful leer. Steven's eyes widened in comprehension. 'Yep, you've got it in one. A pillock like you wouldn't recognise a decent fuck if it kicked you in the bollocks, so I'll give her a good shagging for you. Watch carefully, arsehole, and I'll show you how it *should* be done!'

He turned back to Janice and swiftly removed her blindfold.

'Get your gear off, you bitch—every stitch. Quickly! We mustn't keep boyfriend waiting!' Steven's eyes flashed with anger and disgust. *You filthy bastard!* But he was powerless to intervene.

Petrified with fear and loathing, Janice was unable to move.

Strudwick exploded with rage. He leapt across the cellar, lunged at Steven with the knife and shouted at Janice, 'You've got twenty seconds to strip, you bitch, or I'll cut his fucking throat!'

Fumbling with leaden fingers, tears spilling down her face and soaking the gag, she pulled her blouse over her head, loosened and stepped out of her skirt, took off her bodice and removed her brassiere. Finally, she slowly peeled down her stockings and stepped out of her panties. Completely naked, she faced her tormentor.

Steven agonised. *Some day, you bastard,* he promised himself, *some day!*

Strudwick positioned himself in front of the girl—a little sideways, so as not to block Steven's view—then, deliberately and suggestively, unzipped his fly to expose himself. Soaking in the beauty of the girl who once had surrendered herself to him unreservedly, he reached out to her breasts and fondled her intimately, whilst rubbing himself vigorously in an attempt to trigger arousal.

But Janice was scarcely at her best. She stank of urine, her hair was matted and, with a gag across her mouth, she seemed singularly unattractive. His efforts failed to produce the desired result and it wasn't long before Strudwick gave up in disgust.

'Put your kit back on, you dirty, stinking bitch,' he snarled. 'I don't want you; I never wanted you. I didn't fancy you in the first place, if you must know. It was simply your availability.'

While the relieved girl got dressed, Strudwick returned the knife to its sheath and shrugged back into the harness. He fastened the straps and put his jacket back on.

'I've had just about all I can stand of you pair of shits for one day,' he said, almost cheerfully. 'You think a lot of one another, obviously, so I've decided to do you both a big favour . . .'

He broke off, produced two lengths of cord from his pocket and used one to refasten Janice's wrists.

He shoved her roughly to the floor and retied her ankles.

'You won't be needing this any more.' He grinned and, removing her gag, laughed. 'It doesn't matter if you scream your bloody head off, morning, noon and night—nobody will hear. And what about you, lover boy?' he chortled gleefully, crossing the cellar to Steven. 'You'd enjoy a nice long chat with smelly little shag-nasty, wouldn't you?'

He bent and ripped Steven's gag from his face with a vicious tug. 'Why am I being so kind? Simple. I intend to shut both of you up permanently, but instead of slitting your throats I've a much better idea!'

He rubbed his hands together in satisfaction.

'I'm no spoilsport,' he sniggered. 'You seem to enjoy each other's company, so I've decided to let you spend your last days together. Don't worry, you won't be disturbed. The house is empty and miles from anywhere, and I'll lock it securely when I leave. Of course, you will remain tied up.' He crossed to each in turn and checked their bonds.

'Sorry, no tea or biscuits, I'm afraid, but I'll leave the lamp, it's nearly empty. Don't bother getting up, I'll see myself out.'

Stunned by the ferocity of Strudwick's revelations, the hapless couple looked at one another in dismay as he ascended the cellar steps and slammed the door. Two bolts rammed home and they listened to the sound of retreating footsteps, the muffled 'thud' of what was presumably the front door being slammed shut—then silence. Tears welled up in Janice's eyes and she began to sob bitterly. It was more than Steven could bear.

'Please—don't cry Jan,' he begged, close to tears himself. 'Chin up, Pet. With that damn nutter out of the way, let's see about getting ourselves out of here.'

Aching to comfort her, Steven began to shuffle and 'caterpillar' across the cellar on his bottom. The action seemed so comical that, despite the horror of their predicament, Janice couldn't help but smile.

'I'm sorry, Stevie, but you do look ridiculous, and I'm frightened in case you hurt your bum.'

Grunting with exertion, he smiled briefly, but persevered.

'Don't care,' he retorted, happy she was cheered a little. 'S'only me kecks and a bit of skin.'

Moving surprisingly quickly, he manoeuvred alongside and contrived to comfort her with a kiss.

'Turn sideways, sweetheart,' he said. 'Let's see if we can undo our wrists. I'll have a go first.'

Each with a shoulder against the wall for support, they tried in turn to loosen the knots but, despite their best efforts, neither could make the slightest impression. Even if it had been somehow possible for them to see what they were doing, numb fingers and painfully tight lashings would still have rendered it an almost impossible task. Reluctantly they were forced to give up.

They cast around for something against which to rub through their bonds, but there was nothing. The lamp flared, guttered briefly, flickered and went out, and after a while Janice fell into a fitful sleep, her head resting against Steven's shoulder . . .

Chapter Thirteen

Missing Persons

After an indeterminate period of uneasy sleep, Janice awoke, immediately and painfully aware. Scarcely able to move, the frightened girl groaned and burst into tears.

'Oh, Stevie, what are we to do?' she sobbed. 'I want to go home. I'm so thirsty, I'm cold, I hurt all over and my bottom's red raw.'

Manfully, but with difficulty, Steven did his best to raise her spirits.

'I know Jan, same here. But cheer up, Strudwick's only doing this to frighten us. It's his idea of a joke. He'll be back before you know it, laughing his stupid socks off—but even if he *did* mean what he said about leaving us here,' he added, 'someone's bound to come looking. You'll see.'

Knowing Strudwick as she did Janice remained unconvinced, but for Steven's sake she brightened.

'Do you really think so? I can't wait to get home. I'll wash my hair, have a long, hot soak in the bath—and then for a lovely hot dinner.'

'That's my girl!' Steven declared, trying to sound positive. He tried to kiss her, but failed to make contact when, with a muffled sob, she turned away in the darkness. It seemed a deliberate rebuff and, unwilling to risk another, he didn't try again.

The cellar floor was wet with urine, cold and unbearably hard, forcing the pinioned sweethearts to change position frequently to ameliorate, to some extent at least, the agony of immobilised limbs. Helping one another, they contrived to lower themselves to the floor and lay hunched together in the foetal position, hoping to gain some respite and perhaps even snatch a little sleep. But, far from finding relief, their securely tied hands and feet rendered lying down even more uncomfortable, and it required a sustained effort for them to regain their former positions.

Miserable and in pain, the couple languished in the dark and waited for rescue.

Driving home, Strudwick congratulated himself on the success of a mission which would result in painful, lingering deaths for the hated pair instead of relatively merciful release by means of the knife. Later, at his leisure, he would remove the stinking remains to a suitable location in the dense woodland surrounding the house, thereby putting the finishing touches to another insoluble mystery.

But by Sunday, the serial assassin was having second thoughts. What if the devious pair of shits managed to escape and contacted the police? Or suppose an itinerant burglar stumbled across the property, broke in and discovered the couple? It seemed unlikely, but perhaps he should return to check all was well. Yes, that was it. He might even contrive to be on hand when the couple died; he'd particularly enjoy the death throes of Steven Pearce, the snivelling pile of dog crap.

Robert went to his room to ponder the pleasing prospect when a voice in his mind intervened: *Why dost neglect Pentophiles, thy friend and protector?* Having heard nothing from the being in months, Strudwick was taken by surprise.

'I h-haven't n-neglected you,' he stuttered, idiotically. 'It—it's ages since you've spoken to *me.*'

Have care, Robert William Strudwick, the voice warned, ominously. *Bandy not words ere cause annoyance. Hast dared entertain revenge without regard for Pentophiles? What sayest thou?*

'I thought—I didn't think—the Book. What do you wish me to do?' Strudwick quavered. *Have regard my special preferences,* the unseen being thundered. *KILL! BLOOD! KILL!* The voice tailed away.

'But . . .' Robert began, then realised the entity had already departed.

Uneasily he sat, loathe to tinker with a mission running to plan, a plan devised through careful thought, within guidelines stipulated by the Book, but he grudgingly accepted that to exclude the wishes and desires of Pentophiles was hardly an option. But for Pearce and Pearson he had devised punishment entirely appropriate—that they should continue to enjoy one another's company a while longer. Ever cautious, he checked the Book and was gratified to find no further instructions waiting. He put the matter out of his mind for the time being and retired for the night.

0915, Monday 21st March, 2005: Police HQ, Surbiton

As David Melton replaced the telephone receiver, his eye was drawn to 'Pending', wherein reposed, among other, less challenging matters, *two* unsolved murder files.

Peremptorily, he rapped the glass partition and beckoned his assistant.

'I've just had Sergeant Stapleton on the phone,' Melton told him. 'Would you believe? Another Missing Persons on our patch?'

O'Connor frowned. *What the hell's special about that?*

'Sorry sir, but doesn't it happen all the time?'

'Not when it involves *two* missing persons in one hit it doesn't, nor if they've gone missing from Esher and *especially* from *Lower Green*, no less.'

'You don't suppose? We're not off again, are we?'

Melton nodded grimly.

'It's looking a lot like it, I'm afraid. You see, one of them just happens to be Steven Pearce, the other his fiancée, Janice Pearson.'

O'Connor's eyebrows ascended like rockets.

'The Pennington murder!' he exclaimed. 'The anorak and trainers, the young man we questioned to the limit; who probably knew more about the killer than he chose to admit...' Indignantly, he added, 'Damned if I know why we didn't keep a closer eye on him.'

'The very same,' Melton replied. 'And for your information, Sergeant, we *did* keep an eye on him. To ensure secrecy and with the Chief Super's approval, he was under surveillance by undercover men seconded from Essex. I chose not to advertise the fact, but I thought you might have guessed.'

'Bait sir?'

'Yes, but when nothing untoward happened, the Chief Super downgraded the risk to "minimal".'

'You kept that one pretty dark, sir. I really hadn't a clue. When did the couple disappear?'

'Yesterday—well Friday, to be precise,' Melton replied. 'Stapleton is filing a report, naturally, but the name "Steven Pearce" rang a bell and knowing of our interest he thought it important enough to ring me personally.

'It appears Steven and his young lady went to London for the weekend. Janice left Lower Green by taxi just before five-thirty on Friday to meet up with Steven at Surbiton station. Their coach was due at six and to save time, apparently, he took his luggage to work with him having organised a lift to Surbiton from a workmate.

'The couple were due back at Surbiton at five yesterday evening and when six o'clock rolled round and they hadn't put in an appearance, Janice's mother rang the travel company to find out whether the coach was delayed. They informed her the coach had completed its journey on time.

'She then rang Steven's mother, thinking perhaps the couple had stopped by to visit. This alarmed Mrs Pearce, who had assumed the couple were at Janice's home, and agreed the Pearsons should ring the police should the youngsters fail to make contact reasonably soon. Janice's parents agonised until eight o'clock, praying their daughter would arrive or at least ring, whereupon Mr Pearson finally contacted Esher 'nick' at eight-ten, when Sergeant Stapleton took the call.'

'Do you think Malandra Pennington's killer could be behind this?'

The possibility hadn't escaped Melton, who had long felt a solution tantalisingly close, but couldn't fathom exactly how or for what reason.

'Could be, Sergeant—possibly Bridgwater's too—always assuming the two cases *are* connected.' Melton glared at 'Pending', wishing it was possible to magic away the unwelcome contents. 'But unfortunately,' he sighed, 'it'll take more than supposition to be rid of *those* two files.'

He rose to his feet. These were obvious and compelling reasons for initiating a full investigation.

'But first things first, Sergeant,' the Detective Inspector cautioned. 'There could be a simple explanation and we must check the possibilities before jumping to conclusions. One or the other, perhaps both, may have been involved in an accident, for example, and might be lying in hospital. They may even have decided to stay over without telling anyone. Youngsters *can* be rather thoughtless, you know.

'In any event we deal in facts, and there's little we can do until a few have been established. First of all, get someone to ring all major London hospitals. Once that's under way, ring Mrs Pearson, no doubt she'll be worried. Give her my regards and tell her we'll do everything we can to find Janice and her fiancé. Find out as much as you can regarding that weekend break and try to establish the couple's itinerary.

'And ask her about the taxi. It would either have been a minicab or a cab from Ace. In either event, get somebody to trace the driver in case he or she noticed anything out of the ordinary.'

Melton smiled and nodded meaningfully at 'Pending'.

'I've got a "feeling in my water" about this. The day we ship those files to Records might be nearer. When we do, it'll be worth more than a swift half on the way home, my lad. I'll buy you the bloody bucketful. Now, get a flaming move on and report back a.s.a.p. I'm off to brief the Chief Super.'

At 10.30, DS O'Connor tapped on DI Melton's door. His appearance was sombre.

'Not good news I'm afraid,' he began. 'That weekend break; Mrs Pearson gave me the details.' The DS referred to his notebook. 'The couple were booked on an all-inclusive weekend for two with Cosmopolitan Coaches, a travel-firm trading from Battersea. The package included return fare from a number of pickup points, including Surbiton, two nights hotel accommodation at Wimbledon's Claré del Ortega, tickets for a Saturday-night show and an afternoon's conducted coach-trip around London. It seems Janice booked about a fortnight ago.'

He paused to rub his nose.

'Well, sir, I got the number from Mrs Pearson and rang Cosmopolitan. They confirm the booking, but say neither Mr Pearce nor Miss Pearson checked in. The coach left Surbiton on time, sir, but with two of the seats vacant.'

'Damn! People don't just disappear. Someone knows something, that's for sure. What about the taxi? Any luck there?'

O'Connor looked through the glass screen into the office beyond.

'I sent Graham Gibson to look into that one, Guv'nor. That's him just coming in.'

'Fetch him in here.'

O'Connor went out, buttonholed DC Gibson and returned with the latter in tow.

THE FLYLEAF KILLER

'DC Gibson managed to locate the taxi driver, sir,' O'Connor announced.

'Good morning, Gibson. Glad to hear you found the driver. Well done! What did he have to say?'

Gibson consulted his notes.

'Ace operates from Portsmouth Road, Long Ditton. The owner, a Mrs Fairweather, co-operated. She must have a bloody good memory, begging your pardon, sir. She didn't check a sheet, look in a book or anything, but knew exactly which driver picked Miss Pearson up. That struck me as unusual, sir. I mean, they *are* pretty busy, especially at weekends.

'Anyway, the man's name is Dyson—Henry Dyson, she said—and she called him in by radio. He was nearby, as it happened, in line at Surbiton station waiting his turn for a fare.

'Five minutes later, sir, in he rolled. Ordinary sort of bloke, early thirties I'd say, but a bit shifty, if you know what I mean. Medium build, dark hair, spoke with a heavy cockney accent. I told him who I was and asked him if he remembered picking up a Miss Pearson from Lower Green on Friday evening, and he said:' (Gibson read from his notes) ' "Yus mate, I remember, pretty little tart. Picked 'er up about 'arf pass five and took 'er ter Surbiton station. Dropped her orf abaht twenny-five ter six; 'ad a couple of soot-cases, she did." That's about as close as I can get to the way he spoke, sir.'

'That's OK, Constable,' Melton was amused 'You sounded practically cockney yourself.'

Gibson blushed.

'To be perfectly honest, sir, I doubt whether he *is* a cockney. His accent seemed too contrived and he didn't always drop his aitches. That's the reason I've done my best to imitate him.'

'I understand. Well done, constable. As I always say, what may seem a minor point at the time can become vital evidence later. We could do with more like you. Get your report in as soon as you can.'

'Just how busy are you, Sergeant?' Melton asked, once Gibson had departed.

'So so, sir—why? Have you something particular in mind?'

'Yes, I have, and it concerns Steven Pearce. If you remember, he works at Hadfields, Long Ditton. I'd like you track down the workmate who gave Steven a lift to the station. His mother might know who it was, but in any event, nip round to the factory and ask a few questions. Get the "OK" from the manager first, naturally.

'Find the fellow, put him at ease, but get his particulars—he might be needed as a witness, and ask him to confirm he actually *did* take Steven to the station, exactly where he dropped him off and at what time, as accurately as possible. Ask him whether he noticed anything out of the ordinary. Was Steven intercepted, for example? Did anything happen the slightest bit unusual at the time, or seemed even remotely peculiar in retrospect?

'Time is of the essence, Sergeant. If "chummy" *is* behind this, then with barely two days head-start instead of weeks, or even months . . .' Melton looked at his watch. 'Ten fifty. If you get yourself back before lunch, I just might buy you a coffee.'

'OK, Guv'nor, you're on,' O'Connor said, getting to his feet. '*Anything* for a cardboard sarnie!'

O'Connor was back in good time for his reward. 'The chap's name is George Watson, Guv'nor,' the DS announced. 'He didn't take much finding. Mrs Pearce gave me his name. Apparently George is a close friend of Steven's.

'The manager had Watson paged and gave me the loan of his office. Mr Watson seemed shocked to learn of Steven's disappearance. Said it was the first he'd heard about it.

'But he was emphatic about having taken him to Surbiton on Friday. He says he pulled into the station forecourt at five-thirty on the dot and helped carry Steven's cases into the booking hall where he was due to meet Janice. Significantly, he noted the time, said goodbye to Steven and drove home for tea.'

Leaving his assistant to organise coffee and sandwiches, Melton made a telephone call.

'I've arranged a Press briefing for sixteen hundred hours,' he informed O'Connor on his return. 'I believe Steven and his lady friend are in danger. We can't rely on luck, nor can we afford to shilly-shally. We need media assistance, and we need it quickly.

'I'm going to brief the Chief Super. I'll explain the position as we see it and get the OK to revive public interest in the Malandra Pennington and Francis Bridgwater murders by suggesting all three cases could be linked. Keep the pot on the boil, sonny. I'll be back as soon as I can.'

Twenty minutes later he paused by O'Connor's desk.

'Permission granted, Ben. We're to appeal. Anyone who saw Steven or Janice at, in or around Surbiton station on Friday, 18th March 2005 will be asked to come forward. Mr Jarvis also suggests a second appeal for information regarding any unusual incidents within a radius of ten miles of Esher at any time of the day or night between mid-November and early December 2004. Get your jumbo crayon out Ben. You can draft the appeals while I catch up with routine.'

1600: Briefing Room, Police HQ, Surbiton.

There were familiar faces among the double row of reporters facing Detective Inspector David Melton, most of whom he had greeted by name as they arrived. The significance of further missing persons from Esher was immediately grasped by the majority.

Melton suggested a possible link with the murders of Malandra Pennington and Francis Bridgwater, and a copy of the prepared release was handed to each reporter at the close of the meeting. It read:

SURREY CONSTABULARY—SURBITON DIVISION
PRESS RELEASE No. 7486
Monday, 21 March 2005

The following have been reported missing and relatives are anxious to trace their whereabouts:

STEVEN VINCENT PEARCE Born 29:4:84. Height: 5 ft. 6 ins. Weight: 10 st. 12 lbs. Hair: Brown. Eyes: Grey. Complexion: Fair.

No visible distinguishing marks. Last seen wearing a dark-blue 'Bomber' jacket, light-coloured shirt, grey trousers and black shoes.

JANICE ANN PEARSON Born 15:4:85. Height: 4 ft 11¾ ins. Weight: 7 st. 3 lbs. Hair: Dark brown. Eyes: Brown. Complexion: Pale.

Last seen wearing a bottle-green blouse, grey skirt and brown shoes, Janice left her Lower Green home by taxi at 5.25 p.m. on Friday 18 March 2005 and allegedly arrived at Surbiton station about 5.40 where she was to meet Steven, her fiancé, prior to the couple leaving by coach for a weekend in London.

Anybody who saw either Janice or Steven between 5.30 and 6.00 p.m. on the above date is asked to telephone the special Incident Room number on 0208 112 8484 or contact any police station.

It is believed the disappearance of Steven and Janice may be connected with the murder in July 2002 of eighteen-year-old Malandra Pennington, whose dismembered remains were uncovered in a local garden, and also that of Francis Bridgwater, aged 19, on or around the end of November last year. Francis' corpse remained undetected in a vault beneath St. George's Church, Esher until last month.

Additionally, anyone who has information regarding any unusual or suspicious incident within a ten-mile radius of Esher at any time of the day or night between mid-November and early December should also come forward.

All information will be treated as strictly confidential and informants will not be required to identify themselves if they prefer not to do so.

The couple's disappearance was reported in the late final edition of the *Evening News*, and Thames Television broadcast the appeals during the six o'clock and ten o'clock news.

At 10.40, a Claygate viewer sneered, switched off the television and retired to bed.

Public response was encouraging. Incident Room telephones started to ring shortly after the six o'clock news, and continued sporadically overnight and throughout Tuesday. Despite a plethora of patently spurious sightings and claims, a credible number survived initial screening to merit further investigation. All such reports were channelled to DI Melton, who took personal responsibility for ensuring no scrap of potential evidence was disregarded.

It was tedious, discouraging work and fruitless hours were spent chasing prospective leads until, finally, Melton and O'Connor went home, tired, late—and extremely disappointed . . .

And at the end of a particularly heavy day, Strudwick bathed, dined and went to bed early. Exhausted, confounding habit, he simply couldn't be bothered to confer with the Book.

He slept badly and woke late, tired and ill-tempered. To compound his discomfort, a raging headache came on as soon as he set foot on the floor. Miserably, he sat on the side of the bed supporting his head in his hands. The last thing on his mind was the couple in the cellar. *Mind'st thou Pentophiles, thy mentor and friend, who yet awaiteth, hunger unquenched!*

'Leave me alone,' he shouted. 'I'll do what you want when I'm fucking-well good and ready!' Appalled by his own stupidity, he was immediately, abjectly contrite.

'S-sorry,' he stuttered. 'I'm so very, very sorry. Of course I'll do as you ask whenever you like.'

But the apology either failed to register or was ignored; the voice in his head was gone. Desperately, he tried to persuade the entity to re-communicate, but to no avail.

'Sod you, then,' he snarled, angrily. 'If you can't be civil, why should I bother? Get bloody stuffed!'

Without stopping for breakfast, he banged out of the house still seething. Even now, it didn't occur to Strudwick that he might be courting disaster, nor was he in the least concerned that he had retired the previous evening without having first consulted the Book. Curiously, however, and in response to a persistent sense of foreboding, he resolved to pack his bags immediately, and keep them packed, in readiness to skip town at short notice should it become necessary.

'Here's an interesting one, Guv'nor,' O'Connor declared, holding up a single-sheet report form.

DI Melton looked up from a mountain of routine paperwork.

'Give it a rest, Sergeant,' he snapped, 'I've read those bloody reports twice already.'

'Not this one you haven't,' O'Connor retorted. 'It came in while you were taking a leak.'

'How come it's not on my desk? Oh, what the hell! What is it, then?'

'A witness may have seen Steven Pearce at Surbiton on Friday evening—a Mr Frank Baverstock. He came off the four fifty-five from Waterloo around five twenty and stood inside out of the wind but with a view of the forecourt, waiting for his wife to pick him up. She didn't turn up till a couple of minutes before six that day, on account of heavy traffic.

'He says he saw no sign of a girl resembling Janice, but a young man answering Steven's description got out of a car at around five-thirty and stood close to the clock. He pretty soon began pacing up and down, obviously expecting someone.

'When a black taxi pulled into the forecourt, he grabbed his cases and practically ran outside. After some heated words with the driver, he scrambled into the cab and was driven away. It ties in, sir. But I wonder what provoked Steven—if it was Steven—to go haring off in a taxi?'

David Melton shot to his feet. 'I don't know—but I know a man who might! Henry Dyson, from 'Ace Cars'. Gibson's pseudo-cockney. Haul him in Sergeant. Now!'

No sooner had DS O'Connor departed than a snippet of information phoned in by an anonymous long-distance lorry driver was relayed to Melton. He listened to the tape:

'Last November seventeenth—I checked me log, I ran out of hours and parked up for the night in the service area behind the main shopping parade on Esher High Street. It was around midnight. I was about to settle down, when a light-coloured motor—a Jag XJS, I think—pulled in without lights and parked about twenty metres away. It was too dark to see much, but I'm pretty sure the driver heaved something bulky out of the boot and humped it through a gate towards some old building—a church maybe? I was just nodding off when I heard an engine and I sat up in time to see the same posh motor shoot off towards the High Street, still without lights, the stupid sod! I thought it funny at the time, but forgot all about it till I seen the appeal tonight on me portable telly. I'm in the area, see, but I'm not saying where. OK?' Then the caller had rung off.

DI Melton remained motionless for minutes, thoughtful but uneasy. He glanced at the clock: 9.55. Abruptly, he got to his feet, left the office and rapped on Detective Chief Superintendent Jarvis' door.

DCS Jarvis listened whilst Melton brought him up to date, confessing a long-standing unease about estate agent Robert Strudwick, and proposing a possible connection between the Pennington/Bridgwater murders and the disappearance of Steven Pearce and Janice Pearson.

'All right, but let me get this straight David,' the Chief Super said, eventually. 'An uncorroborated sighting of a car similar to

Strudwick's near the Old Church on November seventeenth clearly aroused your suspicions, yet you dismiss it as mere coincidence and feel certain that, if questioned again, Strudwick will not only turn out to be blameless, but is likely to sue for harassment into the bargain—right?'

'Yes sir, that just about sums it up. I might add that I don't like him. He has a powerful personality and is difficult to question, but that doesn't make him a criminal. Quite frankly, sir, the further we steer clear the better. But I couldn't let it go without seeking your guidance.'

Melton seemed both embarrassed and perplexed by his own hesitancy. Plainly, he needed help. Dithering formed no part of police work and it was difficult to understand why a normally reliable officer was now suddenly so indecisive. DCS Jarvis was no psychiatrist. He merely sighed.

'You want my opinion? Very well. I agree that one unconfirmed sighting doesn't amount to much but, despite your reservations, I think it extremely suspicious and deserving of further investigation. I also accept the possibility of a connection between the young couple's disappearance and the two murders, even though the evidence is somewhat flimsy. But we can't afford to take chances.'

DCS Jarvis thought carefully for a moment.

'Take this as a direct order, David. Have Strudwick in for questioning, and it might help avert claims of harassment if you isolate O'Connor and yourself from any form of direct involvement. We won't be able to hold him for long, and I want him under full twenty-four hour surveillance from the moment he leaves the station—*today*.'

'Yes sir,' Melton replied, getting to his feet. 'Er—what about the taxi driver? He knows more than he's prepared to admit.'

Jarvis gave Melton an exasperated look. What on earth was the matter with his right-hand man? 'If you suspect he's hiding something, oughtn't you to have him investigated? And if he *is* involved, we need to know to what extent. Pull him in for further questioning. Maybe you should give him a good going-over yourself—if you feel up to it, that is.'

DI Melton seemed relieved. He either failed to notice the thinly disguised barb or chose to ignore it. 'Right sir, I'll get surveillance teams organised and a background check put in hand right away.'

Melton took his leave and hastened to implement DCS Jarvis' instructions. Thereafter, the focus of the investigation altered and rapid, unexpected developments caused DI Melton to delay re-interviewing Henry Dyson for considerably longer than he intended.

Still angry, Robert Strudwick was backing the XJS out of the garage when a police car shot into the driveway and slithered to a halt, effectively barring his progress. Cursing, he jumped out and made a dash for the front door but was easily overtaken by two uniformed officers.

'Good morning, sir. Are you Robert William Strudwick?' the taller of the pair inquired. He displayed his warrant card. 'I'm PC Frobisher from Esher and this is PC Fletcher.'

'What if I am? What the hell's it got to do with you? Get that damn car off my property right now, I'm late for work as it is.'

'Please answer the question, sir. Are you Robert William Strudwick?'

'Yes, I am,' he admitted adopting a more conciliatory tone. 'But what's this all about? I really am late for the office, you know.'

'That may well be the case, sir, but we are investigating a serious matter and have reason to believe you may be able to assist in our inquiries. I must therefore ask you to accompany us to the station.'

'And if I refuse?'

'Not a good idea, sir,' Frobisher bluffed, ponderously. 'We'd be obliged to place you under arrest.'

'If I agree, how long will I be? I've got a great deal to do today.'

'No idea, sir. It all depends. Might be an hour or two—might be a couple of days.'

'You can't do that. I've done nothing wrong. I want my solicitor.'

'All in good time sir. Now, shall we go?'

'Very well—but if I'm likely to be kept overnight, I'll need a few things from the house.'

'Certainly, sir. I'll come with you—not that you'd be foolish enough to nip out the back door.'

Strudwick led the way to his room, thinking furiously. Had he inadvertently violated the Contract? Of course not. Was Pentophiles taking revenge for intransigence or insubordination? Extremely unlikely. What then?

Having never meekly submitted to authority throughout his long Custodianship, it was difficult to face the prospect of detention with equanimity. Desperately seeking a way out, he applied his

THE FLYLEAF KILLER

mind to every facet of the situation. The one thing he was sure of was that the police were not to be trusted. That being so, and to ensure his most treasured possession remained inviolate during his absence, he wrapped the important volume in a spare towel and placed it carefully among a selection of overnight essentials. Realising PC Frobisher was watching and concerned that he might object, Strudwick looked up.

'Just a little light reading, officer, in case I have time to kill.'

The policeman did not respond. His brief was to deliver a potentially important witness to Surbiton, allowing no opportunity for communication with a third party, and it made little difference what the man took. Everything would be confiscated pending release anyway.

Strudwick arrived at Surbiton, was booked in and interviewed without delay. Once the line of questioning became apparent, he regained his confidence. He was unable to help. The car seen near Esher Old Church the night of November 17, supposedly a light-coloured Jaguar XJS, was definitely not his. He stuck to his guns and was released unconditionally at 11.05, unaware that, whilst he was being interviewed, a curious PC Frobisher had taken a surreptitious peek at the book so carefully packed by the detainee.

Running down Henry Dyson was simple. DS O'Connor simply drove to 'Ace Cars'.

'Good morning, Mrs Fairweather,' he said to the proprietor, pleasantly. 'I'm Detective Sergeant O'Connor from Surbiton. As you know, we are investigating the disappearance of a young couple and I'd like another word with the cabby interviewed by DC Gibson on Monday—Henry Dyson, I believe. As it's rather urgent, I'd be obliged if you'd call him. I assume he *is* working and not too far away?'

'Yes, he's on station duty all week. Have a chair, I'll call him.'

'Don't tip him off in case he does a runner. Can you make a suitable excuse?'

She nodded. 'Control to oh-five, where are you Henry?'

The radio clicked in response. 'Jest leaving the station. Client wantin' the council offices.'

'OK. Deliver the fare and come straight in. I want a word about yesterday's takings.'

'Right, missus. Oh-five, out.'

220

When Dyson appeared, O'Connor rose to his feet to intercept him. 'Good morning. Mr Dyson?'

Dyson's eyes widened. 'Yus, 'oo wants t'know?'

'I'm Detective Sergeant O'Connor, Surbiton police. Since making a statement to Detective Constable Gibson, certain developments lead us to believe you may be able to help further with our inquiries. I should therefore like you to accompany me to Surbiton police station where additional questions will be put to you.'

''Ere, wotcher bleedin' nickin' me for? I ain't dun nuffink. I tole the uvver copper all wot I know.'

'I'm not nicking you, but if you refuse to come voluntarily I most certainly shall.'

Grumbling about 'Perlice 'arassment' and 'lorst earnings', Dyson acquiesced. However, he stuck doggedly to his story: he had collected the young lady and taken her to Surbiton, just as he'd told the other copper, but knew nothing about some young bloke getting into a cab—how could he?

Insisting that he had knocked off after taking the girl to Surbiton, the indignant man demanded, 'So 'ow the bleedin' 'ell d'yer s'pect me to be in two places at once, then?'

When Sylvia Fairweather confirmed Miss Pearson had been Dyson's last recorded fare of the day, the cabby was released but warned not to leave the area without permission.

Although thoroughly alert to Pentophiles' impatience, estate agency business continued to keep Strudwick fully occupied and it was late Friday evening before he donned an old boiler suit, placed a can of paraffin and a bulky valise in the boot of his car and returned by an indirect route to his isolated house on the outskirts of Claygate, totally unaware that he was discreetly being followed.

On his approach, an indefinable blackness descended upon the property: *KILL! KILL! KILL!* As he neared the end of the gravelled driveway, Strudwick's face contorted into a snarl, his teeth gleamed eerily in reflected light from the dashboard and he licked his lips in anticipation.

A week's incarceration without food or drink in cold, damp conditions found the couple hallucinating and close to hypothermia. They hovered on the borderline between life and death. Neither noticed the rattle of bolts nor the creak of the door and not until the brilliance of torchlight and the sound of footsteps penetrated the veils of tortured exhaustion did either become vaguely aware that they were no longer alone.

They scarcely registered the shadowy form, much less observe him dump a bag on the bench and wedge the flashlight into a niche somewhere near the ceiling. Neither reacted as Strudwick refuelled the paraffin lamp, turned up the wick and brushed it free of charred cotton. A second match was expended before the wick was sufficiently primed to ignite. He replaced the chimney and adjusted the flame for maximum illumination. Unhurriedly, the accomplished assassin returned the lamp to its nail, retrieved the flashlight and consigned both it and the matches to a pocket of the valise.

Only now did Strudwick turn his attention to the captives, and only now did the dreadful condition they were in become apparent. Had he left them too long? His mind raced: *Pentophiles!* What of Pentophiles?

Full subject awareness was essential if he was to regain the approbation of his master. To recreate the conditions for an exchange of personalities and allow his mentor to participate in the climax of the mission, now substantially more difficult than originally intended.

Strudwick dared not delay. He unzipped the valise, withdrew the two-litre bottle of water and set about reviving the prisoners. Janice gagged, spluttered and drank greedily. Steven turned his head away, but when Strudwick grabbed a handful of hair, tilted his head and sloshed water into his face, he too began to drink.

Suddenly, the ill-defined, miasmic blackness lifted. *Thou hast betrayed Pentophiles!* Strudwick straightened up: the water-bottle fell from his grasp, its contents gurgling unheeded across the shadowy floor.

Flee! Flee! Thine enemies are nigh!

His mobile telephone trilled. He jumped. Who was calling? He snatched the instrument from his pocket and squinted at the display: *Bobby Shafto!*

'Hello! What?' He listened intently whilst the informant spoke, then demanded, 'Now? In the morning? Don't you know? What do you mean "They're watching me?"' Strudwick's face paled. 'Right, I'm on my way!'

His mind went blank.

What the hell was his home number? Frantically, he scrolled the memories.

'Father?'

'Yes, Robert.'

'Listen, don't speak. Something urgent has cropped up. I've no time to explain, but I'm going away for a few days. There are two bags inside my wardrobe, packed ready. Get both and put them behind the hedge inside the gates. I'll pick them up in a while. The police will call later tonight or in the morning. Stall them; tell them I'm ill in bed—anything. I need a little time. But don't answer any questions about me. I'll give you a ring when I've sorted things out. Goodbye.'

He rang off. Immediately, he punched in another number.

'Henry? Where are you? Are you free? Good, I need your help. Switch off your radio and pick me up in ten minutes. No, not at the house—Mother is asleep. I'll meet you on the corner. OK? Good!'

It was difficult to think, but he maintained a measure of self-control and focused on the need to escape. Suppressing an impulse to knife the captives there and then, he retrieved the bottle, snatched the lantern from its nail, grabbed the valise and fairly ran up the steps and out of the cellar.

Pausing only to re-bolt the cellar, he slammed the front door, extinguished the hot lantern and threw it into the bushes, slung the valise into the boot of his car and, regardless of risk, drove at breakneck speed down the driveway to regain the road.

'Let him go—for now,' Melton said, newly arrived and parked in the entrance to a farmer's field diagonally opposite, screened from the road by gorse and hedgerow. 'He's heading home and we'll have a word with him later. Right now, I want to know what he was doing up that driveway and why he came out in such a hell of a hurry.'

On his signal, waiting police advanced cautiously and, within a matter of minutes, a muted voice came over the radio to report the discovery of a ramshackle house in total darkness.

'Wait there,' Melton ordered, leaving his car. 'I'm coming in to join you.'

Meanwhile, the water taken by the captives had brought them back from the brink. It was meant only to revive, but may well have saved their lives. Steven was the first to attempt to speak.

'Jan—are you all right?' he managed to croak.

'Just about—are you?' she whispered, hoarsely.

'I'm OK—what was all that about?'

'What d'you mean?'

'Robert Strudwick, just now. That business on the phone.'

'Dunno, couldn't take it in ... Oh, Stevie, I feel terrible.'

'I'm not so good either,' Steven admitted, 'but better after that drink.'

He fell silent. She sighed and leaned sideways in the darkness to rest her head against his shoulder. He smiled. Despite their condition, the couple drifted off to sleep.

They didn't sleep long. Discovery and rescue came not a moment too soon. Their bonds were gently removed. Paramedics arrived in minutes and administered water and oxygen. Both on saline drips, Steven and Janice found themselves in an ambulance—lights flashing, sirens blaring—bound for Kingston General, where specialist medical staff stood by to receive the couple.

It was thirty minutes after midnight. Uniformed police took up station; the property was secured, pending forensic examination. It was time to find out what part, if any, Robert Strudwick had played in the abduction and incarceration of Janice Pearson and Steven Pearce.

DI Melton prodded a yawning DS O'Connor in the ribs.

'It's getting late. He's no idea we're on to him. Sod it! We'll deal with him in the morning.'

'You're having me on, Guv'nor,' his assistant gasped, instantly wide awake. 'You don't intend to leave that bloody animal on the loose overnight, surely?'

'A-ha! You're not asleep, after all,' Melton chuckled.

'Just as well I'm not. Somebody needs to keep an eye on you, obviously.'

There was silence for a moment. O'Connor fidgeted.

'What about Strudwick? That *was* his car, wasn't it? Were you taking the mick, Guv'nor?'

'Of course not. It was his car right enough, and he was driving it,' Melton confirmed wearily.

'Tell you what—radio the team who trailed him here to go nick him and shove him in the pokey till morning. Let him cool his heels for a few hours, minus his braces, belt, shoelaces and dignity while we both grab a spot of shut-eye.' Vindicated, but still uneasy, his assistant nevertheless thumbed the mike switch.

'Oh, we'll talk to Mister Strudwick all right—tomorrow.' . . . a remark which prompted DS O'Connor to let go the key. He was not to know that malign influences heavily affected the DI's judgement, nor, for that matter, that he too was affected, although to a lesser degree. But—and not for the first time—he wondered whether his superior officer was losing the plot.

'Just a thought, Guv'nor,' he ventured. 'What if chummy knew he'd been rumbled? Why else would he scarper in a tearing hurry within minutes of our arrival? Take it from me sir. He'll be miles away by now.' *I'd put my shirt on it!*

Melton jerked himself upright.

'Possible, but unlikely. The surveillance was strictly "need to know". Nobody—apart from you, me and the operatives, and the Chief of course—knew about it until after the subject was shadowed here and we mobilised.'

'Come on, Guv'nor. Get real. Mobile phones? Our probable "mole"? Strudwick could easily have been tipped off. Common knowledge once the teams were briefed.'

DI Melton was unable to contain his irritation any longer.

'I'm in no mood for idle speculation, Sergeant,' he snapped. 'Just detail Gibson and Slade—right now, dammit, before they make it to HQ and knock off for the night.'

O'Connor dutifully re-keyed the microphone.

Meanwhile, at Kingston General, in intensive care, Steven and Janice had stabilised and were resting peacefully under sedation. Neither could yet be assured of full recovery and no further bulletins would be issued for the time being. The frustrated assassin, on the other hand was many miles away, just as DS O'Connor had predicted.

The call came as Melton's car was nearing Hinchley Wood. 'Zebra One—receiving?'

'Zebra Five, go ahead.'

'Problems Sarge. It took ten minutes for the suspect's father to answer the door; he was very annoyed at being disturbed. Refuses to co-operate: says he's not responsible for his son's actions, doesn't know where he is and, what's more, doesn't much care—might still be at the office, or upstairs ill in bed, for all he knows. He told us to leave him and his wife in peace and slammed the door. Could be the suspect has flown the coop. Zebra One, over.'

'Zebra Five, wait one.'

'Roger, Zebra One. Zebra Five to standby.'

O'Connor turned his head. 'What now, sir?'

Melton sighed. 'Tell them to wait there. We'll check it out ourselves. Turn the car round, Sergeant.'

On reaching the gates, Melton was again aware of the strange aura of brooding unease that seemed to surround the property. But tonight he thought it had lessened. He swallowed, suppressed a shiver, and strode ahead.

Flanked by DS O'Connor, with plain-clothes DCs Gibson and Slade close behind, he knocked on the door. Almost immediately, an outside wall light snapped on. There came a rattle of bolts, the door opened, and Strudwick senior appeared, wearing a nondescript dressing gown. If Alfred was annoyed at being disturbed twice within a matter of twenty minutes it didn't show.

'Good *morning*, Inspector—you too, Sergeant,' he said, intentionally sarcastic. 'I must admit I was half expecting you, even though I've already told those two . . .' pointing at Slade and Gibson, '. . . I've no knowledge of Robert's whereabouts. I presume that *is* why you've come knocking, late as it is?'

'Yes, Mr Strudwick, it is—and please, don't play games with me. A very serious crime has been committed and your son may be involved. It is essential we speak with him as quickly as possible. Now, where is he?'

Strudwick blanched, but stuck to his guns.

'I haven't the remotest idea, Inspector, as I've already made clear. Robert went to the office this morning—well, yesterday, to be precise—and hasn't been home since. It's nothing unusual. Robert is often away on business.'

'That isn't true, Mr Strudwick, and you know it,' Melton interrupted. 'Your son arrived home at five-forty and was seen to leave again at nine-fifty. Now, I'll ask you once again, where is he?'

Cornered, Alfred Strudwick almost fell to pieces. He swallowed and tried again.

'You must be mistaken, Inspector. If Robert did come home, I'm sure I would have seen him.'

Clearly, he was lying. Moving closer, Melton pressed his advantage.

'Then if, as you say, Robert failed to come home last evening, who was driving his car? The truth, Mr Strudwick, or I shall require you to accompany us to the police station. Come on, sir. What exactly are you trying to conceal? Why are you lying to protect your son?'

It was enough. Never a good liar, Strudwick realised he was in danger of becoming embroiled in whatever it was his unprincipled son was up to. Clearly, he could stall no longer.

'If you're not prepared to accept my word that Robert isn't here, then feel free to check the house, but that does *not* entitle you to take liberties without a proper search warrant.'

Flushed with affected indignation, he retreated into the hallway and swung wide the door.

'Thank you,' Melton said quietly, crossing the threshold. 'Who, besides yourself, is in the house at the present time?'

'Just my wife, asleep in bed—or at least she was!'

'Having the benefit of your consent we are obliged to check the entire house, but would prefer not to distress Mrs Strudwick. Perhaps you should explain our presence, accompany her to the lounge and remain there with her until we've finished. I trust this is acceptable to you?'

Alfred Strudwick inclined his head. 'I'll go and fetch her. Will you and your officers wait here, please?'

'Of course. But, if you don't mind, I'll wait while my men check around outside.'

Wearily, Alfred acquiesced. He had, after all, done his best. As Strudwick set off up the stairs, Melton turned to the open doorway and the waiting policemen.

'We need a man to cover the driveway, Sergeant—Slade, I think. You and Gibson check the rear, including the garage and outbuildings. Make sure the suspect isn't lurking somewhere outside. Come back here when you are completely satisfied.'

Five minutes later DS O'Connor returned.

'The garage is secured with a heavy-duty pad-bolt and a Chubb padlock, Guv'nor. There isn't a window so we couldn't see inside, but I doubt if he's in there—unless somebody's locked him in!

We also checked the garden shed, but there's barely room for a lawnmower and a few tools, much less a fugitive. If he's here, he's in the house, sir. There's definitely nobody skulking in the garden.'

Beckoning the officers inside, Melton pointed towards the stairs. 'Take Gibson and check the first floor, Sergeant. I'll look around down here.'

THE FLYLEAF KILLER

He opened the door to the kitchen and went inside. Casting around, he noted the door to the garden was bolted on the inside; there was only one possible hiding place—the walk-in pantry. Warily, he pulled wide the door. Nobody lurked within.

The only remaining door opened to the lounge/diner. He knocked and went in.

'Sorry to intrude, Mr Strudwick,' Melton began, with an apologetic smile to Mrs Strudwick.

'We've almost finished, except for a quick look in the garage. Just routine, you understand.'

Strudwick merely stared, as if unable to fully comprehend.

'May I have the key please?' Melton asked.

'I wish you'd hurry it up, Inspector,' Strudwick grumbled. 'Mrs Strudwick and I need to get back to bed.'

He glanced at his wife. Fortunately, she kept her thoughts and opinions to herself these days.

'The key, Mr Strudwick.' Melton insisted. He extended his hand.

'Oh yes, the key,' Alfred muttered vaguely.

He fidgeted uncomfortably, shook his head and sighed. His forehead creased into a frown and he appeared old and careworn. Melton waited, hand extended. Finally, as if he'd only just realised that the policeman required an answer, he said, 'Robert keeps his car in the garage. I park mine outside on the verge, and there's only one key. Robert keeps it with him all the time, Inspector. It's an expensive car—the insurance, you know.'

Strudwick's impassive face concealed a thumping heart and a sense of utter bewilderment: *Robert* never *locks the garage unless his car is inside! Was he, then, still nearby?* He fervently hoped not, but knew better than to warn the police—Robert would be *furious!*

DI Melton's exasperated sigh coincided with the clump of feet to signal the return of DS O'Connor and DC Gibson. Robert Strudwick was not at home.

'No sign of him, Guv'nor. It doesn't look as if he's been here. His bedroom-cum-office—call it what you will—is neat and tidy. The bed hasn't been slept in. I reckon we're pissing in the wind!'

'Maybe so,' Melton conceded, 'but we'll keep an eye on the place in case he should show. Organise a relief for Slade—better still, rustle up another surveillance team. Get them in position a.s.a.p. and I'll clear it with the Chief Super in the morning.' He thought for a moment. 'Let's get back to HQ, Sergeant—I'll drive while you're on the radio. We need to sort things out for tomorrow, and I want to inquire after those unfortunate youngsters before we call it a night.'

He tapped the lounge door. 'All finished Mr Strudwick. Thank you for your co-operation. We'll see ourselves out.'

For the second time that night, DS O'Connor wondered why the Guv'nor deliberately allowed the suspect to escape when he might have been nailed. He could have had him followed: a fast, fully-manned back-up car had waited in a lay-by on nearby Littleworth Common.

Strudwick was a kidnapper and a cruel torturer at the very least. Something (or someone) had startled him into doing a bunk, and it seemed likely he was well out of the area by now. Considering the man was also a murder suspect, it seemed curious that the Guv'nor continued to avoid confronting the possibility that they might be harbouring a 'mole'. He kept his thoughts to himself, however, clipped his seat belt and reached for the microphone . . .

Chapter Fourteen
Fugitive

During the return to Kenward Crescent, Robert succeeded in regaining his composure and with it his extraordinary ability to plan, think clearly and resolve problems, no matter how complex.

Finely-tuned survival instincts and exceptional resourcefulness had produced the spur of the moment decision taken in the cellar: to put as much distance between himself and Claygate as possible and as quickly as possible; to gain time to re-establish relations with his nether-world sponsor and, with his guidance and protection, resume his rightful place in society for the rest of his natural life.

He had come perilously close to discovery, yet quick thinking had undoubtedly averted the ignominy of capture, handcuffs, confinement and trial. But first they had to catch him, and produce some evidence which would prove him 'guilty beyond all reasonable doubt'.

Evidence! he sneered. *What evidence?* Providing Dyson remained silent (he'd better!) and Pearce and his tart either failed to survive or were disposed of before they recovered (which might yet be arranged), the only evidence the police could offer would be entirely circumstantial.

Enemies or acquaintances capable of pointing the finger? None—he had been extremely careful. Of his extensive band of 'assistants', few possessed sufficient information to incriminate him. Fewer still were likely to talk, no matter how closely questioned.

In order of least risk, he eliminated them one by one, including *Bobby Shafto*—privy to nothing of consequence except which side her bread was buttered . . . which left Henry Dyson—who knew far too much for comfort, but had been vital to the kidnap and was equally essential right now. But what had gone wrong? He decided to deal with that question later. He was fast approaching his destination and his first priority was to implement the escape initiative conceived right there in the cellar.

Turning the final corner in third, he slipped into neutral, killed the lights and coasted towards his parent's house. Leaving the engine ticking over, he swung wide through the open gates and trundled with scarcely a whisper the full length of the concrete driveway up to the garage. Making little or no noise, it was the work of seconds to open the double doors, slip into first and edge the big car inside without a nudge of the accelerator. Switching off the ignition, he closed the driver's door with a soft 'clunk', locked the garage and slipped the key into his pocket. Walking on the balls of his feet, he made his way to the gates, picked up the bags and—for the benefit of anyone who might be watching—strolled casually to the corner and waited.

Nor did he have long to wait. Almost on cue, Henry's black cab rounded the corner and stopped, the driver already unlatching the rear passenger door. As soon as it was open, Robert tossed his luggage inside, pulled open the front passenger door and climbed in beside the driver.

'Wassermarra, guv? Scared I might lock yer in?' Dyson sniggered.

'Just drive.' Strudwick grunted.

'Where to?'

'Down to "The Bear" at Esher, turn right on High Street and down the A3 towards the Scilly Isles. Straight across onto Portsmouth Road, past my offices and turn right at the lights towards Surbiton station. I'll direct you from there—OK?'

'S'long way rahnd, innit? Quicker 'f we crosses Littleworth Common.'

'Don't argue, damn you. Just do as I bloody well say ... and there's an extra twenty in it for you.'

'OK, OK! You're the boss.'

Henry drove off, suddenly afraid.

Traffic was light. They passed 'The Bear' and progressed smoothly along Esher High Street. Strudwick glanced speculatively at the subservient pervert who sat close at hand, comfortably within striking-distance of the razor-sharp cook's knife secreted beneath his jacket.

Should he—on the pretext of needing a leak—direct the obnoxious child-molester to a quiet spot somewhere along the Thames and slide the knife between his ribs? Death would be instantaneous; cab and corpse would be under thirty feet of water in a couple of minutes. It was an interesting thought, but the longer Strudwick pondered the more hesitant he became.

Escape required the use of the cab. He could dispose of Dyson and drive himself, but there would be blood, (he licked his lips) not only in the vehicle but probably on his clothing. Moreover, without the cab as a coffin, the body would eventually rise and come to the attention of the police. Furthermore, he would abandon an out-of-district, full-of-clues taxi at or near his destination, there to be spotted by an alert taxi-driver (they really did exist) who would report the discovery to the police. Even bumbling, reluctant DI Melton would connect such a find with the disappearance of Robert Strudwick and call off the search for a white XJS—the very search he was *meant* to initiate. In addition to that, discovery of the taxi might well provide other, more potentially incriminating evidence. He wanted to disappear without trace.

Dyson might well consider himself fortunate—for now. At least he would live to see another day.

Strudwick shifted in his seat, and reflected on the comprehensive way in which he was protected. That seemingly trivial altercation with Pentophiles, for example. Obviously preordained and no mere accident brought about by temper, it served as a reminder that he might one day have need to escape, and prompted his resolve to be packed in readiness for flight at short notice, with the inclusion of the Book and his cash contingency fund amounting to something in excess of £1,000.

He considered his resources and his ability to survive without revealing his whereabouts, by avoiding Barclaycard and the dubious confidentiality of the credit card system—not indefinitely, of course, but certainly for several weeks—if not months. Knowing he might one day need to evade the police—or even flee the country—adequate, accessible funding had long been in place. Far-sighted, intuitive Robert Strudwick had planned well. Apart from around £200 in his wallet and more than £1,000 in his baggage, £20,000 was set aside in a Midland deposit account, whilst his current account balance of around £2,000 was quickly retrievable—in small amounts, using Maestro and automated cash machines anywhere in the modern world. As a further precaution, another £2,000 in cash was stashed in a safety deposit box at a Maidstone bank, accessible by password and coded keypad with no requirement whatever to prove identity. Masked by darkness, Strudwick's unsavoury countenance creased into a self-satisfied smirk.

The taxi trundled on. He was startled out of his reverie when Dyson spoke.

'Cummin' up ter Surbiton station, guv. Where d'yer want me ter drop yer?'

'Pull up by the bus stop. Don't go into the station yet—I need to take a look.'

It was here he intended to pay Dyson off, spelling out the consequences of disclosure, now or at any time in the future. He would cover his tracks in another cab once Dyson was out of sight. But it was late on Friday: most travellers were already home; taxis were at a premium.

Dyson indicated and was slowing in readiness to stop. A solitary cab emerged and rumbled away. Gaining an unrestricted view of the forecourt, he could see clearly that no further taxis were available. Strudwick's innate caution was vindicated—but he would have to trust Dyson yet further.

'Don't stop, Henry. I've changed my mind,' he ordered, brusquely. 'Swing the cab round. Go back to the bypass and run me up to Raines Park tube.'

Glancing in his mirror, Henry spun the vehicle through a hundred and eighty degrees and headed back the way he came. Around 11.15 he pulled up at Raines Park underground, leaving the engine running.

'What's on the meter?' Strudwick demanded, to divert the man's attention.

Dyson switched on the interior light and glanced instinctively towards the meter.

'Nuffink guv, it ain't been on. Look arter the boss, I allus say.'

'Highly commendable sentiments,' Strudwick remarked, drily—and flashed a fearsome-looking knife in front of the man's eyes.

Dyson was terrified out of his wits.

'Wassermarra, guv?' he bleated. 'I ain't dun nuffink.'

'No, and make sure you don't,' Strudwick snarled, his voice thick with menace. 'Keep your bloody mouth shut—or else. One word about me to the police—or anybody else, for that matter—

233

and I'll be back to slit your fucking throat. Make no mistake, I'll get you, no matter what—no matter where you are, no matter how hard you might try to hide. You can rely on it!'

His hand backed off—then flashed forward to stop the blade barely an inch short of the man's nose.

'Christ, you know you c'n trust me!' Henry fairly screeched. 'I won' say a bleedin' word—'onest!'

Slowly—almost reluctantly, it seemed—Strudwick withdrew the knife and returned it to its sheath.

'All right then. Stay schtum, you filthy pervert, or before I cut your throat I'll spill your guts all over the floor.' Dyson was frantic with fear.

'I tole yer guv, yer don' need ter worry abaht me. I swear I won' say nuffink—not ever!'

'You'd better not. Stay where you are. I'm coming round for my bags.'

Satisfied that the disposal of Dyson could now safely be deferred, Strudwick vacated his seat, rounded the front of the cab and pulled open the rear passenger door to retrieve his luggage. Producing his wallet, he thrust five ten-pound notes into Dyson's hand.

'Here you are, Henry' he said casually. 'Ten should cover the diesel, the rest is for you.'

Dyson gulped. 'S'orl right guv. Tole yer I didn't want nuffink. Yer c'n 'ave it back, reely,' he protested.

'No problem, Henry,' Strudwick said airily, waving the proffered notes away. 'You've earned it. Off you go. Just remember you haven't seen me—tonight or any other night.'

'Yus guv—fanks.'

Jerkily, the cab moved off.

Shrugging, Strudwick turned on his heel and strode into the tube, where he followed the arrows for Wimbledon and the City. Midway down the broad, brightly-lit corridor, he slipped through a short connecting tunnel to the southbound platform and boarded the first train to appear. Getting out at New Malden, he crossed the bridge in time to connect with a northbound train. This time he stayed on until Waterloo, where he vacated the lightly populated carriage, surrendered his ticket at the barrier and walked into the nearest public toilets.

In the privacy of a cubicle, he rummaged in his luggage,

swapped his jacket for a raincoat and donned a flat cap. Wearing contact lenses in place of spectacles, he assumed a stoop, shuffled out of the station and set about finding a hotel. As 'Mr William Roberts of East Camberley', he checked into a nondescript three-star establishment just before midnight, and went directly to his room. He locked the door on the inside, leaving the key in place, in order to prevent the insertion of a master from outside.

Placing his phone by the bedside reminded him that calls to and from mobiles were traceable, and that network records were frequently made available to the police. His mobile was an unregistered 'Pay and Go', purchased for cash in Kingston and, therefore, theoretically safe. The number would be known to the company, but they would be unable to connect it with a name. But those in his confidence certainly could, and these were many. What if one should talk? After a moment's thought, he switched the instrument off, flushed the SIM card down the toilet and wrapped both phone and charger in newspaper retrieved from the bin. Craving guidance, he consulted the Book, but without success—the page remained stubbornly blank. Cursing Pentophiles, he retired to bed.

After an uneasy night, 'Mr Roberts' checked out at nine o'clock and limped slowly to Waterloo Station, where he covertly dropped a package into a convenient litter bin.

Leaving his contact lenses in, he put on spectacles and made his way to the booking hall. Fumbling a little, he purchased a single to Tilbury at one kiosk and rounded the carousel to another. There, without glasses and with cap pulled low to mask his eyes, he bought a period return to Folkestone. His train clattered through Clapham Junction a little after 10.15, heading south-east.

Melton's day began badly. DCS Jarvis was in vitriolic form.

'I find it hard to believe you actually watched Strudwick take off in his bloody XJS,' he snorted. 'But if by following your instincts you were instrumental in rescuing those youngsters whilst still alive, I suppose I shall have to overlook it.' He favoured the DI with a sour look and changed the subject. 'I presume you've put out an official alert for Strudwick and his distinctive white Jag?'

Melton shuffled his feet uncomfortably.

'Er—no sir, not yet. I thought it better to seek your advice first.'

'What the devil do you mean?'

'Well sir. I've prepared a photofit and an "All Stations" regarding Strudwick and his car.' He placed them on the desk. '—I propose an early meeting with the Press—with your approval, sir, and plan to get an appeal "on the wire" as quickly as possible, but I'm not sure whether Strudwick ought rightfully to be described as "presumed dangerous, not to be approached". He may yet prove to be innocent, sir. After all, we've no real evidence to the contrary.'

Jarvis' eyebrows clambered skywards. *No evidence? What on earth was wrong with the man?* He leaned back and regarded his one-time star detective thoughtfully. *He* seems *normal enough,* he thought. *Damn ditherer! I* must *shake him out of it, somehow.*

'David,' he said, choosing his words with care, 'I'm worried. Something still colours your judgement where Strudwick is concerned. I'm tempted to take the case out of your hands and refer you to the psychiatrist. However, I've no wish to destroy your self-confidence.'

Melton stiffened, but said nothing.

Edward Jarvis picked up the draft, and read aloud:

'All stations alert. Origin: Surrey County Police, Surbiton. Originator: DI D. Melton

Be on the lookout for Robert William Strudwick, aged 20. 5 foot 4, or thereabouts. Sallow complexion; straw-coloured hair; myopic—generally wears special glasses. Last seen at 10.40 p.m. Friday 25 March 2005 driving white Jaguar XJS registration no. X434RRP. Wanted for questioning in connection with the abduction on 18 March 2005 of Janice Ann Pearson, 20, and Steven Vincent Pearce, 19, both of Esher.'

'Hm!' he grunted, eyeing the photofit with distaste. 'Strudwick? Not much to look at, is he?'

Jarvis tossed the draft towards its author. *Come on, both barrels!*

'Add "Considered dangerous, etc." and get it onto the system, pronto,' he snapped irritably. 'And get this into your head, once and for all. I'm sick and tired of your puerile dithering. Your first and only priority is to nail this Strudwick fellow. Results, we must have results! Don't come bothering me again without something useful to report.'

'Yes sir,' Melton muttered, sheepishly.

Within minutes, the alert was flashed to police forces the length and breadth of the United Kingdom.

Still smarting, Melton was engrossed in paperwork when he gradually became aware of a growing clarity of thought and an encouraging sense of well-being and relief.

No longer plagued by self-doubt, he perceived just how blinkered he had been with regard to Robert Strudwick.

Briefly, he strove to understand why, and in the absence of a more rational explanation, was obliged to conclude that he had been adversely influenced by the man's persona. But what if Strudwick's power diminished with distance? The notion was fanciful, to say the least. But were it so, others too might become less restrained. Then again, had enlightenment been brought about simply through pressure from DCS Jarvis?

No matter. Whatever the reason, Detective Inspector David Melton now felt 'on top of the job', his former indecision a thing of the past. Long-standing doubt gave way to a burgeoning certainty: Robert William Strudwick was their man. The DI strode towards DCS Jarvis' office, practically treading on air.

'Oh, it's you again. What do you want?' snapped Jarvis.

'I thought I should confirm the "All stations" went out and that the media have been fully informed. Robert William Strudwick is now officially wanted in connection with the Pennington inquiry as well as the kidnap of Janice Pearson and Steven Pearce.'

'Of course, just as I instructed. So what? Do you expect a medal?'

'Not exactly, sir,' Melton replied. 'The fact is, I've come to apologise. Strudwick had me completely bamboozled, I'm afraid. I simply couldn't penetrate his facade. You were right. The evidence *does* suggest his likely involvement in the death of that poor young woman—maybe the murder of Francis Bridgwater too. Why I couldn't bring myself to accept it before today I don't know. I'm extremely sorry, sir.'

Jarvis snorted, 'At last. It's about time you came to your senses.'

Melton winced, but went on, 'Sir, I believe we can assemble a strong case, but I'd like first to search his home and turn his bedroom over. Strudwick senior was neither as helpful nor as truthful as he might have been and I'd like to lean on him a little. He might be more amenable after a night's sleep. In any event, may I have your permission to apply for a search warrant?'

DCS Jarvis' countenance broke into a broad grin.

'You certainly can,' he said, enthusiastically. 'Get cracking, David—and good luck!'

Detective Sergeant Ben O'Connor was equally delighted.

'Crumbs, it's about time, Guv'nor! I've been trying to tell you for months. Where do you reckon that creepy little toe-rag has buggered off to?'

'I wish I knew, Ben, but he ought not to get far. That car of his should prove a dead give-away. In the meantime, I've a job for you.'

Melton picked up a file, extracted a report sheet marked 'Confidential' and waved it in the air.

'Any idea what this is, or when it came in?'

O'Connor shook his head.

'Dyson! We should have applied more pressure. I knew there was more to that man than meets the eye—we let him go far too readily. It transpires our imitation cockney is a convicted paedophile.'

O'Connor's eyes widened.

'It seems he worked as a cab-driver in Gravesend and was convicted at Maidstone in ninety-eight. He served three months in Brixton, got slung out of his bed-sit on release and promptly disappeared. How the hell he came by a Surrey cab licence is anybody's guess, but we'll look into that one later. Right now, he's our best chance of getting the goods on Strudwick.' Melton thumped his desk. 'Mark my words, Sergeant. Dyson knows more about the kidnap than he would have us believe. Get off your tail and go nick him. Borrow a "plod" as a witness. Caution Dyson—"Suspected of aiding and abetting, etc."—and let's have his backside in here within the hour. Drag him from his cab if need be. Harass him, allow no time for him to collect his thoughts—or a solicitor. I want him fizzing when I talk to him. While you're out, I'm off to find a magistrate, Saturday or no Saturday. We'll deal with Dyson first, then go a-visiting . . .' He checked his watch. 'It's 10.45—straight after lunch, with a bit of luck.'

Delighting that the Guv'nor was back to normal, O'Connor scrambled to his feet and headed for the door.

Henry Dyson was satisfactorily belligerent.

'Wotcha fink yer playin' at—rotten, bleedin' copper?' he rudely demanded. 'I wos 'aving a nice cuppa when 'e' (pointing to O'Connor) 'came bustin' in ter nick me. Yer costin' me money and 'e won' tell me nuffink 'cept sum bleedin' rubbish 'bout aidin' an' abettin'. I know me rights. I wanner see me brief.'

But David Melton was not to be intimidated.

'Don't push your luck. This chat is informal and isn't being recorded—yet. So keep quiet, speak when you're spoken to, and keep a civil tongue in your head.

'We'll see about a solicitor after the weekend—possibly Monday or Tuesday. Meanwhile, you'd better come clean and tell us exactly what really happened after you picked Miss Pearson up. Both she and Mr Pearce are in hospital, thanks to you. But they're heaps better and will soon be well enough to give us their version of events. Make no mistake, we'll find out the truth, anyway. Do yourself a favour Dyson—save everybody's time. It'll be better for you in the long run.'

The taxi-driver fell silent, weighing the import of Melton's words. But his fear of Strudwick was overpowering. The threatened consequences of 'grassing' just too terrible to contemplate. Terror tightened his throat.

'I dunno wot the 'ell yer on abaht. I don' know nuffink wot I ain't already tole yer. Sorry, copper, yer'll 'ave ter find sum uvver geezer wot duz know sumfink.'

Long moments passed—then, when he judged he'd waited long enough Melton said, 'Come on Dyson, I'm waiting. We know all about your liking for children. The three months you were handed down in ninety-eight at Maidstone Crown Court is nothing compared to the stretch you'll get for aiding and abetting Robert Strudwick—a kidnapper *and* a murderer!'

Dyson turned white.

'M-murder? Robert Strudwick? Wot the bleedin' 'ell yer on abaht?'

'Don't pretend you don't know Robert Strudwick—or that he cruelly killed two local people, one as recently as last November.' He leaned forward. 'Why did you help him kidnap Janice Pearson and Steven Pearce? How much did he pay you? Twenty quid—thirty quid?'

Sensing he'd struck a chord, DI Melton sat back, expectantly.

THE FLYLEAF KILLER

The fear on Dyson's face was evident. He didn't want to answer, but couldn't help himself. His background rumbled, the need to maintain a fake accent disappeared.

'I can't tell yer nothing, s'welp me. Yeah, I does a bit er drivin' fer 'im now and again, but that's all.'

The admission was at least a step in the right direction.

'We know about that, but what about Steven Pearce and Janice Pearson? Look, we realise you're terribly frightened of Robert Strudwick, and rightly so—he's a nasty, vicious killer. But if you help us we can protect you. If not, we might release you and let it be known you've grassed. How do you fancy your chances with *him* at large? Your best bet is to help us catch him. Your testimony might even help to save another life. The sooner he's behind bars, the safer you'll be.'

The power of Melton's logic was unassailable. Dyson cracked. Half an hour later his statement was read back to him and he signed it.

'Make Mr Dyson comfortable, Constable.' Melton said to the officer who had taken the statement. 'Sort him out a decent lunch and a nice cup of tea. We'll be back in a couple of hours. If you're ready, Sergeant,' he said, striding towards the door.

The pair were scarcely clear of the interview room before O'Connor asked, 'What made you suspect Dyson aided and abetted Strudwick's escape?'

Melton chuckled. 'Call it a hunch if you like. I was only fishing.'

'You could've fooled me,' his assistant retorted, 'you seemed absolutely positive.'

'A bluff wouldn't be worth it's salt if it wasn't believable, now would it?'

'S'pose not, but why have half the Force looking for a white Jag if Strudwick legged it in a taxi?'

'Half the Force won't be, shortly,' Melton replied. 'They'll be concentrating on finding Strudwick. We weren't to know . . . Wait here, I won't be a sec.'

He disappeared into the general office, to re-emerge several minutes later with a manila envelope.

'Warrant,' he explained. 'Let's go grab ourselves a couple of clues—and maybe a Jag for a bonus. But we'll need Slade and

Gibson. Pop up to the office and nobble them. It doesn't matter what they're doing, this is important—and make sure Slade brings coveralls and his little bag of tricks.'

Apart from the presence of a couple of reporters keeping tabs on an unmarked police car, Kenward Crescent appeared as quiet and unremarkable a residential street as any other. A stray dog paused at the driveway of number seven. He sniffed tentatively at one gatepost, hesitated, then strolled nonchalantly across to snuffle the other. Satisfied, he deposited his calling-card for the benefit of those who might follow. As he departed, a blackbird swooped from the roof and landed on the lawn. A series of scampers took him close to the hedge, where he began searching the leaf-litter for worms. A little while later, a second unmarked police car, bearing DI Melton and his team, arrived.

'Good morning, Mr Strudwick,' the DI said, pleasantly. 'I'm sorry to trouble you again so soon, but there are aspects to this inquiry which centre on the whereabouts of your son's car.'

'Oh, it's you again,' Alfred grumbled. 'This is getting beyond a joke. Two of your men are watching us, we've been pestered by reporters, and before you ask, we've neither seen nor heard from Robert since yesterday. I'm not surprised you're back, but kindly state your business and then clear off—taking your lackeys with you. I can't imagine what you expect to achieve by this continual harassment.'

'As I explained earlier, your son was observed leaving premises subsequently established to be the venue of a serious crime. He was driving a white Jaguar, X434RRP, at the time. The same vehicle, we have reason to believe was secreted in your garage around 10.45 p.m. last night.'

Alfred had come to the same conclusion. He regarded DI Melton thoughtfully. The awe in which he held his son had largely evaporated and he was beginning to resent the loss of his former position as family head. Furthermore, Robert's adult activities must often have bordered on the illegal. How else, Alfred wondered, could so large a fortune have been amassed by one so young? The police wanted Robert in connection with something serious. But his own position at the bank was his life and must never, ever become compromised. Perhaps he should distance himself while there was yet time?

'You know, Inspector,' he said, slowly, 'I rather believe you may be right. It occurs to me that Robert *never* locks the garage unless his car is inside. I wonder if he's still in the area somewhere.'

'I very much doubt it,' Melton replied, drily, without explaining why. 'Are you *certain* there isn't another key somewhere in the house?' he asked.'

'Absolutely,' Strudwick replied. 'He cut up the spares with a hacksaw the day his new car arrived.'

'Really? Why would he do that?'

Strudwick spread his hands, helplessly. 'Sounds silly, when you come to consider it: to make sure nobody touched the car but himself.'

'Your son's car may have been used in connection with a criminal act, which entitles the law to examine it. New information also suggests the car is concealed on your property and the absence of a key means that access to the garage can lawfully be obtained by force, if need be.'

At this, Alfred Strudwick shook his head.

'I understand what you say, but I cannot allow you to break in. Who would pay for the damage?'

'I'm afraid you've no choice in the matter,' Melton declared. He reached into his pocket and withdrew the magistrate's warrant, displaying it for Alfred to verify its authenticity. 'This Warrant of today's date authorises a search of your property in any way deemed appropriate. Whilst DS O'Connor and DC Gibson are examining the garage, I propose to accompany DC Slade to your son's bedroom in order to conduct a preliminary inspection. On conclusion, the room will be sealed pending forensic examination during the course of the next few days.

'The seals are not intended to inconvenience, but to prevent the room being entered and valuable evidence being disturbed or destroyed. Under no circumstances must those seals be broken. Do you understand?'

'Yes, Inspector.'

Meekly acquiescent, Alfred sighed and pulled wide the door: 'You'd better get on with it then,' he said, resignedly. 'I'll wait in the lounge with Mrs Strudwick.'

'Very well. Sergeant—you have your orders. DC Slade, come with me.'

Ascending the stairs, the DI glanced at his watch—11.30, he noted with satisfaction. As Slade began clambering into coveralls, Melton gingerly opened the suspect's bedroom door.

'Hang on, Guv,' the detective warned. 'Best leave that to me—you're not even wearing gloves.'

'Don't worry, Harry, I'm not going in. I simply need to get the feel of the place.'

While Slade completed his preparations, Melton stood in the doorway and surveyed the room. Singularly ordinary. Bed, wardrobe, bedside table, telephone, writing desk, table lamp and chair. Wooden storage box—hasp, staple and padlock. No computer, no filing cabinet. No books, no pictures, no *atmosphere*. Nothing to suggest the room was used for anything other than sleeping.

'Ready, Guv'nor,' a voice behind him announced.

Melton turned. 'Right Harry, finished. But there's a lot to be done and time is short. I'd like you to concentrate on just one thing for now, then seal up and leave the rest until Monday. OK?'

'OK sir, you're the boss. What d'you want me to do?'

'Hair, Harry—we need some hair. Strudwick's thatch is straw-coloured and he uses gel. If there's nothing doing, you might try the bathroom, but any found here would be more conclusive.'

'Right-ho, sir. Give me five minutes.'

Meanwhile, DS O'Connor and DC Gibson were feeling challenged. Without cutting gear, breaching the Chubb security padlock was impossible, while countersunk coach bolts with internal nuts, fitted through stout, contra-fitted hinges rendered removal of the doors without damage an impossibility.

'OK, Graham, what now?' a frustrated DS O'Connor wanted to know.

Gibson mused aloud: 'The Guv'nor wants confirmation the car is here, not its removal. Garages don't have lofts and those tiles are just plain, ordinary tiles. I reckon I could wiggle a couple out for a look inside, and just as easily wiggle 'em back again!'

It seemed the obvious solution.

'Nice one, Graham. I noticed a ladder behind the shed. Still there, I shouldn't wonder.'

Gibson was right. By easing adjacent tiles, two were readily removed. Producing a penknife, he cut a flap in the underlying felt and peered downwards.

There it was. Unquestionably a car, ghostly white in the gloom. It was just possible to make out a leaping figure on the bonnet—undoubtedly a Jaguar.

Mission accomplished, Gibson was in the act of replacing the ladder when, upstairs, Slade whooped triumphantly, holding aloft a pair of tweezers.

'Just one sir, on the underside of the pillow. Lucky, I guess. The sheets smell fresh as a daisy. Changed recently, I should think. The bed certainly doesn't *appear* slept in, that's for sure.'

Delicately, he placed his find in a specimen bag and sealed it.

'Well done, Harry.' said Melton. I'll go and check how the others are getting on.'

DS O'Connor reported the discovery of the car.

'Nice one, Sergeant. Muster the troops. I'll see if Strudwick senior has anything further to say.'

Melton tapped the lounge door and waited for Alfred to emerge.

'As we suspected,' he informed him at once, 'your son's Jaguar *is* inside the garage. We managed to establish its presence without damaging the doors, but the lock will have to be forcibly removed some time early next week for the car to be taken away for forensic examination.'

Alfred drew himself up in readiness to protest, but was immediately forestalled by DI Melton.

'Mr Strudwick, I feel I must warn you. This investigation has progressed beyond one of kidnap. There is evidence—some compelling—to suggest your son's possible involvement in two cases of murder, and we anticipate further corroborative testimony to become available shortly.

'The Press have been asked to help in tracing your son, which means you and Mrs Strudwick will become liable to media scrutiny. I propose, therefore, to withdraw surveillance and restrict entry to your property by means of uniformed officers.'

Melton produced his card and handed it to Alfred.

'Should your son attempt to contact you, ring this number at any time and ask to speak to me. Meanwhile, I am obliged by law to ask: "Is there's anything further you wish to say?"'

Alfred recognised the cases to which Melton referred. He too read newspapers and watched television. Scarcely able to comprehend, he shook his head.

'No Inspector,' he whispered. 'Did—did my boy *really* do those horrible things?'

'I'm sorry,' the DI said, 'but I'm afraid it very much looks that way. Like most people, I expect your son has a mobile phone. Do you happen to have the number?'

'No, Robert does have a mobile but doesn't care to be disturbed. If he wants anything, *he* rings *us*.'

'I see. Then do you have a recent photo or snapshot we could borrow?'

Strudwick shook his head. 'None since he was quite a small boy. You see, Robert absolutely *hates* being photographed.'

'No matter,' Melton said. 'A photo would be helpful, but we have a reasonably accurate photofit. One last thing, Mr Strudwick. What do you know of your son's financial circumstances?'

'I'm sorry, Inspector, I'm not at liberty to say. Client confidentiality forbids it.'

Melton frowned. 'In cases of criminal inquiry, financial institutions are legally bound to provide such information as may reasonably be required in furtherance of that inquiry. You are surely aware of that?'

'Yes, but not without regional permission—which would hardly be granted without a warrant.'

'That would surely depend on circumstances, if not the wisdom of the bank official concerned.'

Strudwick considered for a moment. 'I'm not entirely convinced,' he said, reluctantly, 'but I'll try to answer your questions—so far as I feel able.'

Melton's opinion of Strudwick's father improved. He decided to go for the jackpot.

'Does Robert bank at the Esher branch of Midland, where you are Chief Clerk?'

'Yes,' Mr Strudwick replied, unhesitatingly. 'My son maintains current and deposit accounts and also uses Barclaycard. But please don't ask me to reveal balances; I might easily lose my job.'

Melton offered his hand.

'Thank you, Mr Strudwick, don't worry. Feel free to call, but I shall keep in touch in any event.'

Mrs Strudwick joined her husband at the door to watch the investigators depart. For years dour, withdrawn and unhappy, she spoke rarely unless addressed directly. But today she seemed unusually animated.

'What did the police want, Alfred? Weren't they here last night? And why hasn't Robert come home?'

'He's landed himself in trouble, I'm afraid.'

'What trouble? Will he be angry? Oh dear, I can't *bear* it when he's angry.'

'Don't worry. He'll be home, but maybe not for some time. We'll have to wait and see.'

'Won't he be home for dinner, then? He'll be hungry. Has he gone off on business again?'

'Never mind that now. I'll explain later.'

Melton arrived back at Surbiton Police Headquarters at 12.15.

'What now, Guv'nor?' O'Connor asked, 'Spot of lunch?' Melton frowned, hesitated—and relented.

'Oh, go on then,' he smiled, 'coffee and sandwiches. I guess we deserve a break!'

'You could say that,' his assistant remarked, wryly. 'I fancy chicken with stuffing, OK by you?'

'Sounds good,' Melton responded, confirming his approval by means of the 'thumbs up' sign.

'Right-ho,' Ben said, 'I'd better go and organise it, otherwise we'll wait all flaming afternoon.'

'OK, but before you go, there's something I'd like you to do—' Melton's telephone rang.

'Melton! Hello—Benjamin? Fine thanks. Good of you to return my call. Yes, I thought so, news travels fast. Local radio *and* TV, you say? Well, any publicity is good publicity—or so they say.

'Anyway, harking back to the *Pennington Murder*, I remember your offer of help. Developments? Yes, quite a story. Prepared statement and interview at three. Interested? Good, see you then. Bye.'

'Benjamin Jopney, Thames Television,' Melton explained, entirely unnecessarily. 'One of the few with a heart, I feel I owe him. Anyway, I'd like you to ring Robin Prendergast. Tell him there's a Press briefing at three. Invite him to attend, but not in my name—he gave me a really rough time this morning, the hard-nosed sod. If we didn't need the publicity—?'

'Yes sir—right away,' O'Connor replied. He returned to his desk and reached for the telephone, leaving Melton free to begin drafting the all-important statement.

Prendergast accepted: Ben visited the canteen; Ben, coffee and sandwiches duly arrived.

Yet again, Melton's telephone rang. 'Melton. Yes, I most certainly will. Put him through.' He began to listen, then interjected, 'Hold on a second.' He signalled O'Connor to pick up the extension, then resumed, 'Sorry about that, Constable, something cropped up. Would you mind beginning again?'

'Not at all, sir,' the caller replied. 'As I was saying, sir, Transport Police, Waterloo. I'm P.C. Melberg. One of the booking clerks, chap named Blessington, came into the station a few minutes ago—still here, actually, if you want a word. Says he came off shift a bit late and went to the staff lounge to eat his lunch and watch telly for a while. When the one o'clock news came on, there was an item about a wanted man by the name of Robert William Strudwick.

'The description reminded him of some four-eyed weirdo who bought a single around nine-thirty this morning. The man fiddled and rummaged for the right money and seemed—well, sort of *furtive*. He wore glasses and had yellow, greasy hair, and when he looked up, Blessington noticed he had big, goggle-eyes, nigh on big as saucers, and black, like knobs of coal. Something clicked. He can't be certain, but Mr Blessington has a funny feeling it was Strudwick. He couldn't remember the man's destination, so he nipped back to the office to check the computer. It seems he sold seventeen tickets between 9.25 and 9.35, but only one single—to Tilbury, at 9.31. Blessington seems intelligent and genuinely anxious to help, sir. Would you care to speak to him?'

'No, thank you,' Melton replied. 'Tell Mr Blessington we're very grateful. Congratulate him on his alertness and powers of observation. Tell him his public-spirited action is appreciated, and we shall make the best use possible of his information. And thank you for ringing through so promptly, Constable Melberg. Please be good enough to render your report through the usual channels.'

Melton replaced his receiver. O'Connor followed suit.

'Well, I'll be blowed,' said Melton. 'What do you make of that?'

'Pretty conclusive, Guv'nor, I'd say. That describes Strudwick to a tee, the crafty bastard. Tilbury! He's legging it to Tilbury, the nearest port. Where to from there, sir? Ostend? Zeebrugge?'

Melton didn't think so. 'No, that's what he *wants* us to think, but for once he's been far too clever for his own good. How did

Blessington put it? 'Black, goggle-eyes, nigh on big as saucers'? *Why*, do you suppose?'

'I haven't the remotest, Guv'nor.'

'I'll tell you why, Benjamin, my boy. Strudwick was wearing contact lenses as well as glasses. It would be difficult to see—he fumbled for money buying the ticket, remember, so I suspect he wore glasses purposely in order to be recognised, which suggests he bought a *second* ticket to a different destination, probably from another booking clerk, this time *without* his give-away goggles.

'Where would he head to from Waterloo? Port, airport? Certainly, but not, repeat *not*, to Tilbury.'

Melton waited, eyeing his assistant. O'Connor fingered his whiskers absently. The more he considered, the more it made sense. What seemed astonishing supposition at first, swiftly transformed itself into a first-class piece of inspirational deduction.

'I reckon you've hit the nail on the head, Guv'nor,' he said.

'Which leads to a rather crafty notion,' Melton went on. He formed a steeple with his fingertips. 'Let's play him at his own game. Let's let him think we've swallowed his red herring. What d'you say?'

O'Connor was quick to agree. 'But how?' He scratched his head.

'Don't look so puzzled,' Melton said. 'I'll explain later. But first, I'd like you to do me a favour. Time is short and I need to get on with this statement. Get back to PC Melberg at Waterloo. Tell him we believe Strudwick bought a *second* ticket round about the same time—let's say within about five minutes. We need to know where to. Ask Melberg to see if he can obtain a printout of all tickets sold between 0925 and 0935—not too vast a number, I dare say. Tell him to ring me personally should he encounter any difficulties. Impress on him that the matter is urgent and I'd like the printout faxed through with the minimum of delay.'

When, twenty minutes later, O'Connor returned bearing a sheaf of fax-paper, Melton was busily finalising the press statement.

Waterloo booking hall had proved reasonably busy, even on a Saturday. Four out of the seven ticket windows had been manned, from which 62 tickets—predominantly returns—were issued between 9.25 and 9.35.

'I dare say you've twigged what we're looking for,' Melton remarked. 'If Strudwick intends to skip, he'll make for an airport: Heathrow, Blackheath, Gatwick or Southend—or, more likely, one of the channel ports with ferry services to the Continent: Southampton, Dover, Felixstowe, Ramsgate, Folkestone or Newhaven. Are you with me?'

'Makes sense, Guv'nor,' his assistant agreed. 'That's where I'd be heading if I were in *his* lousy shoes—France, Belgium or the Netherlands. He knows we're after him, and there are precious few hiding-places anywhere in *this* country.'

'My sentiments entirely, so let's see what we can come up with.'

It helped considerably that the computer records were both comprehensive and self-explanatory. Every ticket sold was date-timed, with multiple sales to individual purchasers quantity bracketed.

Working together, Melton and his assistant swiftly reduced the list to nine destinations: Portsmouth(2), Seaford, Dover(2), Hounslow, Newhaven, Gatwick, Folkestone, Southend and Poole.

'Hm,' Melton murmured, thoughtfully. 'Now which of these seem the least likely?' Answering his own question, he crossed out Portsmouth, Felixstowe, Seaford and Poole. 'Doubtful—too far away,' he explained. 'And scrub out Dover as well—Strudwick is travelling alone. If we rule out airports, and I think we can, that leaves Southend, Newhaven and Folkestone. Southend is out—no ferry services. Newhaven's a bit less likely, but remains a possibility. That narrows things down a bit, doesn't it?'

O'Connor nodded. 'I follow your reasoning, but I can't quite fathom where it's leading.'

'Tactics! We alert all three, publicise Tilbury, but keep Newhaven and Folkestone under wraps. And there's more. Alfred said his son has current and deposit accounts at the Midland, which suggests an opportunity to set a trap. Whether it'll work or not . . . well, that remains to be seen.'

O'Connor was puzzled. 'Sorry, Guv'nor, I don't see . . .'

'We know from experience that Strudwick covers his tracks well and is both clever and recourceful. But, as things stand, he might suppose there's nothing definite to connect him with the kidnap—or anything else, for that matter. He may even plan to return home after a week or two. Who knows? But not if he watches TV or reads tomorrow's papers, he won't. He'll know we really are on to him. That being so, he won't hang about waiting for the dust to settle, he'll head for somewhere remote—a safe haven where he can start a new life. And for that, he'll need money—lots of it. Think about it. He's hardly likely to leg it permanently without realising or transferring his assets, now is he?'

O'Connor's eyes widened. 'Gotcha, Guv'nor.'

'Yes,' Melton said, 'and I've an even tastier trick up my sleeve, but more about that later.'

Informed he was to be released conditionally, Henry Dyson expressed surprise—and some alarm.

''Ere!' he exclaimed, loudly. 'Wot if 'e comes lookin' ter carve me up wiv 'is bloody great knife?'

'Don't worry,' Melton reassured him, 'we'll be watching out for you. But in any case, there's every reason to believe he's miles away by now. But keep that to yourself, it's confidential information.'

'Wotcha mean? 'Ow the 'ell d'yer know?' Dyson demanded.

'All right, I'll tell you—it'll be in tomorrow's papers, anyway. He travelled to Waterloo after you dropped him off, stopped overnight in London and bought a single ticket to Tilbury this morning. Chances are he's making straight for the Continent, so you can go back to your cab and rest easy. The Sergeant will see to the formalities, Mr Dyson.'

Chapter Fifteen

A Promise Made . . .

While DI Melton and his team were setting up a manhunt, Robert Strudwick continued to put distance between himself and his pursuers—alert, wary, careful to avoid arousing suspicion.

Comfortably ensconced in a window seat, his luggage safe in the rack where he could keep an eye on it, he relaxed for a while, taking in something of the scenery as the train moved through the urban sprawl, heading for Beckenham and beyond.

Lulled by the rhythmic clatter of the wheels, he lapsed into thought. It was his first real opportunity to rationalise the who, what or how behind the first-ever failure of a well-conceived 'Mission' and the consequent enforced abandonment of a comfortable existence among his parents, home and friends. More important was the loss of his pride, his enviable position and hard-won, highly lucrative career.

At some stage, and at all costs, the status quo must be re-established, something he realised was next to impossible without the backing of his netherworld mentor, whose patronage he must therefore urgently seek to restore.

Pending that moment, outwitting the police and maintaining freedom must remain his overriding priority. Given his proven survival record, he confidently expected to achieve both.

Not that he didn't recognise—and regret—an extraordinary succession of blunders. What had possessed him to run from the cellar in mindless panic? Why hadn't he stopped to think? *What if Stephen and Janice were to survive? Would fear keep them quiet—or would they talk?* An idiotic question—too damn right they would! Furthermore, Pearce was the one person alive who knew enough to implicate him in the Pennington adventure. So why was the bastard still alive? *Bloody hell!* He cursed, angrily, under his breath. A couple of knife thrusts would have silenced Stephen Pearce *and* his bloody tart permanently.

And what of Henry Dyson, the grovelling, snivelling little pervert who knew far, far too much? Having outlived his usefulness, he too ought rightfully to have been disposed of. *Damn! Damn!* And as for himself—forced to run like a common criminal; revenge abandoned. *Hell's teeth!*

What *had* gone wrong—and why? It didn't make sense. If he really had digressed, then how? He needed help. As Custodian of the Book he surely merited it. Why was Pentophiles so infuriatingly elusive? Clearly he had upset his mentor, but how? He'd been rude before with no lasting effect. Why? Why? He examined and re-examined the happenings of the past few days, but failed to find a satisfactory answer. But he *would* find out—eventually.

Strudwick was still supremely confident, but as the train progressed and the distance between home, office and familiar territory increased, so his confidence began to evaporate.

Nearing Orpington he became anxious, as if events were spiralling out of control. Intuition—some sort of sixth sense—sounded a warning in his mind. He wondered if his escape plan was as foolproof as he had thought?

Doubt engendered fear which constricted his throat, and he became increasingly edgy and uneasy. He ached to know what the police were up to. Were his parents conforming, or not?

His 'spur-of-the-moment' bravado at Waterloo had been needlessly dangerous, and the disposal of his mobile telephone, logical enough at the time, was also beginning to seem like a serious mistake. His unease intensified. Ought he to modify—or even abandon—the escape plan? He was unsure. If only Pentophiles would return to guide him. For all his self-reliance, his ability to scheme and evaluate would surely benefit and he would thereafter know *exactly* what he must do. That Pentophiles *would* relent, he didn't doubt, probably quite soon. Re-empowered and protected, current difficulties resolved, he would return to Claygate in triumph to resume his rightful place.

Probing, questing, his thoughts lit on the informant who urged him to flight: *Bobby Shafto!* She said he had been followed for several days and was under surveillance even as she spoke. OK, she *had* warned him—but why so late in the evening? Why the hell hadn't she alerted him earlier? Had she provoked him into running for no good reason? Thinking back, there was no sign of the police when he left The Beeches, nor was he followed—at least, so as far as he could tell . . . Hm!

He knew she resented his hold over her. Was the warning a hoax, motivated by a wish for revenge? If so, the bitch would definitely become the subject of a brand-new 'Mission' . . . His pulse quickened.

But a 'Mission' needed instructions from the Book . . . He cursed, softly. Abruptly, reality returned, accompanied by an uncomfortable sensation. Damn, he needed a piddle.

Attempting to relieve the pressure, he wriggled, and made matters worse. *What now?* he wondered: *Leave my bags here and have them nicked? Solicit attention by taking them with me to the bog, and risk losing my seat into the bargain, or sit it out and hope I don't end up by pissing myself?* Perversely, he was also becoming extremely thirsty and badly needed a drink. These two simple needs became, collectively, the catalyst for a modified course of action. By the time the train squealed to a halt at Maidstone, his mind was made up.

Hefting his bags effortlessly, Robert mingled casually with the throng of passengers, but he neither crossed the bridge for the Folkestone connection, nor did he make for the exit. Instead, he sidled unobtrusively into the nearest gent's toilet, slipped into a vacant cubicle and securely bolted the door, allowing the platform to empty and free the ticket-collector for his duties elsewhere.

Five minutes later, a bespectacled, stooped figure emerged, shuffled down the platform, passed through the unmanned exit, down the stairs and into the street. Clear of the station, he straightened up, increased pace and headed for the nearest chemist, where he bought a pair of light-reactive designer sunglasses, a bottle of shampoo, a pair of scissors, two pairs of latex gloves and a bottle of brown hair dye.

Shortly afterwards, 'George Kingsley', of Pine Avenue, Orpington booked into The Bell, a dubious two-star, close to the High Street yet within five minutes' walking distance of the station. Going directly to his room, 'Mr Kingsley' locked the door and set to work.

He half-filled the washbasin with hot water and washed the gel from his hair. After towelling, he parted, combed and snipped, collecting the cuttings on a sheet of newspaper. Pulling on the gloves, he proceeded to apply the dye. Having allowed the requisite fifteen minutes for maximum 'take' and after a further, final rinse, he dried, combed and snipped again until the image in the mirror reflected the changes he sought. He put on the sunglasses. Then, almost without thinking, he added the gloves and empty dye container to the clippings and wrapped the lot into an innocuous-looking parcel for disposal later.

Eyeing himself critically, he concluded that, whilst the differences were purely cosmetic, they were nonetheless effective. Encouraged, he shrugged on his mac, pocketed the parcel and used toilet tissue to wipe clean any surface he may inadvertently have touched, before flushing the tissue down the loo. After a final check and a precautionary wipe of the door handles, he vacated the room—leaving the key in the door—and strode the length of the corridor, down the stairs and into the lobby without encountering a soul. To a fugitive with a vested interest in anonymity, it seemed like an omen.

At reception, he rang the bell and waited. Nobody responded. He hesitated. Should he ring again? He glanced around. The place appeared deserted. Could he? ... Should he? ... Oh, what the hell! He picked up his bags and strode boldly out of the building, unchallenged.

Thus, 'George Kingsley' ceased to exist and 'William S. Roberts' (allegedly of Smith Crescent, East Camberley) was resurrected. He dumped an unwanted parcel into a handy bin, walked briskly down the High Street and booked a room for two nights at The Railway Hotel, a comfortable hostelry he had stayed at once before. Registering under an assumed name (of what use were hotel registers when proof of identity was not demanded?), together with his subtle change of appearance, made it less likely he would be recognised.

Leaving the less important of his bags in the wardrobe, he picked up the other, returned to the foyer and slipped quietly out of the building in search of coffee and sandwiches.

He returned an hour later, equally unobtrusively, and switched on the television in time for the one o'clock news:

'Robert William Strudwick', the broadcaster droned, 'wanted for questioning in connection with the disappearance last week of Janice Ann Pearson and Stephen Pearce, both of Lower Green, Esher. Twenty-year-old Strudwick is five foot four, has straw-coloured hair and generally wears glasses. At about ten-forty p.m. yesterday, he eluded capture when driving a white Jaguar X434 RRP at high speed away from premises where Stephen and Janice were subsequently found to be incarcerated. Strudwick is thought to be armed, is unpredictable and dangerous and should not be approached. Anyone who spots the wanted man or his car should telephone the special incident room free on 08041 890890 immediately or notify the police at any police station as soon as possible.'

Robert sneered. Was that *really* the best they could do? A description sufficiently vague to fit thousands and not so much as a snapshot. Did they *really* expect to catch him? Contemptuously, he switched the television off, napped for a while and enjoyed a leisurely bath.

He dined well, slept well and breakfasted well: he felt safe and secure within his new persona. But, on unfolding a copy of The Sunday People, his sense of security abruptly evaporated. Front page banner headlines. Bold, central inset of an uncannily-accurate photofit—*Jesus Christ!* Striving for calm, stony-faced but with thundering heart, he read the article:

SERIAL MURDERER SOUGHT
A report by our special correspondent
The *Body in the Garden*—The *Body in the Vault*

Early yesterday, police named Robert William Strudwick as the chief suspect behind the abduction eight days ago of missing sweethearts Janice Ann Pearson and Stephen Pearce.

As part of a major police operation, Janice and Stephen were rescued late last night, having being incarcerated in a cellar, cruelly bound, for more than a week without food or water. Both were in poor physical condition and are currently in intensive care at Kingston General Hospital.

Detective Inspector David Melton, the officer in charge of the case, revealed that Strudwick is also wanted for questioning in connection with two murders: the *Body in the Garden* in July 2002, and the *Body in the Vault*, the gruesome killing perpetrated towards the end of November last year.

A top employee of a well-known Surrey estate agent, Strudwick, aged twenty, was observed leaving the house where Janice and Stephen were found, and is known to have visited his Claygate home where he concealed his car prior to fleeing the area by taxicab.

It has since been established that Strudwick was driven first to Surbiton and thence to Raines Park, from where he travelled by underground to London, probably using a circuitous route.

A middle-aged man (who cannot be named for legal reasons) was detained early yesterday for questioning, but later released conditionally pending the outcome of further investigations.

At nine-thirty yesterday, a man answering Strudwick's description was spotted at Waterloo by an alert railway employee, who later confirmed that the suspect purchased a single ticket for Tilbury.

The fugitive, who is believed armed and considered dangerous, may be heading for the continent. Police, customs and port authorities have been warned to be on the lookout for him.

Stocky, well-built, Strudwick is about five feet four, variously wears distinctive pebble-lens glasses or contact lenses and has slicked-back, straw-coloured hair—which he might possibly dye.

The suspect should not be approached. Anyone who believes they have seen Strudwick should notify the police immediately. All such reports will be held in complete confidence.

Taxicab! Surbiton! Raines Park! He had little doubt where *that* particular information had come from. *Dyson! The bastard, the snivelling, grovelling little shit. I ought to have slit his bloody throat!* Concealed behind the newspaper, face suffused with rage, Robert remained in his chair, rereading, digesting and analysing the import of the article.

One fundamental truth struck home forcibly: seven years of exciting, challenging brinkmanship with DI David Melton were finally at an end. What's more, given that Dyson had blabbed, it was likely he had also spilt the beans regarding the kidnap. It was too much. Initially stunned and betrayed, 'Mr Roberts' now became angry—very angry. Biting his lip, he pushed back his chair, shot to his feet and made a beeline back to his room. He could barely contain his rage, but he managed to close the door without slamming it—just.'

Drawing his knife, he slashed at the air furiously. *Stuff the plan, I'll cut his fucking bollocks off!* A promise was a promise—the traitor would die before the day was out precisely as promised. He calmed a little as he contemplated the attractive prospect: Henry, down on his knees, crying, gibbering, begging for mercy—not that it would do the arsehole any good. He might even refuse to stand—until a knife up his nostril persuaded him otherwise. And then, back on his feet and with the blade at his throat, he would be ordered to drop his trousers, step clear of his underpants and lift up his shirt—right up. 'Wot the bleedin' 'ell for, guv?' he would probably screech, crying, sweating and shaking with fear. To which he would respond: 'I want to see your guts fall out! Blabbed, didn't you? I promised, didn't I?'

Knife extended, he would move swiftly forward, thrust hard, twist, pull and slash upwards, and step back to avoid the torrent of spurting blood—or maybe not. If theory held true, Dyson would clutch frantically at his belly, but fail to hold his entrails in place.

He imagined the expression on the pervert's face: shock, disbelief, the realisation he was already as good as dead. Hopefully, he would scream in agony as his stomach spilled out. He might even drop back to his knees and raise his head in supplication, thus faciliting the avenging strike—a long, curving slash completely across the throat.

Beyond doubt, retribution would taste uncommonly sweet. Strudwick could hardly wait. He shoved his belonging into his bags and started towards the door. But wait! Native instinct, animal cunning—call it what you will—intervened. No matter what, he needed a plan. Whilst the temptation to leave immediately was compelling, it was nevertheless tempered by caution. Forcing himself to remain calm, he sat down and began to think the situation through rationally.

In order to secure his freedom, Dyson had obviously made a statement. Further statements might follow: from Pearce and Pearson. This changed everything. Lying low for a few weeks was no longer an option. Failing an intervention by Pentophiles, the prospects of returning, either now or in the foreseeable future, appeared slim.

Regrettably, there could be no going back. The contingency

plan must be implemented in full. Those carefully engineered financial arrangements must be triggered first thing in the morning, before news of his flight spread far enough to reach the ears of the banking fraternity. First, he would empty the safety deposit box; then on to the Maidstone branch of the Midland where he would realise assets; buy travellers cheques; close accounts and convert balances into a single banker's draft. Finally, he would exchange the bulk of his remaining Sterling for Euros. That done, he would travel to Folkestone, stay quietly overnight and board a ferry on Tuesday. When the time seemed right, he would contact his father via the bank, grant him powers of attorney with instructions to market The Beeches and transfer the proceeds offshore—discreetly, of course. He would survive, with or without the help of Pentophiles.

But an image of Dyson writhing on the floor flashed into his mind. Greedily, he licked his lips. Yet again, caution intervened. Torn between compelling desires, he vacillated. Maybe he should forget Henry and concentrate instead on making good his escape? It made sense. The police were disadvantaged; they had no idea of his whereabouts. Surely it would be wiser to maintain that advantage and remain here in relative safety, at least until the morning?

On the other hand, Dyson's treachery merited sharp punishment. The stinking pervert had effectively sabotaged any possibility of Strudwick's eventual return. For that alone, he must *definitely* be made to suffer.

For a full minute he stood, hesitant. Then the thirst for revenge overwhelmed him. *Bollocks! I've time to sort Dyson, return here tonight and pick up where I've left off.* Clutching the more important of his two bags, he left the hotel and made for the station . . .

Chapter Sixteen
Come into my Parlour . . .

Following a worrying baby-snatch incident, security at Kingston General Hospital is vastly improved. Cameras now monitor main, emergency and outpatient entrances and every corridor and walkway, including the approaches to maternity and clinic areas, operating theatres and intensive care.

The security office boasts a 'state of the art' monitoring console, manned daily from 8.00 a.m. to 10.00 p.m., with video recording equipment in continuous-loop operation over a seven day cycle. Add one small office adjacent to intensive care, a monitor linked to the corridor camera, tea-making facilities and two alert policemen equipped with digital two-way radios and DI Melton pronounced himself satisfied. Stephen and Janice would suffer no further at the hands of Robert Strudwick.

Protecting a frightened taxi driver without making it obvious was more complicated and difficult to achieve in a short space of time, but DI Melton was decisive, persuasive, and utterly determined. That Dyson's apartment block faced one immediately opposite did help, however, and a substantial bribe secured the flat next to Dyson's for three days. Its unemployed single tenant readily took himself off to Blackpool for the weekend, expenses paid.

Alerted to danger but assured that help was close at hand, Henry blanched.

'If anyone knocks, *don't* open the door,' he was told. 'Just shout "hang on a minute," and sit tight. We'll check it out and see you come to no harm.' Grey-faced, anxious, Dyson simply nodded.

Round-the-clock watchers moved into place, installed cameras and binoculars, set up and tested listening equipment, checked out individual radios, reported readiness—and waited. Strategically-placed back-up units moved into position at 8.00 a.m., the finishing touches to what was probably the most intense, meticulously planned discreet surveillance initiative ever mounted by Surbiton Police. DI David Melton's carefully engineered trap was in place.

After a heavy night with a whisky bottle, Henry obliged by sleeping late, but had he emerged, his every step would have been dogged. Should he climb into the cab parked just outside, an unmarked car lurked nearby, ready to follow at a safe distance, tailed in turn by a back-up crew.

'The importance of this briefing cannot be overstated, so listen carefully,' DI Melton exhorted. 'As you know, weekend leave has been cancelled; few of you fully appreciate why. Before duties are assigned, therefore, I feel you deserve a full and proper explanation. Miserable little creep though he is, it is our duty to keep Henry Dyson safe from harm.

'But if anyone imagines this is merely an elaborate witness protection exercise, they are wrong. It is, in reality, a great deal more.' He paused. 'The main aim is to nail Robert William Strudwick.

'I need hardly remind you of the ignominy of having two unsolved murders on our patch. Working together, it is my belief we can bring about a speedy and satisfactory conclusion to both. At long last, there is mounting and credible evidence to identify Strudwick as the perpetrator. Although he left the area yesterday, there is every possibility he will return—albeit briefly—with the intention of eliminating three people, each able to incriminate him for abduction and torture, but one, we believe, with sufficient information to have him arrested and charged with murder.

'Put simply, Dyson's value as a witness will not escape Strudwick's attention, thanks to the media. A unique opportunity has thus been created to tempt into the open a known kidnapper and probable killer.

'Don't underestimate Robert Strudwick. He's cold, sadistic and cruel, but intelligent and observant. One false move and he'll melt away. There will be no margin for error and I'll accept no excuses. Be under no illusions: Strudwick is evil, devious and extremely dangerous.'

His forefinger stabbed the air.

'Should he succeed in silencing Henry, he will almost certainly go after Stephen and Janice, even though both are in hospital, dangerously ill, and may not survive in any case.

'That fact is unlikely to concern Strudwick, however. He is not given to taking chances.' His measured tones became sterner.

'With luck we shall have a chance to nab him, but one chance only. We cannot afford mistakes. At all costs, this man must be prevented from eliminating witnesses and from fleeing the country. Gentlemen. Be diligent, be swift, and be successful. Good luck!'

At 11.01, the sparsely populated 10.45 from Waterloo squealed to a halt at Surbiton where three passengers alighted. Two were ladies returning from a trip to the theatre and an overnight stay in town. The third was a dark-haired man carrying a single item of luggage, unremarkable, except that he sported expensive designer sunglasses yet wore a singularly scruffy raincoat.

Emerging from the station, the ladies entered a waiting car, whereas the man walked briskly down Westfield Road, turned left on Maple Drive and right into The Mall. Here, he crossed to the left, reduced pace and sauntered on to where two blocks of flats faced one another, just short of the junction with Portsmouth Road.

A familiar black taxi stood opposite. He stopped for a moment, and looked about, warily. There was little traffic, few people. No voice warned of impending danger. Reassured, he moved off again. A few paces more brought him to Portsmouth Road, where he turned left and continued on to the offices of 'Ace Cars', on the corner of Brighton Road. Pushing wide the door, the newcomer walked in and dumped his bag on the floor.

Sylvia Fairweather was on duty as usual. She looked up immediately.

'Yes?' she asked, 'what can I do for you?'

'Hello Sylvia,' he grinned, removing his sunglasses. 'What's the matter? Don't you recognise me? You run a taxi service, don't you? Strangely enough, that's exactly what I want—a taxi.'

To her eternal credit, Sylvia didn't turn a hair.

'Of course, Mr Robert,' she said. 'Sorry, I didn't recognise you. You look different, somehow.'

'It'll be my hairdo,' he retorted, sarcastically, 'cost a small fortune—John Frieda, and all that.'

'Go on with you,' she said, disarmingly. 'Youngsters, you're all the same. You'd tell me anything.'

'More than likely,' he agreed. 'But what about that taxi? I'm rather short of time.'

'I've two working today: George is on airport and Phil's at home on standby. Poor Phil. A drunk spewed in the cab last night. He's cleaning and disinfecting right now, but monitoring the radio in case I need him. Hang on a sec, I'll give him a call.' *What a stroke of luck! Perfect.*

She reached for the microphone, but Strudwick stopped her short.

'No!' he exclaimed, sharply. 'Let him finish cleaning it up; I couldn't stand the smell. I've a better idea.'

His eyes gleamed black. At his most persuasive, he set out to impose his will. 'Give Henry a ring—I prefer his driving, anyway. He is home. I noticed his cab on the way—not another in sight, incidentally—and what I have in mind is right up his street.

'Tell him you've a job for him. Say: "It's bent; fifty quid, back pocket, no questions asked"—there's fifty in it for you, by the way—and don't tell him it's for me; he might be suspicious. Tell him it'll take no more than an hour and has nothing to do with taxis—I'll borrow your spare—so he's to leave his where it is and walk. Impress on him he's to slip out the back and nip through the alley—it's shorter and quicker—and to make sure he isn't followed, or the whole deal's off.'

He fished out his wallet, extracted ten ten-pound notes and placed them on the desk.

'There you are, Sylvia. Real cash, up front. Now, are you on?' he asked, with a knowing smile.

'I certainly am,' she replied, 'nothing like a few extra quid. I'll treat myself to a new handbag.'

She picked up the telephone and dialled. In the still of the office, Strudwick distinctly heard Dyson's answering voice, tinny but unmistakable.

'Yus?'

'Hello Henry,' Sylvia began.

She explained Strudwick's proposition.

'Cor, not 'arf!' came the eager response. 'I'll get me coat an' be rahnd in a minnit.'

The bug installed the previous afternoon performed faultlessly . . . three cars moved quietly closer.

Henry replaced the receiver, put on his shoes, shrugged into his coat and sneaked out of the door. He tiptoed along the corridor and down the stairs, turned left and sidled through the rear entrance. Crossing the parking area, he made it to the alley. Two minutes later, he pushed through the doorway of 'Ace Cars' and blundered in.

'Hi, Sylv,' he said, 'wot's up? Wotcha wan' me ter do? Bury yer friggin' granny?'

'*Hello*, Henry,' Strudwick drawled, from immediately behind, 'nice of you to call. D'you know, I was actually *hoping* you'd pop in. I'd very much like a word—you gabby, snivelling little shit!'

It was a voice with which Henry was all too familiar. His face a picture (as Sylvia afterwards said) he froze momentarily and spun on his heel, offering an irresistible target. Strudwick didn't hesitate. He delivered a single, ferocious back-hander right across the mouth, knocking Henry off-balance. Dyson staggered and slammed hard against the wall.

Panther-like, Strudwick pounced. Twice in succession, he punched Henry full in the mouth. Dyson fell to the floor in a crumpled heap.

'Oi!' Sylvia yelled. 'that's enough. I'm surprised, Mr Robert. I thought you a gentleman. If you *must* fight that's your business, but if you do it in here, it's mine!'

'Shut it, Sylvia,' Strudwick snarled, 'this is nothing to do with you. Just Henry and me, personal. Sit still, keep quiet—or suffer the consequences and I'm sure you know *exactly* what I mean.'

Frightened, and sharply reminded of the debt she believed she owed, Sylvia subsided. Strudwick returned to the cringing wretch at his feet.

'That's just for starters,' he spat, furiously. 'Remember my promise, bastard? Well, do you?'

'Yes, guv,' Dyson snivelled, through split and bleeding lips. 'But I ain't dun nuffink, 'onest!'

'Liar! Copper's nark! Squealing, miserable, ungrateful little shit. You grassed me up, didn't you?'

'No, guv, no. I swear! Melton threatened me, 'ad me knocked abaht—but I didn't tell 'im nuffink!'

'You expect me to believe that? Taxi! Surbiton! Raines Park! Reporters with crystal balls? Bollocks! Come on, you stinking pervert, on your feet. We'll borrow the spare cab and find a nice quiet spot somewhere—somewhere private where I can keep my promise and slice your stinking guts!'

Unquestionably sincere and oozing malevolence, Strudwick

drew his knife . . . It was enough! Sylvia's hand flew to her mouth in horror. Dear God, had she left it too late? Screened by the desk, her knee moved fractionally, located a hidden button and pressed twice.

Linked to a radio transmitter concealed in a drawer, Sylvia's panic button triggered a distinctive series of 'beeps', inaudible—except in the earphones of around thirty police officers. The door to Sylvia's private office crashed open and two waiting detectives burst in at a run.

'Police! Don't move! Drop the knife! Get down on the floor—now!'

Taken by surprise, Strudwick froze and dropped the knife. He made a dash for the door—but was easily outmanoeuvered. In the resultant melée, his sunglasses went flying and were trodden on, he lost one of his contact lenses and collected a couple of bruises. It was soon over. Strong hands clamped his arms and applied handcuffs.

Pulling on gloves, DC Gibson recovered the knife, slipped it into a plastic bag and labelled it. Strudwick was frisked and declared 'clean'.

It fell to DC Slade to 'do the honours'.

'Robert William Strudwick. I'm arresting you on suspicion of kidnap, carrying an illegal weapon, aggravated assault with intent, causing actual bodily harm and attempting to avoid arrest. You are not obliged to say anything but anything you do say may be taken down and given in evidence. It may harm your defence if you do not mention when questioned something you may later rely on in court. Do you wish to say anything?'

Bollocks to the lot of you—especially Melton—and watch your sodding back, copper! Hang on! Why not try a spot of bluff? You can be absolutely brilliant when you've a mind to.

His self-belief was astonishing.

'Kidnap? Assault?' he challenged. 'What the hell are you talking about? You must be mistaken—confusing me with somebody else. My name isn't *Strudwick*, it's Roberts.'

DC Slade laughed.

'Sure, Julia—and I'm Bela Lugosi. If you think we're swallowing that line of crap, you're either off your crust or living in cloud-cuckoo-land. For one thing, Mrs Fairweather knows you and for another—apart from your hair—you match an extremely accurate photofit of—you've guessed it—Robert William Strudwick. What's more, you and I have already met, now haven't we?'

Not the least dismayed, Strudwick changed tactics.

'If you say so,' he muttered. 'But you *could* be mistaken and end up with egg all over your face.'

'I'll just have to chance it, won't I?' Slade retorted, ' 'cos *you*, Mr Strudwick, are *staying* nicked.'

Strudwick shrugged and tried another tack.

'Now I've been arrested, I suppose the next thing you'll do is cart me off to the station—right?' Slade glared. Paperwork, Sunday duty, now this . . . this . . . pillock. What *was it*, with the little creep? Harry had had enough.

'Not if it upsets you. Maybe I should just turn you loose and buy you a ticket to the Bahamas? Of *course* you're going to the station—the nearest one, buster. There's the door, get moving. I've had just about enough of you—and that's putting it mildly.'

He grasped the detainee's arm. Strudwick shrugged him off. His eyes gleamed, he became calmer, rational, persuasive. *The Book!*

'Just a minute, Constable,' he protested, 'I'm being serious. See that holdall, by the wall? It's mine. My pyjamas, shaver and toiletries are inside and it looks as if I'll be needing them. Would you mind if we take it along? I'll carry it—if you take these manacles off.'

'No, I don't mind,' Slade replied. 'You wear your own gear—until you reach the Slammer, that is. But *I'll* look after the bag, thank you.'

He picked up the bag.

'Come on, no more messing. Time to get you to the nick.'

Strudwick merely smiled.

1140, Thames Ditton Police Station.

'Here we are, Sarge,' Slade announced, 'I reckon you've been expecting us. This here is Robert William Strudwick, arrested on suspicion of kidnap, aggravated assault with intent, causing actual bodily harm, resisting arrest and carrying an illegal weapon—i.e., this here knife and sheath.' The Desk Sergeant completed an evidence form which, together with the weapon and sheath, were placed in the safe.

Procedural arrest routine followed, modified to suit Ditton's

THE FLYLEAF KILLER

lack of prisoner facilities. 'Take off your watch. Empty your pockets—money, keys, wallet, handkerchief, and place everything on the counter.'

Strudwick obeyed. Every item was checked and listed, his money counted and everything except his spectacles and his handkerchief went into the cutomary basket.

He signed the receipt and accepted his copy without protest—he wanted something.

'And this is his bag, Sarge,' said Slade, dumping it on the counter.

'OK, Mr Strudwick,' the long-suffering non-com sighed, 'open it up. Everything on the counter!'

Again without protest, Strudwick complied.

Into the basket went a large wad of notes—carefully counted and annotated—passport, travelling alarm, mirror, dressing-gown, shoes and a clothes brush.

'You won't be needing those!'

Suitably crestfallen and compliant, Strudwick asked, 'Then what *can* I keep?'

'Socks, vests, pants, shirts, soap, towel, shaver, toothpaste and brush, and the bag to keep it all in. Hang on a minute. That towel—what's that wrapped up inside it?'

'Just a book I'm halfway through. OK if I keep it?'

'Show!'

Cautiously, Strudwick displayed one edge of the treasured tome. 'OK? Can I keep it—please?'

'Seems harmless enough, all right.'

Outwardly calm, privately elated, Strudwick merely said, 'Thank you.'

On finding himself locked in a cell, however and in the absence of any response from the Book, he became progressively morose and withdrawn. Invited to submit to a saliva swab, Strudwick demurred, but changed his mind shortly afterwards when four burly policemen arrived to commend the procedure. Refusing point blank to co-operate any further, he was moved to Surbiton and interviewed by successive teams of interrogators—including Melton and O'Connor—throughout Monday and again on Tuesday, continuing until late afternoon.

Apart from flatly denying everything, Strudwick remained stubbornly silent. Whilst confession would undoubtedly help, evidence mounting by the hour was beginning to render it unnecessary. When blood and DNA samples were checked and compared, all matched. And when Melton resurrected the envelope from home, it revealed that the rogue hair found on Bridgwater's body conclusively belonged to Strudwick.'

Sylvia made a precise and compelling statement. Henry happily talked his socks off.

With the suspected murderer safely in the can, three major investigations became as one, although for procedural, legal and other reasons, all were to remain separately documented.

Also on Tuesday, to the relief of many, and David Melton in particular, Stephen and Janice were taken off the danger list. Neither was well enough to be interviewed but, with their tormentor safely in custody, it was reasonable to expect both to co-operate fully, with luck in a matter of days. In anticipation, additional charges against Strudwick for murder and other related crimes were drafted in readiness.

Meanwhile, duly charged with the offences for which he was arrested, the prisoner appeared before magistrates on Wednesday, 30 March, 2005. Refusing to plead, he was remanded in custody for seven days pending reports. No application was made for bail.

0930, Thursday 31st March, 2005: Police HQ, Surbiton.

Ejected violently through the open hatch, Strudwick's breakfast tray clattered noisily to the floor, and he began banging on his cell door. Considering the officer on duty was comfortably within earshot, his actions were deliberately provocative.

'Oi, bastard!' he bellowed, determined to attract attention. 'Bastard! Rotten, stinking pig! Wanker, toss-pot, pile of filthy shit!'

The facing door swung open and PC Frobisher appeared. Important prisoner, duty or no, he wasn't the least amused. Co-opted from Esher to help guard, wait on and pander to the whims of someone as odious as Strudwick was bad enough, to be the target of unwarranted abuse . . .

'Shut your row, you noisy sod,' he shouted. 'All you needed to do was press the bleedin' bell!'

'Fuck the bell! Get your fat, lazy arse in here, copper. I want a word.'

Frobisher reddened:

'Not so much lip, Strudwick, or you'll get more than just a word—what d'you want, anyway?'

'For one thing I'm out of bog roll and for another, I'm pissed-off with being cooped up in here. I need exercise; I'm entitled to exercise. Tell Melton I want to go outside and stretch my legs.'

'You'll be lucky,' Frobisher sneered. 'Who the hell do you think you are, Roger Bannister?'

Strudwick ignored the jibe. He modified his tone.

'Just ask, there's a good chap. How would *you* like it, stuck in here? I do have rights, you know.'

'I suppose,' Frobisher conceded. 'All right, I'll see what I can do—in about half an hour when I'm due a break. Meanwhile, keep quiet and behave yourself—or I shan't even bother.'

'Hang on a sec,' Strudwick returned. 'Don't rush off. I want to ask a favour—it might help.'

'What now?'

'Give Melton a message. Tell him I'm putting him up for promotion—that should do the trick . . . and don't be long about it. I'm getting as stiff as a board!'

Arrogant, impertinent bastard! Frobisher glared and slammed the hatch. He was still seething when he knocked on DI Melton's door.

'Good morning, sir. Sorry to trouble you. It's Strudwick. He's demanding outside exercise. How do I deal with it?'

'Yes, he is entitled to an hour a day, but it isn't your problem. Prisons have exercise yards, we don't. With a couple of extra guards, however, we can make do with the car park. Go back to your break, Frobisher, and leave it with me. I'll see to it and have him off your hands in, say, around an hour.'

The DI was as good as his word. At 11.00 a.m., PCs Blake and Bellingham reported to the cells.

'Wotcha, Frobey,' said Blake, evidently none too pleased. 'Strudwick! Exercise! DI's orders. Go get yourself a brew. This Strudwick bloke, he's nothing but a pain in the arse. We'll give him bloody exercise.'

'A couple of miles up the M1 would be nice,' Frobisher commented, 'preferably in the fast lane.'

'You wish,' Blake chortled. 'Come on, Frobey, move it. He's only got an hour.' Frobisher grinned and unlocked the cell.

'Oi, Strudwick,' he said. 'Jesus, you are ugly! Out you come then. Time for w-a-alkies!'

Strudwick glared, got off his bed and emerged.

'Assume the position,' Blake ordered, dangling handcuffs and pointing to Bellingham.

Strudwick extended a wrist, was duly cuffed and conducted to the car park.

'Ere y'are, Cocky,' Bellingham, the taller of the two remarked, deftly unlocking the manacles. 'Steer clear of the cars. Walk, trot, rumba—whatever. Go round as often as you like, but try going further than that wall and you'll be back inside quicker'n lightning. OK?'

Strudwick nodded. Pointing to the boundary wall, Bellingham treated Strudwick to a helpful, if rather vigorous shove.

Strudwick strode his assigned circuit for a solid fifty minutes until stopped by Bellingham.

'That'll do,' he said, 'time's up. PC Blake will take you back. I'm off to lunch.'

Meanwhile, after an enjoyable break, a relaxed PC Frobisher made his way back to the cells. Purely from force of habit, he checked Strudwick's cell—his euphoria promptly evaporated.

'Scruffy sod,' he grumbled. 'Just look at the bleedin' mess.'

His annoyance was understandable.

The bed was unmade, socks and underclothes strewn on the floor, washbasin half-full of dirty water, toilet used but not flushed, shaver on the bed: *deliberate* provocation. The man was a pig.

Muttering, and praying the duty Sergeant was nowhere around, Frobisher set about clearing up the mess. As he was tidying the bed . . . *Hello, what's this? Oh, might have guessed. Strudwick's bloody book! What the hell's he's got this time?* 'War and Peace'? 'Maggie Thatcher's Memoirs'? He smiled at the thought. *Hang on, it's the same as last time. Blimey, he* must *be a slow reader!* Frobisher sat on the bed, opened the book midway and flipped idly through the pages. *I wonder who actually wrote this crap?* Turning to the title page, he read:

BIRDS OF THE WORLD *Pilo Sephten*

Funny sort of name! Impelled by more than mere curiosity, he turned to the first chapter and began to read. Becoming engrossed despite himself, he failed to hear approaching voices and was still reading when Robert Strudwick arrived, cuffed and chatting to PC Blake.

'Hey, what the fuck d'you think you're doing?' he demanded. 'Get your arse off my fucking bed.' Turning to Blake, he ordered, 'Get these bloody shackles off, sod you.'

Scarcely thinking, Blake fumbled for the key and obeyed.

Rubbing his wrist, Strudwick turned his attention back to Frobisher. Then he did a double-take, turned deathly white and clutched at his throat.

'You're reading the Book!' he screamed.

'So what?' replied the officer. 'You're not reading it. Too busy gallivanting while I clean up your mess? I've seen it before, anyway—last time we met. I'm Frobisher from Esher, remember? Took you to Surbiton for interview. Got a bad memory, have we? Hell's bells, and it was only a couple of weeks ago.' He laughed. 'Same stupid book, as I recall, all about birds. Bit of a slow reader, ain't'cher? Here, take your book if it's *that* important.' He tossed it at Strudwick's feet.

Strudwick stared. His eyes bulged, he staggered, almost fell. *God, tell me it isn't true!*

'Y—you've looked at the Book—before?' he stammered. 'H-how? I never let it out of my sight.'

'Easy,' Frobisher sneered, 'while you were at interview. You made such a hoo-hah packing it, wrapping it, treating it like the crown jewels. I thought it was gold-plated or something. Can't see what all the fuss is about. It's only a sodding book, after al—'

He stopped, thunderstruck. Crazed with fear, for all the world like a man possessed, Strudwick had dropped to his knees.

'No, Master, no!' he cried. 'Forgive me. I can explain. It was a mistake, I didn't mean it!'

The cell light flickered and dimmed. The temperature fell. Dank mist eddied and swirled. Strudwick screamed. A long, drawn-out wail—the sound of a soul in torment, a creature without hope. He clutched his head, shook violently from side to side, howled, thrashed and screamed again.

Struggling to his feet, he confronted the watchers. Mouth agape, he dribbled. Dark, viscous liquid oozed from his nose. Vacantly, he turned, lowered his head and charged, crashing headlong into the wall. He howled like a banshee, fell writhing to the floor, limbs thrashing, jerking, shuddering—finally still.

The watching policemen stood helplessly by, stricken powerless, unable to intervene. Time stood still. A moment passed—and another. Neither policeman moved. Strange, archaic words—mysterious, vaguely poetic—entered Frobisher's mind. It was his right, his privilege, his duty. For he had been the catalyst—Strudwick's chosen nemesis.

Involuntarily, he recited aloud: *Another time, another dimension, faint mocking, thundering low, starting with whisper increasing but slow, vengeance as promised by creature none know . . .*

His voice faded. Frobisher shook his head and turned to his companion.

'Christ! That was weird. What about him? Does he need an ambulance?' Blake jumped. 'What? What did you say?'

'Come alive, you dozy plonker! Does he need an ambulance?'

'Nah, too late—he's a goner. Seen it before, Frobey. Only friggin' thing he needs is a meat wagon.'

Skirting the body, Frobisher picked up the book, opened the front cover and examined the label:

SURREY COUNTY LIBRARIES
No: *666   Birds of the World, Sephten*
Date for return: *15:10:98*